Praise for Cordelia Stru

"Smart eccentric prose."

"Often witty and pointedly observant in the face of pain and adversity." (*Newsday*)

"A new word is cropping up on the literary landscape. Strubian. So what does it mean? Unflinching. Chock-full of the unflinching. And funny." (*Georgia Straight*)

"Cordelia Strube homes in on contemporary life and relationships with uncompromising precision and unfailing wit." (Nino Ricci)

"In Strube's work, the characterization is lively and the snappy writing is full of caustic zingers on contemporary urban life and the absurdities of pop culture ... Her comic sense is like a perfectly mixed martini: exceedingly dry and potent." (*The Toronto Star*)

"Strube's prose is unadorned yet not stark. The dialogue is absolutely dynamite ... A unique voice in Canadian fiction ... compulsively readable." (*Quill & Quire*)

"Strube peels back the fast-food, tabloid cynicism that shrink-wraps urban life and shows us the dark matter beneath ... a compelling ride." (*The National Post*)

"Strube has a powerful way of dragging the reader right into her characters' heads ... The story is told with such humour and suspense that it's hard to put down ... As with all her novels, she picks diamonds out of the ashes." (*The Globe & Mail*)

"Most writers either create great characters or propulsive plots: Strube nails both, with gusto, and then does her best to save the planet along the way ... marvelous dialogue and

biting insights that stay with you for a long time."
(*The Ottawa Citizen*)

"Flawless structure, perfectly tuned dialogue and dozens of brilliant cameo appearances by a huge cast of supporting minor characters ... Strube has a rare talent for painting beautiful losers and making you love characters who in real life would be unbearable." (*Montreal Mirror)*

"Strube's portraits of characters caught in urban angst are riddled with laugh-out-loud humour ... her rueful insistence on contemplating human darkness is tempered by a certain wistfulness, a yearning for something finer, a flicker of hope that is never quite extinguished. Strube's mandate has always been to unsettle, not merely entertain."
(*The Edmonton Journal*)

"Wonderfully precise dialogue and descriptive passages weave their magic without pyrotechnics or laboured imagery. Strube's assured prose creates a teeming, ordinary world that is utterly fascinating ... As readers we are walked through contempt, aversion, recognition and then, finally, hope. It's a marvelous journey." (*Halifax Daily News*)

"Strube deftly navigates around the human heart in a way reminiscent of Carol Shields." (*Books in Canada*)

"Strube's descriptions and observations of cultural and urban life are sharp as knives. One of the best novelists around, a writer to rejoice in and embrace." (*Ottawa Xpress*)

PLANET REESE

To Lisa

by cordelia
STRUBE

THE DUNDURN GROUP
TORONTO

Editor: Barry Jowett
Copy-editor: Andrea Waters
Design: Alison Carr
Illustrations: Carson Linnéa Strube Healey
Printer: Friesens

Library and Archives Canada Cataloguing in Publication
Strube, Cordelia, n.d.
       Planet Reese / Cordelia Strube.
ISBN-13: 978-1-55002-684-9
       I. Title.
PS8587.T72975P53 2007   C813'.54   C2007-900086-X

1   2   3   4   5   11   10   09   08   07

Conseil des Arts   Canada Council
du Canada   for the Arts

Canada

ONTARIO ARTS COUNCIL
CONSEIL DES ARTS DE L'ONTARIO

We acknowledge the support of the **Canada Council for the Arts** and the **Ontario Arts Council** for our publishing program. We also acknowledge the financial support of the **Government of Canada** through the **Book Publishing Industry Development Program** and **The Association for the Export of Canadian Books**, and the **Government of Ontario** through the **Ontario Book Publishers Tax Credit program**, and the **Ontario Media Development Corporation**.

Care has been taken to trace the ownership of copyright material used in this book. The author and the publisher welcome any information enabling them to rectify any references or credits in subsequent editions.

J. Kirk Howard, President

Printed and bound in Canada.
Printed on recycled paper.
www.dundurn.com

The author gratefully acknowledges the support of the
Ontario Arts Council.

Dundurn Press	Gazelle Book Services Limited	Dundurn Press
3 Church Street, Suite 500	White Cross Mills	2250 Military Road
Toronto, Ontario, Canada	High Town, Lancaster, England	Tonawanda, NY
M5E 1M2	LA1 4XS	U.S.A. 14150

For B.H.

The magician unwraps a stick of Juicy Fruit and chews on it vigorously. "It's for my ears," he explains. "Otherwise, *kaboom*." He balls the wrapper then palms it, revealing an empty hand to Reese. "I might be working with Buddy Greco in Vegas. It's between me and Ernesto Ventura who's, like, a total loser."

Reese is beside the magician — and not with his wife and children — because, according to the flight attendant with the red eyes and orange lips, the flight has been oversold, the seats assigned. Sitting across from his wife and children was the German in the Tilley hat. Reese, pointing to the back of the plane, asked him to consider changing seats. The German stood, squinted briefly at the magician in the tux and spiky hair, and said, "*Nein, danke*."

The magician is tearing apart his napkin, balling the fragments in his hands. "Need a napkin?"

"I've got one, thanks," Reese says before realizing that his napkin is no longer on his tray.

The magician opens his hand, revealing the shredded napkin whole again. "I'm working on this nail routine, it's kind of like Houdini's Needle Trick. He'd swallow, like, dozens of needles then regurgitate them with all the needles threaded."

Reese peers over the rows of heads in front to see his family. Before takeoff, he managed to hover near them. Roberta had little to say to him, but Clara waved the colouring book the pregnant flight attendant had given her. "Look, Daddy, dinosaurs!" Derek, twitching despite the Ritalin, was absorbed in his Game Boy.

"So my nail act," the magician says, "is like the Needle Trick except that instead of needles I use nails, and instead of swallowing them, I hammer them up my nose."

Clara was the first to spot him. "That's the *magician!*" she shouted. "You are *so* lucky, Daddy! You get to sit beside the *magician!*"

On the ship, Reese had avoided him by remaining on the pool deck, but now, with their arms frequently touching on the armrest, interaction has become inevitable.

"I'm into the classic illusions," the magician explains. "None of that laser crap Ernesto's been doing. Magic's gotten way too safe. You don't see guys in straitjackets dangling from their ankles over major intersections anymore. You don't see guys handcuffed, bagged, crated, and dumped into rivers. Nothing but wussies out there."

Reese smiles politely and glances past the passenger in the window seat who, prior to takeoff, had been speaking heatedly into his cellphone in another language, guttural but unidentifiable. "H'what's your problem?" the man demands. He has an abundance of nose hair.

"I was just trying to look out the window," Reese explains.

"H'what, you never seen sky before?"

The pregnant flight attendant appears to collect their trays. The nose-haired man calls her "sweetcakes" and orders more rum and Coke.

Reese assures himself that it was a successful vacation. He and Roberta didn't fight, and the children were occupied with the Kid's Club, which freed their parents. He slouched on various deck chairs, focusing on his bird books to stop contemplating the effect twenty-five hundred passengers defecating into the ocean was having on the fish below.

Inside their cabin, Reese refrained from voicing his concerns regarding the lack of any windows and their dependency on a ventilation system and elevators. He had come on the cruise to show he could be positive — to prove Roberta wrong. He knew that this was his last chance. Even Greenpeace had called him negative. "You've changed," they said, just before they fired him.

"I'm older," he replied.

There had been complaints about his "leadership skills." When people did stupid things, he told them so.

On the cruise, to his amazement, he was able to behave like a man on vacation, even attending a Fine Arts Auction where he was shown "some of the most beautiful artwork produced in the last century." He put his name in a box and won, yes, actually *won*, a Chagall print said to be worth a thousand dollars.

"That's a lithograph," Roberta told him.

"They say it's a limited edition. They say it's worth a thousand dollars."

"Puh-lease."

Derek and Clara took the upper bunks, Reese and Roberta the lower. It was really quite jolly, Reese thought. The lower bunks came with a slide-together option, but Reese and Roberta hadn't slept together since the separation. The cruise was for the children, particularly Clara, who'd longed for them to be "a family" again. They ate spring rolls and fruit kebabs from the buffet, played minigolf, swam, and watched first-run movies in the movie theatre. Movies overwrought with sentimentality, violence, and the promotion of material gain that, under normal circumstances, Reese would not permit his children to see. But mid-Atlantic, in a stadium-sized boat rigged with stabilizers to free passengers of any sensation of being ocean-borne, the movies seemed appropriate. He enjoyed the popcorn and being in close proximity with his children and even agreed to go dancing, performing the Tush-Push and the Achy-Breaky at the Country Western Party. Roberta, energized from Pilates classes, hot tubs, and foot massages, insisted on attending the Tropical Island Night deck party where she took first place in the limbo contest. Reese joined the Martini Club, which served exclusive designer martinis in ten-ounce martini glasses. He played mystery and trivia games with an oil rig industrial safety consultant and an MP from Alberta who wore a cowboy hat. Not once did Reese mention environmental degradation. Roberta cannot complain.

Although, he *almost* threw a banana peel into the ocean where surely a seagull or some sea creature would eat it. But no, he pushed the banana peel into the chrome trash bin by the elevators. Yes, he has behaved well. And what joy to sit with his family again, particularly last night in Le Bistro. Derek performed his eating eyeball trick, which he hadn't done for months, and when Reese hugged him he didn't recoil. Clara performed her raising-eyebrows-while-wiggling-ears stunt, and Reese, because his children demanded it, did his Porky-Pig-buzzed-on-Smarties impression. Roberta was laughing, *actually laughing* the way she'd laughed before the children were born, when Reese would take her for bike rides, standing on the pedals while she sat on the seat gripping his waist, her long legs stretched out for balance. Only once, in the rain, did they skid into some shrubbery, and even then Roberta laughed. So why hadn't she laughed until their last night on the cruise? Was it because Reese refused to go to the Sock Hop where rumour had it "Elvis" was going to make an appearance? Would it have been different if Reese agreed to attend "Band on the Run," a musical extravaganza featuring music from the sixties, seventies, and eighties? "You don't even like rock," Reese protested.

"That's not the point."

"What *is* the point?"

"The point is we're trying to break patterns, try something different."

Is that what we're doing?

He endured all of it, the Beatles, the Bee Gees, the Stones, the Eagles, Pink Floyd, Creedence Clearwater Revival. Yes, he has behaved well.

The nose-haired man nudges him and signals that he needs to get up. Reese and the magician stand in the aisle while the nose-haired man, off-gassing rum, stumbles towards the toilets. As he squeezes past the pregnant flight attendant collecting garbage, he cups his hands over her buttocks. "'xcuse me," he says, "so sorry." Reese expects the flight attendant to draw attention to this sexual harassment but she only reddens. Since takeoff Reese has felt some concern about her fetus, how it is coping with the changes in cabin pressure. Elevated body temperature due to sexual harassment can only add stress to the unborn. Fetuses, he believes, experience all. Nothing can be hidden from them. When they're forced into Earth's atmosphere, they have supreme knowledge and an awareness that is systematically blunted by human conditioning. They cry out when they are born because they know.

"The bottom line is," the magician states, applying lip balm, "it's one big schmooze fest. That guy Cooney, he's, like, Copperfield's bum boy. That's how he got the three tours in the Middle East. Plus, get this, *eight* winter seasons as head of entertainment at Santa Claus' Village in Lapland."

At the very least, Reese thinks, Roberta will allow him to visit the house and garden again, now that he's proved that he is capable of behaving like a contented family man of the twenty-first century. It pains him that she has let his garden go to seed and feeds their children pesticided, genetically modified, hormone- and antibiotic-saturated foods. "We can't afford anything else," she tells him. "Besides, there's E. coli on organic produce. All that cow shit." She has always been very capable, practical, fearless of plumbing. For this reason Reese was astonished when she told the mediator that she was afraid of him, that she perceived him as uncontrollable. Reese has always felt that he has surrendered to her with little protest. He has even agreed to all of her settlement demands.

The magician is twirling his spikes. "Have *you* had your PSA tested?" he asks. "Everybody should get tested. Get this. The first urologist said there was nothing wrong with me, didn't even order a biopsy. In two years my PSA score *doubled*. Doc number two said, 'We gotta get that tumour out.' A bunch of quacks out there."

The nose-haired man stumbles back and begins to dig around in the overhead compartment. Jackets and bags fall on the magician's head as over the PA system the captain warns them of pending turbulence. The magician stands, stuffing the jackets and bags back into the compartment. The nose-haired man, weaving about, possibly with delirium from the altitude and alcohol, flails his arms, trying to fight off the magician.

"Easy now," Reese says, wedging himself between them. "We have to sit down now, turbulence coming. Time to buckle up." He guides the nose-haired man back into the window seat. Within seconds he passes out. Reese fastens his seatbelt as he should be fastening the seatbelts on his children.

"Every time I fly they do this turbulence number," the magician complains. "Like, what's the big deal?"

As the pregnant flight attendant checks their seatbelts, Reese resists an urge to stroke her swollen belly. He is in awe of pregnant women. They are miraculous, sacred, untouchable. Even Roberta was miraculous and sacred, although had she expressed desire to have sexual relations he would have obliged. Fortunately, she was never particularly interested in sex. Previously he'd been dating an Argentinian accountant who'd believed that multiple orgasms assisted her English Language studies.

The magician unwraps another stick of Juicy Fruit. "Cancer changed my life. Used to be if somebody offered me yogourt, I'd toss it. Now I'm a total low-fat yogourt junkie."

The turbulence begins. Reese fears for his children, wishes he could be with them offering assurances about modern technology and jet planes. In their last stormy exchange prior to the cruise, Roberta had warned him that he'd better stop condemning modern technology because Clara and Derek were entering a modern technological world. "You scare them," she'd said.

"They told you that?"

He'd had them the weekend before, had set up a tent in his basement apartment. They'd eaten Fruit-to-Gos and played Jurassic-period and then Cretaceous-era dinosaurs. They hadn't seemed scared.

"Do you think it makes children happy," Roberta had asked, rhetorically, "to hear about species extinction and loss of wilderness and … and corporate takeovers?"

"Such is the reality."

"The reality is I buy Nike because they're good."

"They make'em cheap and sell'em high."

"I don't want to talk about this."

She always says, "I don't want to talk about this," as though her wants are the only ones worth discussing.

"They think the world's ending," she'd said.

"Yes, well?"

"You don't know that."

"A few thousand Earth scientists seem to think we're at a unique point in a multibillion-year history, that we can proceed to environmental ruin and wide-scale suffering or try to turn it around."

"You're telling them that?"

"The point is our *children* still have a choice. They can take action. They deserve to know that."

Without warning, the plane drops. Despite the seatbelts, Reese's and the magician's heads bang into the ceiling. Women scream, babies wail. The flight attendants, buckled to their seats, are nowhere in sight. The magician falls to his knees in the aisle and puts a blanket over his head.

"I don't think you should do that," Reese says.

"Bug off. I'm praying."

The captain explains that they have dropped fifty feet but that they should be through the worst of it. The magician continues to pray. Reese removes his belt and staggers down the aisle towards his family. A crew-cutted man shouts, "Sit down, dickhead!" at him. Roberta is hunched forward with her arms around both children, who have their eyes squeezed shut. The German is moaning.

"We're alright," Roberta says with that look Reese has come to dread. The look that says, *This doesn't concern you, we don't need you.*

"Go back to your seat, Reese," she says. "It's safer."

He staggers back to the magician.

"Can't you *read?*" the crew-cutted man shouts. "The sign says 'Fasten seatbelts'! Sit the fuck down!" He's wearing a College Girls Gone Wild T-shirt.

Reese squeezes past the magician, who is still praying under the blanket. He decides that if the plane doesn't crash, if they live to see another day, he will do whatever it takes to keep his family intact. No sacrifice — philosophical, psychological, or financial — will be too great. He may even renovate the bathroom. For years Roberta has complained about the chipped pink bathtub and Reese has argued that, though pink and chipped, the bathtub still works, why add it to landfill? He has told her that he has a vision of his children sitting on the pink and chipped bathtub on a massive pile of other discarded but perfectly serviceable bathtubs. "Reese," Roberta said, quite loudly, "it's like we live in a slum. That's a *slum* bathroom."

As the plane stabilizes, Reese vows to renovate the bathroom. Any bathtub she wants, she shall have. Although, he would like one of those water-saver toilets.

The magician crawls back into his seat, his spiked hair flattened by the blanket. The nose-haired man, having slept through the excitement, indicates that he needs to use the washroom again. The magician and Reese stand to let him pass. Reese moves up the aisle to check on his beloved family. All three are blissfully asleep, cuddled. He wants to put his arms around them, cherish them, forever. They are the posts to which he is pegged. Without them he would collapse. He kisses all three of them lightly on their heads while the German stares.

The movie has engrossed the magician. Reese tries to signal that he wants to resume his seat, but the magician remains oblivious. Reese takes the opportunity to use the facilities. As he approaches the toilets he sees the nose-haired man speaking to the pregnant flight attendant. He appears to be looking for something on the floor. As the pregnant flight attendant bends over to help him search, the nose-haired man presses his groin into her buttocks and grabs her breasts. The flight attendant shrieks. Within seconds Reese has grabbed the nose-haired man and pulled him to the floor. He expects other passengers to assist him but they are all asleep or plugged into the movie, iPods, or laptops. In the seats immediately around Reese is a contingent of seniors. He wrestles the nose-haired man, pushes his knees into his ribs. The man vomits onto his hands. The flight attendant disappears, presumably to get help. Reese has no choice but to hang on, inhaling the stench of vomit. A senior nudges him with his white loafers. "What in heck d'you think you're doing?" he demands.

The crew-cutted man in the College Girls Gone Wild T-shirt shouts, "It's a fucking *terrorist!!* Everybody *stay calm!!!*", tackling the nose-haired man's twitching feet. "Way to go, man," he yells at Reese, who is feeling the nose-haired man losing strength. A gnarled woman with brown teeth warns, "Check him for combustible fluids!" Suddenly everyone is panicked about combustible fluids and the terrorist. Reese's only concern is that he keep the nose-haired man away from the pregnant flight attendant or any other unsuspecting females. Roberta, when she wakens, will applaud him for his heroic deed. She has always despised men who objectify women. The co-pilot pushes through the crowd, ordering everyone to return to their seats, then kneels beside Reese. "I think you can let him go," he says. "He looks unconscious."

"Are you sure?" Reese asks. He looks up into the eyes of the pregnant flight attendant.

"Thank you," she says with a timid smile that banishes any doubts Reese has had about forcibly subduing a man.

"I can't feel a pulse," the co-pilot says, pushing Reese aside and beginning CPR on the nose-haired man.

"Really?" Reese asks. "There must be one. I mean … he can't be dead." He looks up, seeking reassurance from the pregnant flight attendant, but it is Roberta who is staring down at him as though he has gone mad.

"What have you done?" she says.

he insists that the limo drop Reese off first. He doesn't argue, is determined never to argue with her again. Clara jumps out of the car and hugs his legs. "Why can't you come home, Daddy? *Please* come home! Mummy, why can't he come home?"

"Get in the car, Clara," Roberta says. Her hair, usually restrained in a knot at the back of her head, has sprung loose.

"You're famous, Daddy!" Clara says. "You're going to be on TV! Junie says you're a hero. She says if her baby's a boy she's going to name him after you."

Roberta pries one of Clara's hands off Reese's legs. "We have to get home, muffin, school tomorrow."

"Do you really think he was a terrorist, Daddy?"

"I doubt it, sweetapple."

"Terrorists *bomb* people."

So does the president of the United States, Reese would like to say, but suspects that Roberta would perceive this as negative.

She straps Clara into the booster seat. "Nobody knows if he was a terrorist."

"I *hate* terrorists," Clara says.

"I'll see you soon, sweetapple," Reese says. "We'll do something on the weekend."

"I love you, Daddy."

"I love you too, angel."

Roberta closes the door. "Have you got everything?"

"I believe so," Reese says. "If not, you can give it to me later."

"What about your litho?"

"My what?"

"The Chagall."

"Oh, right."

Roberta digs around in the trunk and pulls out the rolled-up print.

"You don't think it's worth framing?" he asks.

"I wouldn't," she says. The exclusiveness of "I" is not encouraging, but then she touches his shoulder. "Look after yourself."

"Have you got enough cash for the driver?"

"Yes," she says, swinging open her door. "We'll be in touch."

He planned to comment on the vacation, say, "That went quite well" or "We should do that again sometime." But Roberta's door closes and they drive off and he is alone, with his bags and Chagall, outside the basement apartment. What did she mean by "We'll be in touch"? Whenever someone says they'll be in touch it means they will never be seen again. What did he do wrong this time? Was she angry that he'd used his media moment as a platform? When the compulsively smiling blonde TV reporter asked Reese how it felt to be a hero, he explained that he wasn't a hero, that the real heroes in this world are the ones fighting the global free market.

"The global free market means free to the corporations," he explained to the camera lenses. "*Free* to exploit without restraints or boundaries." The blonde gripped her smile until the light went off. The people behind the lenses then shoved their cameras back into their bags and lit cigarettes.

He can't wash the stench of the nose-haired man's vomit off his hands. He tries dishwashing liquid, and laundry detergent, but still his fingers stink.

He lies on his futon on the floor and sniffs his daughter's clothes, what she's left behind: hairbands, scarves. One mitten he wears on his thumb. His son didn't even say goodbye, despite the hug at Le Bistro. Reese looks at the photo of Derek and himself he has placed beside the futon. Reese is holding the boy at three on his lap. Derek has one hand on Reese's cheek, pulling his father's face down to kiss him. Roberta snapped the shot before the kiss, but Reese remembers the soft trust of Derek's lips. Derek was his sun, a source of brightness and warmth. Now the boy has been diagnosed with Attention Deficit Hyperactivity Disorder. The specialists blame his motor tics — blinking and throat clearing — on ADHD, as they call it. But it seemed to Reese that the motor tics lessened during the cruise. Hadn't Derek been more open? Hadn't there been a truce on all sides? Roberta didn't once refer to Reese's "idealistic efforts to save the planet" running them into a mire of debt. And Reese didn't speak ill of Roberta, not that he ever would in front of the children. Although he has had some concerns regarding the art student. He has seen the art student's car parked outside what was once his home — more than once. He can't speak directly to his children about the art student, can't say, "Is your mother balling a jerk in a Ford Festiva?" He asks casually if she's been giving consultations and they reply "yes" because "we need the money." Derek, blinking and twitching, says this with reproach, the implication being that his father cannot adequately provide.

For months Roberta has been doping Derek, even though Reese has stressed that the long-term effects of Ritalin are not known, that the boy is obviously stressed and in need of special attention. Derek accepts the mind-altering substances from his mother with complete trust, and when with Reese takes pride in remembering to take them himself. Reese watches helplessly as the child struggles to swallow the blue pills, which will vanquish whatever originality of thought remains in his brain.

He opens the only window in the basement apartment. It offers a view to the underside of a deck used by the above-ground tenants, who are singers and dancers. He can hear them now practising *Mamma Mia!* numbers, and probably guzzling light beer. He knows it will be hours before they bunny hop to the bedroom and perform God only knows what numbers in there.

What did Roberta mean by "Take care of yourself"? And why did she touch his shoulder? She looked sorry for him, as though he were a faithful dog who'd bit the mailman and must be put down.

Did she think he'd "lost it" with the nose-haired man? She told the mediator that he'd "lost it" when he smashed the car with the hyper-sensitive alarm system. Parked on the street outside their house, night after night it would go off due to racoons or squirrels or someone farting in passing until finally Reese got out the hammer. Apparently there were no witnesses. Neighbours had watched through blinds, relieved that someone was finally putting the animal out of its misery. Roberta, however, was unimpressed and has used the incident against him, has cited his "losing it" as a reason to keep his children from him.

He doesn't trust the mediator, who takes copious notes during their meetings. Occasionally she'll reprimand him with, "That's not what you said." Reese refrains from contradicting her though he knows she's wrong. She is a cat-lover. Her washroom is decorated with cat wallpaper. Her toilet roll dispenser is a wooden cat holding out its paws.

If, in fact, Roberta and the art student in the Ford Festiva are getting it on, shouldn't Reese reveal this to the mediator? Certainly the art student is a younger man with an artistic and therefore potentially irresponsible lifestyle — possibly a toker, or a crystal meth user. Even a man-hating judge could not deny that this would poorly influence the children. There is also the issue of the anti-depressants, although Reese suspects that many ex-wives take anti-depressants while retaining custody.

He is aware that — should she file for divorce — every passing day strengthens Roberta's position and weakens his. Temporary custody has increased her single-parent experience. Without any custody, Reese cannot effectively contend for same. If his children are being "responsibly" supervised, the Internet has advised him, a judge will not arbitrarily remove the custodian in order to appoint a potentially superior one. To obtain a change, Reese would have to present evidence that Roberta is unfit and that his children are being subjected to detrimental or dangerous conditions. For this reason it is crucial that the separation remain amicable. If she declares war, she will win.

Unless, of course, he can show proof of a dangerous liaison with the art student.

He can't help admiring the husband in New Brunswick who went on an arson rampage to revenge his wife's affair with the local fire chief, setting fire to three storage barns and two covered bridges. He has been found guilty on five counts of arson and vandalism. That the arsonist chose structures in which no life was sheltered endears him to Reese. Unlike the husband in B.C. whose revenge was to burn down his former house with his children in it, leaving his wife screaming in the arms of police. The husband sat in his Buick with the windows rolled up and watched his children burn.

Reese unrolls the Chagall. A red woman wearing a crown and blue shorts is lying upside down. A blue-green chicken is standing on her leg, a blue fish is floating above her, and a green horse is staring at her. There's a sliver of a moon with an eye playing a violin. *What's it all mean?*

He replays scenes, conversations, arguments. He remembers Roberta's irritation when he responded to Clara's questions with information about the dire condition of planet Earth.

"Shoving bad news at them isn't going to improve their quality of life," she'd informed him, dicing onions. "Do you want them to be depressives? They're *children.*"

"How are they going to know if we don't tell them?"

"They're *children*, Reese."

"They're our future."

She pointed the knife at him. "I don't want them turning into you. I'm not going to let that happen."

Prior to the separation, she'd become remote, no longer insisting that they have the occasional dinner out, sitting mutely at a table, fingering their wine glasses. He has always been comfortable with silence. She has not, gnawing words out of the air, questioning when there were no answers, joking when there were no laughs. As she began taking anti-depressants, there were fewer night fears and tears and he realized that he missed the sleepless nights, the silent closeness that they brought. Artificially freed of inner conflict, Roberta slept well on her side of the bed.

He rolls the litho back up and turns on the local news, watching the steel-haired anchor announce surging energy costs, increased taxes, rising homicides, then suddenly, after the car commercial, himself, muted. The steel-haired anchor speaks for him, calls him "a welcome vigilante in this age of terrorism." A passport photo of the "suspected terrorist" is shown briefly. His name was Amir Kassam and he was a Canadian citizen. Surely the autopsy will reveal that he died from some pre-existing medical condition turned fatal due to intoxication and high altitudes. A man doesn't *die* when tackled, it's not as though Reese had him by the throat. Amir Kassam's photo is replaced by slabs of butter, gobs of lard, buckets of bubbling oil while the steel-haired anchor delivers the latest news on fats. Reese gropes for the converter and surfs for Elena's sci-fi show. Elena, his former *grande passion*, who died from some pre-existing, undetected medical condition twelve days ago. Elena, whom Reese might be able to forget were his marriage not in disrepair. With Elena's passing he has gained control of their memories, can edit and revise to his satisfaction. Dead, Elena — unlike Roberta — understands, respects, loves, and desires Reese. He spots her spitting alien venom at a cringing human. Beneath her scales he admires her body, remembers its feel. Her name was Elena, but everyone but Reese called her Lainie. He'd breathed her night and day, and when she became pregnant he saw no reason for her not to have it. Elena saw many, and requested funds to terminate the pregnancy. He protested, sitting helpless in his bath while she sponged makeup off her face. "I'm too young for this," she said. He went with her, sat motionless in the waiting room with the mothers and lovers of equally too-young girls.

It was never the same after that. His complete inability to fraternize with the right people began to irk her. She was ambitious, regularly going through her Rolodex, calling directors, producers, writers, and friends of directors, producers, writers to curry favour. When Reese suggested she walk the dogs of the directors, producers, writers, or the dogs of the friends of directors, producers, writers, she began to go to parties without him, and to stay out later. He continued to pine for her, munching Doritos on the bed, watching *Cheers* reruns. He'd wake in darkness and reach for her, distraught not to find her there. Then she would arrive, rumpled but still Elena, and he would want to hold her, unable to be angry with her, wanting only to possess her. She began to suffocate, as she put it. His attraction for her — his lack of pizzazz, his "groundedness" — became irritating, hindering, and she left on a plane. Now she's dead. He finds this frightening because she still lives in his nerve centres. His lips can still feel the soft hairs on the back of her neck.

He pulled her bio off the Net, and an obituary written by someone called Kyrl Dendekker who claims to have known Lainie for years and who wrote that she was truly a renaissance woman — engaging, sensitive, spiritual, kind, funny, extremely intelligent, and enlightened. According to Kyrl she was an incredibly talented actress and a wonderful and inspiring friend, "a ray of light that has left us too soon." What Reese wants to know is, did Dendekker do her? Photos are included with the bio: Lainie, bare shouldered, gazing at a parakeet perched on her finger, and Lainie as the alien. Reese keeps these pictures on his person. He does not know why. Except that Elena remembered him young.

Kyrl Dendekker has made his e-mail address available for anyone "who needs to talk about Lainie."

What's inexplicable is that she seems more present dead than alive. Because she could be anywhere, flying around watching Reese, observing what a fuck-up he's made of his life. Alive, she was in California, remote in front of TV cameras. Alive, she was mortal and aging. Dead, she will be forever young.

The sci-fi show ends. Reese turns off the TV to hear his neighbours no longer practising *Mamma Mia!* numbers but bumping and grinding in the bedroom. When his children heard these noises and asked what was going on, Reese told them they were moving furniture.

Before they began singing and dancing they must have been frying hamburgers because his apartment stinks of scorched beef. It almost always smells of fried something: potatoes, bacon and eggs, grilled cheese. He lies on the futon. Even it smells of fried hamburgers. He must buy a proper bed, a brand-new odourless bed. He doesn't think he's ever slept on a bed that has never been slept on. The bed he shared with Roberta had been hers. All manner of men had slept on it before Reese. But it was a *quality* bed, she insisted, she'd paid a lot of money for it. He has never bought a brand-new bed because nothing saddens him so much as beds and mattresses put out for garbage pickup. Beds and mattresses full of lust lost and found, destined to be crammed into landfill sites. No, he believes in use and re-use. Sleep on the bed until it collapses beneath you. Roberta's bed saw him come and go. Roberta's bed is harbouring the art student in the Ford Festiva. Even the hamburger-smelling futon was pre-owned by a Greenpeace canvasser who changed her name to Tree when she left for Tibet.

He sniffs his fingers again. They still smell of vomit.

3

The call display feature has robbed him of the element of surprise. Roberta is not picking up. He pictures her seeing his number and continuing on with her day, not to mention her sordid affair with the art student. They probably meet at lunch, fondle each other in the cafeteria, smother each other in the Ford Festiva. Dis*gusting*.

He removes his wedding ring. Immediately his hand feels lost, unhinged. His thumb repeatedly reaches across his palm to feel for it. In its absence there is a white band of skin undamaged by the sun. The finger feels thinner, as though the ring functioned as a girdle. Perhaps now it will spread.

His bus swerves to avoid a small boy running after a ball. The bus driver curses while the father runs into the street and grabs the boy by the arm. "What the fuck did I just say? Are you *deaf?* If I have to tell you one more time you're going to get my boot up your ass."

Love your child! Reese wants to shout through the window, although he suspects his words would go unheeded. Love requires a loss of control, of power, something the shouting father would never surrender. Nor would Roberta. If she felt herself coming loose she would grab a wrench and tighten her bolts. Reese has watched her with their children, always hoping to see a connection between mother and child, the sense that they form a whole. But Roberta pulls back. She cannot tolerate weakness.

When her children falter, she doesn't listen but urges them onward, imagining that this is positive reinforcement. Her unyielding positive attitude has immobilized his children. They fear nothing more than appearing to be "negative" like their father. They tell their mother only the good, and harbour the bad deep in their souls.

When Roberta banished him from the bedroom, he slept on the futon in the basement where Clara would join him for snuggles. The warmth of her, the solid trust of her body gave him strength to go on. Clara would mutter in her sleep, and occasionally wake from a nightmare that Reese would ask her to describe. Often they involved witches and monsters with green hair but sometimes the "dead" dream would recur. In Clara's dreams her parents were dead. "We're not dead," Reese would assure her, holding her closer. "We're not going to die."

"You said nobody knows when anybody's going to die."

"That's true. But I have a strong feeling we're not going to die in the near future."

Unconvinced, Clara would continue to whimper quietly, reminding him of her mother before she took anti-depressants.

Roberta would find them in the morning, groggy on the futon. "You're a big girl, Clara. Big girls don't sleep with their daddies." Roberta's sociopathic mother, whom she loathes, has nevertheless succeeded in programming her daughter into believing that sleeping with children is detrimental to their mental health.

The bus halts in traffic. Beside him, Reese observes a newspaper being read by a sweating man. The headline "Husband Found Guilty in Axe Killing" catches his interest. Between the sweating man's thumbs Reese reads that a stay-at-home-father, who took care of his three children, including a severely disabled daughter, picked up an axe and hit his wife in the head twice, stuffed her body in the trunk of her car, then dropped off the vehicle at Blockbuster Video. They'd been arguing in the garage when she revealed that she'd been having an affair with her bowling partner and wanted a divorce. She said that she would take the boys and that he could keep the severely disabled daughter.

She threw tools at him, hit him with a hockey stick, and kicked him in the groin. In court, the husband admitted that he'd killed her but insisted that it was not premeditated. But the jury had no time for this.

If the wife had axed the husband because he'd been throwing tools at her, hitting her with a hockey stick, and kicking her in the groin, would *she* have been found guilty of murder?

Photos of the axe murderer and his wife show them both in part profile, heavy-lidded, smiling, showing teeth. Their noses are similar, as are their ears. What can this mean? That they grew to resemble each other and in so doing nurtured already well-established self-hatred? Did the mirror-imaging foster mutual loathing to the point that they *had* to throw hockey sticks at each other? Reese has never thrown things at Roberta, but an acquaintance whose cottage they visited two summers ago greeted them with the words, "It's happened."

"What?" Reese asked, disliking the man because he'd been a boyfriend of Roberta's once.

"The transformation," the cottager said, laughing heartily. "You look identical."

Reese did not want to believe this but feared it was true. He and Roberta went to the same optician, same hairdresser, ate the same organic foods, drank the same reverse-osmosis water, walked the same hypoallergenic dog. The transformation was inevitable.

He knows the day will come when his daughter, like his son, will not allow herself to be cuddled by him. He does not know what he will do on this day.

Why are there so few storybooks involving loving fathers? Why is it always Mummy bunny who finds baby bunny? Why is it always Mama bear who tucks in baby bear? Occasionally Papa is portrayed as Mama's assistant, doing the dishes and cooking meatballs, but rarely is he doing the intricate work of soothing the day's pains, rarely is Daddy doing the kissing and hugging.

Reese sniffs his hands. They still smell of vomit.

His father has fallen off the toilet.

"He was trying to transfer himself to his wheelchair," Reese's mother explains, scuttling up the stairs.

It's been some time since Reese has seen their bathroom. The grime coating its formerly shiny surfaces alarms him. He kneels and tries to shift the bulk of his father.

"Bloody hell," Bernie responds while Reese's mother frets in the hall.

"He never even wears underwear anymore," she complains. "It's disgusting. Naked from the waist down. All day he sits in that La-Z-Boy eating croissants and Campbell's soup made with cream and he asks why he's fat."

"The soup's not the same," his father grumbles into the bathmat. "The fuckers've changed the soup."

Reese pulls the hall rug into the bathroom and tries to roll Bernie onto it. "I can't do this by myself, Dad, you're going to have to help me here." His father stinks because he no longer washes. Congestive heart disease has caused neuropathy in his hands, which makes it impossible to grip, to turn taps, open shampoo bottles or toothpaste tubes, put on pants.

"It's like living with a homeless person," his mother says. "Spill some liquor on him and you'd think he was a homeless person."

"They usually wear pants," Reese says. He begins to drag the rug with his father on it into the hall.

"Where do you think you're going?" Bernie demands.

"To the stair glider."

"He doesn't even shave anymore," Betsy says. "I say, 'Use the electric one, what's so hard about that?' But he waits too long. You try to shave now with the electric one and you'll break it."

"Who said I was going to shave?"

"Easy for you to say, I have to look at you all day."

"Stay in your room. She only comes out for booze anyway."

Reese, experiencing twinges in his lower back, drags his father by inches.

"Did you get me my Crispy Crunches?" Betsy asks.

"Yes." Reese has begun to buy them in bulk. At the top of the stairs he lifts his father's legs, swollen with edema, onto the glider. He can't avoid seeing the penis, sagging and purple, meaningless.

How do you know Lainie? Kyrl Dendekker e-mailed.

We were lovers.

She never mentioned you.

"The superintendent wants to rent the parking space," Betsy says, "and even has a buyer for the car, but do you think your father will sell it?"

"You can't drive the car, Dad."

"It's worth three thousand."

"What's he offering?"

"Six hundred," Betsy says, "which we could use right now what with all the cab fares to the hospital."

His father farts. "It's worth three thousand."

"It's an old car, Dad."

"It's a good car. American, you can get your legs in it."

"Ford Escorts aren't exactly hot properties these days."

"I'm not taking a penny less than three thousand."

"That's just unreasonable," Betsy argues. "Reese, tell him that's unreasonable."

"You won't get three thousand for it," Reese says.

Betsy leans over Bernie in the stair glider. "Bernard? Are you listening, Bernard?"

"That's my name, don't wear it out."

"You can't *drive* it," Betsy persists. "Meantime we're paying for insurance and parking, does that seem intelligent to you?"

"She's got a point, Dad. I mean, that's costing you, what, a couple of hundred bucks a month or something?"

"Don't use that tone with me," Bernie says. "The two of you, always ganging up."

"He won't give that car up because it's his manhood. *All* old men have to give up their cars, Bernard. He thinks he's eighty-six going on twenty. You're *old*, Bernard, and you have to go on dialysis or you'll die. He won't even listen to the doctors."

"Let me die, then, if I'm old."

"This is what I have to put up with, day and night. And he stinks. It's embarrassing being seen with him."

Bernie glides to the first floor where Reese waits with the wheelchair.

"Is there anything I can get you at the store?" Reese inquires.

"I have a list," his mother says.

A woman in a hat is shouting at her dog. "Grow up! No other doggie on the street behaves like this. Do you see any other doggies on the street behaving like this?" Reese retrieves a shopping cart. Just once he would like to walk into a supermarket and not hear Karen Carpenter singing, "We've only just begun …"

He looks at the list. The same as last week and the week before that: cream, bacon, butter, cold cuts, white bread, butter and lemon tarts, Ripples (sour cream and onion), canned peaches, cream cheese, pineapple juice, tonic water, Minute Rice, Campbell's soup, croissants, butter pecan ice cream. Their diet would kill normal people.

Nobody offers to help him at the bed store. He lies on several beds in an effort to release neck tension. He tries different positions, different pillows. Looking up, he sees a sombre woman with a name tag that reads Mary Jane Lovering looking down at him.

"I need to buy a bed," he says, uncomfortable at being viewed lying down by a woman standing up.

"That's a Stearns & Foster queen," she tells him. "Very popular."

"It's very springy."

"You don't like springy?"

He sits and bounces up and down. "Not particularly."

"Try this one." She points to an even bigger Stearns & Foster. He sits and checks the bounce factor.

"Less springy?" Mary Jane Lovering asks.

"A little."

"That's absolutely top-of-the-line." She has narrow front teeth that angle inward, providing a flash of rodent.

"How much are these?" Reese inquires.

"With the pad you're looking at five thousand."

"Dollars?" Immediately he realizes how stupid this sounds. He had no idea that a bed could cost five thousand dollars. Clearly this is a *quality* bed, a bed that Roberta would envy. He could mention it in passing: "I slept great last night. That Stearns & Foster queen is top-of-the-line." She would know that he bought a quality bed without her, and that it was a *queen,* which could only lead to more comfort and contented sleeping, a finer state of love with some unnamed woman, and an all-round happier, more productive life.

He had no intention of spending five thousand dollars on a bed. He doesn't have five thousand dollars to spend.

"I can tell you're not in love with it," Mary Jane Lovering observes. "You've got to be in love with your bed." She points to another bed. "The Shiffmans are manufactured more traditionally. They have an eight-way, hand-tied box spring and use only natural fibres."

"Which are?"

"Compressed cotton and wool instead of synthetic foams. Try it."

"Definitely less springy." Natural fibres sound promising. He hasn't really thought about synthetic foams, hasn't really thought about what's in a bed.

She pulls back the duvet. "Make yourself comfortable. It's the only way to find out."

He lies on his side and she pulls the covers over him, sending him back to boyhood, when Mummy had healing powers. Which must be why he wanted her after he killed the pigeon. Which must be why he wanted her after he killed Amir Kassam. Because Betsy, whose chain-smoking has destroyed her circulation, believes her son incapable of ill-doing. Even when she saw Reese's Scout shirt smeared with pigeon blood, she believed that Dudley Dancey did it. Betsy's beliefs are unshakeable. She considers the health warnings on cigarette cartons to be propaganda. A doctor recently cut off two of her toes and advised her that if she didn't quit smoking he'd have to cut off her foot, maybe even amputate to the knee.

"Do you have any allergies?" Mary Jane Lovering inquires.

"No."

She pats the Shiffman. "Then this might be the one for you."

"It feels hard."

"Hard?"

"I can feel my hip and shoulder pushing into it."

"What is your current sleep system?"

"A futon."

Mary Jane Lovering looks saddened for a moment, as though he's just told her his dog died.

"Actually," Reese clarifies, "before the futon I slept on a quality bed."

"Do you remember the brand?"

"No. My wife bought it."

"I see." She averts her eyes, unable to meet the gaze of such a bottom feeder. "Why don't I let you browse?"

"Thank you." Losing conviction, he tries a Sealy with a pillow top, which smothers him. Mary Jane Lovering turns her attention to a young couple in corporate attire who lounge on the beds, together and individually. "How long will one of these things last?" the young husband asks.

"Forget how long it lasts," the young wife interrupts, "we've got to get the bed that *feels* right, we can buy another one later."

"If you buy a bed and don't like it," Mary Jane Lovering advises, "you can send it back within thirty days."

"I already told him that," the young wife says. "Sweetie, people send beds back all the time." She reclines on the bigger Stearns & Foster and takes a call on her cell. The young husband lies beside her while she converses at length with someone else about what she received at her wedding. Will this be their life, on a succession of Stearns & Foster queens, talking on cellphones about recent acquisitions because they can't talk to each other? Acquisitions and beds that will soon be on their way to landfill sites? Like Bernard and Betsy, once the children are grown or dead, will the corporate couple practise tolerance until bowel function becomes impossible to ignore? Is Reese's marriage destined for such a fate? Is he genetically programmed to destroy relationships? Should he remain devoted to Elena who is dead and therefore unthreatening? Whenever he cooks a chicken he thinks of her. They bought the Romertoph together. "A *clay* pot?" he argued. "Do you know how much *energy* is required to heat a *clay* pot for two hours?"

"You'll taste the difference," she said coolly, handing the pot to the cashier.

And he did. The chicken was tender and juicy on the inside, crispy on the outside. They cooked many chickens together and ate them with their fingers then had greasy sex. Roberta still has Reese's Romertoph. He must retrieve it. His daughter used to love the chicken he cooked in it. She used to say it was her favourite dinner. Who's cooking her chickens now?

The Eezy-Rock radio news distracts him with news of a six-year-old girl's abduction. She was dragged kicking and screaming from her grandmother's front lawn. Her dead body has been found, naked and abused. Mary Jane Lovering and the corporate couple seem not to hear this. Reese knows the body is not his daughter's because the abduction happened in Sudbury. Even so, the thought of the little girl's suffering leaves him nauseated, angry, despairing.

He never knows where his children are anymore.

"No lawyer?!" bellows Sterling Green. "Are you out of your mind? It's *war*, boyo. She'll screw you unless you screw her first. Clean out your bank account, hide your assets, valuables, tax statements, cancelled cheques, diaries, debit and credit card receipts, anything she can use to establish a level of consumption that'll justify a level of alimony. She's probably photocopied stuff already, her and her lawyer are probably putting together a financial picture. And no way do you move out."

"I already have."

"Are you *nuts*? She'll argue abandonment, which gives her claim to the house and everything in it."

34

"It's only a trial separation."

Sterling eats more of his Double Whopper. "Wait till she starts talking to her lawyer." He drinks more of his Coke. Everything about Sterling is more. He won't settle for less. Reese didn't want to work for Sterling, Sterling wanted him, thought he would bring credibility to his fundraising-without-morals operation. "You should have driven her out, I'm telling you."

"It's not like that," Reese says. "It's not adversarial."

"It's always adversarial, boyo. Even if it starts out nicey-nicey." He drops an Alka-Seltzer into a glass of water. "And what's with the wetlands people? They're pished, won't get off my ass about you."

The "wetlands people" are gunmen posing as environmentalists because they want to hunt ducks.

"I took their leader out for a brew to cool his jets," Sterling says, "and he got rat-arsed. I had to drive him home. For an environmentalist he's got a pretty pristine lawn, even had one of those little pesticide signs on it."

Reese nods understanding, as he always does, while reviewing results. He has 120 callers working part-time throughout the afternoons and evenings. The call centre seats fifty-two. Some of them barely speak English. They're not supposed to eat at their booths but they do, stashing foreign foods in unlikely crevices. The dialler, a half-million-dollar refrigerator-sized computer, keeps them working non-stop. It is a thankless, repulsive job and only the desperate or truly naive can stand it, and even they never last. Staff shortages are constant. Serge Hollyduke, who supervises the callers, is a sadist and therefore effective at managing for-profit fundraising. They raise money for hospitals, advocacy groups of the right or left, child sponsorships, the Federation of Anglers & Hunters, any disease going, the Humane Society. When a caller's performance is poor, Serge Hollyduke issues warnings and disciplinary notes before terminating them. But there is a pretty girl who has been exempt from his boot camp approach. After checking the data, Reese has no choice but to remind Serge of the response goal of 5 percent. "Has she hooked *anybody*?" he asks.

"She's got a name," Serge says. "Avril Leblanc. And she just started." Serge has a new haircut, very short, revealing a bullet-shaped head.

"She's been here three weeks," Reese says, which is a considerable amount of time at such a repulsive job. "She's spending a lot of time on the phone. What's she talking about?"

"She makes them comfortable. They like her."

Sterling takes a swig of Alka-Seltzer. "They just don't cough up credit card numbers."

Serge fondles the short hairs on his head. "I've got her chasing some lapsed donors. Just give her a chance."

"Fess up," Sterling says, "you get a boner looking at her. It won't do, boyo. We're not here to jack off."

The arteries on Serge's neck begin to bulge.

"Let's reassess in a couple of days," Reese suggests. "I've got mail to write." He must come up with some shift incentives for the dwindling marketers; tickets to brainless events usually go over well. And he must talk to his client service people.

At the coffee station, Avril Leblanc spoons honey into her herbal tea. "Hey," she says.

"Hello." She smells of oranges. She's probably been eating oranges at her booth, dripping juice, leaving sticky fingerprints.

"I'm really enjoying the job," she says.

"Good."

"I like talking to people." She dribbles honey on the counter before licking the spoon.

"Good."

He would like to slide his hand under her skirt. He would like to take her here, on the floor only vaguely dry-mopped by the night cleaners. He would like some distraction.

4

Clara's birth was difficult, different from the boy's. Reese and Roberta had been holding hands when she'd had Derek. When they had the girl they'd been arguing about knives. Roberta wanted to buy a hundred-dollar knife, said that a kitchen without a good knife was useless. Reese had been carving chickens with Canadian Tire knives all his life and saw no need for a hundred-dollar knife. Her contractions started while they were testing blades. They went home, timed the contractions, and waited, barely speaking to each other because of the knife debate. He prepared spaghetti for Derek with a Canadian Tire knife because Roberta said she wasn't hungry and was in too much discomfort. She didn't call it pain because that would have sounded negative. He offered massage but she couldn't keep still. "Why aren't they speeding up?" she said re the contractions. "They should be speeding up." She paced, squatted, breathed heavily. Derek watched in amazement and fear. Reese tickled him and offered to play horsey. The boy climbed onto his back but remained uncustomarily mute while Reese trotted around. Roberta, presumably also wanting to hide her torment from her son, continued her pacing in the backyard while Reese and Derek built Duplo spaceships. Still they could hear her gasping and blurting expletives.

"Is Mummy going to die?"

"Absolutely not, sweetpea."

"Is it supposed to hurt?"

"Yes." Reese pulled him onto his lap and kissed him, holding him tight because at that moment it felt as though Derek was all he had, that he must shield him from whatever lay ahead. Or die trying.

"Why?" Derek asked.

"Why what?"

"Why's it hurt?"

"It's just the way humans are built."

Derek wriggled from his grasp to search for Play-Doh.

Their obstetrician, the one they'd carefully selected, was not on call. They were faced with a frizzy-haired, apparently bored tennis player fresh from tennis camp in Boca Raton who introduced himself as Dr. Cam Phibbs. The woman waiting for a baby in the other bed was also at the mercy of Dr. Phibbs. She won his favour by admitting that she was a financial planner and offering tips on the NASDAQ. Reese feared that the financial planner would take precedence over Roberta, that Roberta would be left with a fetus in distress while Cam Phibbs reviewed his portfolio. But Roberta, contrasting her behaviour at home, was acting with calm and fortitude, and it occurred to Reese that she was attracted to the sporty, tanned hairiness of Cam Phibbs and wanted, therefore, to impress him. The tennis player did at one point address her. "Yo, how's it goin'?" he asked, to which she replied, smiling bravely, "Not bad."

"It's gonna come out," Cam Phibbs said, "don't you worry about it."

"I'm not," Roberta said, which was a lie. Reese could see that she was worried out of her mind, that she was imagining her baby dying inside her. He held her sweating hand but it felt forced. She pulled away to scratch her nose then did not reach for him again. He felt extraneous and found excuses to wander, purchasing water bottles and Trident sugarless gum. His terror of hospitals caused him to urinate frequently. He became familiar with the men's room, and the other expectant fathers wearing baseball caps who appeared considerably less frightened than he was. It seemed to him that even the natal unit smelled of death. Behind a closed door a woman sobbed; Reese tried not to speculate about the cause of her grief.

Roberta began to vomit. Fortunately, the pain was also intensifying for the financial planner. Cam Phibbs located an anaesthetist to give her an epidural then suggested that Roberta have one too while they had her, the anaesthetist, in the room. By this time, Roberta was wailing in pain and had lost all interest in natural childbirth and the sporty, tanned hairiness of Cam Phibbs. Reese averted his eyes as they poked the large needle into her spine. He asked the financial planner's husband, who'd just arrived off a plane, if he could turn down their portable CD player. Reese had been forced to listen to country western music for several hours and felt that at any moment he might terminate the box. The financial planner's husband grudgingly reduced the volume by a fraction. Garth Brooks began belting out another tune. "Isn't he screwing some hussy?" Reese inquired.

"I beg your pardon," the financial planner's husband said.

"All those songs about loving his wife, being faithful and all that, and there's Garth out screwing some hussy."

Roberta began gesturing frantically at Reese. "What is it?" he asked.

"Don't cause a scene," she whispered hoarsely.

"You want to hear this?"

"I don't want a scene."

Twelve hours later, Reese was fastening the strings of surgical scrubs, tucking his hair into an elasticized cap, and slipping paper booties over his shoes. He was no longer of this world. Sleep deprivation and country western music had bludgeoned rational thought. As instructed he followed the nurse into a delivery room so harshly lit it seemed smoky. Roberta, as far as he could make out, had also lost contact with planet Earth. She had the glazed eyes of the dying and he feared he would soon be without her and the baby. He couldn't imagine raising Derek on his own, the silent meals, the relentless void. "No," he protested.

"No?" the nurse asked, bustling around trays of what looked like tools of death.

"Nothing."

She didn't give him a second glance, had no time for his emotional blurting. "Stand by her head," she ordered.

By rote he urged his wife to breathe in, breathe out, push, as he'd been taught to do in Lamaze class, but he could see that he was only irritating her, that if she weren't preoccupied with torturous pain she'd have told him to bite it. The nurse continued to reduce the anaesthetic. "You have to feel it to know when to push," she advised. Within minutes Roberta was screaming. Reese could only watch as violent contortions gripped her. The tennis player, his frizzy hair stuffed into a bulbous surgical cap, became violent as well, crouching between Roberta's legs and barking commands. In exasperation, it seemed, he lifted a pair of surgical forceps, thrust them into her, and began wrenching them back and forth. "She's not a tennis ball!" Reese shouted, picturing an irate Phibbs on the court, slamming his racket into the ground. But then the forceps clanked to the floor and Phibbs stood up with a tiny, purple creature in his hands. Its hair and skin were smeared with fluid, its limbs and head hung lifeless. The neonatal team, shrouded in orange, whisked it away and suddenly it was just them again, Roberta and Reese not holding hands while Cam Phibbs stitched the tear from her rectum to her vagina. "It's just a precaution," he advised, regarding the abrupt departure of their baby. "It's a girl. She'll probably be fine."

Roberta began crying, bereft of pain and baby. Reese tried to reach her across the equipment but it was awkward. And she didn't want him, he could tell. She wouldn't look at him, covered her eyes, forcing her tears to spill around her fingers. They wheeled her back to the room vacated by the financial planner and husband. Reese turned off the CD player and put his arms around his wife. She felt coiled, as though at any instant she could strike. "It'll be alright," he said. "It's just a precaution."

"Go fuck yourself," she said and began to heave sobs he'd never heard before; sobs full of despair and longing that humbled him, that made him resolve to buy many hundred-dollar knives.

He was in the corridor finding ice for her hemorrhoids when the baby was returned. Clara, to his amazement, was no longer purple and knew what to do with her mother's breast, unlike Derek who'd had to be coached. Roberta didn't smile at Reese but she formed a peace sign with her fingers. Reese kissed her palm. All would be well. That's what he thought.

He checks his messages again. Roberta still hasn't returned his call.

"Testosterone gel," Sterling says. "I'm telling you, you got to try this stuff, it's like my cock don't know how to quit."

Sterling paces beside Reese, trying to brainstorm a new angle on yet another campaign for a childhood illness. "This one attacks the lungs, right?" he offers. "So why don't we say something like *with every breath they take*, kind of tie it in with that Police song, you know the one …?" He begins to sing the song. "My ex loved that one." He eats more pizza-flavoured popcorn, tosses a kernel into the air then catches it. Reese's office smells of pizza. "She wants me to loan her some money. I said, 'Get serious.' She says her dogs are freakin' out because she has to keep the house clean for the realtors, says the dogs shit on the floor because it's so clean, it stresses them out. Not my problem, I told her."

Reese is trying to convince himself that Roberta is not ignoring him, that shortly she will call and apologize for her abrupt departure and insist that he take the kids for the weekend.

Sterling waves a newspaper at him. "This is some deal John Travolta's got going, parking his jumbo jet outside his place. It's like a small airport only it's got a swimming pool plus eight bedrooms. What's he need a jumbo for would be my question. Guess he gets off flying big jets."

Reese has been offering free advice to an environmental group in Alberta who can't afford a dialler and who are trying to prevent an oil corporation's development of a wetlands for a relatively small amount of oil. The current government has amended the regulation that prohibited screwing with the wetlands — a unique area that covers less than 1 percent of the province. Once gone, there will be no more endangered plant species, no more

migratory bird habitat, no more oxygen. But John Travolta will
be flying big jets.

Serge Hollyduke shoves an envelope at him. "You've got to
sign for this."

"What is it?"

"Fuck if I know."

"Did I not ask you not to use that word?" Sterling says.

"I don't use it around the callers."

"Don't use it, period. *Capisc?*"

Reese signs the courier's form and looks at the envelope's let-
terhead. *Babb & Hodge, Barristers and Solicitors.*

"Somebody suing you?" Sterling asks, tossing a kernel into
the air but failing to catch it. It lands on Reese's desk, bounces
into his glass of Evian, and begins to swell. "What's up, boyo?
Bad news?"

Reese has opened the letter and has tried to read beyond
"your wife has retained us to act as her lawyer" but the words
blur and breathing has become difficult.

"Easy, boyo. It's the wife, isn't it? What'd I tell ya? Take
action, my man, or you'll be out on the street."

Reese leans over the letter, narrowing his eyes to improve
focus, he *must* focus. Roberta has told Babb & Hodge that she is
concerned because Clara has been acting "strangely," has taken
to turning her dolls over and "sticking things up their bottoms." *What is she talking about?!* In their last meeting with the
cat-obsessed mediator, Reese had carefully presented his prepared statement explaining the reasons why joint physical custody would be in his children's best interests. Roberta did not
object, sat there with a gherkin up her ass while his jaw flapped.
Now, *now* she is rebutting his argument, with the help of Babb
& Hodge, by implying a concern about molestation?! Without
actually offering molestation as a direct objection to joint custody? Without *accusing* him, without so much as *mentioning his
name* she is, by implication, branding him a child molester? This
is madness.

"Get a grip, boyo."

Reese tries to shake his head but it will move in neither direction. He tries to mouth words but is without voice.

Babb & Hodge have recommended that he have no further contact with the children until Clara is assessed by a child psychologist. They provide him with the name and number of the child psychologist should he have any questions directly related to the assessment. They advise him that they will proceed no further until they have received the psychologist's report. Reese grabs the phone.

"No, you don't," Sterling says, covering the dial pad with his hand. "No angry calls, no cussing, she'll record it, use it against you. You call Herman, tell him you're a friend of mine." He scrawls a number on a Post-it. "He ain't cheap but you get what you pay for."

Breathing in short gasps, Reese dials the number of the child psychologist. He leaves a message that he knows is too long, too afraid, too desperate.

"She's got you right where she wants you, boyo. She'll cut you off at the knees."

He scurries off the bus and crouches behind a trash can. If he's seen, he'll be reported by the hostile mothers who will believe Roberta's lies. It's afternoon recess and the children appear to be playing, although he knows they're rehearsing for adulthood; practising numbers on each other, abusing power, testing lies. Derek is ferociously playing soccer, jabbing his feet between players' legs to get at the ball. Clara stands alone, waiting patiently for her turn on the monkey bars. The alpha kids ignore her. Reese sees no noticeable change in her. He longs to make himself visible, to see the shock of surprise as she runs towards him. Although would she run towards him? What has Roberta told her? What *brainwashing* has taken place? Better to stay behind the trash can than discover that his daughter is no longer overjoyed to see him.

He leaves another message from a phone booth. Although his body is vibrating, he manages to keep his voice even. He explains that he hasn't witnessed Clara acting strangely, turning her dolls over and sticking things up their bottoms. If Roberta has, in fact, witnessed this behaviour, it can only mean that Clara's school is not safe, nor the homes of her playmates. He suggests that there be no more sleepovers or play dates until the matter is cleared. Only at the end does he become pathetic. "Please, let's talk about this. This makes no sense to me, I mean I ... I ... you're *killing* me. Please, I mean, can't we talk about this, *us*, can't we talk ...?"

He loiters in the park. Soon Roberta will be dropping Clara off outside the church for Sparks. He must make a plan. Can't think of a plan. A father is helping his small daughter fly a kite that is larger than she is. He pushes the kite into the wind and shouts, "Run away from it, Katie!" The kite, an exotic purple and red bird, surges upward as Katie runs. "Way to go!" her father shouts. "You got it, look how high it is!" Reese has flown kites with both of his children, enjoyed their wonder at their newly discovered power. He wants to fly kites with them again, when will he fly kites with them again? The purple and red bird falters. "Run away from it, Kate! Run!" She does, but the wind has died and the bird nose-dives to the ground. Katie watches, amazed. The father picks up the kite and jogs backwards, away from her, stretching the string, avoiding tangles. "You ready?" He pushes the bird into the wind again and Katie runs. It hurts to watch other people's children. Reese watches anyway, in the same way he picks a scab. He will watch until he bleeds.

Two women with Starbucks cups in hand and two children each take over the bench beside him and discuss wine tours and weight-loss products while their children wander — too far in Reese's opinion. "It's a protein bar," the one in capris says re something that resembles a chocolate bar, which she's shoving into her mouth. "Rick and I are trimming. He's got all these weights." She discards the wrapper, allowing the wind to whisk it across the grass.

"*I've* got to start working out," the other says, sucking on her Starbucks cup.

"Me too, once I get organized. We're doing these mini meals all day long. He makes this protein shake in the morning and takes it to work with him."

"I eat those power bars."

Both women wear slip-on sandals, which they slap against their heels. They are in another world, galaxies away.

"You've got to make sure there's fat in them as well as protein," the one married to Rick advises. A piece of newspaper blows against Reese's leg. He tries to shake it off but it clings to him. Pulling it loose, he's halted by a photo of Pamela Anderson, the woman famous for her breasts, who refers to them as "props." He reads that she contracted Hepatitis C from sharing a tattoo needle with her former husband who belted her outside their Malibu home. The husband pleaded no contest to a charge of spousal abuse and was sentenced to six months in jail and three years' probation. Pamela Anderson has won full custody of their children because of the abuse. *Full custody.*

Reese fears he might belt Roberta if she persists with these lies. Or if he discovers her in the sack with the art student. He almost hit her once, when he couldn't make himself understood and words were choking him. Then he remembered the pigeon, its slippery blood on his hands, the crack of its skull against the rock. He is not a violent man. He must communicate this to the child psychologist, explain that even though he has killed a man and a pigeon, he is in truth quite shy and docile. Maybe he won't tell her about the pigeon.

Or the rat. Although Roberta was an accomplice in the rat murder, helped him corner it then squash it with the two-by-four. It took too long, they had to press harder and harder to make the squirming stop. They had pet rats that crawled over their children, eliciting giggles. But the black rat, the intruder, was brutally killed. Reese has never quite recovered from this, can still see the rat's terror, its bulging eyes. He shovelled its remains into a garbage bag that he deposited in a waste receptacle belonging to the local McDonald's. He presumed that dead rats were not uncommon there.

Below Pamela Anderson's props Reese reads that a Ugandan woman bit off her husband's penis and testicles after he slapped her. Another man in Uganda died after his wife, angered by his inability to provide for her and their two children, cut off his testicles. These acts of aggression are considered to be in response to an increase in domestic violence against women in Uganda. Interesting that, though abused, the women retain access to their husbands' genitals. Soon a multi-national will be marketing Sleep-Eezy Ball-Guards.

The women drain their lattes and leave the cups, plastic lids intact, on the bench for the wind to toss into the grass. "More *landfill!*" a shrill voice in Reese's head scolds. Startled, he can't place the voice although it is unsettlingly familiar.

"It's your brain that gets you through," the mother who is married to Rick the weightlifter says.

"You've got to have smarts," the other agrees. The coffee cups somersault into tulip beds.

"Go 'head," the shrill voice snaps in Reese's head. "Choke the planet with your *trash!*" Reese realizes that the voice belongs to his grade three teacher, Mrs. Ranty — a troll of a woman — who'd told him he was *so* stupid he'd have to piggyback her his *entire* life so she could tell him the times tables. She's on his back now, digging the heels of her old lady shoes into his kidneys.

"Have you tried that new Thai place?" the mother married to Rick asks. "We keep wanting to go but, I mean, what are we supposed to do with the kids? Once you pay the babysitter you're out a hundred bucks. I said to Rick, 'On our anniversary, we're splurging on a spa.' *No kids.*"

"What bliss," the other says. Reese has lost sight of their children.

When he sees the car that was once his park in front of the church, he scrambles from the bench and crouches behind a minivan. Roberta steps out and opens the side door. Clara hops onto the sidewalk in her pink Sparks T-shirt. He notes that mother and daughter don't kiss or embrace on parting. Roberta has never been demonstrative. They exchange quiet words before Roberta pats Clara's head and says, "See you later, kiddo." Clara doesn't appear forlorn as she skips into the church. Reese sees no indication that she is desperately missing him. He has this horrible suspicion that his longing is much greater than hers, that with time she will adapt to a fatherless life, that with time she will be galaxies away.

He hangs his head over the edge of his daughter's bed, feeling his bones being compressed by rigid muscles. He lifts his head then lets it drop back and listens while his connective tissues crackle. It unnerves him that his bones, under his skin, look like everybody else's. Even Clara's bones, were she dead, would look like everybody else's. He wouldn't recognize them. He clings tightly to her pillow.

Amir Kassam had a wife and children. Reese saw them on the news; the wife and daughter had burkas over their faces, but the boy looked vengeful, taut, as though he'd never forget, as though when he reached manhood he would track down and eviscerate his father's killer. Although there was no killer. Only a sick heart that had already been subjected to triple-bypass surgery, "Courtesy of Canada's health care system!" a rabid journalist commented.

Clara's bed feels good, although a bit narrow. He pulls up the fitted sheet to locate a brand name. He can't remember when they bought it, if it cost five thousand dollars. The chicken pot sits on the floor beside him. He only came for the pot, had not intended to doze on his daughter's bed. But the familiar surroundings of her room have soothed him — the stuffies, the books he's read to her, the untidy doll's house that belonged to Roberta when she was a girl. What if Elena is watching him on his daughter's bed, thinking he's perverted, pathetic? "Don't get pathetic on me," she'd say when he resorted to begging. *Killed by a ruptured blood vessel in the brain*, Dendekker wrote, adding that she didn't suffer. How could he possibly know? Didn't Amir Kassam suffer? Didn't he feel his heart exploding, his world ending? Don't we know when we're about to die?

Reese must leave before his family returns from karate. If he is found here, Roberta will call the police, change the locks, terrorize their children with her fury.

Sterling demonstrated his usual lack of discretion by announcing to one of the childhood disease clients that Reese was going through a "ball-busting divorce."

"Been there, done that," the client said. He was very thin with jutting hip bones.

"No, kiddin', Wes?" Sterling said. "So we've all got something in common."

Wes rested a hand on one of his jutting hip bones. "I never see my son anymore."

"Never?" Reese asked.

"I go to his baseball games," Wes said.

"You mean you take him?" Reese asked.

"No. I go so I can see him. We wave to each other."

Reese knows that he cannot live sneaking into his daughter's dance recitals and his son's soccer games. He knows that if Roberta reduces his access to waving in public places, he will have no choice but to take an axe to her head. *Acting strangely and sticking things up dolls' bottoms.* What is she talking about?! Wouldn't he have noticed this — Clara, in pain — there's no way he could not have noticed this. He releases the pillow, now damp with his tears. He turns it over and finds one of Clara's fuzzy ponytail elastics. He thinks of baby teeth under pillows, that panicked groping in the dark while the child sleeps peacefully. It is not possible that this is no longer part of his life. Not possible. He sniffs the ponytail elastic then slips it on his wrist.

"Belly dancing is an art form," the futon salesgirl says. Her midriff is exposed, her belly button pierced. Reese tries out several futons, considering that perhaps he is a futon man after all.

"My boyfriend gives me grief about it," the salesgirl says. "He thinks it's exploitive, like, he just doesn't get it."

Reese thinks of lying on futons with the belly dancer, how much energy would be required. A girl Clara's age somersaults on futons while her parents prod and squeeze them. Reese fears but also hopes that the child will fall and split her head. He imagines that his pain might lessen in the face of someone else's tragedy.

He bought a chicken for the pot. It's warming in a plastic bag beside him, breeding salmonella. He will not cook it, he knows. The Babb & Hodge letter has rid him of any desire to eat well or live long. When Sterling asked him, over his Krispy Kreme, "What exactly are your priorities anyway?" Reese replied, "Don't have any."

"Don't get crunchy granola on me," Sterling said.

Why fight it? Any of it? He's scaring his children. They stopped playing in the yard when he stopped watering the lawn. The city had pleaded with its citizens to water sparingly due to low water levels. Reese appeared to be the only citizen on his block who'd heeded the plea. "The neighbours think our grass is ugly, Daddy," Clara said. "Please, can't we water it just a little?"

"Sweetapple," Reese said, "if everybody waters 'just a little' that adds up to a whole lot of water, which means there won't be enough for everybody."

Mike, the chief complainant and water waster, was hosing down his SUV. "*Your* weeds blow seeds onto *my* lawn." Clara ran into the house.

In retaliation, Reese stopped weeding altogether and witnessed nature's reclaiming of his patch of dirt. In addition to the rampant dandelions at least three different species of thistle flourished, and orange-limbed creepers. A thin intricate spreading vine smothered the grass. Clusters of clover grew, and even mushrooms. They did not demand watering. Mike stopped speaking to him. His children were ashamed.

He is scaring them. *And Clara is acting strangely and sticking things up dolls' bottoms.*

He rolls onto his side on a foam-filled futon to watch the somersaulting girl and the belly dancer. There can't be many years between them. Clara will soon want to belly dance and have her belly button pierced. Clara will soon squeeze her breasts and thighs into tight-fitting clothes and allow herself to be fondled by boys wearing pants falling off their asses, allow them to push their penises into her orifices. Reese shoves his face into a rice-filled pillow, which the belly dancer has assured him is awesome for neck tension.

There is always kidnapping.

At the Bay, he tries to watch a movie in the electronics department. The store is quieter than his basement apartment and he hopes that a movie will take his mind off his children. Unfortunately, there are children in it, and a husband and wife who enjoy getting it on. Reese can't recall ever witnessing a real live couple, with children, feeling each other up while packing their minivan. He senses that a tornado is pending in the movie, but the couple go on Frenching while their children squabble. Sex has been destroyed by its public existence, Reese believes. Too many articles about orgasms. Too much instruction about foreplay and positioning. Too many movies in which actors move seamlessly through fornication, climaxing in unison. Too many print ads of mouths on mouths and naked body parts. An excess of misrepresentation of what should be the most private of acts. He has always imagined that he would try to explain this to his children at the appropriate time. He has always imagined that he would be there.

The garbage piled on the lawn outside his basement apartment has pushed his "War is Not the Path to Peace" sign to the ground. A municipal strike has halted pickup but the singing-and-dancing tenants don't appear to have absorbed this information. One of them, the female, sits scantily clad on a plastic Adirondack chair, reading *Variety*. Reese yanks his peace sign from under the garbage and jabs it into the lawn closer to the house. The upstairs tenant's overabundance of flesh embarrasses him. A dragon tattoo spans her thigh. She ignores him. He has no presence in her mind, he is but a subterranean creature to be trod upon. Her witless arrogance astounds Reese. The world is overrun by such doughy cretins, unable to see beyond their own greed and consumption. He did remind her that he had acquired additional recycling bins — which he had placed in the hallway in front of her apartment — for recycling pop cans and light beer bottles. She has not used them.

In his burrow he studies the printout of Elena. She gazes wistfully at the parakeet, as though she were alone in a deeply contemplative moment rather than inches from a camera lens.

Neither Roberta nor the child psychologist has returned his calls. The cat-obsessed mediator has left a clipped message explaining that it is out of her hands, that he should refer all his questions to Babb & Hodge.

Avril Leblanc appears in his mind, sucking on oranges. Forced to monitor callers who fail to meet the response goal of 5 percent, he'd listened in on her. He learned that she believes in meditation and being with what is. "Just *be* with it," she advises potential donors who offer the usual excuses of financial hardship or previous commitments to other charities. "I gave so much to the tsunami," they tell her. Provided with any kind of opening pertaining to stress-related issues, Avril Leblanc recommends herbal remedies and vitamin supplements. The potential donors do not pledge gifts but do thank her for calling. Serge Hollyduke continually trails Avril Leblanc and, at her suggestion, has begun to wear Birkenstocks.

Reese must sleep, try to sleep. He hears hums. He closes his window but still hears hums. Earlier, the transformer on the concrete pole outside the house was humming. Now it is reverberating through his futon. He tries to picture his children sleeping: Clara with one leg thrown across the bed as though running in dreams; Derek curled tightly into a fetal position. Reese tries to visualize their faces, the shapes of their heads, the curve of their necks. To his horror, the images are fading. He wraps the ponytail elastic around his finger and lies, wired, knowing that sleep will not visit him; that he must endure the hum; that life is full of tests which he has mostly failed; that he has come to expect defeat and that this in turn defeats him.

5

"Put the knife down," Reese says to his mother.

"He kicked me," Betsy protests. "First of all he sends the ambulance away and then he kicks me."

"How could I kick you if I can't move my legs?"

Bernie fell off the toilet again. Betsy couldn't contact Reese because he was in a meeting with the duck hunter/environmentalists. She called Med-merge, who lifted Bernie off the floor and offered to take him to the hospital.

"He hasn't gone to the toilet for *six days*," Betsy explains, "and he says there's nothing wrong."

"It's happened before," Bernard says. "It always rights itself." Bruises have disfigured his face. There are blood as well as coffee stains down the front of his polo shirt, and dried blood and croissant crumbs caught in the white hairs on his thighs.

Betsy gesticulates with the knife. "Not for *six days*, Bernard. You haven't been constipated for *six days*. Every twenty minutes he thinks he's going to go and I have to listen to his grunts."

"Six days is a long time, Dad. Mum, put the knife down."

"I don't feel safe with him, he's crazy."

"Off she goes," Bernie says, "the drama queen."

"Your face is pretty bruised, Dad. What did you do? Smash it into the tub?"

"Of course," Betsy says, "that's what he always does. You've got *two* black eyes, Bernard, and maybe a concussion."

"In your dreams."

"It might be a good idea to let somebody take a look at you, Dad, the cuts on your nose anyway."

"The rat poison makes the bruising worse," Bernie says.

"He means the blood thinners," Betsy interprets. "He says they're killing him like a rat." Bernie went to medical school in 1948 and believes that any advances in medicine since then have been bogus.

"It wouldn't hurt to have somebody take a look," Reese persists.

"Nobody's looking at anything."

"Mum, put the knife down."

"He's afraid they're going to put fingers up his bum," Betsy clarifies. "I told him everybody has to have fingers up their bums some time. Would you rather be *dead*, Bernard, than have a professional's finger up your bum?"

"Why don't you mind your own business? I don't go telling him *your* business, do I? There's a few things I could tell him he wouldn't be too happy about, should I tell him?"

"People *do* die from blocked bowels, Bernard, it's a little different."

"From smoking till they cut off your legs?"

"Can you guys stop," Reese pleads, "just stop?"

They both look at him and ask, "What?"

"Arguing. It's pointless. What's the point? If he doesn't want to go to the hospital, fine, that's his right."

"Easy for you to say, you don't have to listen to him, every twenty minutes ..." She mimics Bernie's grunts.

"Stay in your room and close the door," Bernie advises.

"I brought you more Crispy Crunches," Reese intervenes. "I've got to go. I have a dinner engagement."

"A date?" Betsy asks, excitedly exchanging the knife for the Crispy Crunches. "Are you seeing somebody?"

"I'm still married, Mother."

"Then how come we never see your family?" She follows him to the door. "You were never right for each other. Didn't I always say she should have married a dentist? You're too sensitive for her.

"I'm still married to her, Mother."

"Don't get testy." She smells of cigarettes. There are cigarette burns on her stretch pants.

One of the things that put Roberta off her mother-in-law was Betsy's nostalgia for Reese's old girlfriends. When Clara and Derek came to visit, she'd drag out the photo albums. "Now *she* was a nice girl," she'd say, pointing to a snapshot of a girl she'd barely acknowledged when Reese had brought her home for dinner. Betsy appeared especially fond of a girl named Mitzi who was famous for blow jobs. In the photo, Mitzi is dressed as Princess Leia. "That girl never had a bad word to say about anybody," Betsy would comment, stroking Princess Leia's braids. Her point was that Roberta had many bad words to say about many people, in particular her mother-in-law.

Waiting at a light, the headline "Spousal Slayings on the Rise" in a newspaper box arrests him. Men, apparently, are killing their wives or ex-wives, accounting for 47 percent of all family-related homicides. What does killing the wife do for the men? Beyond the initial adrenalin rush from swinging the axe, what is left? Remorse? Prison rations and no access to their children? Can this be better than negotiating with Babb & Hodge?

He has been encouraged by the judge's ruling in the case of the billionaire. He need pay only $50,316 U.S. a month in child support for his four-year-old daughter rather than the $490,000 U.S. requested by the mother. How is it possible to spend even $50,316 U.S. monthly? Does she own an airport and fly big jets? The judge called the billionaire's wife's request "incredible" and "grossly excessive." Reese had hoped to hear such words coming from the meagre lips of the cat-obsessed mediator. Certainly, in Reese's opinion, Roberta's demands have been incredible and grossly excessive. Already the chains are upon him. It will be a life of penury. The only advantage has been that he's been forced to ride his bike to save on transportation costs, which is better for the environment, providing badly needed exercise and daily near-death experiences. Shying out of the way of opening car doors and right-turning vehicles reminds him that he must want to live, for, although he's thought of suicide — as have, according to a recent poll, one in five Canadians — he would not act on it.

Avril Leblanc also rides a bicycle, with a dream catcher suspended from its handlebars. Reese listened in on her a second time while she was consoling a potential donor who was distraught over a newspaper story regarding the murder of a four-year-old girl. The girl's parents had forced her to drink large amounts of water as punishment; autopsy reports indicated death from "forced water intoxication." Reese felt himself becoming distraught over this information but Avril Leblanc calmly advised the potential donor — and incidentally Reese — to avoid being "reactive" to such items in the newspaper, that perhaps reading the newspaper less frequently would reduce stress in the potential donor's life. Unconvinced, the potential donor — a retired veterinarian — asked if Avril had read about the Iranian man cutting off his seven-year-old daughter's head after suspecting that she had been raped by her uncle. Avril said that she'd made it a policy not to read newspapers and that this had improved her meditation practice enormously. "A post-mortem," the retired veterinarian persisted, "showed that the girl was *still a virgin*." Reese had to disconnect at this point, feeling much too reactive. He reached for his Evian bottle, for the first time perceiving it as an instrument of torture. He thought of children everywhere, beyond the ones making headlines, suffering, and as always he could not understand why.

Peggy and Scott have invited a woman to dinner. As she and Reese are the only guests this can only mean they are intended to mate, which means that Peggy and Scott believe that his marriage is over. Over wine and hors d'oeuvres, they do not ask about Roberta or the children, but speak humorously of Reese's determination to "save the planet" and warn the woman, whose name is Wilda Mims, not to let him catch her idling.

Feeling misled and misunderstood, Reese tries to clarify the situation by mentioning the cruise.

"That was some pricey swan song, Reesie," Peggy says. "Whose idea was that anyway?"

"Oh, I *love* cruises," Wilda Mims says. "I'd like to go to Alaska. I've always wanted to see the aurora borealis." She speaks very quietly, smiling frequently, revealing multiple mercury amalgams. Peggy shepherds them into the living room then hurries back to her convection oven. Although Reese has absorbed that Wilda Mims is a probation officer, he is having difficulty hearing further details of her conversation and says "pardon" several times. He searches for the volume control on the stereo until Scott appears with more wine, enthusing about his state-of-the-art sound and theatre system, then returning to the wine cellar. Wilda Mims resumes speaking words Reese can't hear as he fumbles again to find the volume control. He smiles when she smiles, nodding periodically, acutely aware of his body language, determined to present himself as a happily married man. He notes that Wilda has muscular arms, which suggests that she works out. Reese imagines her smiling as the convicted swear that they are going to rehabilitate themselves, then heading to the gym to pump iron and bat around balls. Her mouth stops moving and she doesn't smile, and Reese realizes that it's his turn to speak.

"Do you believe that pedophiles can be cured?" he almost shouts. Wilda looks very solemn before saying something Reese can't hear, then she smiles. He smiles back.

Conversation over dinner is easier, further from the stereo. They discuss blogs, YouTube, iPhones, personal listening devices, and PCs. Scott wants to upgrade again but Peggy says he's being a booboo pants, they upgraded less than six months ago. "What are you using these days, Reese?" Scott asks.

"Nothing."

"You're kidding?"

"No. I listen to birds."

"And they say *I'm* a radical," Wilda says. Reese can't imagine anyone saying that Wilda Mims is a radical.

"So how are people supposed to get in touch with you?"

Scott asks.

"I have a phone plugged into a wall," Reese says. "Or they could always write me a letter."

"You know what, this might be the new thing," Wilda suggests. "I was reading somewhere that people are spending more time alone, and that even when they're together they're alone because they're watching TV or checking e-mails or surfing or something. My sister's typical. When she's making dinner she's talking on her cell to somebody on the school council or something. Meanwhile Jud is checking his e-mails and the kids are either watching TV or doing homework with headphones on. It's pretty sad."

"Sad," Reese agrees.

"What a pair of whiners," Scott says. "Any information I want is at my fingertips."

"Too much useless information," Reese suggests.

"Too many penises," Wilda says, "and vaginas and breasts. Who needs that with your cup of coffee?"

"All Scott does," Peggy says with unexpected disdain, "is look for deals on eBay. Isn't that right, Lulu?" she asks the cat. Peggy and Scott don't have children, just two cats to whom they speak in baby voices. Lulu does not answer Peggy, leaving a yawning chasm in the flow of chitchat. Roberta has often complained of Reese's dinner conversation, that he will slip into his environmental "rant" unless reined in. As they nibble on an assortment of cheeses, Reese tries to think of some benign dinner conversation. "Good cheese," he says.

"Tell them about Bovine Growth Hormone," Mrs. Ranty urges, digging her heels into his kidneys. "Tell them the cows live two years. They used to live for fifteen!" Sesame seeds from the crackers lodge between Reese's molars. "It's killing *them*," Mrs. Ranty snorts. "What d'you think it's doing to you, *dullards?*" Reese tries to discreetly dislodge the sesame seeds with a fingernail.

"The poor cows are conssstantly *zseeck*," another voice in his head adds, "masstitiss, eendigesstion, diarrhea, cysstic ovaries, utereene problemss, reduced pregnancy ratess, shorter pregnanciess, lower birth weightss." To his dismay, Reese realizes that the voice belongs to his Polish Scout Leader, Igor, who washed Reese's mouth out with soap when he said "clitoris." Igor survived concentration camps and building a plumbing business in Etobicoke. He had no time for "no-goodniks," of which Reese was one. Igor's sibilant "Ss" won him the codename "the Boa" among the no-goodniks.

"You lossers," Igor scoffs, "drink the milk zsucked off thesse zsick, *drugged* cowss!"

"What was that?" Wilda Mims asks, looking at Reese.

"What was what?" Reese shoves another cracker in his mouth. It concerns him that he is hearing voices in his head, but doesn't everybody? He passes the cheese to Wilda.

"Well," Wilda Mims says, "aren't we a chatty group?"

Reese swishes wine around in his mouth to loosen the seeds. "There's pus in the milk," he blurts.

"What milk?" Peggy asks.

"Pus?" Wilda asks.

All three of them look at him as though he has made a rude noise. "I was just thinking about mastitis," he explains. "In cows. The ones given growth hormones. The pus isn't visible, meaning we drink it. Along with the antibiotics plugged into the cows to treat it."

"Oh, Reesie," Peggy says, "don't be such a booboo pants, we're trying to enjoy ourselves here."

Is this where mankind has gone wrong? The pursuit of happiness as a state of being that requires no effort or thought?

Peggy offers more genetically modified crudités. Scott heads for the cellar to scout for more wine.

"I don't usually eat dairy anyway," Wilda admits. "It makes me feel bloated." She smears more brie on a cracker.

"We had brown water at work today," Peggy says. "It creeped everybody out. They couldn't wash their hands or make coffee or anything."

"Why was it brown?" Wilda asks.

"The super said it was something in the pipes. They were

working on the pipes or something."

Third World children crowd into Reese's mind. He sees the brown water they drink daily, and the severely malnourished seventeen-month-old North Korean who was on the reverse side of Pamela Anderson's props. The baby's eyes were half closed; his irises rolled upward, his mouth gaped like a baby bird's. He is probably dead now. Reese gulps more wine.

"Oh, Scott," Peggy says. "Before I forget, the tree guy phoned. He says it's going to cost five thousand to cut them down, dig up the roots, and everything."

"You're cutting down *trees*?" Reese asks, gasping only slightly but feeling a sudden urge to shake his body violently.

"I hate them," Peggy says. "They're always dropping needles and oozing stuff."

"That's sap."

"Whatever, it creeps me out. It sticks to the lawn furniture."

"Trees are *dying* due to development and smog," Reese protests, feeling the wine heating his face. "Trees can't *survive* surrounded by concrete and paving stones! *We* can't survive!"

"Whoa," Scott says. "Why don't you tell us how you really feel."

"I'm not cleaning off those chairs another year," Peggy insists.

"Five thousand's a bit steep I would say," Scott comments.

"I don't care. I want a deck." The cats meow and Peggy speaks to them. "You'd like a deck too, wouldn't you, Lulu and Ricki, so you can warm your tumtums in the sun."

"Did you hear about that guy who stabbed some driver with his car keys?" Scott asks. "He said the guy was driving too slowly. He's being charged with assault with a weapon, property damage, assaulting a police officer, and resisting arrest."

"*You* get psychotic around slow drivers," Peggy snipes.

"Yeah, but I don't get out and stab them."

Over dessert Scott tells of one of his cases; a man suing a strip club, claiming he was injured by a "reckless" exotic dancer who kicked him in the head.

"You're making that up," Wilda says.

"I kid you not. He's seeking damages from the club, claiming it was negligent in not posting signs warning the public of the risk of sitting too close to the stage. He was just sitting there minding his own business when she swung around a pole and kicked him. Fractured his nose."

"My heart bleeds," Wilda says.

"What was he doing in that scuzzbar anyway?" Peggy asks. "Any man who goes to one of those joints *deserves* a kick in the head."

"He was lonely," Scott says, "was just looking for a good time."

"All can be forgiven in the quest for a good time," Reese says, wine pulsing where his blood should be. "Destroy Earth, Mars, whatever's required, as long as we're *having a good time!*" He can't believe he's speaking like this when he has resolved not to, to stop scaring his children. He *must* stop scaring his children.

They all look at him. Wilda Mims smiles. Peggy begins to clear dishes.

"I'm going to a golf day tomorrow," Reese says in an attempt at normalcy, remembering that, in the event of a divorce, he may require Peggy and Scott as character witnesses.

"Lucky bastard," Scott says. "Some fundraising thing?"

Reese nods.

"Do yourself a favour, Reesie," Peggy advises. "Don't start telling them how much water it takes to keep the green green, or how many pesticides they use and how it's killing them through their golf shoes."

"It's a bit of a turnoff," Scott agrees.

"Just try to have a good time," Peggy says.

As Reese leaves them on their pressure-treated, carcinogen-emitting front porch, he knows he will never be invited there again.

Peggy waves. "Take care, Reesie."

"Keep it real," Scott says.

After a near-death experience with a white stretch limo,

Reese, cycling in slow motion, tries to remember who he was seventeen years ago, driving Greenpeace canvassers around in an unheated van. To pay for gas he would buy beer and sell it for two bucks a bottle to the canvassers. At the end of the night, inebriated, all seemed sublime to him, and possible. Seventeen years later, inebriated, nothing seems sublime, or possible. Being without expectation should be freeing. The problem is the children. What happens to the children?

Annoyed, Sterling will not permit him to drive the golf buggy because Reese was late to register and did not bring his own clubs. When Reese explained that he didn't own any, Sterling said, "You were supposed to rent them." Reese could not help noticing Sterling's golf bag bulging with clubs. "You're not using mine, boyo," Sterling said. "It's against the rules."

"Who's rules?"

"USGA. We can't share clubs unless we're a team."

"Can't we be a team?"

"Not on your life. Buck up. Go rent a set."

Plodding back to the clubhouse, Reese wondered if this is what we have come to, a world in which each man must own his own house, car, extension ladder, and golf clubs.

On returning, weighted with clubs, he again offered to drive the buggy because he felt it would free him of the obligation to converse. When he admitted his preference for walking, he noted a certain huffiness from Sterling and the players in the other buggy. Apparently, all must go in the buggy, with their own clubs, their own tees and golf balls, *and* feign amusement at "hooter" jokes.

Teeing off proves easy — driving the ball down the freeway and onto the green. Banging the ball into holes is another matter. The prospect of eighteen holes causes sweat to drip from Reese's nose. He swings repeatedly, digging up turf. Dirt lands in his eye. Sterling, sniffing for business, bonds with the man with hooter humour who owns a chain of dollar stores. "The mark-up would knock your socks off," the man says. "People'll buy anything for a buck."

Roberta is continuing to ignore him; Gwyneth Proudley, the child psychologist, left a message saying that she would "be willing" to meet with him if he felt that there were "issues" to discuss. She sounded weary, as though returning the calls of fathers accused of molesting their children is a task she would prefer to do without. Reese hurriedly dialled her number, but was thrown again into her voice mail.

Sterling and the dollar store magnate lose interest in watching Reese fumble with his clubs when they discover they both own sailboats. As they compare their yachts' prominent features, the magnate's buggy partner offers pointers to Reese in heavily Chinese-accented English, demonstrating when his vocabulary runs out. Reese, hungover and sleep-deprived, rolls his neck to release the tension. He feels the phantom pain from his missing children — his severed limbs — constantly. What would Gwyneth Proudley make of this metaphor? Would she say, "Your children are not an extension of you"? Betsy keeps intruding on his thoughts. And Elena, and Roberta, and Avril Leblanc. Why all these *women*? The fact that he's thinking about them indicates that they have power over him. Roberta has justifiable power, but Elena's dead, his mother's a nicotine junky, and Avril Leblanc doesn't bear thinking about. Avril Leblanc is the kind of woman he avoids, who talks about karma and smells of patchouli. Even the non-reactive upstairs tenant keeps lounging around his temporal lobes. Reese tossed the chicken carcass into the backyard hoping that, in between *West Side Story* numbers, the tenant would stroll in the yard, stumble over the chicken, and scream herself to death. But she didn't leave her deck. The stench of her sunscreen wafted into his window. And the hum continues. Reese has phoned and spoken to much voice mail at Toronto Hydro, eventually contacting Roman Derbish, a supervisor who joked, "Why do transformers hum? Because they don't know the words." When Reese made no comment, Roman said he would "look into it." And the delinquent boys who live next door entertain themselves by dropping garbage into Reese's recycling bins. When the bins aren't available, they litter on the lawn. They play street hockey, shouting and swearing as they slam the puck around. Reese suspects that these are the same teenagers who made the community newspaper headlines by taunting a ten-year-old loner named Barton, hanging his dog by its leash from the top of a piece of playground equipment and leaving it there to die. Barton watched helplessly, screaming for help, until a dog walker called 911.

The Chinese golfer takes a call on his cell and shouts into it. Reese climbs into the buggy with Sterling. "Back in the saddle," Sterling says. "Is this not a beautiful course? They sank a ton of money into it. Beautiful." He takes out his comb and arranges his hair.

"Water," Reese mutters. "They sank a ton of water into it."

"Bee-ewtiful."

"Earth has no more fresh water now than it did two thousand years ago when our population was three percent its current size."

"You don't say. I've never been able to stomach the stuff myself. Those eight glasses a day you're supposed to have. Makes me queasy."

Reese has been reading about native birds. For the most part the birds are hard-working and respectful of their neighbours. Then there are the brown-headed cowbirds. Too lazy to build their own nests or warm their own eggs, cowbirds lay their eggs in the nests of other birds, tricking them into raising cowbird chicks instead of their own. One per nest, which hatches earlier than the nest owner's eggs and therefore demands feeding earlier and grows stronger sooner than the owner's hatchlings. Kirtland's warbler, one of the rarest birds in North America, suffers not only from loss of habitat but because their babies die while the warblers are busy serving the cowbirds. Only the oriole has the sense to eject the cowbird's eggs. The warblers and sparrows continue to feed and protect while the cowbirds, freed of responsibility, have *a good time*. Sterling is a brown-headed cowbird. Duped, the rest of the birds continue to feed and protect. Reese would like to think of himself as an oriole but knows that in his soul he is a warbler.

A donor, who has been making monthly payments for years to the Humane Society, has advised Reese that the Bible warned of an apocalypse, that it is unstoppable and that only the believers shall be admitted into the gates of heaven.

"What if this *is* heaven?" Reese asked.

"What's that?"

"Planet Earth. Maybe this *was* heaven and we destroyed it."

The donor looked at him with the veiled eyes of those who care for the terminally ill. "Bless you," she said and patted his hand. This same donor is one of many who are angry that their donations have been used outside of their communities. They want their money to help only the suffering dogs and cats in their own backyards. Reese has been taking their calls and apologizing for any misunderstandings but inquiring, humbly, if a suffering dog is not a suffering dog? Is a dog undeserving of care because he lives in Parkdale?

Luncheon is even more trying. "Gifts" of wine await guests on chairs at place settings. Piles of dinner rolls are consumed while wine is poured and gulped. Vomit-coloured soup is served, and meat, covered in pink sauce, that Reese suspects is either chicken or pork. A man called Robert Vinkle explains to Reese how his truck came to be vandalized. "The alarm system was a factory-made piece of shite. The frickin' thing didn't go off when they crashed the back window." Reese nods understandingly, although he is having trouble feeling present.

"Never," Robert Vinkle says, tearing apart another dinner roll, "go for a factory-made system."

En route to Golf Day, Reese asked the cabby to drive by the house that was once his. There was no sign of the Ford Festiva. This relieved and yet disappointed Reese, as he was hoping to collect evidence. He had at the ready the portable video camera he'd used to photograph his children. It occurs to him that he should have those videos in the basement apartment. He paid for the camera, the tape. They're *his* videos. He will retrieve them as he did the chicken pot, will even return the chicken pot, which he'll never use because it only reminds him that he has no Clara, or Elena. Robert Vinkle is pulling up his pant legs to show Reese the sutures from his recent varicose vein stripping. "Second time around," Robert Vinkle admits. "The doctor tells me if I don't quit the forty-five-minute drive to work, he'll have to strip more until I don't have any left and they have to cut off my legs."

"Ouch," Sterling says.

"Maybe your socks are too tight," Reese suggests.

"My what?" Robert Vinkle asks, trying to cut through his meat.

"My mother always tells me to make sure my socks aren't too tight," Reese explains. "She says if your socks are too tight you'll get a heart attack. She actually checks my socks."

"Is that right? Well you might want to tell her that I'm supposed to wear *pressure* stockings. A pressure stocking sounds a bit like a tight sock, don't you think?" Pink sauce is collecting on the edges of Robert Vinkle's moustache.

"I'll tell her," Reese says, wishing that his arms did not feel like sponge.

"Who's read *Dracula* around here?" Sterling interjects. "I mean the real thing, the book."

"There's a book?" Robert Vinkle asks.

"I read it," Reese offers. Whenever he speaks, he hears echoes.

"That is one scary book." Sterling says. "I mean imagine being that guy, Harker or whatever his name is, in this big mansion and you're talking to this guy and he looks in the mirror and he's got no reflection. I mean *that's* scary. And these women you can see through keep coming at you. Now *that's* scary."

After the main course there are speeches. Watching lips move, Reese absorbs nothing. He applauds automatically with the other warblers. More glasses are raised, more wine quaffed. A large-buttocked woman in a miniskirt named Wendy Hiscock — "Good thing it's not hercock," Sterling remarks — announces that it's time to collect gifts. Their tickets are numbered, Wendy Hiscock explains, corresponding with a gift on the table. All the golfers check their tickets then swarm the gift table. Reese remains seated, staring at his salad. The golfers, excited, rush back to their tables ripping the gift wrappings off chocolates, mini cheeses, pots of jams, tiny bottles of Bailey's Irish Cream, and trinkets made by Third World children.

To Wendy Hiscock's astonishment there are not enough gifts to go around. She apologizes, clasping her hands over her bosom, suggesting there may have been a mix-up with the numbers, and that perhaps some of the guests would be willing to share their gifts. The guests avoid eye contact as their arms surround their gifts.

"Mine's up for grabs," Reese says, his words resonating off the pastel walls of the banquet hall.

"That's very generous of you," Wendy Hiscock says. "You must be number eighty-nine." She holds up his cellophane-wrapped package.

"That's me," he says.

"Would anyone else be interested in sharing?" Wendy Hiscock inquires. No one puts up their hands. The golfers start leaving with their gifts. Sterling leaps up and offers his to Wendy Hiscock. She visibly warms to him, and actually touches his arm to show her gratitude. Sterling leans towards her, making some comment Reese is grateful not to hear. On returning to the table, Sterling slaps Reese on the back. "I just did it to impress you," he says. "You and Jodie Foster."

"Can we go now?"

"And miss dessert? Get outta here. She's got nice jugs anyway, even if her name's a bit touchy."

Robert Vinkle also donates his gifts. A small crowd gathers around the table on which the donated gifts have been opened. The golfers snatch at the tiny bottles and jars and trinkets. "I think we're going to have to make it one item per person," Wendy Hiscock intervenes, "I'm so terribly sorry." Giftless golfers turn away from the table in disgust.

Dessert is served — fruit crepes with ice cream. "There is a God," Sterling says.

Robert Vinkle waves the crepes away. "My doctor says no more ice cream or I'll fucking die."

Reese begins to worry about the hamster. He's certain that Roberta is neglecting to clean his cage, that Bonaparte has been forced to live in his own filth. And doubtless no one lets him out of the cage to roll around in the plastic ball, or wander a tabletop. Clara is too young to look after him and Derek has adopted his mother's view that the hamster is just a rodent whereas Reese has watched Bonaparte and knows how clever he is. Late at night they would sit at the kitchen table together. To liven things up Reese would place a wastebasket near the edge of the table and Bonaparte would leap into it and tunnel around in the dirty Kleenexes. After a few minutes, Reese would carefully lift him out and put him back on the table enabling Bonaparte to again leap into the wastebasket. Once, Bonaparte escaped. Reese despaired, certain that the hamster would die of dehydration in a crevice. He left the cage open and put it on the floor. Within an hour Bonaparte had found his way back to his cage, his home. Reese told Roberta of this extraordinary feat, hoping to impress her with the hamster's savvy. "How difficult is it for him to smell his own piss?" Roberta said.

It scares him how he is growing to hate her.

7

He did not intend to go drinking with Robert Vinkle, who has insisted that he call him Bob. But the prospect of returning to the basement apartment or loitering in a twenty-four-hour doughnut joint — avoiding headlines about ecological disaster — depressed him. Although, even at Vinkle's — the bar owned by Bob — his eye is caught by "Drug Taint in Canadian Water" and by the man with long fingernails and greasy hair parted in the middle on the other side of the paper. He notices Reese glancing at the headline and taps it. "Whatever happens to the frogs happens to us," he warns. "Boys getting born with no balls."

"Mutations nothing," Mrs. Ranty interjects. "We're talking altered DNA!"

"We're talkeeng *freakss* breeding *freakss!*" Scout Leader Igor adds.

The long-fingernailed man taps a photo of a twenty-two-month-old girl with breasts. Reese looks away, at the television on which a middle-aged Boston couple describe the Cabbage Patch doll they've raised as a son for nineteen years. He has his own playroom and a red Corvette. They plan to send him to university. "He makes friends easily," Joe, the slope-headed father, says. "He's great to know." The mother, Bonny, gripping the edges of her track suit, adds, "He does a lot of things with his dad. He's like most boys." Their real-life daughter, Vicky, an associate at Wal-Mart, says, "He got a dog. *I* never got a dog."

Bob has made it clear that Reese's drinks are on the house. Not that Reese wants more drinks, but he's hoping that several will provide an anaesthetic effect. After pouring them beers, Bob leads Reese to a table in the corner. In the banquet hall, Reese mentioned his trial separation, to which Bob responded, "I'm there, brother." In the truck on the way to Vinkle's, Bob told Reese that he'd gotten "a good hit" off him, which "doesn't happen too often." Reese senses that Bob needs to talk, that varicose veins are the least of his concerns.

"She was jiggin' her assistant," Bob says. "While I was out busting my ass. I heard it from one of the waitresses, she said it'd been going on for months, even before Alicia told me to move out. You know what she said? She said, 'We never see you, Bob, you're always at the bar. I want somebody who can be around.' The whole time she was going at it with her assistant."

"I'm sorry," Reese says.

"So I go over there after work, it's like two in the morning or something, and I start pounding on the door. She won't open it so I break it down. She's in her bathrobe and I say, 'Where is he?' and she says, 'What are you talking about?', that kind of shite, so I push her out of the way and start heading upstairs and she starts grabbing at me and saying 'He's in the closet, leave him alone, we all know you're the big man.' I just about clubbed her." Bob drinks more beer and pushes a dish of peanuts towards Reese. "So, like, at this point I know I can kill him and that this might not be the way to go, so I shout, 'Don't come down here or I'll kill you.' Meanwhile she's gone and called 911."

The beer tastes sour and Reese's eyes are burning from the grease-laden vapour emanating from the kitchen. A waitress with a lip ring and scarlet hair navigates the greasy pathways in the broadloom, stopping before Bob. "Can I have Friday off? I got to take my kid to the dentist."

He winces. "You need all day to take your kid to the dentist?"

"It's at the dental school. It's not like you provide me with health insurance so I can go to a decent dentist where they have actual appointments."

"Whatever," Bob says, waving his hand, looking back at Reese. "So the cops charge me with uttering death threats and breaking and entering. They shove me in a cruiser and tell me they know three cops in jail for the exact same reason I'm going to be wearing the orange jumpsuit. They came home late and found some guy in bed with the wife." Sitting beside a "My Goodness, My Guinness" mirror, Reese shakes his head to suggest disbelief, catching a glimpse of himself that is not cheering. He seems to have aged ten years, and his haircut, done by Corrado the barber for eight bucks, does not flatter him.

"*Four* days I was in there," Bob says. "Had to share a cell with a guy who shot somebody in the head and slugged me if I flushed the toilet too early."

Around them sit couples in various states of courtship. Reese can't imagine being one of them, can't imagine having the stamina for getting-to-know-you conversations and gropings in the dark.

"So now I'm under house arrest for six weeks," Bob says. "I'm allowed to go to work, that's it."

"But you went to Golf Day," Reese says.

"Do me a favour, don't advertise it."

"Sorry."

"So, it makes you wonder, doesn't it?"

"What?"

"Who this person is you hooked up with." Bob eats another peanut. "It makes you wonder."

"It does."

"My mother never liked her."

"My mother doesn't like mine either."

"Is that right? Well, it just goes to show."

"What?"

"Mother knows best."

Reese stares at a Smithwicks Ale mirror. In its reflection he sees a couple leaning into one another over a plate of chicken fingers. Their attentive looks suggest that they have yet to fornicate, that they're in the process of imagining that the earth will move.

"Is your wife zoomin' anybody?" Bob asks.

"It's a possibility, yet to be confirmed."

"Go over and confirm it."

"I don't think so." He would, in fact, like to break down the door to the house that was once his and utter death threats to the art student and Roberta, but he senses that this would not position him well for a child custody battle. And anyway, he still has keys. He gave Roberta his while he snuck the spare set. "Are there children?" he asks.

"One," Bob mutters. "She's only two, she'll forget about me. She'll be calling that jerk-off 'Daddy' in no time." Reese hadn't considered that a new man in Roberta's life — even an art student — might be called Daddy.

"So she gets two chances to show up in court," Bob says, "before they drop the charges."

"Is there a chance she won't show up?"

"I'm hoping she'll come to her senses."

Only now does it occur to Reese that Robert Vinkle might be unbalanced. Only the unbalanced would suggest that his wife needs to come to her senses when he is the one who has broken down a door and uttered death threats. Reese's native bird book has taught him that crows torment owls during the daytime when owls require sleep. With their vision diminished in daylight, the owls are defenceless and have no choice but to endure the jabbing and cawing. Perhaps Robert Vinkle is a crow.

"*My* dad dropped out of the picture when I was three," Bob says. "My mom married a doofus I was ordered to call 'Dad.' When the doofus used to play with my little brothers, *his* kids, kiss them and throw them up in the air and that, I'd ask my mom if my dad ever did that to me."

"What did she say?"

"She said she couldn't remember." Not a crow then, just an abandoned boy.

The thought that Clara and Derek might be watching the fathers of other children kissing and throwing them up in the air, and wondering why their father is no longer doing this, agitates the pooling malt in Reese's gut. Even though they explained the separation to the children, Reese knew it was inexplicable. He said little because he himself didn't understand how Roberta had come to loathe him so. Roberta's "Mummy and Daddy don't love each other anymore" clearly perplexed Clara, who thought that loving someone was forever, like in the storybooks. Derek shrugged, said he'd figured they were going to split up, then stayed in his room, deeply engrossed in cyberspace.

On Reese's last night in the house, on the futon in the basement, Clara asked him if he would stop loving her when he moved away. Reese said that he could never, ever, stop loving her. "How can you know that for sure?" she asked.

"I just know."

"Did you know you'd stop loving Mummy?"

"I'm not sure that I have stopped loving Mummy."

"Then why're you going away?"

"Because Mummy's stopped loving me."

Clara was twirling a lock of her hair in her fingers, a nervous habit she'd only recently developed. "She didn't think she'd stop loving you when you got married."

"No."

"So then you could think you'll love me forever but you could be wrong."

"I'm not wrong. I will love you forever." He knew these words sounded overwrought, that there was nothing he could say that would lessen the betrayal that divorce would bring. He left to prevent war. He is in one anyway. His children are hostages.

The waitress with the lip ring and scarlet hair is poking his shoulder. "Aren't you that guy who saved the plane?"

"What plane?" Bob asks.

"That plane that had a terrorist on it. That's the guy who killed the terrorist."

"Shite, are you kidding me?"

"He's, like, a total hero." She alerts the entire bar, including the man with the greasy hair parted in the middle and long fingernails who leans towards Reese for a better look.

"Why did you kill him?" he asks.

"I didn't do it on purpose."

"Tell that to his corpse."

"Shite," Bob says, "that is so cool. A frickin' hero in my bar."

Soon everyone, even the couples yet to fornicate, are congratulating Reese, slapping him on the shoulder, jostling his exposed nerves. Women press their bodies against him. He feels covered in soot; a body of lies. He considers making a run for it but the mirrors have confused him, as has the beer. He hasn't felt so devoid of soul since his little sister died. The little sister he forgets to remember, whom he neglected, tormented, and whom he watched as she lost consciousness, her chest heaving as she struggled towards death. For forty-five minutes, she twitched and grasped, until there was a rattling in her chest and an explosive jerk of her body. Her chest arched, the muscles of her neck fluttered. Already her skin was turning to ash. He still didn't like her, felt only pity, and guilt for not liking her. Betsy sobbed without pause, Bernie stood stiff with grief. The doctor had suggested that they might prefer not to watch the agonal phase. "I'm not leaving my baby!" Betsy had cried. Born seven years after him, Chelsea got all the love in Reese's opinion. Even now, although Betsy rarely mentions her, Chelsea is the favoured child. Her photos decorate the walls of his mother's house. She is the child who could have been anything — prime minister, neurosurgeon, movie star, Nobel Prize winner. Reese is the good boy, on call to fix toilets.

Bob pours more beer. Red faces leer and sing, "For he's a jolly good fellow." The long-fingernailed man tells Reese about genetically modified foods, specifically peanuts. "They're changing the microbes in our stomachs. You change the microbes, you change the organs. You change the organs you get *mutants*." He eats a peanut.

"Speech, speech," Bob shouts.

"No speech," Reese says.

"How many people were on that plane?"

"I don't know."

"Brother, you must sleep well knowing you saved lives."

"Way to go, dog," a bald man with no eyebrows tells Reese. "Fucking desert people."

"Black gold," the long-fingernailed man says, "will be our ruin." He's still holding a newspaper and Reese observes an ad for a pillow sale, feather or fibre, any size, one price. He will need pillows, once he decides on a bed. The scarlet-haired waitress is staring at him, fondling the lip ring with her tongue and sucking on it. Reese has heard that lip rings provide extra stimulation during fellatio. He feels embarrassed with her standing there, a mother of a child in need of dental work, exposing her tongue. He drinks more beer.

There is something wrong with his television. It has begun to bleed red. He watches it anyway because it offers relief from the humming transformer and random thoughts of death and destruction. A documentary on spinal cord injury shows Christopher Reeves bleeding red while being suspended in what looks like an adult Jolly Jumper. Bleeding physiotherapists move his arms and legs. Superman insists that he's making progress, that a cure for spinal cord injuries will be found within his lifetime. Although Reese pities the Man of Steel, particularly now that he's dead, he can't help thinking about the money involved in trying to mend a severed spinal cord. Money that could be sent to seventeen-month-old babies in North Korea or Iraq or Afghanistan, or to Rwanda where rebels are cutting off the hands of thirteen-year-old girls.

Furniture moving begins upstairs then the stereo blares a song Reese hasn't heard for years, by a band whose name he can't remember. The song, about red wine and staying close to you and not being able to forget, is a song he danced to with Elena. They would cling to each other in nightclubs, absorbing each other through their clothes. *I'm still here listening and you've gone away somewhere!* It's not fair that he has been left behind. She is free in his mind. He wants her beside him, to talk about the things they never talked about. He wants the inexplicable explained. The red wine song ends and he is once again completely without her. A less melodious song thumps through the floor and he begins to howl, softly at first but as his lungs, accustomed to bicycling, expand and take in more oxygen, the howls become louder. He pictures a moon because he can't see one through his window facing the underside of the deck. But in his heart there is a moon, full of displaced passion and woe, and he howls to it. Howls and howls.

Pounding at the door stops him. He considers not answering but the pounding continues and he fears that someone is dead, dying, OD-ing on anti-depressants. He opens it a crack. She's out there, the witless, arrogant entertainer with the dragon on her thigh.

"What are you doing?" she inquires.

"Howling."

"Do you think that's appropriate?"

"For what?"

"For four o'clock in the morning?"

"Do you think it's appropriate to bump and grind and play loud music and wear cleated shoes at four in the morning?"

She puts her hand on her hip where the skin bulges between her tight jeans and tank top. "What are you talking about?"

"Every night. Noise."

"You can hear it?" She actually looks surprised, even slightly embarrassed. Without makeup she looks less trashy, verging on innocent.

"Yes," he says.

"I'm just unwinding. I work in a bar."

"I don't care, it's too loud. *You* make noise, *I* howl." He can't believe he's struck upon this powerful negotiating tool.

"Are you nuts?"

"I'm in mourning."

"You're what?'

"I'm in mourning. Grief-stricken."

"Oh." She adjusts a bra strap. "I'm sorry, like I said I just use it to unwind."

"Never more, or I howl." He waits for her big-shouldered partner in furniture moving to come down and cause blunt-force trauma to his head.

She stares at him. "You are nuts."

"I live in the basement."

She climbs back up the stairs, watching him over her shoulder.

"Sleep tight," he says. "Don't let the bed bugs bite."

Why has his sister entered his thoughts now, along with these other women? Why has he always had women around him, never a proper male buddy to play with? He did try racquetball once but had difficulty with the concept of chasing balls. Perhaps he can become buddies with Robert Vinkle. Certainly Bob made it clear that Reese is welcome at the bar anytime. Perhaps Vinkle's can become a home away from the basement apartment where Reese will meet straight shooters and talkers who will offer tips on how to win child custody cases. He used to creep into Chelsea's room in the middle of the night, holding his hand over a flashlight, creating a shadow of a huge hand on the ceiling. "Mummy!" Chelsea would scream. Reese would dart back to his room. He repeated this offence nightly. Betsy grew tired of the disturbance and stopped answering her calls. His little sister had no choice but to cry herself to sleep while he sat in the dark slowly bringing his hand closer to the flashlight, making the shadow bigger and more terrifying. A crow, devoid of soul.

He eats a handful of Doritos and studies the chemical ingredients listed on the packet, soothed by the knowledge that a long shelf life means a short human life, and that "colouring" involves red dye, which stimulates cancer cells. He eats another Dorito while listening for noises from above; just minor shuffling. He takes out the picture of Elena and tries to gaze into the eyes that stare at the parakeet. The hum resonates through his body of lies. He dials the number that was once his, knowing that Roberta doesn't have call display on the bedroom phone, hoping but fearing that the art student will pick up, his voice husky with sex. "Who's this?" Reese will demand with such force that the art student will have no choice but to give his full name and address.

"Hello?" Roberta says, sounding annoyed, tired, stressed.

Reese can't speak. He manages to make some guttural noises. "Don't phone here, Reese," she says and hangs up.

The dial tone drones. He stares at the linoleum floor, which is getting dirtier daily. He must wash it, buy a mop and bucket. He must do that tomorrow. His neck hurts. And he *must* buy a pillow. Where was that pillow sale — feather or fibre, any size, one price? It upsets him beyond measure that he can't remember. He put a pillow over Chelsea's face once, watched while her legs thrashed. He threatened to do it again if she told on him. He can see the legs now, as slight as Clara's, pathetic in their futility. He knew that if he continued to press down the thrashing would stop and he would lose his mother's love forever. Instead he read "Spiderman" while Chelsea whimpered quietly. "I *hate* you," she whispered.

They are in here, in the basement, the women.

Serge Hollyduke asks to speak with Reese privately regarding Marge Stallworthy, the kindly senior citizen whose walker bumps the chairs of the other callers. "She stinks of shit," Serge explains, "nobody wants to sit beside her."

"Since when?"

"It's been getting worse, it's because she spends too long on the phone."

"She gets pledges."

"She slows things down. Anyway, nobody'll sit beside her. They're threatening to quit."

Reese surveys the pool of callers. Aside from the truly desperate who barely speak English, he sees mostly adolescents without humility or tact, who will undoubtedly spill Coke on their consoles and short the computer. He despairs when he considers that it is entirely possible that he will spend the rest of his life managing adolescents. The ones in Marge Stallworthy's vicinity have angled their chairs away from her. Some of them pinch their noses.

Serge runs his hands over the short hairs on his head. "I've got ten callers on the Crohn's and Colitis program. They're supposed to spend ten seconds per call, Marge is at like six hundred."

"She's doing two hundred percent better than the ones zipping through," Reese says. "It balances out."

"I'm talking mutiny here. Nobody wants to sit beside her."

If possible, Reese would like to shield Marge from youthful cruelty and scorn. He watches the live display that tracks the callers' performances. She continues to out-perform the boy in dreads and the halter-topped girl who regularly presses disconnect when the dialler beeps because she's in deep discussion with her halter-topped neighbour. Surprisingly the team, overall, is not doing badly. Crohn's and Colitis are not easy sells. Marge may have an edge because she's incontinent herself and can genuinely plead the cause. "I'll talk to her," Reese says. In the meantime he sits down with his technician to look at donor history and establish exclusions for the Voice of First Nations campaign. "I'd stay away from the Conservative party," he says. The technician, Wayson Hum, nods as though Reese has given the correct answer. Wayson Hum rarely speaks or makes eye contact with anything but monitors. His father is a grocer in Chinatown. Wayson frequently nibbles on fruits and vegetables Reese doesn't recognize.

"What about geography?" he asks. "Have you set up the time zones?"

Wayson nods as though Reese has given the correct answer.

"Let's suppress all donors who haven't given for two years," Reese suggests. "And suppress all donors who gave over fifty dollars, we'll do them when the team's up to speed."

He spies Marge leaving the washroom and heads her off. "Marge," he asks, "do you have a minute?"

"Certainly. Queer weather we're having. I had to turn up my thermostat to get the damp out of my bones."

He opens the door to the boardroom for her, noticing that she does stink of shit, and waits as she hobbles over to the table. He pulls a chair out for her. "You know how the dialler works, don't you, Marge?"

"The what?"

"The computer that makes the calls."

"Oh yes, very clever."

"The thing is, if one person is spending a long time on the phone it confuses the machine. It reduces the average." Marge blinks, clearly having no idea what he's talking about. "The machine works on averages to time calls," Reese clarifies. "If the average is reduced, the dialler assumes callers won't be ready, which means people are sitting around with nothing to do."

"The young people."

"That's right."

"I do so enjoy them. They're quite lively, aren't they?"

He tries to imagine her young, without humility or tact, in a halter top. She has seen twice as much life as he has and she is still going, still smiling, still talking about the weather. Twice as much life as he has had would kill him. "I was wondering if you'd like to sit by the window," he says. "It's a corner seat, you'd have more privacy."

"Oh that's quite alright, I like being with the young people."

"I understand, but the thing is, we're starting a new campaign and I don't want to mix up bowel disease with Indians, and you're doing so well with bowel disease."

"Yes, well, I do my best."

"I know you do." He can see that she's disappointed, that she doesn't understand why she is being ostracized. "Let's get you set up. I think you'll like it, you'll be able to see daylight."

On the floor, a new caller who works nights at a bakery is distributing day-old Danish, unaware that food on the floor is prohibited. "They're a bit sawdusty," he admits, "but what do you want for free." The adolescents grab at the pastries as though they haven't eaten for weeks. Reese sees Serge Hollyduke fast approaching, his jaw clenched, to enforce discipline. The caller offers a lemon Danish to Avril Leblanc. "Hi, I'm Holden, would you like one?"

"I don't do wheat," she says. "But it's sweet of you to offer."

Holden then offers the lemon Danish to Serge. "Do you do wheat, sir?"

"Food is prohibited on the floor," Serge says.

"Really?"

Serge scowls and turns to Reese. "There's an urgent call for you."

Immediately Reese imagines his children mangled in a car crash. He is in his office within seconds. His mother is on the line.

"It's your father," she says, "he's fallen off the toilet again." Within half an hour, Reese is dragging his father on the hall rug to the stair glider.

Betsy hovers. "Every ten minutes he's straining. Getting himself off that chair and onto the toilet. He's taking laxatives, stool softeners ..."

"How would *you* know what I'm taking?" Bernie demands.

"Tell him you can't pee anymore, Bernard, tell him what's going on, he's your son, he should know."

"What's going on, Dad?"

"She's driving me nuts, that's what."

"You do look paler, Dad, and you seem weaker."

"Why won't anybody leave me alone, would you tell me that?"

"Because you keep falling off the toilet, Bernard."

Reese can't lift his father onto the wheelchair. Two days ago his father could assist him. "You're losing strength, Dad. Are you eating?"

"*You* try eating when there's nothing coming out the other end."

"He had Campbell's soup made with cream. I told him to have plain broth but oh no ..."

"I can't lift you by myself," Reese says. "You're going to have to make some effort here."

His father lets out a small muffled cry of either pain or despair before collapsing onto the stair glider.

"I think we should call an ambulance and get you to the hospital," Reese says.

"Out of the question."

"Do you want to die?" Reese says harshly because he can't do this anymore. "That's what's going to happen, you're going to *die*."

"You don't have to shout," Betsy says.

"How long ago did they tell him he should be on dialysis? Weeks ago. He's losing strength, he can't shit or piss, what do you think's going to happen?"

"He's right, Bernie. It's not right. It could be serious."

His father sits with eyes closed, shrunken.

"I'm calling Med-Merge," Reese says.

A wild-eyebrowed Greek puts his finger up Bernie's rectum and tells him that his bowel must be disimpacted. The doctor leaves to search for a nurse who would be willing to do the disimpacting. Reese waits for his father to sit up. When he doesn't, he puts his hand on his shoulder. "You alright, Dad?"

"They send me a Greek."

"He seemed alright."

"He's incompetent."

"How do you know?"

"He doesn't know what he's doing."

"What should he be doing?"

"Not what he did."

"Did they do it differently in 1948 when you were in medical school?"

"Don't act smart."

A fierce Jamaican nurse appears, ordering them into the corridor.

"Shouldn't we be in the room for the disimpacting?" asks Reese.

"I'm not responsible for any disimpacting. Dr. Panaglotopoulos should have done it when he did the rectal."

"So what do we do now?" Reese inquires.

"That's up to Dr. Panaglotopoulos."

"Where is he?"

"As you can see we're very busy." And she's gone, lost among the patients stranded on wheelchairs and gurneys, waiting for care, beds, death.

"Are you hungry, Dad? I've got a Crispy Crunch."

"Save it for your mother. Maybe if she eats enough of them she'll have a cardiac arrest. Where's the can?"

Reese, hindered by back pain, helps his father onto the toilet. While Bernie grunts and heaves, Reese marvels at the power of the bowel. Ultimately it rules. The aging brain capitulates and can be ignored, medicated, locked away, but the bowel, in all its unpredictability, must be catered to. Someone hammers on the door. "We'll be out in a minute," Reese says, looking at his father's reddening face. "Any luck?" Bernie shakes his head. More hammering on the door while Reese struggles to get his father back on the wheelchair.

"Where have you been?" the fierce Jamaican nurse demands.

"The toilet," Reese offers.

"You were told to wait here."

"No, we weren't."

She shakes her head and grabs the wheelchair, spinning Bernie back behind the curtains where Dr. Panaglotopoulos is waiting. The Greek and nurse position Bernie on his side on the examining table and hoist up his hospital gown. "This has to be done," Dr. Panaglotopoulos says while the nurse slips on latex gloves.

The sight of his father's withered haunches, so helplessly displayed, makes Reese's awareness of his own mortality unavoidable. He feels that he must watch the procedure to ensure that no damage is done, but as the blackened and putrid stool is excavated by the nurse's fingers, he feels the kind of grief reserved for funerals. Because what is his father if not dead? He can take pleasure from nothing, no one. The world is his enemy, overrun by Greeks and Blacks. The ground pushes against him, the sun burns his skin. The last time Reese tried to talk to him about anything beyond food requirements was when Reese was arrested outside the headquarters of Ontario Power Generation during an anti-smog demonstration. The protesters, a total of seven, were charged with criminal mischief for deliberately impeding rush hour traffic. Normally Roberta would have paid his bail, but as they were newly separated, Reese didn't hold out much hope for this option. He phoned Bernie, who seemed willing to let Reese bunk with the junkies, thieves, and scarred men easily excited to violence. "When are you going to stop this messing around?" Bernie demanded. Reese saw no point in arguing, as they had many times before, about the value of peaceful protests.

"Tomorrow," he said. "I'll stop tomorrow." He thought he meant it, that he could no longer tolerate being roughed up by cops who had gone home and found some guy in bed with the wife. But then the judge agreed with the defence's argument that traffic was clogged because of the "massive police presence." The protesters were "validly exercising their rights." Bernie seemed disappointed; the father who'd wanted his son whipped. For years Reese had imagined that on some subliminal level his father was on his side, despite his protestations to the contrary. That day in court, Reese understood that Bernie was one of *them*.

"We've reviewed your test results," Dr. Panaglotopoulos says. "As predicted, your kidneys have ceased to function. You need dialysis. We'll have to do surgery to put in an inner-dwelling abdominal catheter. I can't tell you when because there are no beds."

"Are you sure this is necessary?" Reese asks.

"Without dialysis he will die. In the meantime we'll get an IV into him."

"If there are no beds," Reese asks, "where is he supposed to stay?"

"He'll have to wait in Emergency like everybody else," the nurse says, slapping a diaper on Bernie. "We'll keep an eye on you."

"How long can he live without dialysis?"

"You should have come in *weeks* ago," the Greek almost shouts.

"He's not deaf," Reese interjects.

"Why didn't you come in when you were told to? You were told you needed dialysis *weeks* ago."

Bernie remains unresponsive. Back in the corridor he resumes his grumbling. Reese wheels him into a less populated corner. "Do you feel any better, Dad?"

"You should have let me go."

"Where?"

"Where do you think?"

"Die, you mean? I should have let you *die?* That's still a possibility apparently."

"The bedside manners of apes."

"I think they're fairly stressed, with cutbacks and all that. We should phone Mum."

"I don't want to talk to her."

When a pay phone becomes available Reese grabs the wheel-chair and makes a run for it. "What is this?" Bernie demands. "The Tour de France?"

"Hi, Mum. Everything's alright, we just have to wait to get him on dialysis."

"Let me talk to her," Bernie says, snatching the receiver from him. "The buggers want to cut me open, stick a valve in me."

Bernie, in 1948, trained to be a pediatrician. This did not stop him from performing surgery on his own knees at various intervals in his life. His medical office was at the back of the house and Reese remembers at least twice calling him for dinner and finding Bernie cutting into a knee. Children's screams were often heard through the walls of Reese's house. He feared, more than anything, developing tonsillitis or appendicitis because he knew his father would slice him open.

"They don't know their asses backwards," Bernie says into the phone. He continues to gripe about the Greek and the Black and Reese is reminded of why his parents are still together: because no one else will listen. *Who will listen to me when I'm old*, Reese wonders, before wondering if this matters.

Bernie hangs up and starts to pull at his hospital ID bracelet.

"You should leave that on, Dad."

"Treating me like a goddamn laboratory *rat*."

"There're a lot of people here. You don't want them getting you mixed up."

Bernie continues to pull at the ID bracelet. "You don't have to hang around."

"Sure I do."

"What for?"

"To look after you."

"If you want to look after me, get me out of here."

"I can't do that. And you don't really want that."

"Don't tell me what I want, you and your mother."

Reese looks for traces of the father who dressed up with him for a Labour Day parade. They went as hobos. Bernie painted their mouths and noses with Betsy's lipstick, and burned cork with a match to dirty their faces. Reese remembers the feel of the warm cork as his father rubbed it over his cheeks. Bernie smelled of scotch and wool and pipe smoke. He grabbed a couple of corncob pipes and poked one in each of their mouths. They had a good giggle over that one. Reese felt proud, marching with his father in the parade with his corncob pipe. His mother stood in the crowd with the lump of Chelsea in her belly, also giggling. Good giggles, many years ago.

"Are you hungry, Dad? Can I get you anything?"

"Stop talking about food, you and your mother."

Then there were hard times, less money coming in as patients began to notice that Bernie believed no medical advancement had been made since 1948. Betsy became someone else's medical secretary. Dr. Burrows had a harelip, many small dogs, and, according to Betsy, no interest in the ladies. But because Dr. Burrows presented Betsy with flower arrangements on Secretary Day and Christmas, he was nothing less than an adulterer in Bernie's eyes. Reese would listen to the accusations while Chelsea crawled around on the floor, shoving objects into her mouth. "Did you see what she put in her mouth, Reese?" his mother would ask. "You're supposed to be watching her." He'd allow marbles to roll dangerously close. If Chelsea managed to grab one he'd snatch it from her, causing her to wail. "What did you do to her, Reese, did you do something?" He'd shake his head, clenching the marbles in fists behind his back.

So many people have children who should not. He and Roberta should not have had children.

"What about water?" he asks. "Are you thirsty, do you want a juice or something?" His father has fallen unconscious in his diaper and hospital gown. His face, free of fury, looks strangely smooth. Afraid he might be dead, Reese gently touches his forehead. Though cool, it is not cold, and there is movement behind the eyelids.

The nurse returns with an orderly, a gurney, and an IV pole. Bernie sleeps through the transition from chair to gurney, and even the poke of the needle as the nurse installs the IV. He is completely depleted from renal failure and a week of straining to shit.

While his father was applying the lipstick and burned cork to their faces, Reese felt unafraid, confident that his father was not going to push a swab down his throat or look in his ear or take a scalpel to his abdomen. His father was being a father, taking care of him as fathers were meant to do. They held hands in the parade, did goofy walks and wiggled their behinds. People laughed. Reese's legs grew tired but he continued to clown because he didn't want the fearlessness to end.

Hospital staff swarm a neighbouring gurney. Instruments are applied and mutterings uttered before they cover the body with a sheet and wheel it away. Reese expects to hear wailing from loved ones but there is no one to mourn the lost life. He locates an empty chair, pulling his sleeping father with him. He sits with one hand resting on the gurney, as if it were a cradle.

"Do you have Marshall mattresses," Reese asks, "featuring the original pocket coil?"

The saleswoman is unusually short with wispy hair and eerily white teeth. "Of course," she says. "Canadian-made, an excellent brand, highly recommended."

"By who?" Reese asks.

"What?"

"Who highly recommends it?"

"Customers."

He can tell she's lying, that there isn't an item in the place that hasn't been "highly recommended." She pats a mattress that resembles all the other mattresses Reese has lain upon. "You'll notice the difference," she assures him, flashing teeth.

"What is a pocket coil?" Reese asks.

"A coil that's got a pocket."

Reese waits for further information.

"The coil fits in a pocket," the saleswoman enunciates loudly.

"Is that a positive thing?" He can see that he's irritating her. Her attention wanders to a couple in black leather appraising a black leather couch.

"Excuse me a moment," she says, speeding off on spindly legs.

The Canadian-made mattress featuring the original pocket coil feels no different from all the other mattresses. He is not in love with it, although lying on any mattress is preferable to dozing on a plastic chair in Emergency, listening to a man with massive red hair scream and threaten to kill himself, after overdosing on tranqs and a bottle of Johnny Red. Hospital staff strapped him to a gurney with leather wrist restraints while his bellowing continued to fragment the night, causing those with headaches to moan softly. Clutching their skulls, they lay on gurneys, pleading for more pain medication. What can be said of a world in which people suffer such pain for no apparent cause? Did cavemen get headaches, or was the need for Aspirin born of the modern age?

Bernie is in a room now, beside a man who appears to have had an allergic reaction to medication. His feet are so swollen he can't walk. He tried to get a passing nurse's attention by shouting, "Look at my feet!"

She stared at them. "Has your doctor seen them?"

"How could my doctor see them? I never *see* my doctor." He pointed to his feet. "Look at them!"

On waking, Bernie tried to pull out his IV. Fortunately, the delivery of breakfast provided distraction — whole wheat toast, which he refused because he claimed it contained phosphorous. "People with poor kidney function can't tolerate phosphorous," he grumbled. Reese offered him orange juice. "Orange juice contains *phosphorous*," Bernie said. "The buggers are trying to kill me."

Reese should probably still be with his father and not testing beds. But he had to leave, to breathe, to shower, to appear to be doing his job responsibly. Avril Leblanc has been causing more problems. Although her numbers are improving, she inevitably low-balls. "What do you mean by low-ball?" she asked when he sat her down in the boardroom. She smelled of oranges again.

"If someone has a history of donating substantial gifts," Reese explained, "you don't ask them for ten bucks."

"I would have thought anything would be welcome."

"Well, a hundred dollars would be more welcome than ten. We save the donors with a generous history until last, when the team is comfortable with the script. We count on these donors."

"I'm sorry."

"Maybe it wasn't properly explained to you." He noticed that her skin was extremely clear, unsullied by wheat.

"I'm really looking forward to the Voice of First Nations campaign," she said. "My grandfather is a shaman. Everything is energies to him."

Serge Hollyduke pushed open the door. "Am I interrupting something?"

"Not at all," Reese said. "We were just having a discussion about low-balling donors who have a history of donating substantial gifts. Maybe you didn't cover this in Avril's training session." He waited for Serge to pin the blame on the caller as is his usual custom. But Serge was silenced by Avril Leblanc's orangeness.

She pointed to his Birkenstocks. "Are you finding those comfortable?"

He nodded. "Awesome."

"I wear moccasins at home," Avril said. "That's how the First Peoples learned about the world, by feeling it through their moccasins."

Reese tests the bounce factor of a Sealy Platinum Deluxe. Things are heating up between the couple in black leather and the unusually short saleswoman. They sit on the couch, she sits on the couch, they stand, she stands. They stroke the couch as though it were a large cat, she pats it as though it were a dog. Elena had wanted a leather couch; blood red. It was displayed in a store window on Queen Street and she could not walk by it without uttering a sigh of longing. It cost three thousand dollars and smelled of dead animal. No matter how devoted he was to Lainie, Reese could not buy the couch. She sensed this, and complained of headaches. Reese suspected that the headaches had more to do with the tropical birds she'd agreed to bird-sit for a producer she'd met at a party. There was a lorikeet, an umbrella cockatoo, and a yellow-naped Amazon — birds with big feathers and attitude who reproduced gems of wisdom they'd garnered from TV commercials. "Nine headache sufferers out of ten say Advil works better then Tylenol," the lorikeet would say. The umbrella cockatoo was particularly fond of the slogan, "It's worth the drive to Acton." "Coke is it!" the yellow-naped Amazon would shout. Telling the birds to be quiet only induced jingles, the most popular being, "You deserve a break today, so come on out and get away, to McDonald's!"

Reese e-mailed Kyrl Dendekker again, asked what had been done with Lainie's body. He felt her hand in his while he was standing in the elevator. Unnerved by the sensation, he gasped, causing a man with a goitre to stare at him. The feeling passed but Reese sensed she was still present, watching his exchange with their top salesman, Nick Dizon, who had the Family Values clients imagining massive donations were pending. "What did you tell them?" Reese asked.

"I told them we're going to do great things for them."

"How did you qualify 'great'?"

"Look, it's not my problem what they took from the meeting, I was on the level." Nick is the top salesman because he lies easily, dresses well, and is pathologically outgoing and positive. Nick is the kind of man Elena had admired — was admiring — Reese felt during the exchange.

"It's a mistake to give clients unreasonable expectations," Reese said.

"Family values are hot right now, Reese, where've you been?"

"Hot to who?"

"Everybody. It's apple pie time. You ought to know, you killed a terrorist. They were really excited about that."

"Who were?"

"The Family Values people."

"You told them about that?"

"Why not?" Nick checked his e-mail on his cell.

With Elena watching, Reese felt he had no choice but to assert his authority. "Don't *ever*," he said, "use me as a sales tool." Nick Dizon was engrossed in his upcoming appointments. Nick Dizon met Sterling Green at a resort in Jamaica called Hedonists

Only. They bonded over topless girls and ganja. Reese has no power over Nick Dizon.

There is no question that Bonaparte has been neglected. His cage is in the basement, high on a shelf. No doubt he was moved due to Roberta's hypoallergenic Portuguese water dog, who has never learned to bark but growls at rodents. The dog as well as the mouth guard marked the beginning of the end, in Reese's opinion. The dog would sleep only on their bed, sandwiched between them. He was a good slumber partner in that he never moved and was, therefore, a constant source of warmth. But he was a dog. The mouth guard was the brilliant idea of Roberta's dentist, who believed that she was grinding her teeth in her sleep. Once the mouth guard was installed and the dog was between them, communicating was no longer an option.

He collects Bonaparte's food, woodchips, and dried alfalfa grass in a large Gap bag he finds in the broom closet. A Gap bag? Does his family really *need* to be clothed by a brand name, clothes made cheap by Third World children and sold high by North American teenagers?

The Portuguese water dog will not stop sniffing him.

Reese carries the cage and supplies upstairs and places them beside the chicken pot. He looks for signs of the art student. He studies the notations on the calendar by the fridge, although deciphering Roberta's handwriting has always been difficult. What's *gooling at waven 7:30* mean? Will she hire a babysitter on the night she's gooling at waven? Isn't he entitled to know whom she is entrusting to babysit, who might be causing Clara to stick things up dolls' bottoms?

He thought that he would leave a note for Clara in her slipper. Something simple like *I will always love you.* But she might show it to her mother. A note for Derek is out of the question, he would certainly hand it over to Roberta.

Reese places the chicken pot in its spot behind the clay butter dish Roberta bought at a fundraiser for abused women. He knows that kidnapping Bonaparte will blow his cover, though not immediately perhaps, as the hamster seems to have been for-gotten. Reese takes a hundred-dollar knife out of a drawer and slices the hamster some apple.

They'd also fought over hundred-dollar pillows. He could not believe such a thing existed — that anyone could rest their head on a hundred-dollar pillow when stick-thin Ethiopian children and stacks of corpses were in the news.

He searches what was once his bedroom for signs of the art student. He is not exactly sure what he's looking for — a sketch-pad? An undershirt smeared with paint? Used condoms? There is nothing that does not belong to Roberta in the room. He checks his watch before making what he intends to be a quick visit to his daughter's room. Once again he is soothed by the bed and the stuffies that smell of her. He searches for something small, that will go unnoticed, that he can keep on his person. Socks always vanish, Roberta regularly complains about missing socks. *How can they just disappear?* He finds one under the bed and wraps it around his thumb.

"What is that?" Robert Vinkle demands.

"A hamster."

"You're bringing a *rat* into my bar?"

"It's in a cage."

"Is this like some kind of wife substitute?"

Reese isn't sure why he has come to Vinkle's. He doesn't actu-ally like bars, has spent too many hours outside bars waiting for Bernie, who began to frequent them after patients began to figure out he believed any advances made in medicine since 1948 were bogus. Bernie didn't drink alcohol in bars, instead had the bar-tenders spray-gun countless 7-Ups. But there were people in bars who didn't judge him, expected nothing of him, and occasionally laughed at his jokes. Can Reese find such comfort? He orders a 7-Up. The man with greasy hair parted in the middle and long fingernails nods at him.

"Hi," Reese responds. On television there are shots of an oil tanker that has split in two and plunged to the bottom of the

Atlantic. It was carrying seventy-seven thousand tonnes of viscous fuel oil. Hundreds of kilometres of beaches have been polluted. An environmental worker, wearing goggles and gloves, force-feeds a bird covered in fuel oil. Reese can't watch, looks down at the bubbles in his 7-Up.

"The question is," the greasy-haired man says, "why is a twenty-six-year-old vessel, lacking a modern double hull, plying the waters with seventy-seven thousand tonnes of fuel?"

"So this guy," Bob says, sliding onto the stool beside Reese, "is zooming somebody else's wife in some dive motel. No big news, right? Here's the joke. He gets up to wash the lies off him, slips as he steps out of the shower, and accidentally jams his hand down the funnel of the toilet. He was stuck there for like two hours, firefighters had to rescue him. Is that not gorgeous? True story." He reaches behind the bar for peanuts. "Reese Larkin, this is Linden Prevost, a devotee of Vinkle's. Is that not gorgeous?"

"He must have had a large hand," Linden Prevost remarks.

"Let that be a lesson to you," Bob says, "keep your fingers on your own plumbing." He laughs very hard at his joke, causing the buttons to strain against his shirt.

Before Reese had the opportunity to broach the subject of low-balling with Avril Leblanc, she looked at him intensely and asked, "Are you well?" Having moved beyond sleep deprivation to manic hyper-awareness, Reese feared that she knew something about Roberta's accusations, that she would spread word among the adolescents, without humility or tact, that he is a child molester. "We all have our bad days," he said.

"Challenging," Avril Leblanc said. "A challenging day. 'Bad day' is judgmental and very negative. Try calling it challenging." Reese stared at her and imagined throwing her to the floor and throttling her. She suggested he take St. John's wort for depression, and valerian root to help him sleep. He left another message on Gwyneth Proudley's voice mail, suggesting a time frame in which they might meet. "I'll make myself available," he said, "at your convenience." Then he worried that this sounded too forward, too eager — the guilty trying to buy favours.

The scarlet-haired waitress with the lip ring and a child in need of dental work asks Reese if she can get him anything, and he has an unsettling feeling that he could have her if he so desired — because he killed a suspected terrorist. Bob slaps him on the back, "Have some nachos, on the house."

Reese has not had sex with anyone but Roberta in thirteen years. He wouldn't know where to start. Except with Elena, who's dead. Elena, who, when she wanted him, made him feel handsome and virile. Once, after fornication and French toast, she changed his "look," took him down to Bedo and made him buy blazers with big shoulders, and trousers with pleats. He had shape, suddenly, in the mirror, thought that perhaps this was the real Reese, that he'd never before spent more than a hundred dollars on a blazer because he lacked self-worth. He *deserved* to wear a thousand dollars' worth of clothing at one sitting. They drank spritzers in Bemelman's and he felt comfortable knowing that he was not shaming her. Women looked at him differently in his big-shouldered clothes. Other men in big-shouldered clothes exchanged knowing glances with him. He was part of a club. Until he spoke about dead whales or DDT or climate change. He tried not to speak and began to think it was possible to exist free of concerns for the world at large — to be happy among the beautiful people.

"I had this idea," Bob Vinkle says, "that I should see my kid. I mean, even under house arrest I could have her over, feed her Chinese or something. She loves those crispy wontons. So I thought, what's stopping me calling her? I mean, she doesn't exactly talk a hundred percent yet, but she knows how to say 'yes' and 'no.' So I call, and you know what the sow says? 'After you're in rehab, Bob.' Like, what's she talking about? It's not like I have a drinking problem. I own a bar, so what? I'm thinking, what's this woman telling people about me? The sky's the limit, right? I mean, who's going to believe *me*?"

"I believe you, Bob," Reese says.

"Thank you, brother."

The scarlet-haired waitress leans on the bar, exposing cleavage. Reese has already noticed that her breasts are large and spherical but knows from experience that this could change once the bra is removed. Roberta doesn't wear bras, "harnesses" she calls them. What you see is what you get with Roberta; breasts slightly depleted from having nursed two children. Still beautiful though, vintage. When Reese thinks of the art student mouthing them, he experiences a general clenching. He orders another 7-Up.

Outside the bars, waiting for Bernie, he always feared that his father would appear with a woman on his arm. A woman with red lips and cheeks and bulging buttocks. He saw many such women leave the bar with men who had entered the bar solo.

He has come to the conclusion that Betsy was, in fact, infatuated with Dr. Burrows, the homosexual with the harelip and many small dogs, who gave her flowers on Secretary Day and Christmas. She was infatuated with him because he was courteous and didn't want her. She always spoke highly of him, and quoted him regularly, which drove Bernie to the cellar where he began to make fishing flies. He rarely went fishing, certainly never caught anything, but he became proficient at tying flies. It served as an alternative to operating on his own knees. He took Reese fishing once, but Reese fell out of the boat. Bernie dove in after him. Reese remembers the preliminaries to drowning, the flailing of arms and the kicking, the gulping of water, the growing awareness that sinking was inevitable. Then his father's hands were around his ribs, pushing him to the surface. "Grab the branch," Bernie sputtered. There was one, hanging over the river, but Reese couldn't reach it. He could still feel his father's hands but couldn't see him. He feared that his father was drowning too, that their bodies would be discovered weeks later in mud, half-eaten by maggots. He felt another push from below as his father surfaced again and shouted, "Grab the branch!" Reese did and felt the rough bark tearing his palms. "Now hold on!" his father ordered, rounding up the boat and oars. Bernie pulled him onto the boat and wrapped his L.L. Bean field jacket around him. He did not scold him. He did not take him fishing again.

"Tell him about *your* ex, Lindy," Bob Vinkle says. "Now there's a story and a half. He caught her shagging a bunch of software salesmen."

"She was unstable," Linden says.

"She still comes in here looking for him," Bob says, "like if her computer's giving her trouble or something. 'Has anybody seen Lindy?' You're too nice to her, brother."

Linden drinks more scotch. "She's mentally ill."

"Lindy's had to get her out of padded rooms a few times. She was so out of it, she didn't even recognize him."

Sterling spoke fondly of his ex-wife today. They went mountain biking in Utah. "We had to get our booze out of state," he explained, "it being Mormon country." He looked wistful for a moment, pulling on his ear hairs. "She was a powerful girl then, ran marathons. It nearly killed me keeping up with her." Reese has met Sterling's corpulent and compulsively consuming wife. He could not imagine her astride a mountain bike, could not imagine what had happened between Utah and the divorce courts.

Waiting for Bernie once outside a bar, Reese witnessed a robbery. Two men lifted a television out of a second-storey hotel window and carried it down a fire escape. Reese stood in the shadows, mute, still waiting for Bernie until an hour later the police appeared with the men who'd stolen the TV. The cops noticed Reese and pointed at him. "Did you see anything?" Reese shook his head, fearing that if he identified the robbers they would break his bones. The only person in the world who knows of this shameful act is Roberta. He revealed it to her in trust, believing that they would protect each other's secrets forever. Another reason he must save his marriage. Without their shared history he is just another rejected brother, crying over potato skins.

"If I win the twelve mill," Bob tells them, "I cut you brothers into it. For real. I'll look after you guys. Anybody who's ever been good to me. No joke. Everybody gets a cut."

Reese isn't sure what he has done to deserve such loyalty from Robert Vinkle, who may or may not have a drinking problem, who may or may not be an honourable man. He was the only golfer besides Reese who offered his gifts to Wendy Hiscock with no apparent ulterior motive.

"What do you imagine the money would do for you, Robert?" Linden asks.

"A life of leisure, Lindy, no grind."

Linden scrapes bacon bits off a potato skin. "Wherever you go, there you are."

"What?"

Linden taps his temple. "There's no escape."

Watching the plane take off when Elena left him, Reese was convinced that his hemorrhaging entrails were visible to passers-by. He had no such feeling on the night he carried his bags out of the house that was once his, just a profound sadness as he struggled to put one foot in front of the other. Clara, he knew, was watching from her bedroom window, not understanding. Is it not possible to remain bound at all costs? Is it not possible to endure the rough edges and missing pieces? Roberta said that practising avoidance kept their marriage together. Is that so wrong? Were they meant to crash bumper cars continually? What did cavemen do? Weren't they chasing mastodons or digging for tubers — too *busy* to worry about who said what to whom, and how so-and-so felt when so-and-so said such-and-such? "Who needs that shit?" he hears himself mutter.

"I'm there, brother," Robert Vinkle says.

10

The waitress's breasts tumble over him. Her name is Kyla and her apartment is filled with spiky plants and beaded curtains that have slapped Reese in the face. He feels surprisingly comfortable beneath her, and as her hands, so familiar with beer bottles and greasy plates, begin to fondle him, he experiences arousal. "What kind of bed is this?" he asks.

"What?"

"What brand of mattress? Is it a Sealy?"

"I have no idea."

"It's quite comfortable. Not too bouncy." He tries to suck on her breasts but they escape him. It relieves him that, when he grips them while sucking, her nipples harden beneath his tongue, which suggests that she too is experiencing arousal. Unfortunately, there is Rod Stewart wailing on her CD player, and a synthetic smell that makes Reese mindful of carcinogenic chemicals, particularly the fire-retardant ones that have been found in breast milk. Fire-retardant chemicals that are used on upholstery, carpets, car interiors, baby clothes, toys. Mattresses.

With practised skill Kyla rolls a condom onto his penis and manoeuvres it into her vagina. It amazes him that he is remaining hard despite sleep deprivation, a general feeling of powerlessness, and the knowledge that she is zooming him because he killed a suspected terrorist. While Rod sings about tonight being the night and everything being alright, Reese tries to focus on the task at hand, but of course his mind strays to Bernie, whom he has phoned several times, who has declared him a traitor before hanging up on him. Kyla's hand, massaging Reese's testicles, alerts him to a need for ejaculation. But her vagina feels too spacious, too accommodating, and he feels himself fading, although he performs some last-minute pumping before the blood completely drains out of him. "Sorry," he says. "I haven't slept for days."

"No problem."

He knows that he should make an effort to satisfy her but all he wants is to hide. The strangeness of her naked body spread over his, the complete unfamiliarity of it, suddenly overwhelms him. He feels sobs pending, the kind that should be heard only by bathroom walls. He covers his face with his hands.

"Don't worry about it," Kyla says, gathering the bedspread around her. All he can think is that she is somebody's daughter. Somebody who carried her in his arms. Somebody who would suffer torment if he knew that his baby was offering herself to rejected husbands in bars. "Do you want a coffee?" she asks.

"Sure," he says, recognizing that diversion is needed. While she's in the kitchen he pulls on his clothes, feeling only shame. He should not have come here.

She hands him a cup. "You want to leave, right?"

"Do you want me to?"

"It's up to you."

He sits beside a spiky plant. "I miss my kids."

"Where are they?'

"With my wife. I mean ... I'm separated from my wife. She won't let me see them."

"Oh boy."

"Yes."

"How old are they?"

"Seven and ten."

"I'd just go take them," Kyla says. "If anybody tried to keep my kid from me, I'd just go take her."

"That doesn't work in the long term."

"Sure it does, if you plan it right."

"They'd miss her."

"Yeah, well, Molly's never had a father, makes it easier."

"No father, really?"

"An alligator tore off his arm and swallowed it in Florida, at a botanical garden. They killed the 'gator and got the arm out but they couldn't reattach it. He was a soldier, right, was on leave from Afghanistan. Anyway, he figured without an arm his career was over. So he shot himself in the head. It's just as well, he was a toad." Roberta probably refers to Reese with similar disaffection. It must be open season on things she barely tolerated about him: his books and magazines, his flatulence, his habit of leaving apple cores on surfaces beside his books and magazines. She and the art student must make disdainful comments about him while they pass each other hundred-dollar knives and rest their heads on hundred-dollar pillows.

"I should take my hamster home."

"No hard feelings," Kyla says. "I still think what you did was great."

"What did I do?"

"Kill the terrorist."

"He wasn't ... I didn't ..."

"Canadians are way too nice. We let any dirtball in. Minorities are majorities these days. Pretty soon we'll be outnumbered."

He looks for his jacket, wondering if she — a former soldier's gal — believes in taking justice into her own hands, stashing a .44 Magnum under her pillow. One of the duck hunter/environmentalists advised Reese that he kept such a gun in his house in the suburbs. The duck hunter said it was time to get rid of the middleman, that Canadian gun legislation was outdated and did not take into account how times have changed.

"How have they changed?" Reese asked.

"Street crime."

"But you live in a gated community. Is there street crime in gated communities?"

"There's no such thing as a safe place anymore."

Was there ever? Were there not always predators? Aren't humans biological creatures in need of earth, air, fire, and water? Haven't they, like all animals, been at the mercy of the elements since time began? Why then do humans need guns in their houses in the suburbs? Guns that their children can discover and pack with their lunches?

On the subway the humans look afraid. Eyes avoid eyes, shoulders hunch, backs stiffen. The species that is only fifty thousand years old, that is changing the planet on a geological scale, that is at the apex of the food chain, is afraid. Not because it is degrading the Earth at an unsustainable rate, but because somebody might have a gun, and use it.

Get over it! Reese wants to shout, clutching the hamster cage.

He lets Bonaparte scurry around on the kitchen counter while he searches the fridge for something that might pass for food. He makes a cheese sandwich and stares at it briefly before remembering he must check his e-mail to find out if Kyrl Dendekker has responded to his inquiry. *Contrary to Lainie's wishes,* Kyrl writes, *her body was returned to the land of cold winds, as she called it, and burned. She told me she had always wanted to be put in a tree when she was dead. The Indians used to do this to place them closer to the Gods. Instead they burned her flawless beauty and put her in a stone jar and locked her up in a mausoleum.*

Which mausoleum? Reese immediately e-mails back.

He feeds Bonaparte some lettuce. Gwyneth Proudley has not returned his call but his mother has left several messages. To obliterate thought and the hum he turns on the television, surfs through commercials for cars, running shoes, deodorant, fast foods, hair conditioner, then stops at the dead dolphins. Blackened by fuel oil, they are stranded on a beach. Fifteen thousand birds have been killed. Thick oil has washed up on hundreds of kilometres of coastline. Reese turns off the TV and looks at his cheese sandwich again before offering Bonaparte a grape. He pulls Clara's sock out of his pocket and holds it against his face. The Toronto man who killed his wife and teenaged daughter lived with the decomposing bodies for almost a week before they were discovered. Why didn't he dispose of the bodies? Bag them, burn them, dice them up and stash them in freezer bags? Did remorse immobilize him? Did desolation take over once the anger was spent? And an unbearable loneliness, as he realized that he was no one without them? That without the ties that bind he had come undone? The man was arrested near his home. He did not try to run away.

Linden Prevost admitted to Reese that he still loves his unstable wife, that he has met no one who could pass for her equal. They still, occasionally, have eggs Benedict together and if she's not manic, they converse easily.

"About what?" Reese asked.

"We share beliefs, perspectives, don't have to justify or clarify. We speak freely, without fear of consequences."

Robert Vinkle explained that Linden had been downsized by a major corporation because of his "big yob."

"That's your interpretation," Linden said.

"They wanted you to shut the fuck up — what's good for the corpse is good for you, eat shite and smile. He got labelled 'resistant.' Once you get the resistant sticker, you're toast. Good severance package though, right, Lindy? And an out-placement service. That's how they off-load their guilt, send the resistant off for counselling. I still think you should sue them."

"That's because you know nothing about corporate law."

Bob, by this time, had had several beers. "They wanted to *zap* your frontal lobes, brother. *Nuke* the individual, soon we'll be starting the day saluting Procter & Gamble."

Bob himself, it turns out, has been waging war with a franchised restaurant across the street that has been undercutting his prices. "They can do it," Bob explained, "because it's a no-brainer franchise. They've got the volume. It's ruining the restaurant business. How many independents do you see out there? It's frickin' fast food and coffee joints, all franchised. Big Brother's here and nobody gives a rat's arse about it." Bob began to make large sweeping gestures. "What happened to the corner grocer?

It's frickin' superstores or nothing. What about a gas station owned by some guy who knows how to fix cars, who cleans your windows and checks your oil? What happened to him? What about the hardware store where the guy sells you *one* bolt, the one you *need*, not a packet of them?"

"Bookstores," Linden offered. "What happened to the bookseller who reads the book *before* they make it into a movie."

"We let this happen!" Bob said, banging the bar with his fist. "How come we let this happen?"

Only now, in the basement apartment, does Reese realize that we let it happen because we're afraid, not only of having less than the other guy, not only of other humans with guns or WMDs, but of experiencing something we haven't seen on television. Something unprecedented and unpredicted that might require us to get out of our cars.

Before the cruise, and his new commitment to consumerism, Reese attended a rally protesting drive-through retail outlets: banks, restaurants, even drugstores that enable North Americans to remain in their cars while pumping polycyclic, aromatic hydrocarbons — industrial chemicals *known* to cause gene mutations — into the air. The police watched the protesters from their cars, with the engines running. Reese tapped on a cruiser's window, still gripping his "Honk for Clean Air" sign. The cop rolled down the window and stared at him. "Are you aware," Reese said, "that genetic consequences are being associated with exposure to chemical pollution through the inhalation of urban and industrial air?"

"Is that right?" the cop said, rolling his window up again.

Reese turns the bleeding television back on. A two-year-old Alberta boy has been shot dead by his father. His body was found in a truck beside the father, who killed the boy then himself. The father was estranged from the boy's mother, was looking after his son on a three-day, court-granted visit. Was his gun kept in his house in the suburbs?

Reese continues to surf, trying to rid himself of visions of the father and the two-year-old bouncing in a car seat beside him. "Where we go, Dada?" Did the boy see the gun? Did he

understand? Was there terror? Did the father believe he was saving the son from a life worse than hell? There have been times
when Reese has looked at his children, aware that they will not
have the opportunities that he has enjoyed — the clean air, the
clean water, the freedom — and he has imagined that were the
end in sight, he would take them with him. A classmate of Clara's
had a full-blown asthma attack during a field trip at which Reese
was volunteering. The girl was suffocating and was rushed to the
hospital. No puffer or medication can heal the damage that using
the air as a toxic dump has done.

He must find a way to talk rationally with Roberta.

Pounding on the door wakes him. "Are you in there?"

"Who?"

"You."

"Who is it?"

"Katrina."

"Who?"

"From upstairs. There's no lights. There was this, like, explo-
sion and now there's no lights, no electricity, nothing."

Reese gropes his way to the door. "What do you want me to
do about it?"

"Call the landlord. Do you have the landlord's number?"

"The landlord can't fix the transformer."

"The what?"

"The transformer probably blew. Hydro will have to fix it."

"The house could've caught fire."

His eyes have adjusted to the dark, enabling him to see more
of her. She appears to be wearing a fuzzy bathrobe. "Go back to
sleep," he tells her. "They'll get to it in the morning."

"I can't sleep when it's dark."

"When do you usually sleep?"

"I have to have a light on."

"Oh. Do you have any candles?"

She shakes her head. "Do you?"

He shakes his head. "I guess you'll have to stay awake then."

"It's so quiet. And dark. It's totally spooking me out."

For the first time it registers that there is no hum. No stereo, no television, only moonlight. "How peaceful," he says.

"Can I stay down here?" Katrina asks.

"Why?"

"I'm scared."

"Where's your roommate?"

"He left."

"Is he coming back?"

"Not this century."

Reese looks out the front door and sees lit candles in windows across the street. "It used to be like this," he says. "Peaceful."

"It's totally spooking me out."

"There's nowhere to sit in my apartment," he says. "I only have a chair and a futon."

"Can you come up? I've got a living room set I got from my grandmother. After she died. It's orange. I hate it but you can sit on it." He would prefer to lie on his futon and listen to silence and Bonaparte spinning his wheel. But Katrina cowers like a child about to be forced to sleep in the dark.

He stumbles over shoes and exercise equipment on his way to the orange couch. He loses sight of Katrina, can only listen as she talks about her grandmother's living room set and her grandmother who was a bitch because she had to crawl through barbed wire to get out of Hungary in 1955. "Everything was about how in Budapest you got shot dead for no reason. We were supposed to, like, learn from that."

"What?"

"How lucky we were, duh, not to get shot for no reason. Or hanged. The Communists were hanging people in the streets. Her father was hanged. I know that's, like, tragic but I mean, what am I supposed to do about it?"

"It's still going on," Reese says.

"What?"

"Getting shot for no reason, hung in the streets."

"In Hungary?"

"We learn nothing from history." Which makes him ponder mankind's perception of himself as a superior force that will continue for centuries and millennia. For hundreds of years mankind has looked at time and space in human dimensions. Now it has become clear that time and space are endless, and that everything disappears. Even the stars die, only the cosmos remains. Yet still men fight over gods.

"She talked to her cats a lot," Katrina says. "In Hungarian. Do you want anything? A beer or anything?"

"I'm fine." And he is, on the Hungarian refugee's couch. Lying in darkness while conversing, being free of the compunction to respond with facial expressions, has induced a calm in him. He has left his women in the basement.

"I'm supposed to look like her," Katrina says, "which is, like, a total nightmare."

How can humans not be humbled by time? Time is endless, unimaginable. Time created the life of everything, decided which forms of life would survive and which would disappear. Humans cannot define what billions of years mean. They can say it started with the big bang, but they are not able to imagine what that really means because it is not in human dimensions. So they fight over gods and oil, temporarily defeating their feelings of powerlessness. Would it not be more beneficial for all to respect humanity's space in time rather than fill it with death and destruction?

"She used to watch war movies all the time."

"Did she enjoy them?"

"She said the actors looked too fat, had too many teeth, didn't have lice, didn't shit their pants."

"Did she shit her pants?"

"The whole time she was crawling through barbed wire she was carrying a load."

"I'm surprised she admitted that."

"Oh, she told the whole story, every stinking detail. Her hair got caught in the barbed wire. The creep they paid to get them through it hacked off her braids with a knife. They had to drop their suitcases and run. She remembered every little thing she'd stashed in those suitcases, stuff she'd wanted to give her children who weren't even born yet."

"Why can't you admire her?"

"Because she was a cow."

"She was courageous." He's not familiar with the room and therefore can't visualize where or how Katrina is sitting. She's only a voice in the dark. "Maybe you've seen too many movies," he says. "War movies in which people crawl under barbed wire, dodging searchlights, vicious dogs, and guns. I know I've seen too many."

"They get pretty boring. Nazi movies especially."

"It doesn't mean it didn't happen."

"Duh, like, who said it didn't happen?"

"I think we forget, on some level, otherwise it wouldn't keep happening."

"It's not happening."

"Sure it is, look around you."

"Are you, like, nuts or something? Why were you howling?"

"It felt good."

"You said you were mourning. What are you mourning about?"

"My life. I'm mourning for my life." Isn't that what Masha says? What does she do in the end? He can't remember. She drags her ass around for the whole play then what? Gun in mouth?

"Do you want pretzels or anything?"

Or does she make it to Moscow and drag her ass around there?

"I'm fine."

"Are you gay?"

"What?"

"Lance thought you were gay. I said no way does a gay man wear shoes like that."

"What's wrong with my shoes?"

"Excuse me? They're, like, made of plastic or something."

"They look like leather."

"In your dreams."

He bought the shoes at Zellers, which has become his haber-dashery. "They only cost twenty dollars," he says.

"What a steal."

"They make my feet sweat. I keep meaning to punch holes in them." There was a stooped old man at Zellers, also trying on twenty-dollar shoes. He repeatedly sniffed the shoes and suggest-ed that they smelled of diesel fumes. Reese had to agree but felt that the low price outweighed this concern. The old man advised him of the 40 percent off clearance prices in the slipper depart-ment and the $1.49 coffee and jumbo muffin combo offered until eleven.

"Let me guess," Katrina says, "they're made in China, right?"

"Right." He recognizes that his future will contain many plastic shoes made in China, where human rights are low on the list of priorities. "Can you smell them?"

"What?"

"My shoes."

"No."

He can, particularly when he sweats. He hoped that they would stop smelling over time, like car interiors. Meanwhile he must inhale the carcinogenic chemicals, must constantly be reminded that it has come to this. He did stop for a $1.49 coffee and jumbo muffin combo. The restaurant was occupied by the old and infirm, drinking coffee and eating jumbo muffins, who ogled him as though he were an apparition. On his greasy table, he found a discarded newspaper and on the front page was a photo of a father jailed for child abduction. The man had tried to spirit his eight-year-old daughter to his homeland to win back his unfaithful wife. The judge revoked his passport and declared that the man had used the child as "a sacrificial lamb," that he had committed a criminal act and that he, the judge, was send-ing a message to parents that "you don't deprive the other par-ent of a child." What is Roberta doing then? How is this legal? The man, described by his boss as honest, hardworking, and an old-fashioned family man, after serving time, will face three years of probation. He appeared stunned as he was handcuffed and led from the courtroom. He will not be seeing his daughter.

"I hate quiet," Katrina says. "Makes me feel like I'm dead."

"It used to be like this. People could rest." The quiet embraces him on the orange couch. His muscles soften, his joints loosen.

"You're not going to sleep, are you?" Katrina asks.

Clara never wanted him to go to sleep first. She sensed immediately if he was drifting off and would waken him with details of the school day, details she would never bother to tell him during the daylight hours.

The man who tried to abduct his daughter will not be treated well in prison because he is Muslim. The world will appear different to him when he gets out. He will appear different to his daughter. This is Reese's fear, that Clara will look at him differently, will not know him anymore, trust him anymore. It has already happened to the boy.

"If you snore, I'll scream," Katrina says.

"What was in the suitcases that your grandmother dropped that she was saving for her unborn children?"

"Junk. I don't know. Her father's watch, bits of silver crap that had been in the family for, like, forever. And a music box with a dancing bear on it. She was always singing the tune to us in Hungarian. We were like, 'Speak English!' She stank of sauerkraut all the time. She was always making it and storing it in weird places. Nobody ever ate it."

To have survived only to live a life making sauerkraut and storing it in weird places. To have survived only to be despised by the unborn. To leave behind an orange couch.

Clara's sock has become damp in his grip. He sniffs it to make sure it still smells of her. He doesn't know what he'll do when it stops smelling of her.

In the end only the cosmos remains.

"Are your socks too tight?" Betsy asks. "You wear your socks too tight you'll have a heart attack."

The house smells of cigarettes. "Have you been smoking?"

"I had a couple. It's the stress. He sounds terrible."

"I'd like to clean your bathroom."

"What?"

"Your bathroom needs cleaning. I'm going to clean it."

"Nobody's doing anything to my bathroom."

Under the sink Reese finds a variety of toxic cleaning solutions. He'd intended to bring his environmentally friendly Borax and washing soda combination but was distracted by Lance, the big-shouldered furniture mover, grabbing his feet and shouting, "What the fuck do you think you're doing?" Reese, on the orange couch, had been in as deep a sleep as he can remember having. Katrina, bustling about in her fuzzy bathrobe, protested Reese's innocence while accusing Lance of various offences. It turned out that Lance had forgotten his shaving utensils and other sundry items. The electricity had not as yet been restored although noisy Hydro trucks lined the street.

"Can't we, like, have a civilized conversation?" Katrina asked Lance, who appeared to be searching the apartment.

"This is *mine*," he said, grabbing a model ship in a bottle.

"Take it," Katrina said.

"I should go," Reese said.

"What are we supposed to do about breakfast?" Katrina asked. "We can't, like, make coffee or anything."

"Or shower," Reese realized.

Betsy has the volume on the television set very high. Bernie keeps it muted because he can't hear well and prefers to hear nothing rather than "bits and pieces."

"I'm going to shower first," Reese says, "then I'll clean."

"How's your father?"

"Why don't you visit him?"

"Did *he* visit *me* when *I* was in hospital?"

"Is that a reason not to visit him?"

"He doesn't even bother with Christmas anymore. First he ignores my birthday, then Christmas."

"He gave you Isotoner gloves."

"*I* gave those to me, so you wouldn't worry." The three of them sat around a canned ham and vegetables, pretending that the absence of Chelsea, and children's voices, had not destroyed all appetite. Reese had wanted to be with Clara and Derek. They were at his mother-in-law's who curled and could prepare Christmas dinners for twenty with ease.

It seems to Reese the problem begins with the "I." *I* said this and *I* did that, *I* felt this and *I* thought that. What about the other guy? What about listening? What about trying to understand? Could you bomb people if you really understood them? Could you hate someone whose vulnerabilities you knew like your own? "Love your enemy," Mark Twain said, "it'll scare the hell out of them." Should this be his tactic with Roberta?

"Have you had lunch?" Betsy asks.

"No, I'm not hungry."

"I'll make you a sandwich."

The phone rings. As Betsy hobbles over to it, Reese makes a break for the stairs.

"It's for you," she calls after him. He retraces his steps, wondering who knows he's here. To his astonishment it is Gwyneth

Proudley. He'd left his mother's number with little hope that the psychologist would call. He is breathless for a moment, as though speaking to someone famous.

"Does Wednesday at one-thirty work for you?" she asks, sounding efficient.

"Yes," he says. "Terrific. That's fantastic. I'll be there." She doesn't respond and he fears that he has sounded too enthusiastic, too anxious to win her approval. "Should I bring anything?"

"What would you bring?"

"I don't know."

"Bring yourself."

"Of course."

"Until then."

He hands the phone back to his mother.

"Is that the girl you're dating?" she asks.

"I'm not dating anyone. I'm still married."

"She sounds professional. You could use a change from that artsy-fartsy crowd." His mother has always believed that Reese could have become a brain surgeon had he not "gotten mixed up with the wrong crowd." She pushes a ham sandwich at him. He eats it because he knows one day she will die and he will suffer regret. He glances at the television, which shows the damaged oil tanker oozing foul sludge and more oil-coated dying animals. "Can we turn this off?" Reese asks, pressing the power button.

"I've been thinking about getting his chair re-upholstered," Betsy says, "while he's in hospital. When he's here he never gets out of it. Something cheery, maybe a paisley." If she is aware that Bernie may not return from the hospital, she's not letting on. "Or a stripe might be nice."

Reese puts the sandwich on the plate beside a photo of Chelsea — blue-eyed and hopeful. He used to walk towards her slowly, with arms outstretched like Frankenstein, and grab her throat. "Do you miss Dad?" he asks.

Betsy shakes her head. "Nobody's dishes to do but my own."

Katrina convinced Lance not only that she and Reese had not copulated, but to drive them to Burger Palace for breakfast.

Reese, having slept for the first time in days, felt remarkably hungry. He ordered three eggs with bacon, hash browns, toast, and coffee. Around him sat working people grabbing carbs before another day at the grind while a radio news bulletin informed them that the richest 10 percent of Canadians possess 53 percent of the country's personal wealth, with nearly 50 percent of all Canadians only a few paycheques away from the welfare office. "Good thing they're offering tax breaks on capital gains and stock dividends," Reese said.

Lance was shaking a ketchup bottle over his hash browns. "What'd you say?"

"Tax cuts for the rich. And the corporations of course. They need a break."

Lance began to smack the bottle. "Last week some guy spent fifty-four grand on wine at an auction. Can you believe that? Think what you could buy for fifty-four grand."

"An SUV," Reese suggested.

"Right on."

Why don't the people revolt? Is it because they secretly dream of making it rich themselves and benefiting from tax breaks on capital gains and stock dividends? How can they believe that tax cuts will benefit all when the low income earner will pay twenty-five cents less tax per week while the rich will pay tens of thousands of dollars less? How can people continue to believe that they live in a democracy?

"I'd like one of those Jeep Libertys," Lance said. "That is one mother of a vehicle."

"Three hundred million children are underfed," Reese said.

"What's that?"

"Six thousand children a day are infected with HIV."

"How do you know that stuff?" Katrina asked.

"I work in statistics."

"Statistics are bull," Lance said. "You can fit statistics to any story."

Betsy is pulling up Reese's pant leg to examine his sock. "Maddy's son passed away, did I tell you? Forty-four, had all this back pain, goes to see a chiropractor, comes home, lies down, and has a heart attack. Forty-four." She slides her finger under the top of his sock. "What are you wearing these for? I told you to get Happy Feet."

"These are cheaper."

"They're going to kill you. Buy Happy Feet. Don't take chances."

"I've been thinking of getting you some help," he says, "a caregiver of some kind."

"I don't need help."

"When Dad comes home you will."

"We'll manage, we always have." As far as Reese can make out his parents have never managed. They rarely speak, except to criticize and blame one another for whatever problem is prevalent. The last time Betsy fell, Bernie didn't notice, continued watching his muted television and eating Campbell's soup made with cream while she lay helpless on her bedroom floor. Fourteen hours later Reese discovered her.

It seems to him the problem begins with the blame. There is always somebody — a rogue nation, a terrorist organization, a politician, a spouse, a race — to blame.

At breakfast Lance expounded on the monster truck show.

"Is that, like, where trucks drive over each other?" Katrina inquired.

"You got it."

"Why would you want to watch that?"

"It's exciting. I love the smell of the place, and the noise."

"You're nuts." She pushed her plate away. Assuming that she'd finished, Reese began to eat her toast. "What do *you* want in life?" he asked her.

"Is that, like, a trick question?"

"You practise singing and dancing, you work in a bar. What's the objective?"

"To be discovered, duh."

"You want to be a singing and dancing star? Do they exist anymore?"

"On Broadway."

"Oh, of course. Broadway."

"My great-aunt was in the original cast of *Hair*. I just need a green card." Reese tries to remember if he has ever been this deluded. Lainie was, who is in a jar now. She returned that first Christmas to visit her parents. She called Reese and suggested they have coffee. They met in a café with cuckoo clocks on the walls. Elena complained about the snow while Reese imagined that a proposal was pending, that she would admit she'd made a mistake, that she wanted more than anything to be held in his arms. Instead she told him she was getting married. Cuckoos popped out of clocks and made startling noises. Yes, he has been that deluded. She never did actually marry the man.

"Remember when I gave you that camphor oil instead of cod liver?" Betsy asks. She brings this up annually, seems to need to suffer penance for it. "I'll never forgive myself," she says. "You turned green. I thought you were dead."

"You've told me."

"We got you to the hospital just in time. They had to pump your stomach. I'll never forgive myself." He remembers nothing of the incident except waking in the hospital and being given ice cream and a copy of *Sports Illustrated*.

Does the problem begin with the workings of our own minds, the fabrications, the machinations? "You really don't need to worry about it, Mother. It didn't scar me for life. I enjoyed the ice cream tremendously." What has *he* fabricated and machinated about Roberta? What has *she* fabricated and machinated about him?

"Your father was so upset he made you an ice rink in the backyard." The ice rink Reese remembers, and the sudden popularity it brought. Boys who'd formerly snubbed him became his best friends. Until the thaw. Perhaps he can convince Roberta that he nearly died or is near death and she will want to make him an ice rink. He could tell her that he is headed for war zones to offer himself as a human shield.

His mother leans towards him and speaks quietly, as though someone might overhear. "If he goes, I'm not staying here.

Maddy's got a nice condo above a mall. She doesn't even have to go outside in winter, just takes the elevator down to the mall. There's a Valu-mart and a Laura Secord chocolates and a hairdresser. If he goes, I'm not staying here another minute. It haunts me." She has never referred to the house in this manner. Reese has always thought she was greatly attached to the house and the memories it contained.

"She just walks down and buys a chocolate or two whenever she feels like it."

"Mother, you can hardly walk."

"Who says?"

"You've lost two toes."

"I'll take the elevator."

"Wouldn't you miss this house?"

"What for? Nothing but work, work, work. Maddy says there's a café there that makes lattes. Have you ever had a latte?"

"It's just espresso with steamed milk."

"She says they're delicious. She just walks down and has a latte whenever she feels like it."

He feels several pillows, testers. The salesman has large incisors and appears to be stalking him. "Were you looking for any particular brand?" he asks.

"No. Just comfort."

"Do you prefer firm or soft?"

"I hadn't really thought about it."

"Oh you should. It's quite impossible to shop for a pillow unless you're clear on your preferences."

"I just thought I'd feel them." The testers are grubby from the likes of Reese handling them. He is well aware that the pillows he is currently fondling are in the hundred-dollar range. He has no intention of buying one, only having a cursory experience of them and, in so doing, perhaps gaining a more profound understanding of Roberta. He tried to track her down at the college, searched classroom after classroom until a security guard caught up with him.

"Those are down," the fanged salesman says.

"They're very soft," Reese observes.

"And light, if you prefer a light pillow, some people prefer more density." He points to another tester. "This one has a foam core. Light on the outside, dense on the inside." The advertised feather or fibre same-price pillows lie neglected in a bin near the door to the bedding store and cost only $7.99. Reese did squeeze them in passing.

"What are you sleeping on now?" the wolf asks.

"Umm ... I'm not really sure. It's old, whatever it is."

"Dust mites," the wolf chides. "You *must* change your pillows, particularly if you're sensitive to allergies." He points to several of the testers. "These have bacterial protection." Reese knows this means the hundred-dollar pillows are treated with carcinogenic chemicals. "This," the wolf says, "is a Hungarian Medium White down." He hands Reese the tester. "Definitely in the mid-range."

"Does that mean the geese are Hungarian?"

"That is correct. This" — he hands Reese another pillow — "is a Yukon Extra Soft. Very light, very cozy."

Reese stands holding both pillows.

"You're welcome to lie on one of the display beds to try them."

"Oh good, thank you." With some self-consciousness, Reese puts a pillow on a bed and his head on the pillow.

"Many customers compromise with the Siberian down and feather mix. It's currently on sale, any size, one price, $49.99."

Reese puts his head on another pillow. "How do they get the down off the geese?"

"Pardon me?"

"Do they have to kill the geese to get the down?"

"Of course. Does that disturb you?"

"How many geese does it take to fill a pillow?"

"You might prefer the Hutterite White down. They eat those geese. The Hutterites raise them till they're full grown then eat them."

"You mean the other pillows are made from baby geese?"

The wolf touches his ears briefly, as if to make sure he can still pass for human. "The geese are *raised* for their down," he articulates carefully. Reese imagines the miserable lives of the geese in the Siberian steppes, caged, fed only enough gruel to ensure that they grow feathers.

"Are you a vegan?" the wolf asks, glancing at Reese's plastic shoes. "If you're a vegan, you might be more comfortable with a fibre pillow. The Feather-Likes are quite popular." He passes Reese another pillow. "And washable if you have a tumble dryer. *All* the pillows should be tumble dried on cool once a month to get rid of dust mites." Surrounded by dead geese and carcinogenic chemicals, the children of the drought-ravaged state of Rajasthan crawl into Reese's mind, eating grass to stay alive. Grass that is running out, leaving a trail of dead children. He showed the photographs to Sterling, who frequently claims that there is no such thing as global warming. "The Arctic ice cap," Reese heard himself say despite his better judgment, "has shrunk by twenty percent in the last three decades."

"What's that got to do with wogs eating grass?" Sterling asked.

"Once the permafrost melts, thousands of years of organic matter will break down, releasing huge quantities of methane gas. Up goes the air temperature, down goes the oxygen ratio. Humans'll choke and broil."

"Yeah, yeah, yeah," Sterling said, comfortable in his fabrication that *it can't happen to us.* "Quit with the human-bashing, boyo. Civilization is a bee-ewtiful thing."

The wolf appears ready to pounce. Reese stands, freeing himself of slaughtered geese. "I'll have to think about it."

Bernie can't reach the food on his tray.

"How long has it been sitting there?" Reese asks.

"Who knows?"

"Tell them to place it closer to you next time."

"Who can eat that slop anyway?"

"You've got to eat, Dad." Reese lifts the cover off the food. "It's a cutlet of some kind. I think it's pork, or maybe chicken." He places the tray closer to his father, but Bernie shows no interest.

"If you want to get sick," he grumbles, "go to the hospital. If I soil myself I have to shout at the Blacks to get a change."

Reese tries putting a fork in Bernie's hand but sees immediately that he is unable to grip it. "Let me cut this up for you."

"You should have let me go."

Aware that if he doesn't feed his father, no one will, Reese spears a piece of cutlet and holds it in front of Bernie's mouth. To his surprise, Bernie opens his mouth and eats the pork or chicken.

"I think it's chicken," he says.

Reese continues to feed him as he once fed his children. Bernie has few teeth because he's never gone to the dentist. When tooth pain became unbearable he would extract the tooth himself rather than subject himself to "money-grubbing sadists."

"How about the vegetables?" Reese asks. Bernie shakes his head emphatically. "How about the canned peaches?"

"Let me taste them."

Some peach slips off the spoon onto Bernie's hospital gown. "Sorry," Reese says, trying to retrieve it. The man in the next bed, with the swollen feet, is talking in his sleep.

"The peaches are good," Bernie says. "Fresh."

Reese doesn't question how canned peaches can be fresh. He holds up a bag of croissants and a small tub of margarine because Bernie decided long ago that butter was bad for him. "What else can I bring you? Some fruit?"

"Cornflakes. With cream. They keep giving me bran flakes and orange juice. I tell them people with poor kidney function can't tolerate phosphorous. It goes in one ear and out the other."

"Have they said when they're putting in the abdominal catheter?"

"Tomorrow. The buggers are going to knock me out and do God knows what."

"Save your life."

"Plug me with plastic. What kind of life is that?"

It is impossible for Reese to believe that his own demise, should he live that long, will be any different from his father's.

When his peers complain about their aging parents, even the ones installed in institutions, he marvels that they can imagine it will be any different for them in their golden years. He looks at his father and sees himself, only his father is fearless. Reese will not put up a fight. They'll be able to tie him to a wheelchair and roll him into a corner. When he soils himself, he will not shout at the Blacks.

He joins the few picketers outside the Greenpeace office who have been maintaining a noisy protest against ending door-to-door fundraising in favour of phone canvassing. In so doing, Greenpeace has broken a collective agreement not due to end for another year. The phone positions, Reese knows, offer fewer hours and not the same rate of pay or benefits as the door-to-door work. Only part-time positions will be available to the canvassers, some of whom Reese knows and has worked with — people who actually believe in man's capacity to effect change. They recognize him, pat his shoulder, and thank him for coming. The woman who fired him and refused to give him references walks primly towards them, avoiding eye contact. Reese places himself in front of the door, forcing her to do a little dance to circumvent him. When she does glance up, it pleases him to see that she looks frightened. He stretches his lips into what he hopes is a psychotic grin. "Lucy, you got some splainin' to do."

"Step aside, please."

"Don't you think," he asks, "an organization that expects governments to honour environmental treaties they have ratified should honour a labour treaty that it has ratified?"

"Let me through or I'll call the police."

Reese has coffee with Stan Huckle, a bearded, long-time canvasser who has taken up smoking. They sit outside with the other smokers hunched over ashtrays. "Why did you start smoking?" Reese asks him.

"It'll be over by 2050 anyway."

"That soon?"

"Norte Americanos require twenty-five acres of natural resources *per person* to maintain their non-negotiable lifestyles.

Europeans need about fifteen, Ethiopians less than five, and the Africans in Burundi about an acre. One-third of the natural world's been destroyed by humans over the past three decades. Do the math. Not enough acres."

Stan Huckle was in the Saudi environmental headquarters in Dammam in '91 and saw the first hard numbers hitting the computer screen as all known sources of oil washing into the Persian Gulf were monitored. The 5.5-million-barrel total equalled twenty-five *Exxon Valdez* spills. A third of that oil was the result of allied bombing. Stan flew in a chopper over shores blackened by vast slicks extending beyond the horizon. Half the Saudi coastline was heavily oiled. In Kuwait, his team ventured daily into the creosoted desert, saw spreading lakes of Kuwaiti crude and thousands of blazing and gushing oil wells. He said the forty-six-day war to ensure cheap prices at the pumps consumed some 20 million gallons of oil each day, while releasing another 40 to 60 million tons of globe-girdling, sulphur-laden soot from a thousand burning and gushing wellheads. They burned for two hundred days. Back in Canada, Stan stopped driving a car. He didn't go back for Operation Free Iraq because he felt he'd seen enough charbroiled orphans and landscape to last a lifetime.

"Sounds like you're giving up," Reese says.

"The Third World's collapsing under population and debt. The Pentagon's spending billions on weapons to keep them in line. It's a joke." He lights another cigarette. "Of course, the Democrats are going to change all that." He inhales heavily. Reese waits for the smoke to appear but Stan only stares up at the highrises for what seems like minutes before smoke starts to spiral from his nostrils.

"Ensuring the essentials to *everyone* on Earth," he says, "would cost a fiftieth as much as those dicks are spending on the war machine. If everybody had enough to eat do you think there'd be suicide bombers? The war on terror's a joke, what we need is a war on poverty. It's so basic and nobody's getting it." He leans the back of his head against the plate glass window and closes his eyes. An SUV idles while the driver rushes in to get his latte.

"I met somebody today," Reese says, "who's going to a monster truck show."

Stan Huckle doesn't move, doesn't open his eyes.

"He likes the smell and the noise," Reese says.

"There's plenty more smell and noise coming and he won't have to buy a ticket. It's a throw-away planet. Use it up and chuck it. Nobody's figured out they won't be able to buy another one."

"Do you want a job?"

"At your hellhole?"

"It's a job."

"I don't know how you can do that shit."

"I have a family," Reese says.

"That's everybody's excuse. 'I have a family so it's okay to shit in our water.' What are the kiddies going to drink, guys?"

"It isn't helping me."

"What?" Stan stares at him with searchlight eyes. "What are you talking about?"

"Being an environmentalist. It's turning my family against me."

"Oh, because you make them separate the toilet rolls from the regular trash?"

"It depresses them."

"I'm so sorry. Maybe they'll feel better on a blackened planet." Stan sucks on his cigarette.

"What are you going to do?" Reese asks.

"Most likely I'll get on a plane and make myself useful somewhere. Maybe get blown up."

"It has its advantages."

Reese can see the babysitter through the window, on a cellphone, scrutinizing herself in the mirror. She pinches the exposed skin between her T-shirt and tight jeans, turns sideways and grabs the fat on her ass. She leans in close to the mirror to inspect her skin. Still talking on the cell, she single-handedly squeezes a zit. This is who Roberta has entrusted with his children while she is gooling at waven. He creeps along the side of the house, looking in windows for his children. He finds them in the living room watching television. Were he with them they would not be watching television. They would be drawing or building or gluing or painting. On screen, a man and woman are trying to swallow each other's tongues while removing each other's clothes. Another man, carrying a gun, bursts in and begins shouting. The half-naked couple scramble for their clothes. The tongue-swallowing man places himself between the armed man and the woman, holding out his hand as though trying to quiet a dog. The armed man continues shouting and waving his gun. As the tongue-swallowing man approaches him, presumably to suggest he put the gun down, the armed man shoots him several times. Blood blossoms on his undershirt. Reese watches his children staring at the screen as the tongue-swallowing man writhes in agony. Blood pours from his mouth. The half-naked woman throws herself upon him and sobs. The armed man kicks her and steals away.

Reese stands behind glass, immobilized. Derek appears unaffected by the onscreen events, but Clara's lower lip begins to protrude, which indicates that tears are imminent. And Reese can do nothing. A sickness erupts in him so vile, so potent, that he feels his legs weakening beneath him. He grabs the window ledge and watches as his daughter's tears begin to fall and the big brother sneers and pulls on her ponytail. Reese watches, powerless, clinging to the edge of the cliff, so close but impossibly far away. His legs buckle beneath him. Bricks graze him as he slides into the shrubbery. He will wait here. He will wait.

12

He wakes in darkness with a cat rubbing against him. He is allergic to cats and tries to push it away. It purrs loudly, breathing cat-food breath on him. "Shoo," Reese whispers, but the cat begins to chew on his clothes, possibly catching whiffs of Bonaparte. Reese stands, steadying himself against the house that was once his. The living room lights are off. He creeps back to the kitchen, expecting to find Roberta enjoying a midnight snack and bevie with the art student, but there is no one, only the stove light providing an ominous glow. He moves with stealth to the front of the house and pauses by the lilac bush. He'd intended, of course, to confront her, to intercept her on her return from gooling at waven, to spy her with the art student and accuse her of misconduct and negligence. Instead he fell asleep. Instead his daughter wept alone.

The porch floorboards creak underfoot. He stands motionless for a moment, listening for sounds from within. He inserts the key slowly, turning it gently before applying pressure to the door handle. Inside he stands, trying to hear above the clamour of his heartbeat. It surprises him how well he can see, how streetlight illuminates objects over which he might otherwise have stumbled. The stairs will prove a challenge due to their squeaking. He places his feet close to their edges while clinging to the banister. The ascent is slow as he pauses between each step to listen. The Mickey Mouse nightlight glares at him as he approaches the land-ing. Roberta took his children to Disneyland to spite him, he knows, because prior to the separation he'd refused to support such commercial trash. It was her way of saying "*I* make the decisions now." Beyond the horror of imagining his children being mauled by men in Donald Duck suits, he could not stop worrying about planes crashing. He shuffles along the wall, avoiding floorboards, bumping picture frames. The armed man in the movie, so avidly watched by his children, charged into the room where the other man and woman were swallowing each other's tongues. Will sneaking up on Roberta and the art student be viewed as pathetic? Unarmed, will he pose no threat? Will Roberta laugh outright while dialling the police? Reese looks around for a weapon, a blunt instrument. Only Mickey Mouse leers up at him.

As expected, there is not just Roberta in the bed; another lump lies beside her. With vindication imminent, Reese has difficulty breathing. He'd wanted and not wanted to find her in carnal relations with another. Carnal relations with another should bring closure. But Reese feels only more of what has become a familiar distress, beginning in his plastic shoes and spreading through him. The armed man in the movie didn't hesitate before he fired, but Reese can't spur himself to action; no rage is coursing through him, only disappointment, in her, in himself, in a world in which starving children are running out of grass to eat. He'd expected no better of Roberta, or himself. Lost in machinations and fabrications, they have failed.

Something beneath the duvet moves, causing Reese to brace himself for conflict. Fists form, his knees bend in preparation for a body launch. But then a tail appears, a tail that can only belong to the Portuguese water dog — the slumber partner extraordinaire. How pleased the dog must be to have his mistress and her quality mattress all to himself. If it's relief that Reese is feeling, he finds it difficult to comprehend, hoping as he did to collect evidence. He inches closer to the bed, studies his wife's sleeping face, which carries none of the lines that have become so dominant on her conscious one. He wants to curl up beside her, despite the dog and the mouth guard. He wants to go back, to forget. To go home again. Or smother her with a pillow. A toxicologist used fentanyl to murder his wife then scattered rose petals around her body to make it look like suicide.

She rolls over, towards the dog. Reese remains completely still, alarmed at the rasping of his breathing. Watching her, he tries to understand — to love his enemy. Early on she insisted that sole custody would be better for the children, that they needed stability, that passing them back and forth and sharing decisions about their welfare would only add stress to their lives. "We couldn't agree on anything when we were together," she said, "do you think we'll agree on anything now we're apart?" It seemed to him that they had agreed on many things, but perhaps this was because he was "out of it." "We need a complete separation," she said. "I don't want them being the centre of our conflict, dealing with the contradictions and tensions between us. They've seen enough. They need a sense of security based on living in *one* neighbourhood with *one* set of friends and *one* set of clothes and toys." Initially this gave him pause. She cited a divorced father at the college who'd bungled joint custody, whose daughter had taken to soiling her clothes and whose son had taken to mixing cocaine with Xanax. But the thought of Roberta having full parental authority over his children, meaning he would have no legal right to make *any* decisions concerning their welfare, has become untenable. The words "visiting rights" make him feel as if he is behind bars. "Sole custody is the traditional pattern," Roberta argued, in front of the mediator who was stroking her cat.

"It's the most common method for raising children following a divorce," the mediator agreed. "It means there's no big disruptions in their development and they don't become emotionally disturbed."

Wasn't Derek already emotionally disturbed? Were his emotional disturbances rooted in his parents' conflict?

Reese checked the Internet, learning that non-custodial fathers with legal rights to "reasonable visitation" are frequently prohibited from seeing their children by the custodial mother. Excuses are made — the child is sick, has a birthday party, has to study for an exam. When the non-custodial father seeks a court order to assure visitation by specifying visitation times, he is told that this would constitute a change of custody, that he must first prove that the circumstances are different from those at the time of the divorce in order to change the original decree. Given the difficulty and expense involved in changing court orders, most fathers give up. Reese raised this issue in front of the mediator, but Roberta would not change her stance, said that she was not prepared to sacrifice the children's emotional well-being just so Reese could "feel involved."

Emotional well-being. Is there such a thing? Are not emotional lives fraught with inconsistencies, fragments of euphoria, sunken hopes, miscommunications, fears real and imagined? Does she really believe that banishing him will cause no ripple in their pond?

His knees feel locked and his feet weighted. The dog's tail moves slightly. Stiff-legged, Reese backs out of the room, half hoping that his mother is right about his socks, that he is progressing towards a heart attack and will be found dead at Mickey's feet. He looks in on the boy, even though he has lost him. He lies taut in his fetal position. Reese wants to sit beside him, smooth the furrows from his brow, and talk to him about what animal he thinks he was in another life. When he was five Derek thought that, because humans were animals, it made sense that they would be different animals in past and future lives. Sometimes he favoured being a mole because it lived underground and had few predators. Other times he wanted to be a wolverine because it had "waterproof fur" and all the other animals were scared of it. Reese spots the Ritalin on the bedside table and wants to grab it, smash it. Derek has been programmed to take one immediately on waking. When Reese is not overwhelmed by the odds against him, he has hopes that Derek will come back to him, when he's older and free to think for himself. When he sees that Reese has done nothing, only stood there, waiting for him, year after year.

Clara, as is her wont, has flipped over on the bed. Her head lies where her feet should be and her blankets have slid to the floor. In his past life Reese would have lifted her and set her back on the pillow before arranging the blankets around her. In this life he is afraid to touch her, to wake her, thereby alerting Roberta to his presence. And yet he feels that if Clara doesn't see him, throw her arms around him, love him, he will die. He leans over her waiting, fearing, yearning for her to look up at him. His heart, a swollen, dejected mass, batters his ribs. The tenderness he feels for her that he can no longer express torments him. To think that he could hold her once, kiss her once, extract splinters from her fingers. To think that he stepped on her tiara once, causing torrents of tears to which he responded, "If you leave your things lying on the floor, they're going to get stepped on." A lesson had to be learned, he believed, valued tiaras should be tucked away in drawers. To have that moment back, to pull her onto his knee and explain how sorry he was, that he'd been preoccupied with nonsense from work and had not looked where he was going, to dry her tears and not release her until trust had been restored. Behind glass he can do nothing. He is no longer of his children's world. He picks up the blankets and lays them gently over her.

"Where were you?" Katrina asks.

"What do you mean?"

"I was worried." She's in her fuzzy bathrobe again.

"The lights are on."

"I know, but I'm not used to being alone, like, in an entire house. It's totally spooking me out."

"Oh. Well, I'm back."

"Can you come upstairs?"

"Why?"

"Just to, like, hang out. I'm totally spooked. There was, like, this noise in the backyard and I went to check it out and there was this chicken."

"A chicken?"

"Yeah. Like an entire chicken, raw. Somebody put a dead chicken in our yard."

"I did."

Her eyes widen. "You did?"

"I thought the coons might enjoy it."

"You're nuts."

"I have to feed my hamster. Excuse me." He closes the door gently on her. He needs to be alone. The turbulence inside him has been worsened by caffeine and a chocolate walnut cruller. He is taking pleasure in slowly poisoning himself by eating junk. He checks his messages. There are no calls from the hospital, which suggests that his father isn't dead. His mother has called to ask about his father and complain the Bernard never phones *her*. And Roberta has left an enraged message regarding the hamster she claims he has stolen. "Does this mean I have to change the locks?! Are you *that* juvenile?!" He knows that she won't change the locks because locksmiths cost money. Unless, of course, the art student is a handyman. If there is an art student. Since finding her in bed with the dog, Reese is less certain about the art student.

Noise has begun upstairs.

"Oh hi. I had this audition for *My Fair Lady*. It's only dinner the-atre, I won't get it, but I totally love that song about dancing all night." Clutching a light beer, she begins to sing the song.

"This creates a disturbance downstairs."

"Oh, don't be such a sad ass. Watch a Fred and Ginger movie with me. I've got the boxed set. What's your favourite? *Top Hat*, *The Gay Divorcee*? Ginger's favourite was *Swing Time* because it was the only time a director treated her like an actor. Usually they treated her like she was this dumb blonde with legs. Some things never change. Ouch." She examines something purplish on her ankle. "I got this tattoo today and I keep forgetting about it. You're supposed to treat them like a wound first off. It's a butterfly. I got the guy to put more purple in it. It was more like orange, you know, as in monarch. No way was I paying seventy-eight bucks to get orange poked into my pores."

"I need to sleep."

"Really?"

"Really."

"Okay, I'm sorry."

"That's alright. Please, no more dancing."

On the futon he listens to her constricted movements as she tries to manoeuvre soundlessly. His pillow, filled with dust mites, offers little comfort. He hadn't realized the consolation that a hundred-dollar pillow filled with slaughtered geese feathers could bring. His ear begins to hurt where it makes contact with the depleted, $5.99 pillow. His hip aches where it makes contact with the depleted futon. He flips onto his back and contemplates the Texas dentist, a former beauty queen, who ran her Mercedes over her orthodontist husband in the parking lot of a hotel where he'd gone with his dental assistant. The beauty queen/dentist insisted it was an accident, that she'd stopped at the hotel to buy sugarless gum. They had no children although they'd been married eleven years. Was the beauty queen/dentist devastated by her infertility? Did she run over the orthodontist because she couldn't stand the thought of him spawning with the dental assistant? It must have been startling, feeling his body thud under the wheels, hearing him screaming in agony.

Reese should have returned his mother's call, as she is the only person left who cares if he is alive or dead. There was fungi growing in her bathroom, she who used to spring clean. They would all have to cooperate, move furniture, tidy, store the winter clothes, shake out the summer. Betsy would scrub the walls. The house smelled fresh afterwards. What happened to that person? Who is this woman missing toes with fungi in her bathroom? Where's his mother? He wants his mother. She had a way of stroking his forehead that could soothe all ills.

He sniffs, noticing that the basement apartment smells of decay. If he thinks ahead, to a life lived in basements, a paralyzing despair begins. Better to think of beds, and the meeting with Gwyneth Proudley, who may be very charming and compassionate. She may shake his hand and immediately feel a connection with him.

Possibly their eyes will meet with unspoken understanding. He will not have to explain about killing a man, or a pigeon, or a rat.

He tries lying on his side again but within seconds his hip and shoulder resent the absence of a quality bed. He saw an ad for "pressure-relieving Swedish mattresses and pillows that have been proven by doctors and health professionals worldwide to be beneficial to circulation, muscles, and solid sleep." He must try one of those.

"Hi," he says.

"I'm trying to be quiet."

"I know. I mean, I can hear you trying not to make noise."

"You must have bat ears or something. Like, what am I supposed to do, stop moving?"

"No, not at all. I thought maybe I'd watch that Fred and Ginger movie with you."

"Are you serious?"

"Quite."

"Which one?"

"Whichever." He hopes to escape Elena, his mother, and Chelsea, who keeps appearing as a child with a runny nose. "Find your sister a Kleenex," Betsy would say. He wouldn't, the snot would continue, and Chelsea would lick it. "That's dis*gusting*," Reese would sneer. Her upper lip would become red and chaffed from the licking.

"*Top Hat*'s the most popular," Katrina says, inserting a DVD into a player. "Ginger gets to wear the ostrich feathers. They gave her such a hard time over that dress because it kept shedding. Fred used to totally freak if Ginger's clothes were upstaging him. Everybody was against the ostrich dress until they saw the rushes. Even then nobody said, 'Wow, Ginger, you were right about that dress.' People can be so small. Fred gave her a gold feather charm, though, for her bracelet. On the card he wrote 'Dear Feathers, I love ya.'"

Fred, who has been in deep discussion with another man in tails, begins to tap dance, disturbing Ginger who's trying to grab some shut-eye in the hotel suite below. "It's just like you and me except in reverse," Katrina observes. Ginger, wearing an elaborate peignoir, storms up to Fred's suite and scolds him for making noise. Fred, immediately stricken by her beauty and spunk, can't stop smiling at her.

"They were chemical together," Katrina says.

Reese, on the orange couch, feels remarkably relaxed and free of ghosts. Perhaps he should offer to buy the orange couch. Or is the orange couch only therapeutic while above ground, beyond decay?

"Nobody knows if they ever actually got it on," Katrina says. "Fred always said they were just friends, but Ginger said he took her out dancing and even kissed her, which he never did in the movies, well, just once because the public was like, 'Why don't they ever kiss?' And that kiss was for, like, a split second. They had to slow it down on film to make it last longer. Fred's wife was, like, totally mental about him being with Ginger all the time. She used to go on set and knit while they were rehearsing. The clicking of her needles drove Ginger nuts."

Ginger, her bleached hair unruffled, gets back into bed. Fred spills sand from an ashtray onto the floor of his suite and begins tapping and swishing a gentle lullaby. Below, at first angered but then mellowed by the soft sounds, Ginger goes to sleep.

"Her hair used to be brown, that's why they called her Ginger. That's when Fred dated her, when she had brown hair and was just a Charleston girl. He was this big stage star and she was, like, a nobody. He was probably threatened later on, when she turned up blonde and a movie star."

Fred's clarity of movement, his elegance and grace, have calmed Reese. He watches as he imagines the thousands watched during the Depression. They lined up to see Fred and Ginger dazzle on shiny white sets rather than face hunger and strife in the dull grey of their real lives. "Do you watch these movies often?" Reese asks.

"Only when I'm, like … *really* depressed."

The beauty queen/dentist was sentenced to twenty years in prison. The jury could have sentenced her to ninety-nine but, after six hours of deliberation, they found that she'd acted in "sudden passion," which under Texas law put the maximum at twenty years.

"What do you think made them chemical?" Reese asks.

"They were totally different. The truth is they didn't even want to do movies together. Fred didn't want to be teamed with anybody after being teamed with his sister so long. And Ginger wanted to be a serious actress. It just happened they were both under contract with RKO."

Were the beauty queen/dentist and the orthodontist different? Were they chemical? "Sudden passion" sounds chemical. What does it take to sustain chemistry? Or is it an illusion, like Fred and Ginger who beneath the glamour were just contract players who may or may not have got it on?

Roberta has told him she doesn't want the children being the centre of their conflict, dealing with the contradictions and tensions between them. Is a chemical-free existence a realistic goal? Listening in on Avril Leblanc, Reese learned that "it's important not to suppress emotions but to embrace them." She quoted her teacher, Lama Ole Nydahl: "Let emotions be like a thief who comes to rob an empty house." Reese couldn't quite get his head around that one, nor could the potential donor, who said she had to pick up her dry cleaning.

Roberta has a way of tilting her head when she doesn't understand something that Reese continues to miss. And when she cuts vegetables, she sings quietly to herself, songs nobody sings anymore like "Fly Me to the Moon" and "On the Street Where You Live." He misses her singing.

Fred and Ginger dance close and fast around a shiny white hotel lobby. Their steps are light and clean, leaving no trace on the sparkling floor.

"Sometimes," Katrina says, "it's like they're one person."

That's part of it then. Without Roberta he is missing what he thought was a part of himself. He had entrusted her with his failings and weaknesses. His heart. She knew all, knows all, and won't hesitate to use it against him.

Avril Leblanc advised the potential donor in need of dry cleaning to think of herself as an onion, and to continually peel away layer after layer, seeking the simplicity and sweetness at the core. Avril Leblanc stressed, however, that the core is not the goal, the *peeling* is the goal.

So it must be with Reese. Let Roberta's wrath shake the ground beneath him. He will be an onion.

"**A**re you getting your teeth cleaned?" Betsy asks. "Get your teeth cleaned or you'll have a heart attack. The infection goes down from your gums to your heart. It happened to Peggy's cat."

"Dad's having surgery this morning," Reese says. "I thought you might like to come."

"What for? He'll start telling me I'm doing something wrong the minute he sees me."

Why do his parents constantly point out each other's failings? Did the mutual loathing grow out of their isolation resulting from Bernie's dwindling practice and finances? Shunned by the world, they could only vent their anger on the other outcast. They did not let their emotions resemble thieves who come to rob empty houses.

Avril has requested a private meeting with him. He doesn't know why and has said that he is unavailable due to his father's surgery. He is not sure that he can handle a private meeting with Avril Leblanc. He fears that she will penetrate the facade that he is struggling to maintain — revealing that he is not being a good onion.

"They were talking about heart attacks on TV," Betsy says. "Next time you shovel snow, make sure you jog first. Men have heart attacks shovelling snow because they don't get the blood going first. The blood vessels tighten in the cold and can't take all that action all of a sudden."

"Do you need anything from the store?"

"Did you bring me Crispy Crunches?"

He hands her several. "I'll call you from the hospital."

Bernie accuses someone invisible of incompetence, shouts at another to watch the road, asshole, tells another he has other fish to fry.

"Dad?"

"Where's Chelsea?"

"What?"

"Where's your sister?"

"She's dead."

"What?"

"She died."

"You should've been nicer to her."

Another possible reason for Bernie's lack of faith in modern medicine is that it let his daughter die. For months afterwards he went to his office, devoid of patients, and did not come out until Betsy called him for dinner.

"I brought you Cornflakes in little boxes," Reese says. "And cream. You just pop the box open on the dotted lines and pour in the cream."

Bernie stares fixedly at the red and green rooster on one of the boxes.

"Did you eat the croissants, Dad?"

"I feel terrible."

"Is there anything I can do?"

"I feel like I'm dying."

"You have to rest."

"They keep feeding me goddamn brown bread. They don't listen about the phosphorous."

"I'll talk to somebody."

"Nothing but coloureds. I eat the jam and peanut butter, without the bread."

"I'll bring you some white bread."

"Sliced, none of that crusty stuff."

"Does the catheter hurt?"

"The what?"

"The abdominal catheter, can you feel it?"

Bernie gropes under his hospital gown. "They got it in me."

"Good, that means you'll be able to do dialysis at home."

"What?"

"The dialysis you're going to do while you're sleeping, at home. They're going to hook you up to something."

"Who said that?"

"That's why they put in the inner-dwelling catheter."

"Buggers."

"Are you thirsty? I brought 7-Up. It's not cold. Maybe I can find some ice." Reese used a nail to punch holes in his plastic shoes this morning. For this reason it dismays him to feel perspiration trickling between his toes. "Dad?" Bernie has closed his eyes again.

There is no staff person available to ask for ice and the sick, over-breathed hospital air is clogging Reese's air passages. He takes the elevator down to street level and hurries through the revolving doors in search of oxygen and a convenience store. Spring should be evolving, there should be optimism in the air, but people stare at the pavement. He feels no kinship with them. As much as he knows that suffering exists greater than his, he cannot see beyond his own. At the convenience store an obese woman buying cigarettes and a Mr. Big complains to the Korean behind the counter about her diabetes and heart condition.

Reese first sensed that his feet were still sweating despite the holes when Sterling told him that one of the bequest donors for the Humane Society had been complaining about the distribution of funds. She, like the born-again Christian who believes that the apocalypse is imminent, resents aid going to animals outside her neighbourhood. "She was pretty miffed," Sterling said, "started hyperventilating, I thought maybe we were going to lose her right then, which would've been convenient. Anyway, lest you forget, the bequesters are at the top of the pyramid. We don't want to go putting their backs up."

There was a time when Reese dreamed of sabotaging whaling ships.

He sits with the bag of ice on a bench. The meeting with the Family Values clients did not go well this morning. Devout Christians, they seemed convinced that their beliefs were right and everybody else's wrong. Discussing the script, it became clear that room for innovation was limited. Mom and Dad, the kids and Fido were the golden standard. When Reese raised the issue of same-sex marriage, Sterling showed signs of irritation. During the break he muttered, "Don't make me regret making you Creative Director, Marketing." Reese had resisted becoming Creative Director, Marketing, had been content being Managing Director, Operations. It was Sterling who pushed him into what he called "the creative side." Reese had already begun to loathe the office, its beige walls and carpets, its chrome chairs, its Robert Bateman reproductions, its hypocrisy. Although where is there not hypocrisy? Who cannot be bought? *He* has been bought. He looks down at his shoes and sees a tear beginning at one of the nail holes.

A third patient has been wheeled into Bernie's room. A man with a pointed head who says "Oh my, my ..." repeatedly in response to pain. Usually he gasps and winces before saying "Oh my, my ..."

"Do you want some 7-Up with ice, Dad?"

"Where's your mother?"

"At home." Reese tears open the bag of ice and the packet of plastic cups. Never before has he bought plastic cups. It is a signal of his defeat that rather than hunt down hospital staff for a glass, he has purchased plastic cups.

Chicken à la king is served by a black woman who doesn't look at Bernie or Reese or the man with the pointed head or the man with the swollen feet. Reese places the food within Bernie's reach. "Do you want to try any of this?"

"Wouldn't feed it to my dog."

"Vegetables might help your bowels."

Bernie eyes the peas mixed in with the chicken à la king

before picking at them with his fingers. Reese avoids contemplating the last time Bernie washed his hands.

"So Mum's doing alright."

"Why won't she come and see me?"

"You didn't visit her in the hospital."

Bernie gives no indication that he's heard this. He carefully picks out more peas. "These are fresh, they must shell them here." How he can imagine that there are Blacks in the basement shelling peas, Reese can't fathom. But he says nothing, knowing that it's best not to argue. All his life he has believed it's best not to argue. Maybe he should argue more with Roberta. He has avoided a confrontation over the hamster issue. Does she perceive his avoidance of conflict as being "out of it"?

"Oh my, my ..." the man with the pointed head says. Reese rolls his neck. What does conflict accomplish anyway? Wars are fought, children killed, women raped, land destroyed, hatreds reinforced, what is gained?

Bernie pushes the plate away, chicken untouched.

"There's applesauce," Reese says.

"Put Splenda on it."

Reese tears open the packet of artificial sweetener and shakes it over the applesauce. What is it about sweets and old people? Why is his mother addicted to Crispy Crunches? As humans regress into infantile states do they crave the sweetness of mother's milk? "I guess they want you to take these pills," he says.

"Laxatives."

"I guess you'd better take them." He offers the little paper cup to his father. "Come on, Dad. Unless you want fingers up your butt again."

"Oh my, my ..."

Bernie takes the pills. "Ask them when I can go home."

"I will. If I see a doctor."

"I feel like a robot with this thing inside me."

"It'll save your life."

"Did I ask them to save it? You should have let me go."

"Do you want me to dial Mum for you?"

"She doesn't want to talk to me."

Reese dials her anyway, knowing that no one can understand his parents as they understand each other. He leaves Bernie griping at length to Betsy who, no doubt, is smoking while chewing Crispy Crunches.

In a dream on the orange couch Reese was in a plane with Clara. They were wearing parachutes and it was imperative that they jump. Like parachutists in war movies, they stood battered by wind in the portal of the plane. Reese could see that Clara would be unable to reach her rip cord, and was trying desperately to think how to pull it for her. They could jump together, he hanging on to her until he could pull her cord, then his own. But he feared that once in flight he would lose his grip on her, and they would spin away from each other.

"You spend a third of your life in bed," the saleswoman tells him, "that's if you plan on living to a hundred." She smiles in what he fears is intended to be a humorous way. "Restful sleep helps your back, boosts your immune system, and reduces stress." She bears an uncanny resemblance to Harpo Marx. "And you don't need me to tell you what it does for your sex life."

He tests the mattress in question. "Do you have any of those space-age mattresses?"

"Any whats?"

"They're Swedish. They're supposed to be proven by doctors and health professionals worldwide to be beneficial to circulation, muscles, and solid sleep."

"Never heard of them."

Reese suspects that she's lying, that she knows perfectly well where he might purchase a Swedish space-age mattress.

"Stretch out, turn over, *relax*," she orders. "We sell only *quality* mattresses here, no flavours of the month." She pats a mattress. "Heavy-gauge springs, resilient, high-quality foam and cushioning tucked inside cotton blend ticking for a natural touch."

"Heavy-gauge springs don't sound too natural."

"All mattresses have springs."

"Not the Swedish space-age ones. They're supposed to mould to your body."

Harpo shows minor irritation while adjusting a pillow top. "All our mattresses are made to *exacting* specifications and meet *strict* international standards for quality, comfort, and safety. Do you have a partner? You should bring your partner. Sharing a bed means you need a mattress that absorbs movement so you don't disturb each other."

Why was it imperative that he and Clara jump from the plane? She was frightened and shivering but she trusted him. "We can hold hands, Daddy." He knew that he couldn't hold her hand, that in flight it would create too great a distance between them for him to reach her cord. He'd have to grip her body harness but had no way of being certain it was secure. The harness would tear and Clara would fall away from him at deadening speed. What would Gwyneth Proudley make of this dream?

He buys a pair of plastic sandals at Zellers, planning to wear them at the office while keeping the plastic shoes in a desk drawer for meetings. Outdoors, the shoes emit less odour as there is less heat, which of course will change with global warming. Heat waves, according to scientists, will increase ten to forty times due to droughts and lower lake levels. If so, plastic shoes will be untenable. He tries to remember the brand of "breathable" sandals Roberta buys that costs over a hundred dollars. "You can't compromise on shoes," she told him. He *has* compromised, and is managing quite well, thank you, his sole concern being that the sandals might slide off his bike pedals. He has noticed that the plastic shoes, having smooth soles, tend to slip. The sandals, he's pleased to note, don't smell of diesel fumes, but of nylon; nylon with plastic accents.

He orders the $8.97 Cajun Turkey Sandwich with beverage and choice of cookie. At the next table, a man his age in a wheelchair, with a plaid blanket over his knees, studies his lottery tickets. His feet are strapped to the footrests. He begins to peel a banana. What dreams do buying lottery tickets offer him? A better wheelchair? A custom-fitted car? A palatial mansion to roll around in? Reese can see no anger in him, no resentment or bitterness about having useless legs. He is being with what is. A chinless man with hair sticking out in tufts greets the man in the wheelchair and advises him not to watch television because it's propaganda. The man in the wheelchair nods while eating his banana. "What kind of sick person watches WWE wrestling anyway?" the chinless man inquires. "What kind of psycho?" He notices Reese. "Do you watch that shit?" Reese shakes his head, not wanting to admit that his father is a WWE wrestling addict. He tries to hide behind the newspaper left on the table, but encounters a photo of an oil-coated dead whale. Men are plugging the leaks in the hull of the sunken tanker. The oil will lie at the bottom of the sea until the patches deteriorate, at which time it will begin leaking again. Reese quickly turns the page. Beside the ad for Royal Doulton figurines, he reads that an American shot five members of his family to death in his suburban home, including his three-year-old son, who was found in his dead mother's arms. The man is claiming that the shooting was perpetrated by his wife. How can America grieve over American casualties of war when daily Americans are shooting their wives and children? Why the children? Why bomb entire countries of children to eliminate one demonic leader? How can the genocide be swallowed, stomached, eliminated, and forgotten? The images of children with burned faces and stumps for limbs never leaves him. He is in a state of constant grief for the children. His children.

He is scared, so scared, he will never hold them again.

He stands by Elena's tomb. There are no chairs. He brought real flowers, but a sign in the mausoleum states that only plastic flowers are permitted. Clusters protrude from the wall vases, coated in dust. Elena's urn is stored in one of the many compartments with a marble front. Her plaque reads, "Beloved daughter, always in our hearts." He met her parents once. They tried to be civil while serving salmon and pinot grigio, but it was clear that they had no time for a young man wearing a "Just Say No to Drug Companies" T-shirt.

A memorial crowd has gathered in the chapel and Reese can hear them speaking well of someone called Clement. Some refer to him as Clem. One man chokes up as he describes a particular golf game he played with Clem. Another says Clem drove a hard bargain but if you could trust anybody, it was Clem. Clement's sister says Clem was a bastard at Monopoly but otherwise was as great a brother as you could get. Is any of this true, or do they in fact feel that the world's a better place minus Clem? Do they owe him money, which they hope his widow doesn't know about? She speaks last, thanking them all for coming, assuring them that Clement would be overcome by the turnout. He'd had no idea he'd touched so many lives.

Reese is trying to *be* with the fact that Gywneth Proudley has postponed the meeting due to "a family emergency." Her voice message was without remorse. Reese cursed her in the basement apartment and called her all manner of names. Now it occurs to him that something horrible has happened, a fatal illness, a car crash. Is Gwyneth, at this very moment, at her child's bedside trying to explain that death is a part of life? "Don't be afraid, sweetheart," she's saying while grief rips through her. Reese presses his cheek against Elena's crypt, thinks about their aborted child who would be a teenager now, warring with authority and hormones. The aborted child who would have prevented Lainie from flying away, from dying young. They didn't speak during the cab ride back to the apartment. He felt eviscerated. She looked grey and lifeless and slept for hours. He sat at the kitchen table listening to time passing, mourning the fetus that he could not stop visualizing in a garbage can. He has always wanted children. There is no point to any of it without children.

He sits on the stairs outside the mausoleum and watches Clement's associates depart in their German cars. The service has ended with a kilted bagpiper playing "Danny Boy." Clement's associates talk loudly over the bagpiper into their cellphones, arranging meetings and social engagements. Clem's memorial service was only a minor glitch in their busy schedules. When the bagpiper finishes "Danny Boy," a woman in a large-brimmed hat mutters, "Thank God for that."

"At least they didn't have kids," says another wearing big sunglasses.

"*She* wanted them."

"Clement was her kid. Let's hope the life insurance makes it worth it." The woman in the big sunglasses notices Reese. "Have we met?"

"No," Reese says. He can see his boxed self in the lenses of her sunglasses.

"I'm Hailey Daley." She glances at his sandals.

"I'm Reese Larkin."

"It was a beautiful ceremony, I thought."

"Hailey," the woman in the hat intervenes, "I've got a three o'clock, I've got to run."

"Call me," Hailey Daley says, lingering, trapping Reese in her lenses. "Please don't repeat what I said."

"My lips are sealed."

"It was completely inappropriate."

"But accurate."

"Do you think so?"

"Nobody knows but the dead man's wife."

"God bless her. And may he rest in peace." She offers her hand, which feels barely alive. "Nice meeting you."

"Likewise."

With Clement's friends and the bagpiper gone, Reese is alone with the birds and the squirrels who bite off the heads of the tulips. Beyond the shrubs and the trees of the cemetery the internal combustion of the city is still audible. He longs to be free of that rumble, to take his children to a forest where there is no sound but wind in trees and bird song. He failed to identify Clement's wife in the crowd, there were so many women showing signs of wear. Childless, she will return to their mansion, uncertain of how to fill her days without Clement to care for. She will no longer be in demand. No matter how much she despised and feared Clem, he was in need. This gave her purpose.

Without purpose, without an appointment to see Gwyneth Proudley, Reese looks down at his toes, which seem to have developed an apish quality. Were they always this hairy? Sterling has advised him that getting old means getting hairy, "Except on the pate," he'd added. Sterling has been tweezing hairs from his eyebrows only to discover that this encourages growth. Reese must *be* with his hairy toes. Elena often complained about the prospect of aging, the sags and bags. She'd lean in to a mirror and pull at her face, exaggerating laugh lines and crow's feet. She had a horror of developing what she called "droopy butt syndrome." "Suddenly it's just there," she'd say. "You're going along and suddenly your ass has dropped." You're going along and suddenly you're dead.

His parents, through all of it, have sat on their porch in summer and watched the street. They angle their chairs slightly towards one another in case discussion should arise. Neighbours have come and gone during his parents' watch. Most of their peers have died. Reese can't imagine Betsy alone on the porch, missing toes, nodding at passersby. Perhaps this is why she is speaking of the condo above the mall with the chocolate store. She can't face the porch alone. This shows a kind of devotion.

Gwyneth Proudley said she would phone him to reschedule in a couple of days. He tries to believe he can wait that long. A woman in black exits the mausoleum carrying a large memorial wreath. She stumbles on the stairs and Reese hurries to assist her. "Thank you," she says. She has the look of someone in unfamiliar surroundings. "Do I know you?"

"No."

"Oh. That's good. It's very heavy," she says regarding the wreath. "I had no idea."

"Can I carry it for you?"

"Really? Oh, that would be so kind. I think I should take it. I don't think I can just leave it here."

"They don't want live flowers in the mausoleum."

"Really? Well, these aren't exactly alive, are they?" She laughs a small, tortured laugh. "Do you work here? My car's over there. I must say I'm glad it's all over."

"Yes."

"From now on I do what I want."

He doesn't tell her that, with no one's wants to attend to but her own, she will shiver in vacant rooms. That without the harness of Clement's needs she will wander aimlessly, with droopy butt syndrome, spending Clem's money, seeking gratification that cannot be found.

After he loads her wreath into her German car, she tips him a loonie. "To be honest," she says, "I've never really liked carnations. Funeral flowers." She drives off into her delusion. A red carnation tumbles from her trunk. Reese retrieves it and slips it into his buttonhole.

14

He deliberates over which toxic substance to ingest. So engrossed is he in his examination of candy bars and chip packets that he doesn't smell Avril Leblanc's orangeness. "How *are* you?" she asks, looking searchingly into his eyes. "You look stressed. Is your father okay?"

"As near as I can tell."

"That's great news." She's holding a bottle of water. "I switched shifts with Rashid. Is that alright?"

"Of course."

"You look anxious."

"Not at all." He grabs a Kit Kat bar.

"Do you eat chocolate often?" The Sri Lankan behind the counter takes the widow's loonie. "I find it really hard on my system," Avril confides. "Caffeine leaches calcium from your bones. And all that toxicity sits in your joints."

He can't shake her. She matches his stride to the office and beyond. She speaks of herbs and digestive enzymes, probiotics and psyllium hulls. She watches as he pulls the plastic shoes from his desk drawer and exchanges them for the nylon sandals. He forgot to bring socks. He will have to face the Cystic Fibrosis clients without socks. Not only is his script poor and without innovation, his apish ankles will be visible.

"Aren't you wearing socks?" she asks.

"You'll have to excuse me," he says, "I'm expected in a meeting."

"Can we talk later?"

"Of course." He plans to be gone later.

The meeting is all fabrication. Nick Dizon is present, smelling strongly of cologne, singing the praises of the new dialler, quoting untraceable statistics. He is wearing avocado green socks that match the tiny green diamond pattern of his yellow silk tie. He should not be at this meeting. As the salesman his job is complete. Reese can only assume that Sterling asked him to be present because Sterling is losing confidence in Reese's ability to produce "Wow Factor." During Reese's presentation, Nick Dizon regularly intervenes with unyielding positive energy. The clients turn to him as though to the sun. Reese, in shadow, sockless, feels sweat pooling under his toes.

"Are you avoiding me?" Avril Leblanc is dripping honey into herbal tea again.

"Not at all."

"It's really important that we speak in private."

"Of course. I'm in a meeting just now."

"They left."

"Who?"

"The people in the boardroom."

"Really?"

Nick Dizon looms alpha male. "Way to go, Reeso, they think you're great, just *love* your ideas."

"They didn't want to say goodbye?"

"They got Blue Jays tickets, you know how that one goes, snooze you lose parking-wise."

"Of course."

"They think you're the man."

"Good."

"They got really excited about the terrorist."

"What terrorist?"

"The one you killed."

Avril Leblanc stops stirring her tea. "You killed a terrorist?"

"I told you not to tell them that."

Nick Dizon leans against the counter like a catalogue model. "You told me not to use it as a sales tool. They're already sold, man. I was just giving them background information."

"You actually *killed* somebody?" Avril Leblanc's unsullied by wheat complexion has lost its glow.

"Not on purpose."

"How could you kill somebody?"

"He saved a planeload of people doing it. Security's a joke in this country. Ali Baba and his forty relatives are flying into Pearson because they can't make it into the States." Avril Leblanc hasn't moved in several seconds. "Bye, sunshine," Nick says, winking at her.

"I can't believe you killed somebody."

"He was sexually harassing a pregnant flight attendant," Reese explains. "I don't even know if he was a terrorist."

"That's no reason to kill somebody."

"No, well, as I said, it was an accident."

"No human has the right to kill another human."

"I agree. Or animal for that matter."

She rinses her spoon and places it on the draining board. "I should get back to work."

"Of course." The door swings closed behind her. He stares at it briefly before searching for a clean cup in which to pour caffeine that will leach calcium from his bones and put toxicity in his joints. There are no clean cups. He washes one with Charlie Brown on it. While pouring the coffee he makes the mistake of resting his hand on the counter, which is sticky from her honey. It is no longer important that she speak with him in private. He unwraps his Kit Kat bar and tries not to care.

"So I'm telling the guy," Robert Vinkle says, "I don't want a new phone. This one's still under warranty, why would I want a new one?" Reese notes that Bob has had several beers. "The fact is," Bob elaborates, "you schemers sold me an extra warranty for *five bucks*. Last time I looked, one plus one equalled two, meaning I got another whole year and a half under warranty."

"Robert," Linden Prevost intervenes, "you're supposed to be under house arrest."

"Ah, fuck that noise. So the guy says, 'It only costs forty dollars, they're getting cheaper all the time.' 'Read my lips,' I say to him, 'I want a *battery* for this phone. No new phone, just a *battery*.' 'We don't carry them,' he tells me. He was a Jap, right, nothing could rattle him. I say, 'What do you mean you don't carry them, you sell the phones, you must sell the batteries?' 'Most people upgrade before they require batteries.' He says this like I'm a cretin. 'The battery costs twenty-five dollars,' he tells me, 'you might as well buy a new phone for forty, they're more compact, better quality …' 'Excuse me,' I say, 'why the fuck did you sell me an extra warranty for five bucks if you knew in five minutes the phone would be obsolete?' 'Some people like the security,' he says. Is that a crock or what?"

"A crock," Linden Prevost agrees.

"They just want to sell you stuff, that's all it's about."

"A disposable society," Linden Prevost says.

"And I'm thinking, we're doing this with people now," Bob continues. "I mean, *everybody's* replaceable, right? Nobody gives a toad's butt if you keel over and die, they'll just order another one."

"Online," Linden Prevost adds.

"Some dumb fuck who'll eat shite. That's all they want, some yes-man who won't ask questions. He was a fucking pod. I told him, I said, 'You know where you can stick this phone.'"

Bob's wife, Alicia, answered when Bob called to invite his two-and-a-half-year-old daughter over for crispy wontons. He begged and pleaded with Alicia but she would not let him speak to Hilary. Reese suspects that it is for this reason that Bob revealed his anger to the cellphone vendor. "Why do you need a cellphone?" Reese inquires.

"What?"

"Why bother having one?"

Bob looks at him as though he's just posed a complex mathematical problem.

"They've been linked to brain cancer," Reese says.

Linden eats another peanut. "They leak cadmium into landfill."

"Africa," Reese says, "is choking on our discarded cellphones."

"What's Africa got to do with it?" Bob asks.

"The tech trash we throw out gets loaded on boats and dumped in Africa."

Bob appears to be trying to visualize lions and wildebeests surrounded by cellphones. "I'm in the restaurant business, brother. They need to be able to get ahold of me."

"You're always here," Reese points out. "It's like walking around with a ball and chain. Try doing without it."

"I remember a time," Linden says, "when there were no answering machines. You would phone someone and it would ring and ring suggesting that they weren't there. You'd phone them again later. It would require great effort because there were only rotary phones in those days and your finger would get tired." Bob looks at him as though he too is trying to recall those days but having some difficulty. "There was no caller ID," Linden continues, "you'd have to actually pick up the receiver to find out who was calling."

"Barbaric," Reese says.

Bob pulls his cellphone out of his pocket and drops it in the bar sink. "I'm sold, brothers. No more techno-junk."

Kyla asks if they want anything else. "Another round," Bob says. Kyla has been ignoring Reese since their encounter on her bed surrounded by spiky plants. Why men and women cease to be civil to one another after troubled forays in the bedroom Reese has never understood. He says please and thank you to her anyway.

"So the Queen," Bob says, "the richest sow in the universe ..."

"Not the richest," Linden interjects.

"Whatever, *rich*, okay, the woman's got more than the three of us times a hundred. Anyway, she's got it into her head that terrorists are going to attack her so she's getting high-tech 'panic rooms' installed at Buckingham Palace. Guess how much?"

Linden doesn't look too interested and Reese has no idea.

"Come on, guess," Bob persists.

"Five hundred thousand," Reese says.

"One-point-five mill *each*. We're talking forty-six-centimetre-thick steel walls. They can take bombings, gas attacks, even direct hits from light aircraft. She's planning to take her corgis in there with her. She's got enough food for her and the dogs to last a week."

"A noble sovereign," Linden says. Linden's bipolar ex-wife is in a psychiatric ward again. When he went to visit her, she didn't speak.

"Maybe that's where it's going," Bob muses. "The rich'll get panic rooms and the rest of us will die in the streets. It's like with all these diseases. The rich don't get'em. They don't ride the subway."

"You don't either, Robert," Linden says.

"I know, but you get my point. They're all going to have panic rooms with food for their dogs in them."

"You might want to market that," Linden suggests. "Custom-built panic rooms."

The idea of a panic room is inviting to Reese, not for protection but as a place to panic unseen or heard. Because panic is ugly. When panicked, mankind creates havoc. Much better that they stay in their rooms with their dogs.

He met Roberta at a rally protesting Bush senior's war. Reese disliked her because she was articulate and striking in a batik dress, and attracted more attention than he could muster. The crowd listened intently to her rhetoric until tear gas was used. Later she stood by Reese's bed, on the other side of the oxygen tent. By that time his eyes were less swollen and he could see again. "Why are you here?" he asked her.

"You looked lost," she said. She offered him grapes and touched his hand. Her father had just left her mother for a former Miss Winnipeg Blue Bomber and Roberta was having difficulty accepting this. Reese's mouth still didn't quite feel like his mouth, and talking through the tent was awkward, but he nodded sympathetically. She took charge after that, arranged dinner engagements and outdoor activities. Greenpeace had been all-consuming, he'd had no time to factor in relationships or social events. Roberta became part of his day, a lifeline to a world without environmental causes. They went to repertory cinemas and watched movies from the sixties and fifties because movies were still about something then. Afterwards they would walk for hours, talking. He'd never talked with anyone as he did with Roberta. The agility of her mind awed him. She knew what he meant before he even said it. A comradeship formed. A trust.

They stopped talking when the boy started school, when it became undeniable that he wasn't like other boys. Roberta wanted him to fit in, conform. Reese wanted him to bust out, be different, suffer the consequences. She has always wanted to spare her children suffering. What does she think she is doing to them now?

"You want another?" Bob asks.

"Are you?"

"It's not like anybody's waiting up." He taps two more drafts. "What I always tell myself is it's cyclical."

"What is?"

"The whole outfit. It's all relative."

"To what?"

"Sometimes I get so sick of it, I mean *so* sick of it, I'm thinking bullet. Do you ever get that?"

"Not a bullet exactly."

"Pills?"

"I haven't worked out the details."

"So she grows up thinking I'm whatever that witch wants to make me, right? Am I right?"

"You're right."

Bob drinks more beer. "I've got a gun."

"Really?"

"It's an old Colt. Been in the family for years."

"Does it work?"

"It's got bullets. If you want to use it, brother, it's yours." Bob stares deeply into his beer. "Sometimes I put it in my mouth."

"Does Alicia know about this?"

"She wouldn't let me keep it in the house. It's behind the bar." Bob pulls up a trouser leg to scratch under one of his surgical stockings. "This may be way out there but I have a feeling it has to do with that sister of hers being married to the meat-packer. He's not like a meat-packer, he *owns* the meat-packers. Anyways, it turns out he's been jiggin' their real estate agent and wants a divorce. He told the kids while they were watching the Academy Awards. He muted the set and said, 'Your mother and I don't have fun together anymore.' The sixteen-year-old wanted to know what he meant by fun. 'I like to go to plays and concerts,' the meathead said, 'your mother likes to go shopping.' Anyways, now the bastard won't leave. He's holed up in the nanny's old room, buying stuff on sale for his new place if he ever gets it. He's got two TVs in there, one for the cottage he's renting with the real estate agent and another one for the nanny's room. He's hardly ever home, doesn't drive the kids to soccer or karate or anything. He's freeloading. Most nights he stays out until the wee hours. Alicia's sister says when he's around he acts like a teenager all excited about getting laid and moving into his first apartment. She calls it Freedom 55."

"But he's not leaving."

"No. Go figure. I think he wants her to get so pissed she turfs him, which means she'll get less alimony. Like if she changes the locks or something, he'll hose her. Son of a bitch. Anyways, I'm thinking Alicia's convinced herself that I'm this guy's clone or something, you know, women do that, get it into their heads that all men are assholes. Well, I'm not an asshole, am I? I don't think I'm an asshole."

"You're not, Bob."

"Thank you, brother."

They both stare into their beers. The Eric Clapton song comes on about how wonderful you look tonight with your long blonde hair. Reese has heard this song a thousand times before, too many times. "Why are the songs always about how they look?" he asks.

"Who?"

"Women, in the songs, it's always about their hair and legs. No wonder they hate us."

"Who?"

"Women."

"Oh." Bob appears deep in thought. "Do you really think they hate us?"

"You just said they think we're all assholes."

"I said that? I think I qualified it, didn't I? I think I said *some* women. Hey, Kyla, do women think *all* men are assholes?"

She stares at him as though he's panhandling. "Yeah."

"I should get going," Reese says.

"Never, *ever*," Bob interjects, "let a woman plan your vacation. You'll be looking at every fucking artifact in the place. Alicia's a ceramic freak, she's always chasing after pots, masks, sculptures. We have to bring them back in carry-on. Security goes nuts over them."

"Bob?"

"Yeah?"

"Do you think it might be possible that we're better off without them?"

"Who?"

"Women."

Bob takes a deep breath and holds it for several seconds before releasing it in an extensive sigh. "I don't know, brother. It's the kid thing, the kid's the problem. You get my point?"

"Yes."

All the lights are out in the house that was once his. He sits on the curb across the street and sends his children what he hopes are healing energies. Avril Leblanc told a potential donor with rheumatoid arthritis that her shaman grandfather was able to project healing energies over great distances. People would phone him and talk about their illnesses and he could heal them over the phone. Avril had tooth pain once and phoned him. What was it, Reese would like to know, that she needed to discuss in private with him that suddenly wasn't worth discussing? He's seen too

many movies in which people declare affection hitherto undetected by the recipient. Nonetheless, it's not beyond the realm of
possibility that Avril wanted to become intimate with him, invite
him out for chai, which would explain why the news of his capacity for murder caused her to lose interest in a private meeting.
Prior to the news of the murder, Reese wasn't under the impression that Avril Leblanc considered him an asshole. Now, of
course, it's game over. Not that he wanted to be in the game, he
doesn't think.

Reese has never been offered a gun before. Aren't Colts the
ones with barrel cartridges? Would a few spins of Russian
roulette make the time go faster?

A man with a cat on a leash stops by Reese's bicycle. "You could
lose your legs sitting on the curb like that," he says. The cat sniffs
the tires. "What're you doing sitting around here this time of night
anyway?" The man has a jutting lower lip and sagging clothes.

"I used to live here."

"You don't anymore?"

"Not at the moment." The cat begins chewing a tire.

"So, what're you doing sitting around here this time of
night?"

"I was just leaving."

"I should hope so. Go to bed, like normal people." He
resumes walking his cat. "Get a move on," he tells it.

"Where were you?" Katrina demands, in her fuzzy bathrobe.

"You have to stop asking me that."

"But it's like three in the morning. The doorbell's been ringing all night, jerks selling something. I kept answering it because
I thought maybe you'd forgotten your keys."

"I never forget my keys. I'm without transport without
keys."

Her meatiness is made larger by the bathrobe. It will be awkward squeezing past her to enter to his panic room.

"Let me guess," she says, "you have to feed your hamster?"

"That's right. And give him exercise."

"I'm, like, totally wired. I tried sleeping but my legs kept twitching and stuff."

"Try taking Gravol. My mother takes Gravol when she can't sleep." He begins to move towards her and is relieved to see that she steps back. He offers her Clement's widow's carnation. "Goodnight, I must try to get some sleep." He closes the door as gently as possible. He brushes his teeth to rid himself of beer breath. He checks his phone messages. His father is not dead and his mother's toilet is plugged again. Reese releases Bonaparte and places the wastebasket by the table. Within minutes Bonaparte skydives into it, which brings to mind space-based missile defence. "Where's proof," Reese asked Sterling, "that multi-layered shields of anti-missile missiles can defend North America from an attack?"

"Who needs proof?" Sterling said.

"It's going to cost a trillion dollars."

"Yeah, but just think of all the weapons they'll get to sell to all those rogue states who'll have to keep up."

"How can anyone," Reese persisted, "imagine that missile defence will do anything but encourage the proliferation of not only nuclear weapons, but of weapons to *protect* the weapons?"

"Just so long as they keep drivin' to the mall," Sterling said, looking at the sports pages. "You got to take a duck and dive approach to the thing, boyo."

Reese turns on the bleeding television, is lulled into a stupor by commercials for cars and Coke and mutual funds. Then, without warning, Iraqi children are shown collecting unexploded bomblets left behind by American cluster bombs. Unexploded bomblets have resale value. A group of women in burkas wail over the death of a five-year-old girl and her two-year-old brother who found a bomblet in their front yard. A thirteen-year-old boy who picked one out of the mud stares mournfully at Reese. Both his hands were blown off. Reese turns off the television. He rolls onto his side on the futon, gripping Clara's sock. He stares at the photo of Derek sitting on his lap, touching his cheek.

She's dancing upstairs.

"I'm trying to be quiet," she tells him.

"I can't sleep either."

"Do you want to watch Fred and Ginger?"

"Sure."

"This is the part where they did forty-eight takes and his rug fell off."

"I didn't know he wore a rug."

"He went bald early. He was a worrier."

"Really?" Another illusion lost.

Fred, smiling and confident, swings Ginger around the sparkling floor.

"He was, like, a total workaholic. Everything had to be perfect or he'd make them do it again. You can't see it but her feet are bleeding in this number."

Reese settles on the orange couch while Fred and Ginger dance as one. Ginger's lissomness provides the perfect foil for Fred's extraordinary precision and grace. Forty-eight takes and not once do they look out of breath. Katrina tries to imitate their steps. "It was all in one take, right. Fred didn't want cuts in his dances so it was all or nothing. Watch how her dress wraps around his legs. It used to drive him nuts. They'd rehearse in pants then shooting would start and he'd have to deal with the dresses. She wore one that was all beads that kept tripping him." Katrina swings past Reese, flinging her head back while extending one leg. "Will you come to my ballroom dancing class with me? Lance was supposed to but there's no way that's going to happen and it's not like I can get my money back."

"I can't dance."

"Duh. That's why you go to a class."

"I don't want to go to a class."

"You're just shy. Come on, it'll be fun. It's beginner, right, you won't be the only klutz." Fred and Ginger spin up separate staircases that meet centre stage. "This is where his rug fell off," Katrina explains, spinning herself, causing her bathrobe to flap around her.

"It feels as though the world's ending," Reese says.

"Right now?" She flops into the easy chair and stares at him. "Everybody should know how to foxtrot."

"Why?"

"Because it's civilized. Because the people who know how to do it are old and are going to die and we'll be left with Britney Spears."

Fred and Ginger's dance ends with Fred leaning over her, cradling her in his arms. Reese envies their closeness. Whether or not they got it on, they knew each other's bodies and rhythms, had a feel for each other that no one else could share, an intimacy that no one else could touch.

Katrina is still staring at him. "Pleeeeze?"

Reese has been trying to forget about the son of the woman who was killed while waiting for a bus. A car drove up on the curb and threw her twenty metres. Reese heard about this on Wayson Hum's radio. She'd just dropped her six-year-old son off at school and was on her way to work. All day, in and out of shifting realities, Reese has been aware that the little boy didn't know yet, that he was playing, and printing letters and numbers. All day Reese has wanted to stop time. The little boy must know by now.

At least his children know he's not dead.

"If *you* start composting," Reese says.

"What?"

"You compost, I dance."

"Get out."

"And use the recycling bins."

She narrows her eyes.

"That's the deal," Reese says.

Standing in line at the checkout, clutching sliced white bread for Bernie, Reese stares at a *People* magazine that reads "Who's Having a Baby?" Several actresses with swollen bellies pose in mini dresses and stiletto heels. Reese grabs an Oh Henry! The Cystic Fibrosis script is stalling, as is the asthma campaign.

"Tell them about *toxic* environmental exposures," Mrs. Ranty snaps.

"Pessteecidess," Scout Leader Igor adds. "Dioxeenss, PCBss ..."

"Mercury," Mrs. Ranty chants. "Manganese, solvents ..."

"Are theess *healthy* for junior?" Scout leader Igor demands.

Reese tears open the Oh Henry! and chews rapidly. He thought the voices had stopped. He rolls his neck. Fudge sticks to his dental work.

"Are you in line?" a woman with angular hair and glasses demands.

"Yes," Reese says, moving forward.

"With just one item you should use the U-scan register."

"I prefer human cashiers."

Her lips tighten as she grips her assortment of deli-wrapped cheeses.

Reese unplugged Betsy's toilet, went at it with a plunger for some time before succumbing to reaching down and pulling out banana skins. "Why," he asked, "are you throwing banana peels down the toilet?" His mother was wearing lipstick, smeared in places.

"They get fruit flies if you leave them lying around."

He bought his parents a composter years ago. Bernie stores old paint cans in it.

"My hair's a mess," Betsy said to the mirror. "You've got to take me to the hairdresser's." Normally Bernie takes her, sits with the ladies in the waiting area, telling jokes and offering medical advice. Betsy regularly complains about Bernie's flirting. Until recently she believed that one woman in particular, Verna Petty, had her eye on Bernie. "Wait till she finds out you're broke," Betsy said. "Then she won't be so interested."

"It's my body she wants," Bernie responded. He kept the Verna Petty thing going until Verna's children put her in a home in Mississauga.

"Is the hairdresser's open in the evening?" Reese asked.

"How would I know, I always go in the mornings."

"Yes, but *I* can't go in the mornings." When does the change occur from nurturing parent to self-absorbed old person? As with droopy butt syndrome, are you just going along then suddenly you're geriatric and can't see beyond the next Crispy Crunch? Nothing has replaced the pillar that was his mother. He suspects that were he properly formed, an inner strength would have developed, a confidence, a self-sufficiency, that would have filled the gap where mother love used to be. Improperly formed, he still yearns for the security his mother's youthful hand in his brought. The feel of her grip is clearly marked in his sensory memory. The world was vast and threatening until he grasped his mother's hand.

"How are you feeling?" he asked her.

"What do you mean?"

"Are you feeling alright?"

"Why wouldn't I be feeling alright?"

"You had toes amputated."

"Oh that. I get around. It'd be easier in that condo above the mall I was telling you about."

"With the chocolate store."

"And the Valu-mart and a hairdresser's. I'd just have to take the elevator to get my hair done."

"Have you talked to Dad about this place?"

"He won't leave here."

"Have you asked him?"

"He won't leave Chelsea." The name, always thought, never spoken, jolted Reese. Her room is still as it was. Betsy used to dust it while Bernie vacuumed. It was a shared devotion. Is that all there is, in the end, threads of shared devotions holding a marriage together, despite the resentments and boredom?

"How was your date the other night?" she asked.

"What date?"

"You were going to dinner."

"Oh. Fine, it was fine."

"Are you seeing her again?"

"It wasn't ... she wasn't ... I'm still married, Mother."

"It's not too late to start another family." Her tendency to pack up the old and bring on the new irritates him where his children are concerned.

"I *have* a family," he said.

"Could've fooled me."

The cashier picks up the phone to get a price check on a bonus-size bottle of barbecue sauce. The bulging, bug-eyed man purchasing the sauce has insisted that it is on sale. They all stand and wait for a pimply price checker then wait longer for his return. The woman with angular hair and glasses breathes heavily behind Reese.

Betsy told him about Wanda Hubbard's son whose ex-wife accused him of molesting their three-year-old daughter. Reese immediately feared that Betsy somehow knew of Roberta's accusation and was offering Wanda Hubbard's son as a cautionary tale. "He's only allowed to see her for two hours every second Saturday."

"Do we know that he *didn't* molest her?" Reese asked.

"Waddy? You remember Wad. Nice boy. Always washed his hands." Reese's only memory of Wad Hubbard was that he would shamelessly eat his scabs.

The bonus-size bottle of barbecue sauce is not on sale. The bulging, bug-eyed man accuses the cashier of false advertising. She stares at him, unmoved. "You want it or not?" she asks.

"Pass," he says, waving his hand as though never before has he encountered such chicanery. The woman with angular hair and glasses nudges Reese with her deli-wrapped cheeses.

"Don't touch me," he says.

"The line is moving forward," she says. "If you're in line, you should be moving forward."

"I *am* moving forward."

"This is an express line."

"I *know* that." She is the kind of woman who has always caused him distress, who plays by the rules, who cannot see beyond the goal posts, who bleaches her whites, who irons her jeans. She is the kind of woman who got him fired. "Touch me again," he warns, "and you'll be choking on brie."

"Are you uttering verbal threats?" Her increased body temperature has caused her assortment of cheeses to off-gas. He would like to grab her and plug her mouth with cellophane-wrapped gorgonzola. "It's your turn," she says, her disdain particularly audible on the "t" in *turn*.

Is this what it has come to? A world in which people will kill one another at the checkout counter? Next time he will use the U-scan register.

"I brought you white bread, sliced."

"The buggers are cutting me open again."

"Why?" His father looks paler, smaller.

"To take the thing out."

"What thing?"

"I didn't want it in me in the first place."

"What are they taking out?" Reese asks.

"The tube."

"Why?"

"I cut it."

"What do you mean you cut it?"

"I cut it. I didn't want it in me."

"How could you cut it?"

"With scissors."

Reese is having difficulty absorbing this information. Hospital staff on the elevator were discussing a ten-year-old girl whose body parts are being discovered wrapped in plastic in the lake. "Oh my, my ..." the man with the pointed head in constant pain says.

"Dad, I don't understand. You *cut* the catheter?"

"Damn right, nobody asked my permission, did they? A god-damn tube sticking out of me."

Reese, who had been hoping the worst was over, looks for a chair to support his suddenly insupportable weight.

"*You* try having a tube sticking out of you."

"It was supposed to save your life, Dad."

"Who says it's worth saving?"

"Where did you get the scissors?"

"One of the Blacks. Had to ask her about a hundred times."

Reese stumbles into the corridor to find someone, anyone to scream at. At the nursing station sits a mouse-haired woman who looks as though she's been sucking on lemons. "Who gave my father scissors?"

"I beg your pardon."

"Someone gave my father scissors."

"We generally give patients what they ask for."

"Bullshit! You never even *see* the patient!"

"Would you like me to page a doctor?"

"He won't show up. Why bother having hospitals anymore? Why don't you let us die peacefully at home?!"

She stands, revealing massive thighs. "Sir, you'll have to keep your voice down."

"What kind of moron would give my father scissors?"

"He said he wanted to cut something out of the newspaper."

"Did he even have a newspaper? Did the moron look to see if he even had a newspaper?" A small crowd has gathered, geri-atrics in hospital gowns dragging IV poles.

"I'm going to have to call security," the nurse says.

"Go'head, maybe *they'll* change my father's diaper." This gets a laugh from the crowd. The nurse punches numbers into her phone. Reese walks away, back to his father who will die without dialysis.

He wakens to the sound of Bernie gumming white bread. "Sweet dreams?" Bernie asks.

"How long was I asleep?"

"How should I know? They came looking for you."

"Who?"

"Hilda of the S.S. and her man in uniform."

"Did anybody change your diaper?"

"You got to pay extra for that."

"Dad, you have to let me change it."

"Doesn't bother me." He gums more white bread.

"You're going to get a rash."

Bernie points at his food tray. "What do you suppose that is?"

"I don't know. Shepherd's pie, maybe. Do you want some?"

"Let's have a look."

Reese places the tray within his father's reach. Bernie pushes the mashed potato to one side with his fork and digs around in the meat as though searching for something. "Nah," he says, "give me the fruit." He eats the canned peaches with his fingers. "These are good, fresh. They must can them here."

"Has a doctor been to see you?" Reese asks.

"Why?"

"To make sure you're alright."

"I'm alright, it's the fellah in the next bed I'm worried about, hasn't said boo for ages. Have a look at him. Go on, have a look."

Reese slowly pulls back the curtain on the man with the swollen feet who appears to be unconscious. "I think he's sleeping."

"Check his pulse."

"I'm sure he's alright, Dad."

"Check his pulse!"

Feebly, Reese lifts the man's swollen wrist, which feels colder than he would like. He can't find a pulse, adjusts his grip thinking he's misplaced his fingers. "I can't find a pulse."

"Put your head on his chest for God's sake." Reese would prefer not to do this because the man smells of rotting meat. All his life his father has forced him to do things he'd prefer not to do. Against his ear there is no heartbeat, no chest movement. "I think he's dead."

"Oh my, my ..." the man in constant pain says.

"Get a nurse," Bernie orders.

The only one available is the mouse-haired lemon-sucker. She looks ready to sound the alarm when she sees him.

"The man in the bed next to my father is dead."

She springs into action. Dead patients get service.

"What did you say to Avril?" Serge Hollyduke demands.

"What do you mean?"

"She hasn't been the same since you talked to her." Beads of sweat sparkle on his upper lip. The air-conditioning isn't working. They've been waiting all day for a repairman.

"Are her numbers improving?" Reese asks.

"It's no joke, you upset her, and I, as the caller supervisor, am entitled to know what went on between you."

"Nothing went on." Reese resumes looking at the before and after photos of a woman with Huntington's disease. In one she looks young and vibrant, in the other, wheelchair-bound, she looks ravaged at the age of forty-three. She anticipates having fifteen years of mental and physical deterioration before she dies. Her father died of it, her son has a 50 percent chance of getting it.

"*Something* went on," Serge persists, "because she's acting totally different."

"Dizon told her I killed a terrorist."

"And that upset her?"

"Apparently."

"Jeez."

"Serge, I have to work now." The literature claims that a cure for Huntington's disease is imminent, that with extra funding final steps can be taken. Reese knows this is a ruse. Drug companies like to keep diseases going for years.

"Everybody *I've* told thinks it's great," Serge says.

"What?"

"That you killed a terrorist."

"Who have you told?"

"It's not like it's a secret."

"There is no proof that he was a terrorist. Please don't tell anyone that I killed a terrorist."

"People need heroes, man."

"I have to work, Serge." The heat, Reese believes, is making everyone less cooperative. Serge stands firmly in his Birkenstocks.

"Did she say anything about me?" he asks.

"Who?"

"Avril."

"Should she be saying anything about you?"

"I was just wondering."

"I have to work." Reese continues his Huntington's reading knowing that, with time, Serge will depart. Clearly the key is to home in on the hereditary aspect of the disease, make the potential donors aware that as long as the gene multiplies unchecked, their children and their children's children may copulate with carriers and consequently produce children with Huntington's disease. Reese has found that, in for-profit fundraising, scare tactics work wonders. No sooner has Serge departed but Sterling's butt and thigh appear on Reese's desk, his knee inches from his face. "How'd it go with the Cystic Fibrosis crowd?"

"Fine."

"Nicky says you seemed a little undercharged. Getting enough sleep?"

"Yes."

"We can't afford to lose clients."

"No."

"It's showtime."

"Yes."

"She's a cougar, that Arlene, been after Nicky since he first talked to them." Arlene, to the best of Reese's memory, is a demure woman embittered about the amount of funding being poured into AIDS research. That she has been after Nicky explains why Dizon was at the meeting. "What we don't need to tell her," Sterling says, "is that the Nickster never mixes business with pleasure."

"Of course."

"Your divorce working out alright? Did you call Herman?"

"I'm not getting divorced."

Sterling pulls out his comb and adjusts his hair. "I'm sure you don't need me to tell you we can't bring personal problems to work."

"Right."

"We had a guy in here, a Rasta, not bad on the phone, thought he was Bob Marley. One night he throws hot fat on his wife and her boyfriend. Guess where *he's* sleeping?"

"Jail."

"You got it. It ain't worth it, my friend. You get yourself all worked up and another year's gone by. From here on in it's just a waiting game."

"For what?"

"Whatever. The End." He slaps Reese on the back. "I'll leave you to it."

Reese is aware that Sterling has issued a warning, that he must perform his duties with more conviction or suffer the consequences. As much as he would like to starve Roberta for funds, he cannot do this to his children.

Avril Leblanc, flushed, appears. "I'd like to file a complaint regarding sexual harassment."

Reese can't recall so much as touching her and is without a heartbeat for a moment. An accusation of sexual harassment will not sit well beside an accusation of child molestation. Perhaps the Rasta was onto something. A man going down can do worse than to cause lasting disfigurement. "I don't understand," Reese says.

"Your supervisor follows me around."

"That's his job."

"He's constantly onto me about everything. I don't see him doing that to any of the other callers."

"I'll talk to him," Reese says.

"He told me I'm coming on too strong about the First Peoples, but the fact is they were here first, we drove them off their land."

"Yes."

"They harmonized with nature, we've destroyed it."

"Yes." She is distraught. He feels an unsettling impulse to kiss her forehead.

"They carried their dead with them," she says, "they didn't leave them behind. They *thanked* the animals they killed. They had respect for each other and the world around them. Not like white people." She says "white people" with loathing while wiping what might be a tear or sweat from her cheek. "The First Peoples didn't bridle their horses, didn't use whips, didn't *force* them to do anything. White man had to go and shove metal bits into their mouths, and use whips to show who's boss. The First Peoples didn't care who was boss." Reese considers how this line of rhetoric might work for the Voice of First Nations campaign. Certainly heartfelt pleas can get results. The challenge with Native issues is to rid the potential donors of visions of drunken Indians on street corners.

"They didn't even have saddles," Avril continues. "White man had to strap himself to horses but the First Peoples just threw blankets over them."

"There are things to be learned from their ways," Reese suggests.

"We can't just forget about them."

"Perhaps that's the line to take in the campaign — here is a culture that must not be forgotten, a way of life from which we can learn."

She looks at him with new interest, giving him hope that he will not always be just a terrorist-killer to her.

"They did just fine for thousands of years before white man showed up," Avril says.

"Bringing disease and alcohol."

"And guns."

They remain silent for a moment, the white man haters. Urgent knocking rattles their solidarity. Serge Hollyduke, purple-hued, pushes open the door. "What's going on in here?"

"See what I mean?" Avril says to Reese.

"Serge, can you wait outside for a minute?"

"No way, I want to know what's going on in here!"

"Nothing's going on."

Avril walks past him, avoiding bodily contact. "You are a very aggressive person," she says. Serge starts to follow her.

"Serge, sit down," Reese says.

"What'd she mean by that?"

"You have to get off her case. She's feeling harassed."

"No way."

"Yes way. You have to give her some room."

"Somebody has to keep an eye on her."

"Not you. I'll watch her."

"You just want to jump her."

Reese isn't sure that this is true but doesn't argue. "Maybe it would be best for all parties if we let her go."

"No way. I *love* her." The word *love* is said with such emotion by the young man with the bullet-shaped head that Reese feels his anguish, remembers his passion for Lainie and the agony it brought.

"If you love her," he says, "leave her alone, otherwise she has to go. We can't have sexual harassment charges."

"She actually used the word sexual?"

Reese nods.

"Man, I haven't even touched her."

"Once charges are laid, it doesn't matter what happened. The damage is done." He dreamed last night that, like Waddy Hubbard, he was awarded only two hours every two weeks to see his children. Derek refused to see him but Clara agreed. Reese, confused about the allotted time for the meeting, suddenly realized he was forty-five minutes late, and that it would take another forty-five minutes to reach her. By the time he arrived at the house that was once his, the car was gone from the drive and no one answered the bell. He had failed her. Again.

"I never thought it would happen to me," Serge says. "The love thing, it's so … *huge*, it's like … nothing else matters, you know, all the stuff you used to shit your pants about." He looks about him in wonder, seeking the words to describe his condition. "You just *can't believe* you used to shit your pants about that stuff." Reese remembers feeling something like this, although the memory is faint. Mostly he remembers the blood on the sheets after Lainie had been sleeping for hours. He touched it, what remained of their baby, and rubbed it into his face. She was in the bathroom applying makeup, continuing on.

He realizes that this has been a recurring problem in his life; the reluctance to continue on. It all happens so fast, he's never ready for the change. He wants to linger, to hold his babies longer, to listen to the rain, to finish his cup of coffee, to not think about tomorrow. Because tomorrow always comes, robbing him of today. He has grown to fear tomorrow because it will only bring more of the stuff he shits his pants about. Unlike Serge Hollyduke, he is no longer capable of the love thing, no longer fooled by its hugeness. It will pass, tomorrow will come, and only detritus will remain.

"It moulds to your body," the salesman tells him. Reese notices the chunky gold wedding ring on his hand and envies it, the weight of it, the statement it makes. His thumb feels for his own minimalist ring. After taking it off on the bus, he put it back on, felt unmoored without it. What has Roberta done with hers? Tossed it down the sink? He wants to ask the salesman, whose name tag reads Luther Irving, about his marriage, if conversation still comes easily, if it is felt that the workload is evenly split, if his children are on Ritalin, if sex has become arduous.

"The high-tech foam," Luther Irving explains, "was designed by NASA to protect astronauts during the excessive G-forces of takeoff."

"Is that necessary? For us, I mean, on Earth?"

"We're talking high-density, viscoelastic memory foam," Luther Irving emphasizes. "The first time I tried one of these, I thought I'd died and gone to heaven."

"What about your wife?" Reese asks.

"My wife?"

"Doesn't sharing a bed mean you need a mattress that absorbs movement?"

"Oh, we don't have one of these at home, my wife prefers Beautyrest." A discordance over the matrimonial mattress signals dysfunction, despite the substantial ring. This cheers Reese somewhat. "If I had my druthers," Luther confides, "I'd be using the Tempur-Pedic system. It's proven by doctors to be beneficial to circulation, muscles, and solid sleep."

The tragedy of being forced to sleep on a Beautyrest when your heart belongs to the Tempur-Pedic system does not elude Reese. "Which Beautyrest?" he asks.

"The Victoriana. Don't get me wrong, it's a quality mattress, I recommend it to seniors with osteo. I bought one for my mother. She loves it." So there it is, Luther Irving must sleep on his mother's mattress — an old lady's mattress — while longing for the space-age. Briefly, this seems to Reese a fate worse than his own. "Do you read in bed?" Luther asks. "You can adjust it to the recliner position." He demonstrates, making the bed resemble a dentist's chair.

"Actually," Reese admits, "I prefer to read on my side. I don't like having to hold a book, I like to lie it flat."

"I understand," Luther says, adjusting the bed to the horizontal position. "Try it," he urges, "pretend you're reading."

Reese, accustomed to being viewed supine by mattress vendors, rolls onto his side and leans on one elbow as though he were reading a book lying flat before him. The mattress is not uncomfortable but he doesn't feel that he has died and gone to heaven. He lifts his arm and notices that there remains a dent in the mattress where it moulded to his elbow. "Is it supposed to do that?" he asks.

"What?"

"Leave a dent?"

"What dent?"

"My elbow left a dent, from where the bed moulded to my body."

"I don't see a dent."

Reese is beginning to doubt Luther Irving's word.

"We have other products," Luther says, desperation edging into his voice. "You might want to try the Perfect Chair. Its zero-gravity seating position is recommended by doctors to help relieve pressure from the spine and stress from the entire body." He strokes the chair. "And it's a beauty."

"Which doctors?" Reese asks.

"Pardon?"

"You keep mentioning doctors, which doctors?"

"Doctors familiar with the products."

"Have you got any names?"

Luther looks as though he's been caught with his fly undone. "Not off the top of my head." An old lady begins to thump the space-age mattress next to them. Luther points to another chair that looks even more like a dentist's chair. "You might want to check out the Ultimate Robotic Massage Chair with human touch technology. It's the most advanced robotic massage system available. The massage discs move three-dimensionally to approximate human touch." Reese has a vision of the wealthy few in their panic rooms with their dogs, masked and gloved in full-body protection gear, waiting for Armageddon, reclining on Ultimate Robotic Massage Chairs because human touch would put them at risk of infection. A quiet desperation is driving the Western world's insatiable quest for the perfect chair and mattress, a quiet desperation Reese recognizes in himself as he slides into the chair. I shop therefore the world isn't ending.

"How's it feel?" Luther Irving asks.

"Not like human touch."

"I know what you're saying but you know something? I actually prefer it. With human touch you're always worried they're getting tired. These chairs don't get tired."

"You could be massaged all day."

"That's right."

"Who needs human touch?" For the first time Luther Irving visibly takes note of Reese's nylon sandals with plastic accents. "Humans get dirty and sweaty," Reese adds, "and want you to talk to them, *do* things with them. A chair's a lot easier." He caresses the arms of the Ultimate Robotic Chair. "I should've married a chair."

Possibly sensing that he is in the presence of a chemical imbalance, Luther Irving glances around for other customers who might be experiencing a general malaise from which human-touch technology might provide a cure. The old lady is talking loudly to the saleswoman about a six-year-old girl who's in a coma after a metal bar thrown from a balcony pierced her skull. "Now what are the chances of that?" the old lady asks lying on the space-age bed. "Imagine tossing a metal bar off a balcony? What kind of person would do such a thing?" A quietly desperate person, Reese thinks. Of all the fears he has for his children, flying metal bars piercing their skulls is not one of them. "They can't find her father," the old lady informs the saleswoman. "He's separated from the family. Imagine that, him not knowing his little girl's dying?" Why bother to fear anything when there is always something more horrendous readily available? Reese finds a phone booth and checks his messages to make certain that Clara does not have a metal bar in her skull. There are no messages. He remains in the phone booth, relieved but without direction. A young father strides by with a small girl on his shoulders. Confident that she will not fall, she flaps her arms like a bird. Clara used to do this.

As a parent there were always places to be, errands to be run, children to be carried, driven, fed. Now there are only beds.

The ballroom dancing teacher has slender legs and a large girth. When she asks Reese to help demonstrate a forward step, he has difficulty finding a concave area around her waist to hold. "Don't be shy," she tells him. He rests his hand on one of the rolls of flesh around her middle. While she guides him through the forward step, he tries to avoid inhaling her frizzy hair. "Nice and easy," she says, "no rush." Her name is Edwina Pendleton. "Long neck," she tells him. "I start with the right, you start with the left. *Glide*." They collide several times. Katrina leans against the mirror, laughing into her hand. They almost didn't come because they'd begun arguing about terrorists. "They're dirty," she said, referring to the Pakistani family across the street. "Have you ever smelled them? And it's totally sick what they do to women." Reese doubted that the Pakistani family was comprised of terrorists and suggested Katrina examine the Western world's partnership with several repressive regimes — ones retained for the work of torture in the War on Terror. "*Glide*," Edwina Pendleton says. He also suggested she take a look at those corporations friendly to neo-conservative political zealots, which have racked in billions of dollars in contracts leaving millions with little food, clean water, or electricity, no jobs, and children missing limbs and faces. "I don't want to talk about it," she said. "Let's just go dance." Reese didn't feel like dancing, would have preferred to go to Zellers for the Shanghai Surprise Chicken Salad, and perhaps a slice of lemon meringue pie. Noting the pie beside the paraplegic studying his lottery tickets the other day, it seemed quite fluffy. Betsy used to make lemon meringue pie, would beat the egg whites until they formed peaks. It was Reese's favourite dessert. If Betsy was making lemon meringue pie, Reese knew he hadn't disappointed her. She stopped making it after Chelsea died. "Head up," Edwina says. Her heavy makeup makes her eyes resemble exotic beetles. While her mouth is smiling, her eyes appear ready to crawl off her face. Before class started, she was swilling coffee.

Reese is one of two men in the group. The other has a hump but seems eager, although Reese suspects he doesn't have the reach required to circumvent Edwina's girth. For this reason, Reese fears he will be asked to assist Edwina frequently. "Now let's try the backwards step," she says. "I lead with the right, you lead with the left. *Glide*."

"That wasn't so bad," Katrina says afterwards. She takes the corned beef out of her sandwich. "No carbs till I lose ten pounds. I'm supposed to eat, like, all this meat. It's totally gross." Reese assesses the fish and chips on his plate.

"Go'head," Mrs. Ranty taunts, "chow down on those PCBs."

"I liked doing the Macarena," Katrina says. Reese didn't like doing the Macarena. All the jiggling and turning around reminded him of the hokey-pokey, which he barely tolerated while his children were under four. "We should practise at home," Katrina says.

This reference to "home" as a place where they both belong unsettles Reese. He checked his messages again. Gwyneth Proudley's family emergency must still be in progress because she hasn't called to reschedule. He shoves deep-fried fish into his mouth.

"Mercury, deeleessciouss," Scout Leader Igor smirks.

A fish bone jabs the roof of Reese's mouth. He digs for it with his fingers while Katrina dissects her corned beef, discarding the fatty bits. "Apples are packed with carbs," she says, "and so are grapefruits. Can you believe that? Grapefruits, I mean aren't those supposed to be like a *diet* food? My sister was on some grapefruit diet, was eating grapefruits before every meal. It was totally gross."

Reese pushes several French fries into his mouth and jabs at the toxic fish, welcoming heart disease and cancer. Will Roberta visit him on his deathbed, contrite, begging forgiveness? He will reach towards her, caress her forehead, but say nothing, leaving her in earthly torment.

"I've got to get back to my dancing weight," Katrina says. "It was having Lance around that did it. He's, like, a total pizza junky."

There is always someone to blame.

In an effort to impress Avril Leblanc, Reese has been working intensively on the Voice of First Nations campaign. His angle will be to pose the question: how is the war booty of modern times — oil — any different from the theft of native resources by past colonial empires? If potential donors feel for the bloodied children of Iraq and Afghanistan, why not cough up for the aboriginal orphans of the past?

Why is he so keen to impress Avril Leblanc? Because she's young and unsullied by wheat? Because Serge Hollyduke is ready to lay down his life for her? Because Reese's own life has become so disjointed that Avril, with her dream catcher and herbal remedies, offers a hub to which he can join his spokes?

"I've got to move more," Katrina says. "Maybe start jogging again. I just get so sick of guys looking at me when I run. It's like they've got nothing better to do than stare at women."

"They probably don't."

"What?"

"Have anything better to do."

"Drop dead would be my suggestion."

His nylon sandals with plastic accents are giving him blisters, made worse by the ballroom dancing. His inability to locate inexpensive but comfortable footwear defeats him. Comfortable footwear has become as unattainable as a comfortable bed. "I have to get some Band-Aids," he says. Katrina seems not to hear. She's inspecting the pickle on her plate. The speaker above their heads is blaring the Stevie Wonder song he wrote for his baby daughter, about how lovely she is. Reese feels pressure in his chest, which he suspects is heartache, but hopes is the precursor to a massive heart attack. He has been noticing that black cats are continually crossing his path.

"What does your ex-wife do?" Katrina asks.

"She's not my ex-wife." Robert Vinkle's gun continues to entice him. He'd like to fondle it, maybe put it in his mouth. Or Roberta's. Could he do that? Would it free him from this hell on earth?

"Like, does she have a job?"

"She teaches art."

"Get out."

"Seriously."

"What a wank."

Reese can tell that Katrina is still hungry, that the corned beef and the pickle did not offer the sustenance that carbs can bring. "*I* don't think you need to lose weight," he says.

"Gee, thanks. Like, I'm only size fourteen."

"But you're a big person."

"Large boned, right?"

"Yes."

"I'm *fat*. Just plain fat." The potency of her self-loathing reminds him of his own. And what for? Why should she hate herself? He knows from experience that there's no point in shitting on yourself because there's a whole world out there willing to do it.

"You're too hard on yourself," he says.

"Yeah, well, who isn't?"

"Lots of people."

"I've got to get away from food."

She follows him around the drugstore while he looks for Band-Aids. An old man in shorts and knee-high bright yellow socks asks him about corn plasters. "I don't work here," Reese tells him.

"Doesn't mean you don't know a thing or two," the old man says. He has a large growth on his temple. To avoid staring at the growth, Reese peruses the corn plaster options, surprised to see that there are so many.

"Get the foam doughnuts," Katrina advises.

"Do they stay stuck?" the old man asks.

"Definitely." She hands him a packet.

"Thank you most kindly." He shuffles down the aisle, studying the corn plaster instructions.

"Why do you suppose he wears yellow socks?" Reese asks.

"They go with the yellow swirly pattern on his shirt."

"You mean he worked that out? He's got this *thing* growing out of his head but he's still coordinating?"

"What else is he supposed to do?"

"I don't know. Die."

"Maybe he doesn't feel like it." Why not? What's wrong with oblivion? What luxury to be able to screw up then dissolve. Reese yearns for the innocence of perfect oblivion. The B.C. man who burned his children must have experienced a similar yearning. He'd intended to shoot himself after killing his children. He'd felt that they would all be safer dead than with his estranged wife, whom he claimed tied the children to furniture. He told the court that the only way they could all be together was if they were dead. Unfortunately, Reese doesn't foresee such a reunion with his children should he kill them and himself. The allure of annihilation is that it offers the ironclad assurance that, once dead, he will no longer have to care. But its prospect does not bring his children closer.

They watch *Shall We Dance*. Fred's crush on Ginger makes him follow her to the dance studio where she teaches. He pretends to need lessons. Reluctantly, she agrees to teach him.

"Why doesn't she ever like him?" Reese asks. "He's always really nice to her and she gives him the cold shoulder."

"That's the plot. He has to win her over." Katrina is gnawing on celery stalks.

"Why though? What's her problem with him in the first place? He seems perfectly charming."

"She doesn't trust him."

"Why not?"

"Duh. He's a man." Fred starts to dance as only Fred can.

Ginger stands back, mouth agape. Her boss appears, who, in a previous scene, had been poised to fire her. Impressed by Fred's dancing and Ginger's apparent teaching skills, he gives her back her job.

"See what I mean," Reese says. "Fred's being nice to her."

"He tricked her."

"So, he got her the job back."

"Doesn't mean she can trust him."

Reese suspects that he lost Roberta's trust some time around the adult video. She'd been asking him to pick one up from their local video store because she thought she might use it in some art class or other. "Get it yourself," he'd told her, having no interest in adult videos because a college roommate had rented them continually, causing Reese considerable lack of sleep. But Roberta of the can-do approach to life was too bashful to ask Sook, the Korean video store owner, if she could make a selection from the back room. So Reese, under pressure, did the deed, thereby permanently damaging his rapport with Sook who hitherto had considered Reese a video renter of some sophistication. From that day onward, when Sook recommended a film, he would always add conspiratorially, "It's a little bit ewotic." When Roberta rented a video, he treated her with similar familiarity. "What did you say to him?" Roberta demanded.

"I asked to see his adult videos."

"You could have told him it was for my art class."

"Do you think he'd have believed me?"

"I can't trust you to do anything." They watched part of it together, stone cold on the bed. Roberta was repulsed and saddened. Reese switched it off. Just like Fred, he could do nothing right.

"Have you ever been heartbroken?"

Katrina hands him a celery stalk. "You mean like over a guy?"

"Anything."

"I was wrecked when my cat died. She had cancer and went blind. It was brutal watching her smash into things."

"Have you ever been wrecked over a human?"

She shakes her head. "I don't let anybody get too close. Like, nobody really knows me."

"Is that your preference?" Fred and Ginger are dancing close again.

"I had big ears when I was a kid," Katrina says. "The brats at school called me Dumbo, Big Ears, forced me to sing dirty songs. It made me figure out humans are bad news." She points to the television. "That was Ginger's idea, that step, and nobody ever gave her credit for it. It was always Fred, Fred, Fred."

"Your ears don't look big to me."

"Duh, like, I had surgery."

"When?"

"Fourteen."

"Did it hurt?"

"I was asleep."

Reese chews his celery. The delinquent garbage-producing boys are playing hockey in the street, shouting obscenities at cars that dare to pass.

"Nobody really knows me either," Reese admits.

"We're supposed to be *substantive communicators*," Sterling says. "That means you make people feel good, you don't go telling them about frigging Arctic ice shelf's breaking up."

"It took forty-five hundred years to form," Reese says. "A century to destroy."

"My heart bleeds. Look, I respect your opinions but do me a favour: don't go bringing them to work. The Family Values people are starting to wonder about you." Sterling has begun to use an escort service, and wear cologne that off-gasses carcinogenic scents. "I have a lot of respect for you," he says, which Reese knows to be untrue. When people talk of respect, it is never present. "I'm just concerned about your performance with clients." When did performing become the verb of choice when talking with people? Sterling points at him. "You're going to that seminar."

"Seminar?"

"'Staying Competitive in the New Normal.' Don't pretend I didn't tell you about it. I want you to go and *learn* something. We're not saving whales here."

"When is it?"

"Tomorrow, bright and early, no excuses."

"Will I need golf clubs?"

"Just do your job, Reese. I don't want to have to get heavy." He is already heavy, buttocks spreading on Reese's desk, hairy fleshy fingers flipping through the Voice of First Nations script. "Why the hell are you mentioning Iraq?"

"There are some interesting parallels."

"The people *here* don't care about the people *there*. Don't go victim with the Indians, nobody cares."

"They *are* victims."

Sterling sighs heavily and crosses one weighty leg over the other. "I've been in this business a long time and one thing I know is, donors want something for their money. Make it sexy, make it like there's something going on besides Indians sitting around drinking Lysol. Make it like *Dancing with Wolves*, did you ever see that? Great movie. Indians were sexy in it. Even though they were being massacred, they were sexy." Reese did see *Dancing with Wolves*. He thought it was manipulative and shallow. He doesn't remember the Indians being sexy. "Am I making sense?" Sterling asks, furrowing his brow in the manner of a substantive communicator. "Whatever it takes, we make the client happy."

"I'll take another run at it," Reese says, knowing he won't.

Sterling puts his hand over his heart. "Thank you. I don't want tensions between us."

"Me neither."

"We're a team."

"Of course."

"What's that smell?"

"Smell?"

"Like tires burning or something." He sniffs several times. Reese knows that the smell is emanating from his plastic shoes contained in the drawer beneath Sterling's buttocks. Reese doesn't want to draw attention to the shoes with the nail holes because Sterling will undoubtedly suggest that a substantive communicator wear substantive footwear. Sterling approaches the window and sniffs. "Probably some asshole burning garbage."

"Probably."

After the surgery to remove what remained of the inner-dwelling catheter, Bernie appears pasty and despondent.

"Aren't you glad it's out?" Reese asks. "At least you don't feel like a robot."

"You should have let me go."

"Next time."

"Promises, promises."

"Oh my, my …" the man with the pointed head in constant pain says.

"Try the tortellini, Dad. It smells alright." He places the tray within Bernie's reach.

"It looks disgusting."

"Really? I don't think it looks that bad."

"*You* eat it."

"I've eaten in the last seventeen hours. You haven't." Reese forks a tortellini and holds it to Bernie's lips. "Come on, at least try it, you love noodles." Bernie allows the tortellini in his mouth then immediately spits it out. "Now do you believe it's disgusting?"

"Oh my, my …"

Were Bernie to die, Betsy would be able to move to the condo above the mall with the chocolate store. Does Bernie knows this? Is he attempting a slow suicide, a final selfless act?

Avril Leblanc called in sick today. Reese had been hoping to show her the Voice of First Nation's script. He'd hoped for a shared moment of understanding between them.

"What's your mother up to?" Bernie asks. "She never calls. You'd think I was dead already."

"I think she's afraid if she calls you, you'll start yelling at her."

"Why would I yell at her?"

"You criticize her."

"Is she so perfect she's beyond criticism?"

Reese has made this mistake before, allowed himself to get caught between them, to be used as a shield or a weapon. "I'm taking her to the hairdresser's."

"I'm lying here sick and dying and she's going to the hairdresser's?"

There's no winning with either of his parents. Reese knows this and yet comes back for more. Is this devotion stemming from a sense of duty or the need to have an effect in someone's life? To matter? He watched Roberta eat falafel today. She often has lunch at a Lebanese hole in the wall close to the school. He's been scouting it regularly for signs of her. Suddenly there she was, chewing pita and dripping yoghurt as though nothing had changed in her life. He braced himself to approach, to have a rational discussion. She was reading a magazine, *how could she be reading a magazine?* He felt his fists clenching, a primal scream pending. He strode towards her, thinking of Bob's gun. Then she was gone, her escape hidden by a delivery truck. He biked to Zellers for pie but couldn't dent the meringue with his spoon. The paraplegic was eating a piece of Chocolate Volcano cake. Did he have inside info on the baking schedule and knew when items were fresh? Reese wanted to ask him, but as the paraplegic was intently reading the sports pages, dripping chocolate sauce over photos of men who could move their legs, he felt this might be intrusive.

Holden, the bakery night-shift caller, is showing poor numbers and Sterling wants Reese to fire him. Holden is good on the phone but tends to veer from the script into other subjects such as the novel he's writing about the boy who journeys from Nova Scotia to Toronto, finds out he's gay, and returns to Nova Scotia to tell his mother. Everybody likes Holden, because of the free Danish, and because he's invited everyone to a party he's planning, even Marge who stinks of shit. It will be unpleasant to fire him. Reese could ask Serge to do it but Serge has not been himself since Avril told him he was a very aggressive person. His hangdog expression has become grating. He no longer preys on her but watches dejectedly from a distance. Reese knows that he should have a conversation with him about professional ethics, but has no energy for it.

The belly-dancing girl with the multiple piercings is not at the futon store. Desolation sets in. Reese squats on a beanbag chair, thinking that nothing can be counted on in life. But then she's there, as committed to futons and rice-filled neck pillows as ever. She doesn't recognize him. He hadn't expected her to, although he hoped she would. They have the quality mattress versus the quality futon conversation again. She explains that there are futons made with coils, kind of half mattress, half futon. "Some people aren't ready to commit to straight futons," she explains. "Which I don't get. I mean, I'm happy on my rock-hard futon."

Reese isn't happy on his rock-hard futon but doesn't admit this, feels this would weaken him in her eyes. He does, however, mention the mildew.

"Is the futon in the basement?" she asks.

"Yes."

"Does it *have* to be in the basement? Because futons shouldn't be in basements. It's too damp down there." He doesn't want to admit that it has to be in the basement. "Is it on the floor?" she asks. "Never put a futon on the floor in the basement. It needs air circulation. You have to get it at least six inches off the floor."

"Maybe you should advise people of this before you sell them futons," he suggests. "I suspect many customers put their futons on the floor in the basement."

"Why would you say that?" she asks, her tone chilling.

"It's a relatively inexpensive alternative to a bed," Reese says. "People like alternatives in their basements. For guests and ... pets."

"What people do with their futons is not my problem." She is withdrawing, retracting her belly button. "Use lemon and water," she says. "Or water and vinegar. It'll get the mildew off, but then you have to make sure you get the futon dry. Use a hair dryer. And you might want to get a dehumidifier. If you're planning to leave it in the basement." She says this with scorn. Only the truly ignorant put futons in the basement.

"I guess mildew is one of the reasons people prefer mattresses," Reese says in way of self-defence.

"Anything *organic* is going to rot. If you've got untreated wood down there and it's damp, it'll get mildew." Another customer has arrived, a lean and tortured youth in torn jeans. The belly dancer shimmies towards him. They start feeling futons together.

It has begun to rain and Reese has no raincoat. Moisture will seep into him, into his basement, his futon.

Anything organic is going to rot.

The hairdresser's waiting area is limited to three chairs. Reese sits wedged between two old ladies who are sharing lemon cookies and discussing Cleopatra. "People forget," the one with fire engine red fingernails says, "that she was first and foremost a queen."

"She was a slut," the one supplying the lemon cookies says.

"That is just not true, Sylvia."

"First Caesar and then Marc Anthony."

"She *loved* them."

"The two men she thought could save her? A bit of a coincidence, don't you think? Caesar's whore." Sylvia offers Reese a lemon cookie. She looks very proper in a hat not unlike the ones worn by Queen Elizabeth of the panic rooms.

"Thank you," Reese says, biting into the cookie, feeling it corroding his teeth.

The old lady with fire engine red nails reaches across him for one. "I can't believe," she says, "that you're slandering the greatest queen of all time."

"She murdered her brother and sister."

"Only because they would have murdered *her*."

"Two wrongs don't make a right." Fearing they might ask his opinion, Reese attempts to look engrossed in *Chatelaine*'s cottage-living tips. He's worried about his mother who has been eating only Glosette raisins, Crispy Crunches, and the occasional bacon, lettuce, and tomato sandwich. She doesn't fry real bacon but prefers the microwave variety, which is ready in three minutes and is saturated with toxins. She appears painfully frail in the hairdresser's chair, smiling meekly, showing no signs of her drag-on self. If Bernie dies, Reese isn't certain that Betsy would be able to look after herself in the condo above the mall with the choco-late store.

He has begun to litter. After withdrawing funds from his dwindling account, he discarded his Caramilk wrapper. On his way to Zellers, he dropped a can of Fruitopia, listened to it bounce and rattle on the pavement. He has, in the past, confront-ed litterers, said things like "Who do you think is going to pick that up?" to which the litterers would usually respond, "How 'bout you, asshole?" Reese's littering is an act of revenge, on whom he doesn't know. As landfill drops from his fingertips, he feels thrilled and mortified all at once. In the small appliance department, as he tried to select a hairdryer, a pair of identical twin Zellers clerks vaguely offered to assist him. One twin had a stud pierced through his eyebrow, but otherwise Reese couldn't tell them apart. He kept looking from one to the other as he asked about various options. They stared at him as though he were alien, the pierced eyebrow twin speaking only if the other spoke first, the two then speaking simultaneously in monosyllables. Perplexed, Reese selected the hair dryer with the "super-plus-power" option and, starting for the checkout, nearly collided with a woman crying. Her blotchy face indicated that she'd been in tears for some time. Reese wondered what could have caused such sorrow. Loss of a child, a husband, a home? A lover's betray-al? Fumbling in his pocket for a Kleenex, he found one dampened by rain and offered it to her. She looked at him with lizard eyes. "Get the fuck out of my face," she said.

"Catherine the Great," the old lady with fire engine red fingernails says, "now *there* was a leader."

"She was a whore."

Big ears forced Katrina to figure out early on that humans were bad news. Is there shelter to be found in such a revelation?

When you no longer hope for signs of intelligence, compassion, or kindness are you safe from harm?

Betsy teeters towards him with her hair tightly curled. "How 'bout we get some dinner? I'm buying."

"We should probably talk about Dad."

"Why?"

"He may die."

"He wouldn't do that." She wanted steak, has been sawing interminably at a piece of meat.

"Would you like me to cut that for you?"

"I'm not a two-year-old."

A stuffed moose's head leans over their booth. On a small television attached to their table a hemp-clothed environmentalist whose wife ate too much tainted fish — causing their unborn child neurological damage — has made it to the hourly news. "Each Canadian," the environmentalist says, "is responsible for emitting five tonnes of greenhouse gases into the atmosphere every year." He holds his palms upward like a beggar. "If *all* of us," he pleads, "cut back by *one* tonne, it would reduce ..." Reese quickly changes the channel. "Have you got enough mystery novels?"

"I'd like more of those ones set in the desert, with the Indians, those are good."

"I'll see what I can do." He tries to sample what's on his plate: a pasta dish that seemed palatable on the menu but on the plate looks predigested.

"The woman who owns the hairdresser's," Betsy says, "died climbing a mountain. Her daughter's running the place, doesn't like it, wants to sell it. All those years her mother worked to build the business and now the girl's going to go and sell it." The moose eyes Reese. He tries to think of something to say to his mother that would hold meaning, that would support the bulk of years between them. She points her fork at him. "Did you buy Happy Feet?" He nods, looking back at the TV, at a dog on its hind legs wearing a bikini. "You're lying," Betsy says. "Why won't you go and buy Happy Feet? You keep wearing socks with tight elastics, you'll have a heart attack."

"I *will* buy Happy Feet. I just haven't got to it yet."

"What have you been doing all day?"

"Working, Mother. I work, remember?"

"Don't act smart. Maddy told me a friend of hers' son had a heart attack in an airport limo. Fifty-seven years old."

Reese tries to eat the pasta. He remembers being small and running to Betsy, throwing his arms around her waist, feeling her soft warmth against his face. "We have to think seriously about getting you a caregiver," he says. "When Dad gets back. You won't be able to manage him on your own."

"I'm not having a stranger in the house."

"She won't be a stranger for long. She won't have to sleep there. She can do housework for you, and cook." He has no idea how he will pay for this.

She tucks into her fries. "In that mall I was telling you about, they also have a deli. You can get egg salad, macaroni, tuna, anything you want." The condo-above-the-mall fantasy gives her the will to live. Where is *his*? Why is he without the capacity to dream? *Head up*, Edwina Pendleton told him repeatedly while he stared at the floor. Why is he walking with head bowed? Because of Roberta? Because there is no certainty he will hold his children again? Because nylon sandals with plastic accents give him blisters? Because the pie at Zellers could not compare to his mother's and his mother will never bake a pie again? "Remember those lemon meringue pies you used to make?"

She nods. "Those were Chelsea's favourite."

"No, they weren't. They were my favourite. Chelsea preferred butter tarts."

"Lemon meringue was her favourite."

"No, it wasn't."

She glares at him, ready to fight. He looks away, at the stuffed fish on the walls. He is not ready to fight. The dead child always wins.

"I don't mean to intrude," Katrina shouts to be heard over the hair dryer, "but this just seems kind of retarded."

"It's what they told me to do at the futon store," Reese shouts back.

She starts peeling another hard-boiled egg. "Like, why don't you just junk it? Get something that doesn't get mouldy, like a regular mattress."

"I am not putting this in the garbage. The garbage goes into the Earth. The Earth doesn't need more garbage. The Earth is bursting with garbage." His hypocrisy astounds him.

"Suit yourself, but you can get sick from mould. People die from it, like they can't breathe and stuff." With hard-boiled egg in her mouth she is muted briefly and this relieves him. He doesn't understand why his panic room has become an extension of her living room.

Sterling keeps weighing in on him, punching holes through his consciousness. Reese is aware that he didn't behave well with the Family Values people, that he should not have mentioned the Bible-thumper's wife who drowned her five children in the bathtub, one by one. She pleaded insanity and got off with life imprisonment, in Texas where they still execute the convicted. Had it been the husband who had drowned the children in the bathtub one by one, he would, Reese has no doubt, have been sentenced to lethal injection.

The Family Values client with the rectangular head wanted to know what Reese's point was, and Reese covered by suggesting that he wasn't sure what family values were, exactly. The rectangular-headed man's nostrils began to flare. Nick, who has no wife or children, interjected with, "Till death do you part and all that jazz, Reeso. For better, for worse, in sickness and in health, etcetera etcetera."

"I'm just not sure that that's possible," Reese said. "I mean, you can live for years with someone and think you know them then find out you don't know them at all."

"It's your duty to get know them," the rectangular-headed man said.

"What if you find out you don't like each other, that on some fundamental level you disagree?"

Nick Dizon slapped Reese on the back. "You make do, Reeso, that's what it's all about. Keeping the family together." The B.C. Bible-thumper who burned his children was upset that his wife was taking yoga classes. Her friends said that she'd begun to find herself, but he felt that she was becoming too familiar with a male neighbour.

Katrina is shouting at him again. "Are you going to be doing that all night?"

"It's very musty."

"The hairdryer might explode or something. It's not supposed to be on for, like, forever."

"That's a point." He switches it off. The room becomes unbearably quiet. Bonaparte begins spinning on his wheel. Reese stopped at a pet store to pick up cedar chips for his cage. In line were people who looked like animals. Reese suspected that he himself was beginning to look like a hamster. He became aware of his nose twitching. A cat woman stared at him without blinking. A dog man farted and scratched behind his ears. "I have to get the futon off the floor," Reese says. "Do you have any milk crates?"

"Why would I have milk crates?"

"Some people use them as shelves."

"What about chairs with a board between them?"

"Have you got a door?"

They work together to create his bed. She lends him the door to her bedroom, and two chairs that belonged to her Hungarian grandmother. With difficulty they lift the sagging futon onto the door. "Looks alright," she says.

"I'll have to be careful how I distribute my weight." He wants her to leave, or at least tell him why she seeks his company — company which he himself can hardly stand. She has revealed to him that she works in a topless bar, maintaining that it is "no big whoop"; the sizeable tips make it worthwhile. The thought of her arriving at work and removing her clothes to serve chicken wings sickened and aroused him all at once. He looked away from her, and her breasts, took out his newly purchased mop and bucket to begin cleaning the floor.

"Aren't you lonely down here?" she asks. "I mean, it's not like there's any furniture or anything."

"Does furniture make us less lonely?"

"It's *totally* depressing."

Bonaparte's wheel spins. "I think I should probably try to sleep now," Reese says.

He can't, of course, once she's gone. He listens to her trying to do song and dance numbers soundlessly. Forgetting that he must be attentive to his weight distribution, he rolls onto his side. The futon and door crash beneath him.

Robert Vinkle has released mice into the men's washroom of the franchised restaurant across the street. His glee at having committed this violation worries Reese. Not only did Bob disregard house arrest to procure the mice from the pet store, but he has also admitted that he is planning to release mice into Alicia's house. "Alicia craps herself around rodents," he said, cackling. Beer has normalized him somewhat. He's telling them about a regular who screwed around on his wife. "No big news, right? The wife turns a blind eye. But then he goes and stuffs her *niece*. The wife demands a divorce. So the guy gives it to her but the wife's a mess, tells her friends she'd had no idea how happy she'd been while she was miserable with this jerk. She's fifty-something and not getting any invitations. So, guess what?" He looks at Reese then at Linden Prevost, who appears to be absorbed in televised highlights of the mayoral debate.

"I have no idea," Reese says.

"Come on guess. Like, what would be your biggest nightmare?"

"She doesn't let him see his children?"

"Shit, no, he doesn't care about them, they're teenagers."

"His willy drops off," Linden suggests.

Bob leans into them, heightening the dramatic tension. "He goes *blind*. He gets macular degeneration. The doctors try stuff, none of it works. Guess who comes to his rescue?"

"I have no idea," Reese says.

"Come on, guess. Like, who would be the most unlikely person to want to look after him?"

"His wife?" Linden offers.

"Bingo. Is that not gorgeous?"

"Each to his own hell," Linden says.

Reese can see himself performing such an act of apparent selflessness. He can see himself rushing to Roberta's side were she in need. Why? Because of his great love for her? Because there is no one else? Because the only role he recognizes is that of enabler? He imagines the blind man accidentally knocking over a glass of orange juice and cursing the betrayed wife who says, "I'm so sorry, darling, I'll get you another one."

Bob has discovered a chat room for men who have been betrayed by their wives. According to the participants, they've all been greatly wronged and misunderstood. "This one guy," he says, "only gets to see his daughter for two hours on Sundays and it has to be in his ex's house because the ex says he molested the kid."

"Did she prove it?" Reese asks.

"Who needs proof? You think guys molest their kids with witnesses around? Anyways, it gets sicker. The wife's got some dead-end job at a bank and is figuring out that being married to a lawyer wasn't such a bad idea so she's coming on to him again. Is that not putrid?"

"Does he want her?"

"Shit, no. After what she put him through? But he's playing along so she'll loosen up on visiting rights." Bob still hasn't seen his daughter Hilary. He has placed a framed photo of her by the bar phone. When it gets splattered by mixers, Bob wipes it tenderly.

Who needs proof? You think guys molest their kids with witnesses around?

Reese dreamed about Gwyneth Proudley. She was very tall and inexplicably drawn to him. She pulled his face into her breasts. Hoping to give her pleasure, he placed his hand between her legs. Her vagina was large and all-consuming, swallowing first his hand, then his arm. He lost all hope of ever satisfying her, of convincing her that he did not molest his daughter.

"You don't look too good, brother," Bob says. Mayoral candidates, sweaty and untrustworthy, debating on the TV above the bar, begin talking at once.

"My employer," Reese says, "wants me to develop a market-driven perspective. To take a fast track to personal and professional growth."

"He wants you out is what he wants."

"I have to go to a seminar."

"Yikes."

Kyla tells them that the kitchen is closing, that they better order if they want anything. "Bring us some nachos," Bob says, drinking more beer. "So my car mechanic is buying a frickin' Firestone Tire franchise. He's painting his place up red and silver and wearing this little red vest that says Firestone on it. This guy has been, like, an inspiration to me, you know, with Canadian Tire and Wal-Mart breathing down his neck, not to mention Mr. Lube, this guy has *stayed in business*. And you know why?" One of the mayoral candidates has eyes that ceaselessly shift. "Because I can trust him," Bob says. "Because I know he knows how to fix cars. Today he tells me he doesn't have time to work on cars anymore because he's so busy with this Firestone bullshit, learning the corporate way. I've never heard this guy take crap from anybody, he's Sicilian, wiry. Today I hear him on the phone with some Firestone higher-ups and he's eating shite. I could not believe it."

"Another icon shattered," Linden says.

"I said, 'Tony, bigger is not better. Do not sell your soul to some label.' Guess what he said."

"I have no idea," Reese says.

"'I have to create and capitalize on a sustainable competitive advantage.' Like, what kind of talk is that? Like, what does that *mean*?"

"Screw the other guy," Linden says.

"Meanwhile his blood pressure's going up. By the end of the day his ears are pink and he's ready to pass out." The mayoral candidates shout at one another. The big-haired female moderator looks alarmed. "Gentlemen," she keeps saying. Kyla delivers the nachos, says she might be late tomorrow because her kid has a fever and might have to go to the doctor. "Whatever," Bob says. He picks up the photo of his daughter and wipes it. She has his look about her, the same bafflement. How will she feel about a house full of mice?

"She's beautiful," Reese says.

"Thank you, brother." Bob leans heavily on the bar, staring down at the photo. Reese is drawn to the header "Sleepless in Toronto" in the newspaper beside the photo: 35 percent of Canadians average less than six hours a night; 50 percent of Canadians feel sluggish two to three times per week. The article offers tips to mattress selection. *First, stretch out on the mattress with your back against it. Then, take the flat of your hand and slip it under the small of your back. If your hand slips in and out too easily, the mattress is too firm. If your hand fits snugly, then the mattress will offer the right amount of back support.* This has been Reese's mistake, he realizes, testing mattresses lying on his side. Had he tried them on his back he may have found the ideal bed. He feels flooded with possibility; the doors of mattress stores reopen before him. The mayoral candidates shake hands and force smiles.

"The word *democracy*," Linden says, "has been debased."

"I'm there, brother." Bob taps more drafts.

"Democracy," Linden says, "has become less a process than a result. You're democratic when you're on *their* side, when you're the product of something *they* did. Democracy is like religion, or freedom, or morality — a value to be enforced rather than a tool for discovering the popular will."

"Hear, hear," Bob says. Kyla sits at the bar, cashing out. Reese wonders how she can be so calm knowing that her child is feverish. When his children have fevers he fears they have meningitis. He imagines them weakening before him until breathing itself defeats them. He sits them in tepid baths and sponges them with cool water. Roberta will not have the patience for this. Roberta will dope them with Tylenol and leave them with the pimple-squeezing babysitter while she's gooling at waven.

"I said to Tony," Bob says, "*when*, in your experience, has bigger been better? Guess what he said."

"I have no idea," Reese says.

"He told me his wife shops at Wal-Mart because the prices are better. I said by how much? Two cents? Is it a buck eighty-seven instead of a buck eighty-nine? They dupe you with those numbers."

The article says sleep studies have proved that healthy sleep is the single most important determinant in predicting longevity — more so than diet and exercise. If you live to be eighty and sleep an average of eight hours a day, you will have spent twenty-six years in bed. Reese hears the "I am your lady, You are my man" song on the sound system. He has heard this song many times before over many years. Sometimes a man sings, "You are my lady and I am your man." Sometimes a man and a woman alternate phrases in the song. The woman sings, "I am your lady" then the man sings, "I am your man." Reese loathes this song. "Can I see your gun?" he asks. Bob shares a deeply understanding look with him before digging around behind the bar. He places the gun wrapped in a dishtowel on the bar. "Take a peek," he says, "but don't go advertising it. Linden's already seen it." Linden watches the television. Another car bomb's exploded, fifty-two people dead. Reese lifts a corner of the dishtowel.

"Isn't she gorgeous?" Bob asks.

"I've never seen one before. Up close, I mean."

"Touch her."

Reese strokes the Colt, admires the solidity of it, the engineering.

"Go on," Bob says, "pick her up."

It is heavier than Reese would have imagined. An arm would soon tire holding it.

Kneeling beside his daughter's bed, he leans closer so he can smell her. She sweats in sleep because she likes to be covered by several blankets. Consequently she smells slightly animal. He loves this about her. Unconscious her face is completely without guile, defenceless. Hugged to her chest is the stuffed dog Reese bought because he liked its squiggly tail. He bought it because Clara had strained her hip jumping off the roof of a playhouse. The kindergarten teacher phoned him at work because she couldn't reach Roberta. She said she'd cautioned Clara more than once not to climb onto the playhouse but Clara hadn't listened. Seeing his daughter limping badly caused a strangulating panic. He embraced her, lifting her off the ground until they reached the car. They had to wait for over an hour in the pediatrician's waiting room. Clara hobbled from toy to toy. People watched with pity, thinking she'd been born disabled. Reese was reminded yet again of how lucky he was to have healthy children. How lucky he was.

"What's going on?" Katrina asks.

"I have no bed."

"There's blankets on the couch."

"Thank you." He sits on the couch but doesn't look up at her, at anything.

"What's wrong?" There's something like a noose around his neck. When he tries to speak, it tightens. "You look seriously fucked up," Katrina says. "You want a drink or anything?" He shakes his head. "Do you want to watch a movie?" He shakes his head. She sits beside him, causing the orange couch to sag and their thighs to touch. He doesn't want to touch her, he wants his children. Katrina pats his knee. "You know what's really good? Ovaltine. It's, like, full of vitamins and helps you sleep. Do you want me to make some?" He nods, if only to make her move away from him. He saw Roberta's neck exposed, her artery persistently pulsing. He thought of sharp implements, gushing blood. The gun. Escaping with his children in his arms. "You brought tapes," Katrina says, picking them up and handling them loosely. He snatches them from her. "My children," he says. Each year they shed versions of themselves, versions that he is never ready to lose. He can look at the videos but that child is no longer there, has been replaced by another version of the child he is not ready to lose.

The earlier versions might as well be dead.

"Do you want me to put one on?" Katrina asks.

He has been afraid to look at them, afraid of grief hemorrhaging inside him. She fits a tape into the player. Clara is there, fat and happy toddling in the grass. Derek, as yet undiagnosed — unlabelled — digs intently in some dirt. The garden, still young, looks barren. Now it's a forest. "I can't watch," Reese chokes, turning away, lying on his side facing the back of the orange couch. He thinks of all the suffering worldwide since time began. He thinks of war and famine, hurricanes, floods, forest fires, earthquakes. He thinks of the wife of the B.C. man running towards the flames screaming, "My babies! My babies! He killed my babies!"

He knows it could be so much worse.

He feels a blanket laid over him. "Try to sleep," she says.

18

The seminar attendees are conservatively suited, sporting substantive footwear, the men in jackets and ties with understated patterns and the women in skirts and blazers with discreet shoulder pads. They mingle around a stack of muffins on the banquet table in a windowless, colourless room. Some of them exchange greetings, attempting to shake hands while clutching muffins and Styrofoam cups of coffee. Most simply nod at one another. Reese suspects that they are the veterans of many seminars who have failed to achieve a sustainable competitive advantage with innovative marketing strategies. He can feel the Band-Aids on his blisters, loosened by sweat, coming loose in his plastic sandals. As he approaches the muffin table, the group parts, without apparently seeing him. He selects a fruit and fibre muffin then pours himself a coffee.

He left Katrina in a heap of blankets. She refused to get out of bed for a Burger King audition. "Like, how many times do I have to go through that shit knowing they're going to hire a size two with perfect teeth?" Reese didn't respond. He knew that he'd gone through many things too many times, that he would go through many more things he'd already gone through too many times. She refused coffee or orange juice. When he invited her to Holden's party, she merely grunted.

He wonders what part the muffin he's eating will play in the reproduction of his cells, which are constantly being renewed. He is not the same mass of cells he was ten years ago. His children are not the same cells they were in the videos. This impermanence should offer reassurance. Despite the regressions of the mind, the body forges ahead. A woman nearby spills coffee on her blouse while brushing muffin crumbs from her skirt and gasps in horror, prompting Reese to offer assistance. Aghast, she thrusts her coffee and muffin at him and rushes to the ladies' room. Reese resumes his seat, placing her coffee and muffin under his chair for safekeeping.

A couple enters the room confidently and, with a sense of well-being, greets everyone enthusiastically. The woman, with pointed breasts, narrow hips, and bright blonde hair that doesn't move, smiles without pause. It's not difficult to visualize her in a cheer-leader's uniform. Her partner resembles the Six Million Dollar Man.

"Hi. This is Victor G. Boone and I'm Bambi Ootes, welcome to the seminar. We're very excited about having you all here. Before we begin, has everybody helped themselves to refreshments?" The conservatively suited nod and murmur assent.

"The first step to empowerment," Victor G. Boone booms, "is to be here."

"Right on," Bambi Ootes cheers.

They begin a PowerPoint presentation in which a soccer team is used to illustrate a high-PERFORMing team. "The most important function of a high performance team is to *perform*," Bambi says. On the screen appears:

P for "PURPOSE"
E for "EMPOWERMENT"
R for "RELATIONSHIPS AND COMMUNICATION"
F for "FLEXIBILITY"
O for "OPTIMUM PRODUCTIVITY"
R for "RECOGNITION AND APPRECIATION"
M for "MORALE"

The coffee-stained woman still hasn't come out of the wash-room. Reese imagines her frantically drenching her conservative blouse and skirt in an effort to remove the stains. Bambi and

Victor G. take turns discussing the need for clear but challenging goals that are relevant to the PURPOSE. They remind Reese of the man and woman taking turns singing the "I am your lady" and "You are my man" song. They use the words *strategize, achieve, challenge*, stress the importance of committing to a common PURPOSE. Reese feels the need for another coffee and muffin as a slide showing members of a female soccer team hugging flashes on. Bambi and Victor G. speak of team members feeling a personal and collective sense of power, having mutual respect and a willingness to help each other. Are *they* a team, Reese wonders? After stressing the need for team members to express themselves openly and honestly, do they rut? Where? And on what kind of bed?

Team members must listen actively to each other, Bambi emphasizes, with warmth, understanding, and acceptance. On screen, members of a male soccer team pat each other on the back. Reese approaches the muffins by way of the ladies' washroom. He opens the door a crack and whispers, "Everything under control?"

"I'll be right out," a small voice responds.

He chooses a cran-apple muffin then resumes his seat. On the chair beside him a newspaper headline, "Canada Losing Pollution Fight," threatens him. Below this, before he can avert his eyes, he reads, "From 1995 to 2005, toxic emissions pumped into air, water, and land rose 50 percent." Mrs. Ranty digs her heels into his kidneys. "Hel-*lo!*" she says. "We're not just talking lead here."

"Or arsseenic," Scout Leader Igor adds, "assbesstoss, mercury, benzene ..."

Mrs. Ranty grabs hold of Reese's ear. "We're talking a whole *new* batch of chemicals they haven't even tested yet!"

Then the unmistakable glass-shattering voice of Mrs. Steinman his piano teacher joins in, "Four *billion* kilograms a year spewed out of industry's anus! It's a dis*grace!*" She told Reese he was a disgrace. He called her Mrs. Stinkman.

"Is a *team effort* required for such destruction?" all three demand. "A commitment to a common PURPOSE?!"

Reese shoves the newspaper behind his seat.

F for FLEXIBILITY. On screen a goalie demonstrates flexibility by catching a ball while lying on his stomach. "Team members must be adaptable to changing demands," Bambi emphasizes. "Team members must share the responsibility for team leadership and team development."

"Not *one* of us is as smart as *all* of us," Victor G. booms.

"No development stage is bad," Bambi says. "Each stage the team makes is part of the journey. But you must have a Team Development Game Plan."

"Number one," Victor G. booms, "determining vision. Set goals."

"Number two," Bambi cheers, "diagnosis. Determine the development level of the group. Its productivity and its morale." The woman comes out of the washroom, water-stained and wary. Reese waves to her, pointing to the seat beside him.

"Have I missed anything?" she asks.

"Not much. I saved your coffee and muffin."

She looks startled, as though fearing he might pitch them at her. "No, thank you." It takes Reese a moment to notice that Bambi and Victor G. have stopped talking and are staring at them. "Is everything alright over there?" Bambi inquires.

"Fine," the water-stained woman says. "Sorry for interrupting."

"No problem."

Reese observes the men's ties, knowing that a tightly knotted tie presses to such an extent on the jugular vein that it raises blood pressure to the eyes, causing glaucoma. Ophthalmologists are particularly watchful for this problem among white-collar professionals. Glaucoma destroys optic nerves and causes blindness. Blind men can't drive cars. Will they stop polluting if they go blind?

During the break one of the men in a tightly knotted necktie complains that his car has been vandalized *twice* since he bought it three months ago. Both times passenger windows were broken, causing glass to shatter over his leather seats, which then required two hundred dollars' worth of detailing. Nothing was taken from the car. According to the necktied man, whose name tag reads Raul Tuttle, the culprits know the alarm doesn't go off if you don't touch the car or the sound system. The guy at Speedy Auto Glass told him they must have used a baseball bat to break the glass because it's coated in a film tint, which makes it impossible to break with bare hands. "In my own driveway," Raul Tuttle says. "I told my wife, 'Clean out the garage, I'm moving in.' She's got all kinds of crap in there, strollers, old exercise equipment. I told her, 'If I see *anybody* touch that car, I'll kill them, I'm not kidding, I'll kill them.'"

"You and your car," Mrs. Stinkman scolds, "will consume the products of 7.9 hectares of land in your lifetime!"

"Your American cousin," Mrs. Ranty adds, "is going to suck up 12.1 hectares."

"And zsome poor Afghani schmuck," Igor intones, "ees going to usse up .9."

"There are *only* 12 billion hectares of bio-productive land left," they shout in unison. "With the current population at *6 billion!* That leaves nothing for junior, or *other* species!"

"It's a dis*grace!*"

Reese stuffs more muffin into his mouth.

"That's the first car I bought for *me*," Raul Tuttle emphasizes. "The wife's got the minivan, I even let my sister use my name to buy a car because she's got a lousy credit rating. This was the first car I bought that had *everything* I wanted." He shakes his head, clearly distraught. "I *love* that car. If those little fucks so much as touch it again, I'm going to kill them." Other tightly knotted men nod sympathetically. Reese, crippled by blisters, leans against the wall, beside a plastic plant.

"Did you hurt your foot?" the water-stained woman asks. Her name tag reads Bobbi Galindo. "Hi, I'm Bobbi. Thanks for saving me a seat."

"No problem."

"I had a bunion once. You really appreciate your feet when they hurt." She has a chronically startled look about her. "Is it your ankle?"

"No, actually, it's just blisters. These sandals aren't very comfortable."

"That's unusual. Sandals usually are."

"Yes, well, these are made of nylon."

"And plastic," she observes.

"Yes."

"I find it's best to buy leather. And they have to feel good in the store. You can't break shoes in, they break you." He senses that she's talking to him because no one is talking to her. They are the undesirables at the dance. Bambi and Victor G. laugh heartily at something that Raul Tuttle says. Not far from them, a wide woman in a pantsuit is speaking forcefully to a skinny-assed man with a goatee. "When somebody disagrees with me," she says, "I know they're stupid. It's that simple. Why beat around the bush when you know *you're* right and *they're* wrong?" Bobbi Galindo leans against the wall beside Reese. They both face the dancers. He rolls his neck. Were he not hampered by blisters, Mrs. Ranty, Igor, and Mrs. Stinkman, he might take the opportunity to practise his forward and backwards steps. Katrina was emphatic that he practise. "Don't embarrass me," she said. But there's little space for dancing in the basement apartment. And Katrina's living room is too crowded with her Hungarian grandmother's furniture.

"This is my first time at something like this," Bobbi admits. "It's really exciting. I think Bambi and Victor are dynamite."

The wide woman in the pantsuit is shaking her head. "I don't suffer fools gladly." The skinny-assed man nods, pulling nervously on his goatee.

Bobbi Galindo turns towards Reese. "Are you in marketing?"

"Yes."

"I think it's the way of the future. I mean, if you think about it, absolutely everything has to be marketed." Reese feels a headache coming on, knives being thrust into his skull. "I'm just a medical secretary," Bobbi confesses. "I really want a change. I mean, people are sick in the office, and they cry and that and I have to give them Kleenexes and glasses of water and it's just ... it's really stressful. I mean, besides the germs and that, I know everything on their charts. And I have to call them all the time, like, not if there's a serious problem. The doctors get them to come in if it's serious. But I have to tell them if their iron's low or something and they get all freaked out and start asking questions and I don't know what to tell them. I have to practically hang up on them."

Reese wishes Avril Leblanc would look searchingly into his eyes again. In the paper there was an eighteenth-century drawing of Mississauga Indians in feathers signing over their lands to white men in wigs. Reese wanted to show it to Avril, and tell her that the white men in wigs had to intoxicate the chiefs before they'd consent to make their mark. In the drawing the Indians didn't look drunk.

"Do you enjoy marketing?" Bobbi Galindo inquires.

"Not particularly. Actually, if you'll excuse me, I should use the facilities."

A tightly knotted man is standing at the sink with his pants unzipped, washing his genitals. On seeing Reese, he hurriedly pulls up his pants while muttering apologies. Reese doesn't want to ponder what this means.

As Reese returns to the office, Sterling Green is in the midst of placing his new chairs in the waiting area, busy trying one arrangement, assessing it, then, dissatisfied, trying another. So engrossed is he that he doesn't notice Reese come in, allowing Reese time to meet with Wayson Hum to look at the figures. Sadly, Avril Leblanc has not returned to work and, consequently, Serge Hollyduke no longer walks the floor, shouting orders. He has bought an I Ching book and is repeatedly tossing coins to determine what action to take. But a sound not unlike that from a stabbed bull is heard from the waiting area, and Reese feels obliged to investigate. Sterling has turned the chairs upside down and is examining their undersides closely. "Is there a problem?" Reese inquires.

"They're not leather!" Sterling exclaims.

"Are you sure?"

He points at Holden. "Ask *him*."

Holden shrugs. "They're some kind of composite stuff."

"They look like leather," Reese says.

"Smell them," Holden suggests. Sterling, on his knees now, begins sniffing the chairs.

"Does it matter that they're not leather?" Reese asks.

"I paid eighty bucks apiece for them."

"If you paid eighty bucks apiece," Holden says, "they're definitely not leather."

Sterling begins scratching the imitation leather with his thumbnail.

"I wouldn't do that," Holden advises. "It'll just chip the coating."

"Never again," Sterling says, "do I trust a Jew."

"Did he tell you they were leather?" Reese asks.

"What are you talking about, they look like leather."

"Yes, but the salesman didn't *tell* you they were leather. You *assumed* they were leather."

"Plus they were cheap," Holden points out, "so you went for it. They look okay to me. I'd move that one over a bit." He looks around. "I think the room needs a plant. One of those snake plants. All the dry cleaners have them. They grow anywhere."

Still on his knees, Sterling is stricken.

"Can't you return them?" Reese asks.

"They were final sale."

"Well, I think they look fine." Already he can smell them off-gassing. Already they are on their way to landfill. "Where are the old chairs?" he asks.

"Waiting for garbage pickup."

"I'll take them," Reese says.

"What for?"

"To sit on. In my apartment."

"They're a bit eighties," Holden cautions.

"Where the hell are your shoes?" Sterling demands.

Reese, defeated by his footwear, has been going barefoot, exposing his apish feet. "I'm having a problem with blisters."

"Buck up, you can't go around barefoot."

"I realize that, certainly not in front of clients."

"Not in front of anybody. What kind of message does that send? We've got Third Worlders working here. Pretty soon they'll all want to go barefoot."

"I need some Band-Aids that stay on. The ones I bought come unstuck."

"That's because your toes are hairy," Holden advises. "Band-Aids don't stick to hair."

"Am I actually having this conversation?" Sterling asks.

"No," Holden says. "We are."

Sterling ignores him and looks at Reese. "How was the seminar?"

"Fine."

"Stimulating?"

"Absolutely."

"Got any ideas?"

As Reese was leaving, Bambi Ootes, still smiling, said, "*You* take care." For a moment he thought he'd misjudged her, that she perceived his despair and felt a need to express particular concern for him. Then he heard her say, "*You* take care," to the skinny-assed man with the goatee.

"We paid good money for that seminar," Sterling says.

"I'm just going to let it sit for a bit," Reese says. "Lots to think about."

"They truly believe," Holden says, "they've been up in space capsules and that aliens have given them anal probes. There's like eight thousand hits on the site. Eight thousand people think aliens have looked up their anuses. What's that tell you about modern man's mental health?"

Reese pulls his plastic shoes out of his desk. "How's the job going?"

"I don't mind it. I'm not really a phone person but I'm getting used to it. Avril says I have to learn to *be* with it. There's something really mercenary about it, like, I mean, where does the money go? You're chasing some old lady for twenty bucks and you want to be able to say it's going straight to that sick kid or whatever, but the whole time you're pretty sure it's padding some suit's expense account."

Reese isn't up to informing Holden that he is failing to meet the response goal of 5 percent. He puts more Band-Aids over his hairy toes before trying on the plastic shoes.

"That would be cool though, wouldn't it?" Holden asks. "Being convinced you were in outer space? I mean, even if you didn't go, it wouldn't matter because you *thought* you did. They remember every detail. Like what the aliens were wearing and the control panels and stuff."

"Who's to say they didn't go?"

"Exactamundo. Like, maybe the anal probe is to study humans' dietary habits. Maybe the aliens are fascinated by our forty-foot intestines."

Reese puts on the plastic shoes and stands. Immediately, he is in pain.

"You need socks," Holden points out.

"Don't have any."

"Take mine, I don't need them." He starts taking off his running shoes.

"You don't have to do that."

"Chillax, it's no problem They're fluffy inside, my mum buys them." He hands Reese the socks.

"They're Happy Feet," Reese observes.

"They're supposed to have special features, like cushioned heels and sweat absorption."

"They don't kill you," Reese says. "My mother believes that tight socks can kill you." He knows that he is PERFORMING badly, that he should be effectively problem-solving where Holden's numbers are concerned, generating alternative solutions, and analyzing consequences, action planning, and evaluation. Bambi spoke of the importance of the Group Climate — the feeling or tone of the group. "All team leaders need to practise the skill of being a participant observer," she said. Reese has no idea what this means. He knows only that history shows that mankind works best alone, that discoveries are made as a result of one man or one woman's obsession. His son, before he was labelled and drugged, created elaborate projects that didn't blend with the projects of less enthusiastic students. His teacher did not applaud or encourage him, said only that he didn't need to do so much. Derek was upsetting the Group Climate.

"Aha," Holden says, "I see the aliens haven't finished *your* anal probe. Earth to Captain, do you read me?"

Aren't wars about Group Climates? Didn't Hitler create an excellent Group Climate? Aren't the Taliban team players?

Bobbi Galindo says absolutely everything has to be marketed. Why? Can we not see what is before us? Must we be told what to eat, wear, think? Can we not sit alone in our panic rooms and figure out who we are?

"I wouldn't mind being probed by an alien," Holden says. "As long as I get to go to outer space. I wonder how they make their selections."

Winston Churchill pissed off his generals. Was he practising the skill of being a participant observer of the team?

Reese removes the shoes and puts his sandals over the Happy Feet. "I'm going to collect those chairs."

19

They sit on Sterling's discarded chairs on the subway platform.

"This novel spans three generations," Holden tells Reese. "Women keep having babies and the men go off to war and get their faces blown off. It's pretty boring. A lot of landscape, though, if you're into that. It's not my idea of award-winning." The PA system crackles and a man with a Pakistani accent makes an unintelligible announcement. "Must be a delay," Holden interprets. "Jumper." A crowd begins to form. To make room, Holden and Reese stack the chairs and stand on either side of them. Several feet away is a woman in a burka who repeatedly leans over the tracks to see if a train is coming. Her children, a boy and girl the age of Reese's own, push and pull at each other while her back is turned then resume saintly expressions when she faces them. Her eyes look full of relentless sadness. Stan Huckle told Reese that he never saw Middle Eastern women cry. He said they looked haunted, and always kept their children near them, even in sleep, so that if a bomb struck they would all be killed. Instinct tells Reese that the woman in the burka on the platform is Amir Kassam's widow.

"One of the characters is a fisherman," Holden adds, "always getting on boats so there's endless description of the sea as well. And fish."

Once again, the woman in the burka leans over the tracks to look down the tunnel but this time she falls. It takes a moment for this to register. She is there, then she isn't. No one in the crowd seems to have noticed, even her children continue to torment one another. Reese waits to hear her screams but there are none. Holden continues to denigrate the award-winning novel. In the haze caused by sleep deprivation and the knives being thrust into his skull, Reese runs to the edge of the platform and jumps onto the tracks. Women scream, but not Amir Kassam's widow. On her knees, she is silent and shaking, inches from the 600-volt power rail. Reese looks up at the platform, hoping for aid, extended arms, anything. But the onlookers are frozen, their mouths black holes, and a train is coming. "Don't move!" he shouts to the woman. "I'm going to get you, don't move. Please!" He steps over the tracks to the woman and wraps his arms around her. She is mostly fabric, the skin and bones of her he can hardly feel. He grips what he believes to be the bulk of her and tries to stand. She is muttering in her language, perhaps praying. "Put your arms around my neck," he says, but she only continues to pray. On the platform, people are screaming that a train is coming. Holden, on his stomach, reaches towards them. "She's too heavy," Reese says, "I can't lift her." Back pain jabs him. The rumble of the train reverberates through his plastic sandals. Once again he looks to the platform for help but sees only the woman's daughter wailing and trying to run towards her mother while the boy restrains her. Reese murdered their father, he will *not* let their mother die. With strength unknown to him, he hoists the woman onto his hip and stands, wavering slightly, looking beyond her skirts at the power rail. Afraid he might stumble if he tries to turn around, he steps forward, over the cable, and carries her to the wall. The shrieking of emergency brakes and humankind continues until the train stops 1.5 metres away.

Holden arranges the discarded chairs in the basement apartment. They sit on them for several minutes. "I'm starved," Holden says. "You got anything to eat?"

Reese is having an out-of-body experience. The fire captain frightened him, had the protruding eyes indicative of a thyroid condition, and no understanding of personal space requirements. He shadowed Reese, threw an arm around his shoulder and repeatedly called him a bona fide hometown hero. The press arrived. All his adult life Reese has struggled to draw press to protests. During the "Stop the War Against the Poor" demonstration he threw fake blood at the Parliament Buildings knowing that he'd be hauled off by police but believing the press would get there first. Unfortunately, Cher was in town. All his adult life Reese has been pushed around by the likes of the fire captain. He gave him his name, which he would not have done had he not been accustomed to giving his name to men in uniforms.

"Where've you been?" Katrina demands.

"Out, I've been out, that's what I do, I go out then I come back."

"You don't have to get snippy." She's in her leotard and dance skirt. "I've been working on my sashay, it's really coming together." Reese realizes that the door was open; even so he would prefer that she knock.

"Chairs," she observes. "What'd you do, rob a dentist's office?" She sees Holden. "Hi."

"Howdy. Do you live here too?"

"Upstairs."

Amir Kassam's widow didn't speak English. When she regained consciousness, she called for her children. They huddled around her while the fire captain and press swarmed them. When Reese looked again, they were gone. He couldn't walk for several minutes, was without balance. Medics prodded him with instruments despite his protestations. He stared at his Happy Feet in sandals.

He did save her life. This he knows.

He mixes some Swiss Miss, watching his hands that belong to somebody else. The hands carry the cups to his guests. "Delicioso," Holden says.

"You know how many calories are in those?" Katrina asks. "Like, my allowance for an entire day."

"He just saved somebody's life," Holden says. "Jumped on the subway tracks and grabbed her."

"Get out." Katrina stares hard at Reese who is looking at his sandals again.

"Seriously," Holden says. "He's been acting a bit like an alien ever since."

"He's always like that," Katrina assures him.

They talk about and around him. They expect nothing of him. This provides relief. Always, he is trying to be somebody, at work, even in the house that was once his. He can never drop all vestiges of apparent knowledge and power and just *be*. For once, he is being a good onion.

Fred is in hot pursuit of Ginger again, being snubbed at every turn.

"He doesn't look good in a sailor suit," Katrina comments. Holden has never seen a Fred and Ginger movie before. He sits inches from the screen and makes Katrina replay the dance sequences.

"Wait till you see him in tails," Katrina says.

Reese's phone began ringing as reporters made the connection between the terrorist killing and the subway rescue. "Maybe they'll make you into a movie of the week," Holden said. Katrina took the calls, speaking rudely in Hungarian. One of the callers was the husband of the woman in a burka, who wanted to thank Reese. He spoke little English but was able to say "much thank you" many times. This meant that the woman was not Amir Kassam's widow. Reese has been trying to *be* with this.

It's Betsy's birthday tomorrow and he has forgotten to buy her a present. He can't give her more Royal Albert china, the "Olde Country Rose" pattern, because she has all the pieces. Last year he bought her "Olde Country Rose" oven mitts and dishtowels. The year before he bought her a matching tea cozy. There are no more "Olde Country Rose" options. And Pierre Berton is dead. As a backup he has always been able to buy Pierre Berton books.

Fred decides to put on a show to raise money to save Ginger's sister's ship. Sets and costumes materialize, and Fred in tails. "See what I mean?" Katrina asks.

"Sharp," Holden says. Fred reveals a gun while beautiful people mill around him, oblivious to his suffering. Fred fondles the gun, spins it on his finger, then points it at his head. Ginger appears in a shimmering gown. Unaware of Fred, she stands looking forlornly at the sea. Fred watches, entranced by her beauty and grace. Abruptly she prepares to jump into the turbulent waters, but Fred stops her. He pitches his gun and they begin to dance while Fred sings about the possibilities of trouble ahead, and music and moonlight and love and romance. Katrina joins in when he sings, "Let's face the music and dance." Soon Holden too is singing the refrain. By the end of the number even Reese is humming let's face the music and dance. Then it's over. They're back in a world devoid of music and moonlight and love and romance. Katrina offers to boil broccoli for them. Holden turns on the news. A man has abducted his ex-wife, grabbed her by the hair and dragged her at knifepoint, screaming, from her apartment. Their toddler is in the care of the Children's Aid Society. Reese turns away from the television into the couch. He sees the woman in a burka sleeping with her children around her. He sees his own children unconscious of a world gone horribly wrong, believing that there will always be more water, more air. Food. And he wants to pray for them only he doesn't know how as he believes in no god. Prayer comforted the woman as she knelt before certain death. Reese was the answer to her prayers. His act has reaffirmed her faith.

The limited space available on the orange couch confines him, inducing sleep. But something wakes him in the dead of night, not a noise, not a movement, not even a fallen blanket. It is a feeling similar to what he felt when he lost Clara at the airport, on the departure level, seeing his parents off to Florida. They'd just come up the elevator from the parking garage and were standing on the terrazzo floor between the elevator and escalator, simultaneously trying to find a luggage cart and locate the Air Canada desk. Betsy had been holding Clara's hand when she stooped to check a troublesome zipper on her suitcase. After fiddling with it for several seconds she enlisted Reese's assistance. Bernie had wandered off in search of John Grisham novels. Reese bent over the suitcase, lost in an anxious miasma caused by the hazards of getting his geriatric parents to the gate before takeoff. Betsy, perceiving the malfunctioning zipper as yet another tragedy in her life, grew sullen while complaining of Bernard's disappearance. Only then did Reese realize that Clara too had disappeared. "Maybe they're together," Betsy said, but Reese knew this to be unlikely as Bernie's interest in the four-year-old was limited to the condition of her ears and throat. With white noise pressing in on him, Reese began calling her name, first loudly and then louder. As his terror became increasingly public he dreaded the involvement of strangers, the appeal to people in authority in whom he had no trust. Loudspeakers. The call to Roberta. Wanting to run but with no idea to where, he stood surrounded by pedestrian conversations, announcements, the mundane rolling on of a world that was irrevocably changed. Every second took her further away from him. He imagined her screams as she realized she was being taken from Mummy and Daddy. He imagined child slavery, pornography, sacrifice. Only then did he remember her fascination with escalators. In an instant, he had checked the down and found her on the up, smiling proudly. He did, of course, chide her for wandering off, but all he wanted was to hold her, forever. On the orange couch he tells himself that his current loss is not irrevocable. She is in bed, sleeping soundly, hugging the stuffed dog with the squiggly tail.

His mouth tastes of ashes. He finds a glass in the kitchen and drinks tap water, savouring the chlorine. The bathroom light is on. Out of habit he attempts to switch it off but then sees that she's in there, pulling out bottles of pills from the medicine cabinet and lining them along the sink.

"What are you doing?" Reese asks.

"I have a headache."

"You don't need all those."

"I don't know what half of them are. Lance was always taking them. He had pills for everything. I was hoping there was something with codeine in it." She swallows several pills.

"Is that the suggested dosage?" Reese asks.

She opens another bottle and takes more pills.

"I think that's too many," Reese says.

She opens another bottle. "That's awesome that you saved that woman, especially with her being Muslim. Her kid would just look like a mini suicide bomber to me." She swallows more pills. "Did you know that their idea of heaven is being surrounded by little boys and girls they can screw? That's what they're told will happen after they blow themselves up. One big fucking kiddie orgy." She starts to swallow more pills.

"You have to stop that," he says.

"Why?"

"Because it won't kill you. It'll just make you sick."

"It's not me I want to kill." She opens another bottle. "I figure a cocktail's the way to go."

He grabs the bottle from her and sweeps the remaining bottles to the floor.

"That was macho," she says, bending down to pick them up.

"Why are you doing this?"

"None of your fucking business. Who the fuck are you, anyway, some weirdo who howls because his wife turfed him. I felt sorry for you. Don't go thinking you can do numbers on me."

"That won't kill it," he tells her. "Pills will only brain-damage it. Or cause deformity."

"What do *you* know about it? You don't know shit. Don't bother me." Clutching the bottles with one arm, she starts shoving him out of the room. He braces himself against the door jamb, knowing that if she gets him out she can lock the door.

"I've seen those children," he says. "My wife was interested in adopting a child no one wanted. We saw tapes of children whose mothers took drugs, smoked, drank. Some were blind, retarded, had misshapen skulls."

"It's not a child, okay?"

"What is it then?"

"A fucking disaster."

"Then do it right. Go to a clinic." He knows that he has no right to interfere, that it is her body, her life, but the thought of the toxins seeping through the placenta, crippling and blinding, makes him hold his ground in front of the door. "I worked with a couple who couldn't have a baby. They tried everything, hormones, test tubes. Conception's not a disaster."

They hear a dog barking, racoons snarling, and a domestic dispute between the parents of the delinquent garbage-producing boys. "I'll fucking leave now!" the husband shouts. "You fucking do that!" the wife shouts back. Reese gently removes the bottles from Katrina's grasp. "Do you feel like dancing?" he asks. "Do you think you could show me your sashay?"

"Are you nuts?"

"Abortion clinics aren't open this late."

She lets him lead her like a child into the living room where he moves the coffee table and pushes the orange couch against the wall. He puts on the CD she bought from Edwina Pendleton, which features the music of "Edelweiss" arranged as a waltz. "It's three-quarter time," he tells her.

"Like I don't know that."

"How do you want to start?"

She stands without moving for several seconds, staring at his plastic sandals.

Edelweiss, Edelweiss, every morning you greet me.

"I feel like shit," she says.

"Maybe we should try the forward and backwards steps first," he suggests, "before we attempt the box step." He takes her hands, which feel hot, and he remembers the heat of Roberta when she was pregnant, how she would fling the duvet from the bed. "Gents start with the left," he says.

"Duh."

"Remember to shift weight on every step."

"Don't fucking tell me what to do, alright!"

Small and white, clean and bright...

She allows him to lead. She feels different to him, breakable. They step slowly, as though medicated. He hopes that the movement will cause her to vomit. He tries not to think about the damage she may have done to the life inside her.

Bloom and grow forever.

"Head up," he says.

20

"Can I help you with anything?" a lipsticked, large-bosomed saleswoman asks him.

"I'm looking for a gift for my mother."

"Isn't that nice. Would this be for her birthday?"

"Yes. Usually I buy her china."

She nods understandingly. "You're looking for a change."

"Yes." It gives him some comfort that abortion clinics aren't open on weekends.

"We have some wonderful Mexican glass. Does she enjoy wine?"

"Gin and tonic, actually." He follows her past shelves of useless items made cheap in Third World countries. He should not have entered a store called Gifts 'n Things. His hands feel like his own again and he has not heard from Mrs. Ranty, Scout Leader Igor, or Mrs. Stinkman. But his body, wasted from a ceaseless yearning for his children — and waiting to hear from Gwyneth Proudley — has lost its dependability. Without warning a knee or an ankle will buckle beneath him.

"These are hand-blown," the saleswoman says, pointing to the Mexican glass. She reminds him of one of his high school teachers, a constantly smiling woman who never made sense. He would listen and watch her lips move but absorb nothing. "Or how about some artwork? A nice framed print?" If he could convey to Katrina the smell of death in the abortion clinic. If he could describe the aftermath, the unending grief; Elena bleeding on the bed. "Cowboy is very in right now," the saleswoman says. "We have some cowboy prints that look fabulous in those tricky areas. I put one in my vestibule. It really brightens things up." Reese stares at the cowboy prints. Brightly coloured, they do not resemble cowboys. "They're abstract," the saleswoman explains. She points to some angular shapes. "Those are horses." She points to other angular shapes. "And these are cowboys." Time is running out and he has no present.

"I would like to give her something useful," Reese says.

"Useful?" The woman's red lips contract.

"Something that she can use," he clarifies.

Apparently perplexed, she cocks her head slightly. "You mean … like a napkin holder?" She displays something wiry and beaded. "This is terrific on a table, and doesn't take up too much visual space." The radio barks that the dead bodies of nine Afghani children have been uncovered from a compound flattened in a bungled U.S. air strike. Reese grabs at some paperweights. "Aren't those lovely?" the saleswoman asks. "I especially like the ones containing wildflowers." The ex-wife who was abducted at knifepoint has been seen buying feminine hygiene products. The police believe her to be in great danger. A boy was beaten and stabbed to death by several other boys who took turns kicking his head. "Or a vase," the woman says. "You can't go wrong with a vase." Reese has been trying to think of a good argument for allowing the baby to live in a world rife with horror.

"These are inlaid glass. It gives that stained glass effect without the cost. It looks marvellous with long-stemmed roses." The Americans want to put a man on the moon again despite their deficit of trillions. They want to put a man on the moon again because the Chinese are going to put a man on the moon. What happens when China stops buying America's debt? The saleswoman is thrusting candle holders at him. "These are from India, they do wonderful brass."

He still has the ultrasounds. He found them in the back of a drawer as he was packing to leave the house that was once his. Grainy images showing mottled, shadowy figures with big heads and spindly limbs.

After viewing the tapes of the unwanted children, Roberta became speechless in the car. One child's skull was misshapen not because of what her mother had done to her in the womb but because her father had beaten her head repeatedly. A fourteen-year-old girl who'd been force-fed salt by her mother and raped by her father begged to be adopted. "I just want a family," she said tearfully. Some of the younger children affected by prenatal substances appeared normal but potential parents were advised that problems would ensue. It was a lifetime commitment, they emphasized.

"I don't think I can do it," Roberta said finally.

"Me neither," Reese agreed.

And yet here he is, hoping to save a life that may already be lost.

"What is it?" Betsy asks.

"A cowboy print. Cowboy is very in right now. I thought it might brighten up your vestibule." Betsy looks closely at the print as though deciphering its hidden meaning. Reese rolls his neck. "I figured you had more than enough of Olde English Rose." Betsy holds the print at arm's length and squints at it. "I can return it," he says. "They have all kinds of things in this store."

She starts to wrap the print up again. "I'm going to save it. I want a whole new look for the condo. I like the cowboy idea. That Tex-Mex look, maybe get some Mexican rugs. Bernard doesn't like colour. All my life I've lived beige."

"Did he call today?"

"To make sure I'm picking up the junk mail. He's worried I'll leave it on the porch and we'll get robbed. 'Help yourself,' I'll tell the robbers."

Bernie has never bothered with her birthday.

Reese takes her to Swiss Chalet because she wants barbecued chicken. She says that's another thing you can buy in the mall under the condo.

"Dad isn't dead yet, Mum."

"Who said he was?"

"Does that mean you're planning to take him with you to the condo?"

She arranges a napkin over her lap. "Maddy has a corner suite with *two* balconies."

"What about Dad?"

"What about him?"

"You can't buy a condo unless you sell the house. You can't sell the house unless you *both* move to the condo."

Betsy tears a roll into small pieces. "You don't know what it's like living with him."

"I have some idea."

She dips a piece of the roll in the barbecue sauce. "I don't want him back. Too much work."

Reese has always imagined that beneath the turbulence of his parents' marriage ran a current of devotion. "Mum, he lives there. That's his home."

"Why can't he stay at the hospital?"

"Because it's a hospital."

"What about a home? He'd be happier in a home. He could bore people with his jokes." Why on earth didn't his parents divorce after Chelsea died? What bound them other than the shared duties of maintaining her room? Betsy stopped cooking, which meant they no longer sat down to dinner. To eliminate tensions over viewing rights, Reese bought Betsy a TV for her bedroom. Perhaps that was a mistake, perhaps if they'd been forced to fight over *The Young and the Restless* versus WWE wrestling, they would have separated and found new resources elsewhere. As it was they became too depleted to move beyond their front door. Betsy began referring to the characters in *The Young and the Restless* as personal friends.

"I dreamed about Pierre Trudeau last night," she says.

"How was he?"

"We were dancing. I've never understood what he saw in that

guitar player with the hair." She dips another piece of roll before reverting to informing him of the dead and dying. Her neighbour with bowel cancer who is having more of his gut cut out. And her hairdresser suffers pain in the shower, can't tolerate the pressure of the water against her skin. "It turns out it's the thyroid medication," Betsy announces. "The doctors have been poisoning her with thyroid medication. *Poisoning* her. Now they say her blood cells are oval instead of round. They say it could be that thing with the blood, what's that called?"

"Leukemia?"

"It could be that. Nice woman, looks the picture of health." She picks at more fries. "Maddy's got pains in her joints. She gets massages. I'd like to try that. This fellow comes to the condo. He's coloured but she says he's very nice."

This eagerness of his mother to ditch his not-yet-dead father creates a general feeling of bloodlessness in Reese. "You can have a masseur over with Dad in the house."

"He'd kick up a fuss. 'Massage is for massage parlours,' he'd say."

"Who cares what he says?"

She drains her gin and tonic, dabs at her mouth with her napkin then rearranges it on her lap. "He cheated on me. I never told you because I didn't think you needed to know. But that's how it is."

"You mean with Verna Petty?" Reese assumes this is just another of his mother's fabrications.

"Not her. Long ago. She was a drug rep. He was always getting free samples from her. They were in his office humping, that's the truth of it."

"How do you know this?"

"He knocked her up. Mercy Mayers. A mousy thing, thought he was some kind of genius because he cut out her ingrown toenail."

There is too much information coming at Reese too fast, and too little blood in his body. He pushes his plate aside, puts his elbows on the table, and rests his head in his hands.

"No elbows on the table," she says.

"I'm not feeling very well."

"Eat something. It's your blood sugar."

"I still don't understand how you could know all this."

"Because he wanted me to adopt it," she says as though this were obvious. "Mercy was scared of getting rid of it, coat hangers and whatnot. She was hoping he'd leave me and take her on. She didn't know what a selfish bugger he was. He likes his comforts, a faithful wife who finds him socks and underwear. Besides, he figured if Mercy was messing around with him there was no guarantee she wouldn't do it with somebody else. Did we order coleslaw? I like the coleslaw here."

Reese tries to get the attention of the Filipina who's carrying many dirty plates.

"And another drink," his mother says.

He manages to stand and pursue the Filipina. She speaks limited English but he thinks he makes himself understood. When he resumes his seat, his mother looks intently at him. Her smeared lipstick is working its way into the wrinkles above her lip. "Sometimes you've just got to let it go, son. Let it go, otherwise you burn your wagons."

"What happened to the baby?"

"Bernie did the abortion. That was the end of Mercy."

"You mean he killed her?"

"Heavens no, just no more hanky-panky."

The image of his father pushing metal instruments into the vagina of the woman carrying his baby, dilating her cervix and scraping out the fetus while the woman, gassed, moves in and out of consciousness, creates a heaviness of limb in Reese. He slouches against the banquette and stares up at the ceiling tiles which he knows are off-gassing toxic chemicals.

"I didn't want to tell you," his mother says. "But you're a grown man now. I just didn't want you thinking I owe him any favours."

The waitress sets down the gin and the coleslaw. Reese watches his mother drink and chew. Shreds of cabbage dangle from her lips. How is she not an accomplice in the murder? What was she doing while Bernie was dilating and curetting? Eating

Crispy Crunches? Did she think she was protecting Chelsea and himself from a bastard sibling? How would they have known unless it was explained to them? It could have been an adopted child, just another sibling for Reese to torture. It might have grown into an ally for Chelsea. His little sister might not have felt so alone, so despised. She might not have died of cancer.

"I've upset you," his mother says.

"I'm alright."

"People do strange things. No point making yourself sick over it."

Reese felt touched that Holden wanted to be his friend, but judging from the invitees of the party, Holden wants everybody to be his friend. Sterling corners Reese to tell him about his trip to Las Vegas to visit his friend Darren who performs as Elvis at the Stratosphere Hotel and Casino. Darren took him backstage to meet the original Elvis band members who were backing up Greg Page. "That alone was worth the trip," Sterling says. "A dream come true." He drinks more of Holden's punch.

"They must have been old," Reese says. Avril Leblanc is here but hasn't acknowledged him. He doesn't know if this is because he killed a terrorist.

"Who?" Sterling asks.

"Elvis's band."

Sterling sucks in his gut. "Age is a state of mind, boyo. You've been looking pretty antiquated yourself lately."

Reese visited Bernie, who was unconscious. He wanted to grill him about Mercy Mayers. About killing a baby. He wanted to shout at him, hit him. The massive-thighed, lemon-sucking nurse said Bernard was doing well on dialysis, that he was enjoying the attention of the nurses. She said this as though sharing a joke with Reese.

"You've got to see my fifties-style diner's booth," Sterling says. "I even put down black and white floor tiles. I've got *two* commercial turntables, *two* jukeboxes, and scads of rock and roll and Coca Cola memorabilia." He gyrates his pelvis. "My ex hated the stuff, it's been sitting in boxes waaay too long."

A karaoke machine has been hooked up to the television, which displays the words to the songs. Nick Dizon is singing "I Left My Heart in San Francisco." Before this Sterling was crooning "Don't Be Cruel." What makes singing in front of strangers universally appealing? A giddiness occurs, far away looks, wavering voices. No one becomes violent while singing off-key. Could peace on earth be found if karaoke machines were available to the masses?

Katrina wasn't home. She's working at the topless bar, exposing her unborn to the basest of human urges. Reese doesn't want to think about how she must position her near-naked body to earn tips.

To prevent an anxiety attack due to not hearing from Gwyneth Proudley, and to find distraction from his ceaseless yearning for his children, he did test a mattress briefly — a Simmons Beautyrest Enthuse. He'd just eaten a Wunderbar and had ejected the wrapper outside the store. What had been marketed as "a peanut and caramel experience" left him hyper. He twitched while Mary Jane Lovering advised him that the queen mattress set, regularly priced at $2799, was on sale for $1399 Saturday and Sunday only. Attracted by the price Reese tried the Enthuse, lying on his back as suggested in the article. His hand slid easily between the mattress and his lower back, which he knew meant the mattress was too firm. Mary Jane Lovering watched him with revulsion. "If you purchase the set and have it delivered," she grumbled, "we'll give you a discount equivalent to the cost of standard local delivery."

A woman displaying cleavage and a large tongue, singing "New York, New York," catches Sterling's attention. Reese moves to the punch bowl to look engaged. A blonde showing black roots in tight jeans and what looks like a plastic T-shirt is anxiously mopping up spilled punch with a soaked napkin. Her body seems to resent containment and escapes wherever possible.

"I think you need another one of those," Reese says, looking around.

"This always happens to me," the woman says. Reese finds a

Zellers napkin in his back pocket and mops up the punch.

"I don't usually go to parties," the woman confides. "My counsellor says I have to go out more, make my own friends. She says that's all part of the healing."

"From what are you healing?"

"My husband." She slaps her forehead with her palm. "See, that's what the counsellor's talking about. I keep blaming him. It takes two to tango, right?" She eats several pretzels. "He's been way better since the restraining orders. That and being detained. That totally humiliated him. He said the cops threw an Egg McMuffin at him." She eats more pretzels. "It's not about *me*. I have to forgive. That's what I learned in church. The counsellor wants me to leave him. She says, 'He drags you around by the hair, calls you dirty, why would you want him back?' She doesn't understand. That's okay. I forgive her."

"You said 'restraining orders.' Were there more than one?"

She nods. "Every month I'd see the judge and say I wasn't ready."

"Did you have to say why?"

"No way. He put me in hospital, gave me a cardiac arrest. He made me so stressed I got a stomach ulcer." She slaps her forehead again. "There I go again. It's not about *me*."

"Who is it about?"

"He's really trying now. He even takes the kids in his truck sometimes." She wipes her hands on her jeans. "There is no such thing as the perfect man. I learned that in church."

"Is it easy to get a restraining order?" Reese asks.

"Sure. Just say he's abusive."

"You don't have to prove it?"

"I know a woman who gets restraining orders even though her husband's never hit her. Meanwhile she's getting most of his pay. Last I heard she was scootering in Bermuda with some guy."

Reese suspects that Roberta is within easy reach of a restraining order — that soon he will be in a prison being pelted with Egg McMuffins. He notices Nick Dizon speaking intensely with

Avril Leblanc. She looks smaller, weaker, in need of rescue from the alpha male. "Excuse me," Reese says to the blonde who is slapping her forehead again.

"Reeso, the man, wha's happenin'?"

"Hello," Reese says.

"So I got out my pick and shovel," Nick continues, turning back to Avril, "and lowered the level four to six inches. That was some workout. Next I levelled it with roadbed material, compacted it then lay, *single-handedly*, three thousand inter-locking bricks."

Reese suspects that Nick is hoping to impress Avril with his connections to the Earth. "What's wrong with grass?" Reese asks.

Nick drinks more of the Sleemans he must have brought because no one else is drinking any. "We're talking landscaping here."

"I'm talking grass in landscaping," Reese says, "chlorophyll, oxygen. The First Peoples didn't require interlocking bricks." He hopes for a shared look with Avril, a wan smile.

"Let me ask you something," Nick says, "do you sleep better being so fucking negative?" Reese has never heard Nick use such an expletive before. Nick is a model of self-control and salesman-ship. He is not wearing his usual coordinated sock and tie arrangement but jeans and a V-necked sweatshirt, which reveals his hairy chest. "Because it's *fucking* tedious. We're just trying to have a life here, share a few laughs."

"Laughing is difficult when you can't breathe."

"If it happens, it happens, alright. Who gives a fuck?"

Reese notices a heightened redness to Nick's complexion. "It won't just happen," he says. "It is happening. Global warming is killing off hundreds of thousands of people. The death toll will double in the next thirty years."

"Listen to him, are you hearing me? We *don't care!* People like you fuck with progress."

"All that freaky weather in the news, you know droughts, floods, ice storms, avalanches. It's all due to radical shifts in the way heat circulates around the planet."

"Somebody turn him off," Nick says, "or I'm going to do it."

Reese leans closer to him. "What part of the Hotter-Planet-equals-Worse-Air-plus-More-Air-Conditioning-equals-Hotter-Planet-which-makes-Worse-Air equation don't you get, boyo?"

Nick grasps the air as though about to grab Reese's throat.

"Nick," Avril intervenes. "*I* care."

"You do?" Reese asks, feeling a torrent of affection for her.

"It's wrong, Nick. It's not about us."

Nick, considerably redder, points his finger at Reese. "Fucks like you have caused me problems my whole life." He continues jabbing the air with his finger. Reese remembers being confronted in a similar manner during an anti-war demonstration. The father of a soldier who'd been a victim of friendly fire broke a "Honk for Peace" sign over Reese's head. Reese hopes that Nick Dizon will express similar aggression, knock him unconscious, which would free him of thought but also, perhaps, cause Avril Leblanc to cradle his head in her arms.

"Looks to me like somebody's opening a can of whoop-ass," Sterling observes.

"Stop!" Avril says. "Just *stop!*" Her voice sounds shrill, no longer honeyed by herbal tea. She spins away from them, into the Jerry Lee Lewis fans who shake around her. Reese considers following her as he has seen Fred follow Ginger. They meet on balconies and have meaningful tête-à-têtes. Marge is pulling on his sleeve. "Lovely party," she says. "I don't get out much. Too many people dead these days." She sips more punch. "Shouldn't be doing this, terrible for digestion." Reese hears the theme for *Mission: Impossible.* It's Nick Dizon's cellphone. He takes the call, losing interest in Reese. Sterling joins the woman with the cleavage and large tongue.

"Do you have children, Marge?" Reese asks.

"Oh yes."

"Do you miss them?"

"Not particularly."

"I miss mine constantly."

"That's because they're little. They turn nasty when they're older." Does his mother regard him with similar disaffection — the nasty son who won't let her buy the condo above the mall with the chocolate store?

For a brief instant, when Avril said that she did care, Reese felt as elated as he'd felt when chosen to star in his kindergarten play about healthy eating. Miss Seabrook selected him to be the boy who wouldn't eat his vegetables. All the other kindergarteners had to play the vegetables and convince him that they were better to eat than hot dogs. It had so surprised Reese to be chosen. He'd felt a general tingling. But now, with Avril lost among the shaking bodies, the tingling ebbs. There is only Marge, stinking of shit. "What are your thoughts on abortion?" he asks her.

"Are we going to be raising money for abortions?"

"No. It's just I have a friend ..."

She nods knowingly. "I see."

"No, it's not like that. We're just friends."

"Of course."

He has no idea why he is blurting in this manner. Sterling is shaking close to the large-tongued woman with cleavage. He clutches her buttocks.

"It was an accident," Reese explains. "She split up with her boyfriend."

"I don't think it's too difficult these days. They have a sort of vacuum cleaner."

In the mattress store a parched couple was also testing a Beautyrest Enthuse. The parched woman was concerned about feeling her husband's movement in the bed. "I'm *feeling* you," she said. "I shouldn't be *feeling* you."

"What kind of bed do you sleep on, Marge?"

"Oh, something or other. I've had it fifty years."

"You shared it with your husband?" Here, at last, is a love story. The devoted widow who never remarried.

"Which one?"

"Which what?"

"Which husband?"

Serge Hollyduke appears, looking shipwrecked. "Is she

here?"

"Who, dear?" Marge asks.

"Avril."

"She was."

"Where did she go?"

"The powder room, perhaps."

He turns on Reese. "*You* know where she is."

"I don't. Wish I did."

"Why? So you can stuff her? Talk about *Indians*? You fucking hypocrite."

Holden offers hot dogs. "There's nothing like a steamy," he says. Reese takes one and has to admit that there is nothing like a steamy. Bernie used to buy him one occasionally from a street vendor. Father and son would stand on the sidewalk, united in their chewing.

"Everybody wants to try out for *Canadian Idol*," Holden says. "I think that's sad."

"Have you seen Avril?" Reese asks.

"She's on the fire escape. What's biting Serge? Frankly, I think Commando Hollyduke would benefit from some pharmaceuticals." Ketchup drips from his steamy onto the carpet.

Avril sits cross-legged, very still, with eyes closed. Reese realizes that she is being with what is and that he has no business being with her unless he too can be with what is. But "what is" is so huge, so insurmountable, so wrong, he can't just be with it. He wants to tear it apart with his hands, his teeth. He wants to kick the shit out of it.

He doesn't see Katrina at first. Women naked except for thongs push past him. Fetid air burns his eyes. All the tables are occupied by slouching men, many of them alone, awaiting special treatment from the dancers. Reese, sickened but forced to stand, feels a knee about to buckle. He no longer sits, is always moving. He used to sit, when he had children. He would come home from work and sit with them and inquire about their day. They would say, "I forget." Derek would bond with his Game Boy. Eventually

Clara would ask, "How was *your* day?" Reese would pretend that he hadn't felt defeated by the previous nine hours, frightened by a world so intent on self-destruction. Roberta would have turned on all the lights. She felt unsafe unless every room was illuminated regardless of whether or not she intended to use it. He would turn off several, giving Derek the opportunity to shout, "How am I supposed to *see?*"

He secures a vacant chair beside a frowning fat man who is speaking to a smiling skinny man. The skinny man nods continuously as the fat man talks. "Do you mind if I sit here?" Reese asks.

"I don't own it," the fat man says.

Reese checked on Katrina this morning, to make sure she was breathing. Asleep, she had the smooth face of a child. Her leg was poking out from under the sheets, revealing her butterfly tattoo. What would it be like to have a mother with a butterfly on her ankle and a dragon on her thigh? What would it be like to watch the mother's skin age and the tattoos lose their edges? What makes him think Katrina is fit to be a mother? What if she becomes involved with a man who enjoys beating children's heads? What makes him think the baby would be better off alive than dead? He removed anything remotely lethal from her apartment, bicycled with bottles of bleach and Drano in plastic bags dangling from his handlebars. He pushed them into a dumpster outside an apartment building. An old man in slippers chased after him, shouting, "That's against the law!" Reese did not turn back. Like the worst of mankind, he was dumping in someone else's backyard.

He sees her, tinged red from the lights, distributing pints of draft to the slouching men who stare at her breasts. Breasts that embarrass Reese, that should be restrained and not flopping around. Breasts that should be reserved for the mouths of babes. He wishes he were driving a streetcar. He often fantasizes about driving a streetcar, having his wheels in tracks. "The boss leaves this note telling me to make clam chowder," the fat man beside him says. "I hate the stuff. It always separates. He's not around so I figure I'll make tomato." The skinny man continues nodding and smiling. "Only it turns out there's not enough tomato," the fat man says. "So I look in the fridge and, what d'you know, there's chicken noodle left over from yesterday. So I toss it in with the tomato and buzz it." The skinny man appears shocked and stops smiling briefly. "I've never gotten so many compliments on soup. 'What'd you put in it?' the customers kept asking me. 'Chef's secret,' I told them." The cook snorts while repeating "Chef's secret," several times. Like a politician he has pulled a fast one. How did we arrive at lies? Or has lying and cheating been business as usual since civilization began, only more visible now because of the communication age? When Reese told Derek and Clara that women lost their lives fighting to get the vote, Derek, playing *Grand Theft Auto*, said, "What's so great about voting?" Which made Reese consider his own methodology — vote for the least detestable candidate in the hopes of preventing the election of the most detestable. He feels no excitement at the voting booth, no hope of change. The ones who speak of change before the election inevitably have different views once in office, feigning surprise about the size of deficits and blaming the previous government for bungling finances. In the end, it is the same wealthy oligarchy who rules.

Katrina asks the fat and skinny men if they want anything else. She hasn't noticed Reese and tries to ignore the fat and skinny men who are ogling her breasts as she collects empty glasses. Sparks shoot through Reese. "A couple more drafts, angel tits," the cook says, copping a feel as though he were testing a melon. She slaps his hand and he apologizes with mock sincerity. "I didn't do it on purpose," he says. Reese is on him in an instant. He clings to his balding, seborrheic head, which is sweaty and therefore slippery. The skinny man begins to squeal. Reese tries to hook his legs around the cook.

"What are you doing here?" Katrina demands.

It's like scaling a mountain, but there is no rock underfoot, only blubber. The cook grabs Reese's hands and yanks them off his head. "This your boyfriend?"

"Get serious," Katrina says.

A large-gutted man with biceps appears to escort Reese off the premises. "It's a strip joint, buddy," he says. "You might want to stick to the Keg."

Reese thinks of streetcars going around and around. Would Roberta approve if he became a streetcar driver? He dreamed of Gwyneth Proudley again last night. She was an old lady. When he shook her hand, he crushed her bones. He apologized profusely but knew that she would assume that, if he could crush her bones, he could molest his daughter.

One of the last conversations Reese had with Clara was about aliens. Sidona at school had told her that they did exist.

"How does she know?" Reese asked.

"She has a photograph. They have big heads and kidnap you."

"It couldn't have been a real photograph," Reese said. "There are no aliens." As with ghosts, he didn't know this to be true but didn't want frightening visions flourishing in his daughter's imagination.

"It *was* real. It has all kinds of eyes. She said it can see everywhere."

"They use computers to make things look real," he explained. "It's digital."

She said no more and he knew that she doubted his word. He'd run into conflict with Sidona's word before regarding heaven and hell. Sidona's parents were churchgoers, as was Sidona. "There is no heaven or hell," Reese told Clara but she looked away, as her mother does.

What life could the baby possibly have, surrounded by fetid air and men who lie? Better dead than tolerated, strapped to various devices. A baby died in a car seat. The father, late for work, forgot to drop the baby off at daycare. On a day of smog alerts, he turned off the air conditioning, failing to notice his sleeping infant.

Better dead than forgotten.

"Do you buy that line about marrying your mother?" Bob Vinkle asks.

"Not really." Reese is on his second beer. He littered again on his way here, even tried to kick over a trash can, but it was securely tethered to a parking sign.

"Because I hate my mother," Bob says. "But then I got to thinking about it and figured out I hate Alicia."

"Doesn't your mother hate Alicia?"

"That's right. So what's that about? If I hate my mother *and* I hate Alicia?"

Alicia appeared in court on Friday to lay charges. She arrived late, providing Bob with the opportunity to hope that she'd forgiven him. She did not look at him. "It was like I did-n't fucking exist," Bob said. He has been planning the mouse infestation.

"Maybe it's true about the mother thing," he says.

"Stop making excuses, Robert," Linden says.

"Do you hate your wife, Lindy?"

"No."

"Not even when she's like … psycho?"

"Not even."

"That's romantic," Bob says, before turning to Reese. "What about you? Do you ever hate her?"

"Frequently."

"That's more normal," Bob declares. "See, I don't buy this long-term devotion crap. Like, who came up with that one? It's a control thing, right? Keep us paying our mortgages for our women. It's bullshit."

"Some people enjoy sharing a history," Linden says.

"That's true," Reese agrees. "Some people don't like starting over." Himself, for instance.

"That's a chickenshit attitude," Bob says. "That's *fear*, brother, right there. Fear of the unknown. Life's about challenges. There's this dating service for nature lovers, you go for walks and shit, look at birds. I'm thinking I'll check it out."

"I didn't know you loved nature, Robert," Linden says.

"I want a down-to-earth girl, none of this it's-got-to-be-Prada bullshit. I want, like, somebody who can be a friend."

"Who you also want to fuck in half," Linden suggests.

Kyla, scowling, orders two Jack Daniels.

"It's not about sex," Bob protests. "It's the soulmate thing."

"You've been watching *The Bachelor*," Linden says. "Soon you'll be listening to your heart."

Bob pours the Jack Daniels. "So this New York millionaire killed his wife then left town disguised as a mute woman. One night he's in a bar, lights up a cigarette, and sets his wig on fire. Is that not gorgeous? Next he skips bail, flees to Philadelphia, and gets arrested for shoplifting a sandwich and some Band-Aids even though he's got $523 U.S. in his pocket plus forty thousand greenbacks in his car."

"Are you planning to kill your wife, Robert?"

Bob doesn't respond so Linden repeats the question.

"I went by the house," Bob admits. "And I keyed that asshole's Toyota."

"Now that's constructive," Linden says.

"It felt great. Next I do the tires."

"Robert, you're under house arrest."

"I want to kill that bitch, I'm not kidding, I want to fucking *kill* her!" His vehemence surprises even Bob. Linden picks up the photo of Hilary and waves it in front of Bob's face. Bob turns away and starts loading beers into the fridge. Kyla, expressionless, orders two Heinekens and places the Jack Daniels on her tray.

"Bob," Reese asks after what feels like an interminable silence, "do you ever go to topless bars?"

Bob shakes his head while popping the caps off the Heinekens.

"I know somebody who works in one," Reese mutters. "I don't want her to."

"Does *she* want to?" Linden inquires.

"Bob, could you use her here?"

"She'd make less money."

"She's pregnant," Reese blurts. Bob and Linden both look at him then away. Bob shakes his head sadly.

"It's not like that," Reese explains. "She's a friend."

"A nature lover?" Linden asks.

Bob dries some glasses. "What's it to you where she works then?"

"I don't think it's a good place for a baby."

"This may surprise you," Linden says, "but it can't see."

"That's not the point."

"The truth is, brother, training somebody then having her go off and have a baby is not good business. I had a pregnant cook once. The fumes dried up her amniotic fluid, I had to give her time off. After the kid was born it got even worse. Kyla's kid's always got something wrong with it. Don't get me wrong, she's a great waitress. I just don't want more hassles."

"You expect your wife to drop charges against you for breaking into her home," Reese says, "and yet you won't hire a pregnant woman?"

"Where's your compassion?" Linden says.

"What's she doing working in a bar anyway?"

"She wants to be on Broadway. She sings and dances." Again both Bob and Linden look at him then away.

"A pregnant Rockette," Linden says.

"Her great-aunt was in the first production of *Hair*."

Like a bartender in a movie with a dishtowel draped over his shoulder, Bob leans on the bar. "Are you in love with this girl?"

"No." He can see that Bob doesn't believe him.

"Because, if you're in love with her, I'll give her a job."

"Why won't you give her a job anyway?"

"You know how many people *apply*? People with *restaurant* experience? This girl's used to showing her jugs and passing out beers. What's she know about handling food?"

Linden holds a peanut between his thumb and forefinger. "There's not a lot to know, Robert."

"Forget it," Reese says.

"She can have a job. If a shift comes up. There's nothing going right now, but Kyla's kid's bound to get bird flu or something."

A regular named Vito leans over the bar to present Bob with a wedding invitation. It's a photo of Vito and his bride-to-be standing beside a convertible in front of Casa Loma. "You better be there, hombre," Vito says.

"Wouldn't miss it for the world, buddy." Bob places the card on the bar while he pours more beers for Kyla. In the photo Vito stands with his arm around his fiancée while she smiles meekly. They're both in jeans, he with a spreading gut, she with an ample behind. They will only expand once married, eating regular meals and reproducing. "Is that his car?" Reese inquires.

"Shit, no, that's a Jag he borrowed for the shot."

"He's got the car and the woman," Linden says.

"It's not *his* car," Bob repeats.

"It's symbolic, Robert."

Bob adjusts his surgical stockings. "You know what gets me is on the day I really thought it was forever. I mean, you got to think that, right? Why else would you do it?"

"Because everyone else is," Linden says.

"Not everybody. There's all kinds of singles out there."

"Social lepers."

"*I* believe it's forever," Reese says.

"How d'you figure that?" Bob asks.

"She knows me, all my faults. There's nowhere to go but

up." They both wanted children. She'd been through two near marriages that had stalled due to her eagerness to procreate. They talked at length about children and agreed on how they should be raised. They agreed until the boy tried to strangle his sister. "*I* tried to strangle my sister," Reese argued in an attempt to stop the drugging of his son. "I even tried to suffocate her with a pillow. Once I tried to get her to swallow a marble." Roberta stared into the darkness of his soul.

"Is that a reason to stay married?" Bob asks. "Because she knows all your faults? You are jaded, brother."

"*Your* faults were a surprise to Alicia, I gather," Linden says.

"Alicia has high standards." He carefully sets the photo of Hilary back on the bar. "Speaking of lepers," he adds, "there's this colony in Iran where they're all missing hands and feet and noses, well guess what?"

Linden doesn't guess, so Reese asks. "What?"

"There's this couple in it who truly love each other. She's blind because leprosy ate up her eyelids and her eyeballs dried out. He's got no legs but he brushes her hair since she can't because she's got no fingers. He says he loves to touch her hair. And she says she loves it when he brushes her hair. Is that not romantic?"

"Romantic," Linden says.

"So it's possible, brothers. Do not despair."

"We're not despairing, Robert."

Outside the house that was once his Reese is confronted by the cat-walking man. "You again!" he almost shouts. "What're you doing here this time of night?"

"That's my house."

"I thought you said it *used* to be your house."

"It's still my house."

"Then why aren't you in it?"

"I needed some air."

"Go to bed like normal people." He pulls on the cat's leash. "Get a move on," he tells it, "I don't have all night." He takes several steps before turning back to Reese. "You're not that shoplifter, are you?"

"No."

"We don't want shoplifters around here. My neighbour sat on him till the cops came. This is a Neighbourhood Watch community. We don't put up with any monkey business."

"I'll go back in shortly."

"You do that." The man nor the cat move. Reese can hear the wheeze of the man's breathing. "You know what I think? I don't think you live there. I think you're planning a burglary. I think maybe I'll just walk on over there and ring the bell and tell whoever's in there about you."

"No. I'm going in."

"Is that right? Well, we'll wait here and make sure you get in safe." The man and the cat stare at Reese. He steps as quietly as possible onto the porch while trying to appear as though he is not trying to step quietly. He turns the key and steps inside, standing away from the door window. After a moment he peeks out. Under the streetlight, the man waves at him. The cat rolls on its back in the grass.

It still smells of home. He wants to lie on the couch, reach for a magazine, eat some soy nuts. He looks out the window. The man waves again, smiling this time.

Two weathered women eating Zellers Tuscan Tuna specials were discussing the newly discovered body of the little girl who was abducted from her bedroom. "Who could have done such a thing?" one of them said. "What kind of *monster*?" A man who watches violent television, Reese wanted to blurt, and kiddie porn on the Net. A man who equates the abuse of power with pleasure. A man who only feels vital while destroying the vitality of others. A man like many others.

It wouldn't hurt to look at his children.

Once again the stairs squawk beneath him and Mickey glares. On the off chance that there might be a man in her bed, he looks in on Roberta. There is only the dog. Roberta's mouth gapes and he wonders if she has swallowed her mouth guard. He steps closer to ascertain that she's breathing. He contemplates shoving the mouth guard down her throat. Her arm jerks suddenly, as though shooing a fly. He remains so still he can hear the numbers changing on the clock radio. The room smells different. If he were a dog he could piss to reassert his territory. He backs out. Once in the hall he resumes breathing and thinks about taking his children to Bob Vinkle's fishing cabin. Bob offered Reese the use of it, said he used to fish up there before Alicia but Alicia hates bugs so he never goes. Reese imagines himself and the children canoeing. He could teach them how to paddle and Derek would admire him. It would be something father could pass down to son, away from urban hell. They would collect firewood and search for non-toxic mushrooms and fiddleheads. They would sit in the rain and watch droplets form circles on the lake. They would listen to the loons, which his children have only seen on the face of coins.

Clara is talking in her sleep and tapping her knee with her fist. "Saw it off," she says. The tapping turns to hitting. She is hitting her knee in her sleep. "Saw it off!" She has often talked in her sleep, sometimes uttering commands like "Move the wall over there!" Commands that made no sense to Reese but seemed logical in Clara's dreamscape. But he has never seen her hit herself before. Afraid to touch her for fear of waking her, he allows the knee-pounding to continue until it becomes evident that she may cause herself harm. He grabs her wrist and holds it steady while stroking her forehead with his other hand. He doesn't speak, hoping that she will think that he is Roberta, that she will not wake up and shout "Daddy!" He hears noises that could be Roberta picking up the phone and dialling 911, that could be Roberta ensuring that he will never see his children again. Already he feels Egg McMuffins pelting his skin. Clara calms and rolls onto her side, abruptly reaching for his hand. When they shared the futon they would hold hands in sleep. He would say, "Where's that paw?" and she would slip her hand into his. "Where's that paw?" she demands now, with eyes closed, and he has no choice but to take her hand. Her grip is firm but her hand still small, in need of protection, *his* protection. He kneels beside her, waiting for her grip to loosen, for his moment to escape.

He wakes feeling someone pulling on his hair. It is Clara making little braids all over his head. "What're you doing here?" she asks. "Is it morning yet?"

"Shhh, sweetie, how are you, baby?"

"Good."

"Were you dreaming?"

"I forget. Did you see what I made?" She jumps out of bed and turns on the light. "It's a dream catcher," she announces. "I made it at Sparks."

"That's great, sweetapple," he says. "But we don't want to wake anybody."

In seconds the barkless dog is barking and Roberta has Reese by the neck. "Get out!" she's shouting, digging her fingernails into his skin. When he has difficulty getting up she begins to kick him with her bare feet, jab him with her heels. Clara starts to scream. "Stop, Mummy! *Stop!*" Then Derek is at him, yanking on his arms and kicking him.

"She was having a nightmare," Reese explains. "She was hitting herself in her sleep." Roberta is pulling on his braids. Clara screams in a voice raw with pain and abandonment. "Stay Daddy, don't go, Daddy!" She grabs Roberta around the waist and tries to pull her from him. "I don't want him to go, Mummy, why does he have to *go?!*"

"Don't spaz out," her brother says.

"Why can't he stay, Mummy? I want Daddy! I want *Daddy!!*" Her face, a dangerous shade of red, is dripping with tears. The mother releases the father. The son, full of confused rage, continues to pummel Reese.

"Stop it, Derek," Roberta orders.

"It's alright," Reese says, trying to stroke Derek's forehead. When he was younger Reese could calm him by steadily, lovingly stroking his forehead. But the boy jerks his head away and continues to kick his legs. How did he come to hate him so? The power to resist leaves Reese. He drops his arms and welcomes the blows. He deserves no better.

"Stop it, Derek," Roberta repeats. It is the norm to have to ask him several times. "Stop it, Derek. *Now*. That's enough!"

"You're an asshole," the boy says, giving one last punch. Without their fury to hold him Reese slumps to the floor. Clara throws her arms around him and hides her face in his chest. He clings to her as a drowning man clings to wreckage. Around them is only sharks.

"How often have you been here?" Roberta asks. She has allowed him to sit on the back steps while the children eat breakfast. Two starlings have been collecting bits of dried grass in their beaks. They look suspiciously at Reese but do not flee from him. Their nest must be built, regardless of human dysfunction.

"Just to pick up the hamster," he says.

"You're lying."

"Why tell the truth, you don't believe me."

"I could have you arrested."

"I know."

"What were you doing in her room?"

"Holding her hand. She was hitting herself in her sleep. Hard. I was afraid she'd hurt herself. What do *you* do when she has nightmares? Do you hear her?"

"She doesn't usually have nightmares."

"All kids have nightmares."

"Oh, so suddenly you're the authority." Her wraparound skirt flaps in the breeze, showing a familiar thigh that has grown veins since he first knew it. During her pregnancies the veins became swollen and caused her pain. She lay like a tumbled Humpty Dumpty with her legs propped up against the wall.

"Do you really think," he asks, "that I could hurt her?"

"I think we should have her assessed."

The killing of baby seals has been made legal again. In his mind is bloodied ice.

"I don't understand why you hate me," he says.

"There's a lot you don't understand."

"Explain it to me."

"I tried, Reese, for twelve years." She covers her eyes with her hand to shield herself from him or the sun. "After I take them swimming, I want you out. And don't come back, or there'll be consequences." She has always issued this warning to the children *or there'll be consequences.*

"I'm dying without them," he says.

"I'll come to your funeral."

"Clara needs me."

"Children adapt, they *will* adapt if you stop interfering." She speaks with such conviction that he believes that yes, he has been interfering. Then he remembers that he hasn't even spoken to them. Clara pushes open the back door and climbs onto his lap. The feel of her, the weight of her, the softness of her hair against his cheek is balm to his tortured soul.

"Can you make us chicken, Daddy? We never have chicken anymore. Just the barbecued kind."

"Is everything in your backpack, Clara?" Roberta asks. "Towel, flip-flops?"

"Can Dad take us?"

"He has to go to work."

"It's Sunday," Clara says. "You should see my front crawl now, Daddy."

"I can take them swimming," Reese says.

"This," Roberta spits, "is exactly what I didn't want to have happen."

"Why can't he take us?" Clara asks. "Please …?" She begins to redden again, meaning that tears are pending.

"Mum's right," Reese says. "I've actually got some things to do."

"What things?"

"To do with work. Don't want my boss getting mad at me." He hugs her hard, disbelieving that he will be able to let her go. The starlings hop around them. He can't let her go. "I love you, sweetapple."

"I love you, Daddy. Can I come over to your place later? I don't mind that there's no furniture."

He can't let her go.

"Come on, kiddo," Roberta says. "Or we'll be late."

Clara releases her grip and kisses him on the lips, which has always irritated Roberta who believes that parents and children should kiss only on cheeks. Roberta holds out her hand and, for an instant, Reese thinks she is offering it to him. "Give me the keys," she says.

They drive away and he is left with the birds in a Chekhov play, with a burnt-out crater where his heart should be. *We must work, Uncle.* What good will he be to his children if he collapses in despair? What case can he plead if he allows himself to rot? The grass is covered in decaying leaves. He takes a rake from the shed and begins to form them into piles.

Katrina doesn't answer and the door is locked. He knows she's in there because the television is on. "I've got some wanton soup and some spring rolls," he says to the door. "I've never figured out why they call them spring rolls." The door opens suddenly.

"What do you want?" Her bathrobe has a dark stain down the front.

"What did you spill?" He wants to be sure it isn't blood.

"None of your fucking business. What do you want?"

"To make sure you're alright."

"Of course I'm alright."

"Do you want some soup?"

She grabs the bag from him and takes it to the kitchen. He follows, looking for evidence of a homestyle abortion. He's not sure what this would be; a coat hanger? turkey baster? bottle of gin? paint thinner?

"What's with your hair?" she asks without looking at him.

"Oh. My daughter braided it. She likes to braid."

"You saw your daughter?"

"Just briefly."

"I thought you weren't allowed to see her."

"I'm not."

"So you did something illegal."

He leans against the wall, feeling the weight of the house pressing against him.

"That's brilliant." She hands him one of the Styrofoam containers of soup and a plastic spoon.

"Please tell me if you did anything to the baby?"

"What baby?" She stares at him with eyes that have witnessed too many callous acts. "You almost got me fired."

"I'm sorry."

"Don't pull a stunt like that again." She takes her food into the living room. On television a fitness instructor is kicking up her knees to a sped-up version of *Pretty Woman*. She shouts "Awesome" and "Excellent." Katrina lies on the orange couch and chews on a spring roll. At least she's eating. "I hate Sundays," she says. "It's like everybody's waiting for Monday to happen. Saturday you can kind of forget about it."

With the orange couch occupied, Reese feels displaced. He slinks into an orange armchair. The springs are shot. He feels himself sinking. Minutes go by, maybe hours, certainly time passes because when he looks at her again she is no longer eating. "They caught that guy," she says, "who kidnapped his wife at knifepoint. I wonder what he did that made her hate him, I mean, before he kidnapped her."

"He probably wonders that too."

"They must've been hot for each other at some point."

"You'd think."

"I wouldn't mind," Katrina says, "meeting somebody and falling in love and all that. It never happens though. I just get tired of them. Maybe she was tired of him."

Reese has no doubt that Roberta is tired of him, after trying to explain "it" to him for twelve years. On TV, before and after photos of women who have had plastic surgery are displayed. A plastic surgeon with closely set eyes describes what he terms as not at all complicated procedures. "Some woman died," Katrina says. "Went in for a spring lift and had a cardiac arrest." She turns off the TV. "I hate doctors." She rolls onto her side and stares at him. Outside the garbage-producing delinquent boys are playing hockey. A dog barks and they tell it to shut the fuck up.

"I wouldn't mind dying," she says. "Like, if it was over fast. You?"

"I have kids."

"What if you didn't?"

"I wouldn't mind. If it were over fast."

"And painless."

"Definitely painless." Bob Vinkle also talked of suicide. Clearly there is comfort to be found in considering this option. Katrina continues to stare at him but she doesn't seem to be seeing him. "My grandmother died of strokes," she says. "She kept having them and she'd sort of recover but something wouldn't work anymore, like one side of her face or an arm or something. She thought there were men coming and taking food out of her fridge. And using her towels. She said she didn't mind making sandwiches for them but she didn't want them using her towels. I asked her how they got in and she said they had a key. I said 'Who are they?' and she said, 'They won't tell me.' She said they left their dirty socks for her to clean. I'll probably end up like that. Everybody says I'm just like her. Same fat ass. I can't get excited about hanging around until I'm making sandwiches for invisible people."

"I wouldn't worry about it," Reese says. "Mankind will probably have exterminated himself by then."

"Maybe we'll all get nuked." She rolls onto her back and stares at the ceiling.

"That's a possibility."

"I've had an abortion before. They say it doesn't hurt but it does."

"I'm sorry."

"Will you come with me?"

"Where?"

"To the clinic?"

"When?"

"They said to call Monday. Sometimes they get cancellations."

"I'll come with you."

"You feel like a total reject waiting for it. They think you're scum, even though they don't say it. And there's always some jerk with a sign out front." Driving past the abortion clinic on Gerrard, with Clara alert in the back seat, he'd hoped that the pro-lifers would go unnoticed but his daughter said, "Why do the signs say 'Please, Mummy, go home, let me live'?" He tried to explain that some women didn't want babies and that it was their right to decide. "Why wouldn't they want babies?" Clara asked.

"Maybe they don't feel capable of looking after them. Babies are a lot of work." She accepted this explanation, lame though it was.

"It would have been eight by now," Katrina says. "I didn't want it because I wanted a career and all that shit. What a joke."

She rolls away from him, into the couch. He wonders if she is mourning the loss of the life, imagining the eight-year-old as he so often imagines Elena's ever aging child.

"What are you thinking about?" Katrina asks, still with her back to him.

"Nothing."

22

Sterling pulls his belt tight. "Last notch," he says. He has been on a European juice diet. "I do isometrics in the car." He demonstrates by gripping an imaginary steering wheel and tensing his arms and shoulders. The fax machine has broken down again and Reese is having difficulty making this clear to the service rep, who's wearing an oversized black suit. His head and neck move independently of the suit, which remains stable like a box. Reese involves Wayson Hum, who is fluent in techno-speak. Wayson and the black box huddle over the fax machine.

"V8 juice, I'm telling you," Sterling says, patting his gut. "Everything you need is in that can."

All morning Reese has been waiting for policemen — his wife's henchmen — to take him away and pelt him with Egg McMuffins.

His mother phones to tell him that Maddy who owns the condo above the mall with the chocolate store has a man friend. They play cards and go to movies together. "It's never too late," Betsy says.

"Have you called Dad yet? I think he'd like to hear from you." Reese isn't certain that this is true. When he visited Bernie he wasn't speaking well of "that mother of yours."

"What's to stop him picking up the phone and calling me?" Betsy asks. "All he does is lie around all day."

"I think he's feeling pretty lousy." This is not true. Bernie is responding very well to dialysis and to the dialysis nurses, to one in particular whom he refers to as his Funny Valentine. He's swearing less and obediently taking a laxative with every meal. An occupational therapist came to assess whether or not Bernie could manage at home. He asked Bernie to repeat three words. Bernie couldn't remember them or the day of the week. He told the occupational therapist that he'd studied psychology in 1948 and that there was nothing the therapist could tell him about psychology. The therapist suggested that they complete the tests another time. "Twerp," Bernie said before he'd left the room.

"I think he needs to know that you miss him," Reese says.

"Who says I miss him? Too much work."

"We're going to get somebody to help you with that."

"I don't want a stranger in the house."

"You'd let a masseur in," Reese says. "What's the difference?"

Sterling takes out his comb and adjusts his hair. "Next I'm going for the hair graft," he says. "When that bitch sells the house. I told her if she can't get her dog to stop shitting on the floor every time a real estate agent drops by, *I'll* take care of the dog."

The service rep in the black box appears to be leaving.

"Everything working?" Reese inquires.

The box hands Reese a business card. His name is Cody Hendricks. "If you have any problems, just give me a ring."

"I do have a problem, Cody," Reese says. "Your company said it would recycle our old photocopy machine. I bought the new copier on the condition that you would recycle the old one."

"No one's come to pick it up?" Cody Hendricks inquires, swivelling his head as though looking for someone who might pick it up.

"No. Your company delivered the new one but did not take the old one."

"That's weird."

Reese realizes that here, finally, is someone he can kick around. "Had I known, Cody," he continues, raising his voice, enjoying the increased blood flow that kicking someone around induces, "that your company would not recycle the old one, I would have bought a copier from Minolta, who has better prices. I bought from *your* company because you profess to be '*green*.'"

"We are green, absolutely."

"Then why have you not recycled the old photocopier?!" Reese almost shouts, lunging towards Cody Hendricks, who stumbles backwards into one of the eighty-dollar chairs. "I hope you're not one of those green-washing companies who run around *pretending* to be green when the fact is you're feeding the waste inferno just like everybody else." Before he could turn it off, Betsy's television shouted at him that the government has announced that the bottle-nosed whale, of which only 148 remain, will not be put on the endangered list because it would interfere with explorative drilling for oil.

"I'll get right on it," Cody Hendricks says.

"Yearly," Reese blurts, "twenty-five million tonnes of wasted oil drip from sewers into lakes and oceans."

Cody Hendricks nods briefly before hurrying out. Wayson returns to his monitor and Chinese vegetables. Sterling, looking worried, puts a hand on Reese's shoulder. "Are you cracking up or something?"

"No."

Apparently unconvinced, Sterling continues to eye him. "Is that true about Minolta having better prices?"

"They don't recycle."

"Do I look like I care? What's the matter with you?"

"The price difference was negligible."

"How much?"

"I can't remember. Maybe a hundred bucks."

"A *hundred* bucks?" Overwhelmed, Sterling sits on one of the fake leather chairs. "And what's all this about a wireless mouse?"

"Wayson wants one."

"What's wrong with the one he's got?"

"He's our hardest worker," Reese says. "He's responsible for massive amounts of data. I think we can get him a wireless mouse."

"Make sure he shops around."

"He already has. He's found one in Chinatown for twelve dollars less than the average price."

"Good man." Sterling rearranges the fake leather chairs again. He stands back to view them. "No more expenses without my approval, you understand?"

Reese has never had to ask Sterling for expense money before. This prospect causes a general tightening of Reese's pores.

"Understand?" Sterling repeats.

"What about Post-its?"

"What about whats?"

"Post-its, that we write notes on and stick on things."

Sterling points a finger at him. "You're walking a fine line, boyo. I've given you a lot of slack. No more."

Holden appears with a sickly palm in a plastic pot. "Look what I found! Somebody threw it out just because it's got a few dead leaves. I figured it would look fabulous with the chairs." He moves one of the chairs that Sterling has just arranged and sets the palm on the floor. He tears off some dead leaves before stepping back and admiring it. "Is that cool or what?"

There is no denying that the bottoms of Reese's pants are frayed. He has been trimming them with nail scissors. He sensed that Sterling was looking at them when he found himself blurting about wasted oil to the service rep. It concerns Reese that Sterling asked him if he was cracking up. Why is he blurting envirobabble, despite his new commitment to being a litterer and junk-food consumer? He managed to restrain from ranting at the air conditioner repairman about the need for renewable alternative energies. But when the repairman admitted that his wife was expecting twins and he was nervous about this prospect, Mrs. Ranty jumped onto Reese's back. "You *should* be nervous, lardo," she snarled to the repairman. "Soon there will be nothing left for your little Johnnies to plunder!"

The trousers at Zellers feel as though they're coated with a toxic substance. A label describes them as "no-iron," which would be useful as Reese has no iron. He's hopeful that if he wears new pants to the meeting with the asthma people, Sterling will worry less that he is cracking up. His presentation is quite good, Reese thinks, focusing on recent research involving non-steroidal medications. It's crucial that he avoid blurting inflammatory statistics.

"Oh," Mrs. Ranty intrudes, "you mean like ninety-three percent of the carbon monoxide in Toronto comes from *motor vehicles?!*"

"Or that keeddiess," Scout Leader Igor adds, "in high-zsmog zoness are *five timess* more likely to develop assthma than keeddiess in clean-air zoness?"

"It's a dis*grace!*" Mrs. Stinkman shrieks.

Reese grabs at more trousers. He knows that the asthma people believe in medicine, research, drug companies, and God. The woman, puffy and placid, often says "God willing" or "with God's help." Reese plans to smile beatifically. The fortune in his cookie said that fortune truly helps those who are of good judgment. Katrina's cookie said that she had great physical powers and an iron constitution. "Yeah, right," she said, chewing on bits of broken cookie. When Reese asked if she thought that he had good judgment, she snorted.

"Isn't judging judgment highly subjective?" Reese persisted. "I mean, who's to say who has good judgment?"

"Why ask me then?"

They watched *The Story of Vernon and Irene Castle.* Katrina explained that it was Fred and Ginger's last movie together for RKO. Things were tense between them as they wanted to be stars on their own and yet feared separation. There was no telling what the future would hold when they were no longer a package. Knowing their frailties, Reese watched the movie intently, looking for signs of wistfulness — a glance here, a touch there. He found himself dreading the end of the movie, the end of Fred and Ginger. Then suddenly Vernon got on a plane to fight the Hun and died. "How could they do that?" Reese protested. "He's the star, how could they do that?"

"It's based on a real story."

"So, it's still a Fred and Ginger movie. You can't kill off Fred in a Fred and Ginger movie."

"Vernon and Irene Castle were *real* people."

Sunken in the orange chair, Reese did not want to be real. "What about the baby?" he moaned. "The baby will be fatherless."

"Don't throw a hissy fit about it." A silence descended as she ejected the DVD. He wanted to know what became of Irene and the baby — if they lived in poverty. Katrina had told him that it was hard for female dancers to make a living without a partner. Did Irene find another partner? Did she continue to wear those funny little hats?

"What do you make of those?" an old man in a stained cardigan asks him, pointing at the pants with the toxic coating.

All day he has been fearing that she has called the abortion clinic.

"I'm not sure," Reese admits. They both grope the pants. Reese realizes that this is the same old man who advised him that the plastic shoes smelled of diesel fumes and tipped him off re the jumbo muffin and coffee special.

"There's something on 'em," the old man says. "Smells like diesel fumes." He feels other pants. "What in hell's wrong with plain cotton? Why can't they make *plain* cotton?" Mrs. Ranty grabs Reese's ears. "Hel-*lo!* Little brown cotton-pickers get sprayed with pesticides!"

"It's a dis*grace!*"

Reese points to the "no-iron" label. "You don't have to iron these."

The old man leans in to him. "So the hooker says to the fellah, 'For a hundred bucks you get half an hour.' The mistress says, 'We've only got half an hour.' What do you think the wife says?"

"I have no idea."

"'Beige. I think we should paint the ceiling beige.'" He nudges Reese in the ribs. "Hot chicken sandwich served with veggies and real mashed potatoes only $7.29." He winks at Reese as he heads for the restaurant.

Avril will not come out of the washroom. Serge, gripping his shorn head, paces outside it. "I think you should go away," Reese says.

"Why?" Serge demands. "So you can *brainwash* her? What have you been telling her about me?"

"Nothing. Absolutely nothing."

"Fucking classic this."

"Serge, I don't know where you're getting this idea that there's something going on between Avril and me."

"I've seen how you look at her."

"She came to me because she felt that you were harassing her."

"Oh, so guys aren't supposed to open doors for girls anymore, right? We're not supposed to help them with their coats or carry their bags, right? I bought her flowers, is that so wrong?" He shouts into the washroom door, "Is that so *wrong?!*"

"Serge, this is a work situation. We work here. We don't court."

"Is that right? So what is it you're doing in the kitchen with her all the time, and your office, and the boardroom."

"Discussing work-related issues."

"I don't see you discussing work-related issues with any of the other callers," Serge says. "It's *my* job to discuss work-related issues with the callers."

"Well, you haven't been doing your job terribly well lately."

"Is that a threat?"

"No. I just wish you would calm down and leave Avril alone. She wants to be left alone."

Serge crosses his arms. "You leave her alone then."

"She's in the washroom. Other people need to use the washroom. She can't stay in there."

Serge falls against the door and begins to slam his head into it.

"Stop that!" Avril screams, opening it. "Stop it! You're insane."

"I love you, is that a crime? Is that a *crime?!*"

This exchange reminds Reese of Fred and Ginger. Despite verbal and physical abuse from Ginger, Fred is never dissuaded from pursuing her. And he always gets her in the end. Unless he's real and killed by Huns.

"I don't love you," Avril says. "I've never given you any reason to think that I love you. If you try to follow me one more time, I'm calling the police."

"You've been following her?" Reese asks.

"I happened to be going in that direction."

Avril clasps her hands and holds them under her chin. Stillness surrounds her. Reese suspects that she is being with what is. Serge watches her with awe. Marge hobbles towards them. "Awfully quiet all of a sudden," she says before closing the washroom door on them.

Katrina told Reese that Fred, on first reading the script of *The Gay Divorcee*, objected to Ginger slapping him. He felt it made his character look stupid. Reese didn't think Fred looked stupid, only supremely confident that he would get the girl. Serge does not look confident that he will get the girl.

"I don't want to have to say this," Avril says. "You are *forcing* me to say this. I don't like you. You are a very aggressive person with issues."

"What issues?" Serge demands.

Reese steps between them. "Let's get back to work."

Serge pushes him aside. "*What* issues?! That I'd *die* for you? That I can't think about anything but you all the time? Night and day I'm thinking about you." Reese hears Fred singing *Night and day, you are the one, only you beneath the moon or under the sun.*

"That's not her concern," he says.

"Who asked you? You, the king of the fuck-ups. We all know about *your* marriage." What do they know? Avril heads down the hall. Serge starts to follow but Reese grabs his arm. In seconds they're on the floor. Reese feels Serge's hands around his neck and remembers Elena telling him that a lover once put his hands around her neck during sex and that it freaked her out. If he allows Serge to strangle him, he could be with Elena. He hears Avril screaming as he relaxes into Serge's arms. "You've killed him," she gasps.

"No way," Serge responds, releasing Reese, whose head hits the floor. Avril kneels beside him and begins slapping his face. Sterling, suited for the meeting with the asthma people, appears with his cop friend — one of the duck hunter/environmentalists. "What's going on here?" the cop demands. Reese plays dead, hoping to go unnoticed, but Avril won't stop slapping him. "Please stop that," he whispers.

"You're alive!" she says, loudly.

He waits for the cop to grab him as he has been grabbed so many times at protests. He's always amazed at the apparent enjoyment they feel, brutalizing people. But the cop doesn't seem interested in Reese. He has Serge up against the wall and is speaking to him in gruff tones.

"Please leave him alone," Reese says.

Sterling silences him. "I want you in that meeting in ten minutes. Look at you, you're a mess."

"I bought new pants."

"I'll alert the media," Sterling says.

Reese senses that the asthma people are not wowed by his presentation, although the puffy and placid woman punctuates his statements several times with "God willing." The small-headed man wants to talk about Plasmacluster Ion Technology. More research needs to be done, he says, now that Plasmacluster Ion air purifiers are available in Canada.

"With God's help," the puffy, placid woman says.

"Before they were only available in Japan," the small-headed man explains. Reese is trying to remember his name; he thinks it's Darwin or Dirwin.

"By creating a positive and negative ion shower," Darwin or Dirwin explains, "Plasmacluster Ion Technology recreates the natural process that purifies the air in the Earth's atmosphere. It can inactivate most airborne particles."

"Stupendous," Sterling says.

"More landfill," Reese blurts. His toxic pants are chafing his crotch.

"I beg your pardon," Darwin or Dirwin says.

"We can go on polluting as long as we can drive to Wal-Mart to buy our Plasmacluster Ion Technology."

"He's being funny," Sterling says.

"Technology cannot save us," Reese adds, too loudly, while his arms begin to saw the air. "Technology cannot produce water or land or air."

"He's a greeny," Sterling says to Darwin or Dirwin. "I warned you."

"Are you saying," Darwin or Dirwin interjects, "that we should not continue to research air purification?"

"I'm saying," Reese says, not wanting to say it, "that we should stop *contaminating* the air in the first place." He tries to think of something else, the Nachos Supreme special at Zellers, apple caramel pie, beds.

Mrs. Ranty digs her heels into him. "Tell them America is *weakening* pollution controls, bonehead!!"

"Tell them 440 coal-fired generatorss," Scout Leader Igor says, "are being retrofeetted to meet 1971 emeesssion-control zstandardss."

"Hel-*lo!*" Mrs. Ranty shouts. "Let's gas the kiddies!"

"It's a dis*grace!*"

"Yes, well, in a perfect world," Darwin or Dirwin interjects.

"In a perfect world," Reese blurts, "all the asthmatic children could stay inside their houses beside their boxes of Plasmacluster Ion Technology. They'd get fatter and sicker but at least they'd be able to breathe."

"God willing," the puffy, placid woman says.

"The Dalai Lama says if you can't do good in the world, then don't do harm." Avril is sipping a freshly squeezed juice called a Smooth Feeling. It's made with beets and is very red. "I'm doing harm without even *doing* anything," she says, "just by being."

The juice bar smells of rotten vegetables and has no air conditioning. Reese's toxic pants and plastic shoes are creating a general meltdown. He'd hoped to change after the meeting but Avril left in haste and he feared, if he didn't stop her, he would never see her again. She seems unaware that Serge Hollyduke is following them. Reese has noticed him ducking into stores and phone booths. Currently he is squatting behind some newspaper boxes.

"Maybe it isn't harm that you're doing," Reese suggests. "Maybe it's a lesson in Serge's chain of being."

"He's so primitive. Although I shouldn't say that because that's a judgment." She sips more Smooth Feeling. "He isn't evolved at all. I don't think I've ever met anyone so primal."

Reese feels somewhat primal himself what with his urges to kill Roberta and shout at the asthma people. After Fred was killed by Huns, Reese surfed while Katrina slept. On *Biography* Captain Bligh was being deconstructed. It seemed he was actually a quiet man who kept to himself and wanted to spend all day with his charts. He was an extraordinary navigator but not very good at hustling sailors on rations. Rather than ordering whippings, he stayed in his cabin with his charts and meticulously kept his journal. Fletcher Christian, on the other hand, was political and visible. As the *Bounty*'s troubles mounted, Bligh became more remote and Christian more present. When Bligh did appear he would lose his temper. This was his tragic flaw. Sunken in the orange chair, Reese suspected that this was his own tragic flaw. A memory he can't repress is the night he took Clara to the Bon Marché for waffles with ice cream. It was to be their special night together but he became incensed when the host insisted that he take two cards for their staff to stamp. "She's with me," Reese argued. "Why do we need two cards?"

"That's our policy."

"But she's my daughter. *I* will be paying for the waffles. We don't need *two* cards."

"Everybody gets a card." The host had pitted skin.

"Why?"

"That's our policy."

"Oh, I see. So let's cut down *entire* forests so that each of your customers can have their own card."

"I want you to leave now," the host said.

"I don't want to leave now!" Reese felt his arms beginning to flap. "I want to buy my daughter a waffle!"

"You must leave now."

Clara, mortified, grabbed one of his arms. "It's okay, Daddy." On the pavement, she said she never wanted to go to that restaurant ever again. Her loyalty disarmed him, he wanted only to buy her a waffle, nothing else mattered except that he get her a waffle. They searched for waffles until her legs were tired and she pleaded that they stop. "I don't need a waffle, Daddy."

"Do you like me?" Avril asks.

"What? Yes." Serge's Birkenstocks poke out from behind the newspaper boxes.

"You're not just saying that?"

"No." Reese has, in the juice bar, managed to refrain from bellowing regarding the absence of a recycling bin for the plastic cups and straws.

"Because you don't even know me." Beet juice stains the corners of her mouth. "So how can you like me?"

"I think sometimes it's easier to like people you don't know very well." Is it really possible that Betsy imagines she will acquire a man friend in the condo above the chocolate store? Is that what it's all about in the end, having another body to play cards with and sit beside at movies?

"I think I have to quit," Avril says.

"Oh, please don't."

She twists her plastic straw. "I'm not good at it."

"I'm confident you'll hit your stride with the Voice of First Nations campaign."

"I'm a total loser, I've never been good at anything. All I've ever wanted was to be good at something. I see other people and they're good at things."

"I think you're good at being."

"That's just one big lie. I can't stop my mind. I'm a total fake." She drops her head onto her arms and begins to make injured animal noises.

"*I'm* not good at what I do," he offers, wondering if he should pat her shoulder in way of consolation. "I think a lot of people fake it. We're all so busy faking it we don't notice that everybody else is faking it."

She looks at him warily. "You say that like it's okay."

"Well, I think it is. I mean, it keeps the wheels turning."

"I don't want that. I *hate* that. I would rather *die* than fake it."

He considers all the times he has suspected that women were faking orgasms above and below him, how he has always felt that the ability to fake sexual pleasure sets women apart from men more than any other gender difference. Women can hide. He has always had difficulty finding them. The puffy and placid woman touched his hand before departing with Dirwin or Darwin. "She liked your passion," Sterling told him. "Otherwise you'd be out on your ass." Sterling was particularly upset because his newly ordered BlackBerry did not fit its holder. He wasted Wayson Hum's valuable time by instructing him to e-mail the company to rectify the error. Mrs. Ranty started yanking on Reese's hair. "Eighty percent of the world's farmlands are severely damaged, *half* the planet's forests have been cut down, CO_2 emissions are climbing sixty percent by 2025, but *stop the world*, Sterling's BlackBerry does not fit its holder!!"

Reese doesn't touch Avril but leans over the table, so much so that his gut, swollen from Zellers' hot chicken sandwich with veggies and real mashed potatoes, pushes hard against his toxic pants. "I can't do the Voice of First Nations campaign without you."

She looks at him with smudgy eyes. "Really?"

"Really."

She places her hand against her chest. "That's the nicest thing anybody's ever said to me. I think I'm going to cry."

Serge is striding towards them. Avril, deeply moved and busy sucking up her Smooth Feeling, doesn't see him right away.

"Not after her, eh?" Serge shouts. "Not looking for the first opportunity to turn your crank!"

Reese stands, immediately feeling the toxic pants chafing his crotch. "Serge, I didn't press charges because I didn't think it was necessary."

"Why won't you give me a chance?" Serge pleads, falling to his knees before her. "I'm a nice guy. I get emotional sometimes but I'm working on it. You're right. I have issues. I'm sorry."

Avril, very still, with her fingers clenched around her plastic cup, looks to Reese for assistance.

"That's enough, Serge," he says.

"Let *her* talk."

"She doesn't want to."

"You were nice to me before," Serge says. "You told me about the sandals, and I ... I stopped eating wheat."

"I was trying to help you," Avril squeaks.

"You *did* help me. I'm a new man, totally."

"Let's talk about this tomorrow," Reese says.

"Yes, let's," Avril agrees.

"You mean you're not quitting?" Serge asks, his habitually intense expression lightening briefly.

"Reese needs me for the Voice of First Nations campaign."

"Oh he does, does he?"

"Serge ..." Reese says.

"Okay, okay, as long as you're coming back."

"She's coming back."

"Cool." Serge stands, apparently embarrassed by his display of passion.

Captain Bligh found his way to land in a rowboat with the few loyal or fearful sailors who didn't die from exposure and dehydration. Fletcher Christian stayed in the tropics to spread disease among the natives. The cruel irony is that Bligh had wanted Christian for the voyage. Christian had bounced Bligh's children on his knees. Bligh ordered fewer whippings than did Captain Cook. But Bligh will be maligned into eternity because of his temper and primal urges. As Reese shall be forever condemned by Roberta. And possibly his son, and Gwyneth Proudley. She was a midget in his dream last night. He kept tripping over her. "Goodnight, Serge," he says. "We'll see you tomorrow."

He had to suppress a primal urge to shout at Betsy because she couldn't find her slippers. He knew from experience that she'd probably put them in a plastic bag somewhere. She puts everything in plastic bags. He wanted to shout, "Why do you put everything in plastic bags?" but he couldn't, couldn't be *real* as it would only cause disharmony. Avril says she would rather die than fake it. As a young man Reese felt a similar disdain for artifice. Now it seems his only chance for survival. He must control his urges and blurtings, acquire the aura of a man confident of the value of his life's quest.

"Thanks for the Smooth Feeling," Avril says.

"Would you like me to walk you home?"

"That's okay."

Does she fear he will shove his tongue down her throat? Elena told him she'd been having a drink with a screenwriter when suddenly he was shoving his tongue down her throat. A rage brewed in Reese, not unlike the rage he suspects that Serge is currently experiencing. But Reese has no desire to shove his tongue down Avril's throat. He has no desire. Only concern for the baby. All babies, his babies. In Iraq and Afghanistan there are villages of babies with no one left alive to look after them. In the cities women are holding up dead children and saying look what America has done.

"Are you finished?" a green-haired youth says fiercely. "We need your table."

Before the medication, Derek couldn't get to sleep at night because he thought his throat was closing and that death was imminent. He'd hold a mirror up to his mouth and announce, "See, it's closing!"

"Are you finished?" the youth repeats.

Reese is. Finished. "It's all yours," he says.

Betsy is eating SpaghettiOs from a can.

"Shouldn't you heat that up?" Reese asks.

"Who needs dirty dishes?"

"I'll do the dishes."

A SpaghettiO falls from her spoon and sticks to her slipper. "Maddy's man-friend took her to Casino Rama to see Englebert Humperdinck."

"Englebert Humperdinck? Is he still alive?"

"He looks exactly the same, she said."

"I didn't know you liked Englebert Humperdinck."

"He was wearing a white satin tuxedo made by a cowboy tailor."

Katrina didn't answer her door. Is it possible that she went out, that she is not lying in the bathtub with blood congealing around her?

"I never go anywhere," Betsy says.

"I'll take you to Casino Rama. Where is it?"

"Englebert's not there anymore."

"Well, somebody must be booked."

"Herman's Hermits. Who wants to see them?"

It's Katrina's night off, and the evening of their ballroom dancing class. He went, hoping to meet her there, endured the Macarena while watching for her. When she didn't appear he tried to leave, but Edwina Pendleton paired him with a small woman in silver shoes who smelled of cat. Where would Katrina go with a baby in her belly? What will she do to it?

Betsy shoves the empty can into the garbage. "When Maddy's cousin's husband passed away, she got herself a sports car, had the house redone, and bought a parrot. Maddy says the parrot just sits on her arm and says 'I love you, I love you' over and over. They live for a long time, parrots." Betsy begins to sing, "Please Release Me, Let Me Go."

Edwina chose Reese rather than the humpbacked man to demonstrate the foxtrot, the very dance that Katrina had been so eager to learn. "Step forward between the lady's feet on the second step," Edwina instructed. "Lady steps between the gent's feet on the first. Head up." She was playing the music from *Mame*. "Now the gent steps between the lady's on the first, the lady steps between the gent's on the second. Slow, slow, quick, quick. Head up." Reese couldn't bear being without Katrina. Inhaling cat, he began to cough and had to excuse himself.

"Mum, I need to know you won't make it difficult for Dad to come home."

"Why would I make it difficult? As long as he looks after himself, he's welcome."

"He can't look after himself. That's why you need help. I've been talking with an agency that provides caregivers."

"If he needs caregivers, he should stay in the hospital." She opens a box of Glosettes and chews energetically on them.

At the drinking fountain, the humpbacked man told Reese about his pigeons — tumblers, he called them. He has bred them for thirty-five years. He lets them out of their coop once a day. They fly up into the sky and then tumble, somersaulting towards earth then swooping up again. When they're too old to tumble he gives them to an Italian who eats them.

"You've been smoking," Reese says. "I can smell that you've been smoking."

"One or two can't hurt."

"What did the doctor tell you? Didn't he say you have to stop smoking or he'll cut off your feet?"

"He just says that to scare you."

"Mother, I can't help you if you won't help yourself."

"Who asked for your help? I can look after myself."

"No, you can't. You *know* you can't. Why are you doing this?" He remembers the feel of her arms around him when he got hit in the mouth by a baseball. He remembers her calm as she wrapped ice in a cloth and held it to his bleeding mouth. Where *is* that woman? Who is this Englebert Humperdinck fan? She bends down to pull at the SpaghettiO stuck to her slipper.

"I guess you found your slippers," he says. "Were they in a plastic bag?" Do the pigeons know that, when they are no longer able to tumble, they will be eaten by an Italian? Consequently, do they tumble when it is no longer fun, when their joints ache, because they fear being taken from loved ones and roasted?

"Maddy's daughter's getting divorced. Her husband hates budgies and she hates thrillers. All these years they've been putting up with each other but last week they couldn't agree on a wall unit so that was that." All his life Reese has been waiting for something to fall into place. Was this delusional? "I never liked the look of him," Betsy says, "all that talk about being in rehab with Diana Ross." She drops a Glosette and inadvertently steps on it with her slipper. "Maddy's dyed her hair out of a box. It's called Natural Light Golden Brown with built-in highlights. You should see her, she looks twenty years younger." As he was approaching his mother's house, a neighbour with orange hair was shouting at her yapping dogs and trying to push them inside her house. "What did I tell you about barking?" she shouted at them. She's been a neighbour for years but has never acknowledged Reese and has always had orange hair. Reese doesn't know if he can handle Betsy with Natural Light Golden Brown with built-in highlights.

"Is there anything you need at the store?" he asks.

"It's by Nice'n Easy, number 216A. I wrote it down." She hands him a much-fondled scrap of paper.

Bob Vinkle has paid a teenaged boy to spread the word about the mice at the franchise across the street. He has also paid him to puncture Alicia's assistant's tires. "Next I use the gun," he says.

"Is that wise, Robert, while you're under house arrest?"

"Wise is for fucking losers, Lindy. I've been fucking wise all my life and look where it's got me. Fucking assholes across the street putting me out of business, a fucking asshole in my bed ..."

"Thank you for sharing that with us," Kyla says. "I need two rum and Cokes."

Beside Reese are two tightly necktied men, one of whom has been to Africa and put inside a cage, underwater, to observe a great white shark. "When I saw those teeth," he says, "I got pretty emotional, which is unusual for me. You know your place around one of those bastards. I mean, it's you in the cage and them." What amount of money is required to send tightly necktied men to Africa so they can climb into cages and look at sharks? Are there not heart-stopping experiences closer to home? The mother of a severely disabled child, for example, being paralyzed by a bullet in a drive-by shooting? Why does the tightly necktied man need to face a shark through a cage to get pretty emotional? And what does he mean about knowing his place? Did the shark humble him? Did he return from Africa with humility and a deeper understanding of the frailty of our oceans? Is he washing his car less frequently?

"You know what gives me hope?" Bob says, pouring rum into glasses. "Ryan and Farrah getting back together. Twenty-five years after they started dating. They say they found true love while helping their heroin-addicted son, Redmond, in rehab."

"Sorry to disappoint, Robert," Linden says, "but Ryan and Farrah are splitsville."

"Who says?" Bob demands, spray-gunning Coke.

"Farrah's been occupied battling cancer, Ryan's been busy assaulting his son and his son's pregnant wife."

"Redmond?"

"No, the older one, Griffin, star of *Assault of the Killer Bimbos* and *Ghoulies III*. Apparently, he went at his father with a fire poker, so poor Ryan had no choice but to fire at the banister."

"Are you shittin' me?"

Linden shakes his head gravely. "Hard times in Malibu."

Bob pushes the drinks at Kyla. "Life sucks, no matter which way you slice it." He tried contacting Hilary at her daycare, but the formerly friendly childcare workers had been warned against him.

"Next," the tightly necktied man says, "I want to go on safari, see some elephants."

Bob drops his head onto his arms on the bar and appears to be convulsing. Reese worries that he is experiencing a heart attack due to his tight surgical stockings.

"He's crying," Linden whispers. "He does that sometimes."

Katrina still doesn't answer her door and Gwyneth Proudley still hasn't called. Reese flings himself on the futon in an effort to *be* with his anger and frustration. He hears Bonaparte shuffling around and lets him loose on the kitchen counter. Within seconds the hamster is diving into the garbage can. It must be the equivalent of skydiving for humans. A young woman died skydiving. Her father said he couldn't believe it when her chute didn't open. Grounded, he watched helplessly as she plummeted towards earth, struggling with her cords. He must have prayed that she would swoop upwards, like the tumbler pigeons. What can it be like to know that your daughter will, in an instant, be crushed? The father is demanding more regulation of skydiving clubs. Why, Reese wants to ask him, did your daughter feel a need to jump from planes? Did life on a planet plagued by violence not offer enough peril? Did terrorists beheading yet another hostage not offer enough of a reminder that life can be here one instant and gone the next? Or has decapitation, like all atrocities once familiar, lost its effect? He hears movement upstairs. She is home, was home when he knocked on her door. She doesn't want to see him.

The identical twin Zellers clerks assisted him in locating the Happy Feet section but seemed to panic when he asked if they knew anything about Nice'n Easy Natural Light Golden Brown with built-in highlights. They'd pointed in the general direction of the hair care aisle where Reese went in search of Number 216A. A yellow-haired woman, his mother's age, was also studying the packages. She said she was in a hurry because she had to organize a church supper. "*I'm* the organizer," she stated several times. "The same fellahs have been coming for nine years. They're always asking me to marry them. That's because they know my husband died. Just two cigarettes a day killed him. Do you smoke?"

Reese, staring at the boxes, which all had bare-shouldered, shiny-haired, digitally perfected young women smiling seductively, shook his head.

"The doctor said to me, 'Margaret, it's the cigarettes that killed him.' Anyways, one of the boys told me he had just one wish. So I told him to tell me since I'm the organizer and might be able to organize it for him. He said, 'Margaret, would you kiss me?' Can you believe the *nerve?*"

Reese found Number 216A but was having second thoughts about buying it for his mother. He considered pretending it was unavailable but then pictured her disappointment. "Do you use this?" he asked the yellow-haired woman.

She shook her head. "I'm a blonde."

"No, I mean the dye itself, is it easy to use?"

"Are you worried about your greys? Because there's rinses for men."

"No, it's for my mother."

"Oh, well, she'll know how to use it."

"She doesn't. I mean, she never has."

"Is that what she tells you?" She winked and waddled away with her box. Reese took refuge in the restaurant. He ordered a Swiss Marvellous omelette followed by a Divinely Decadent butter tart because the paraplegic was eating one while scrutinizing the skateboards on the Zellers flyer. When Reese handed the Nice'n Easy to his mother, she became girlish at the prospect of turning naturally golden brown. Why, Reese wanted to know, must we always yearn for what we do not have? Is it not possible to stand back and say *enough*, I have enough?

Furniture moving begins upstairs and he realizes that she is not alone. She is with child, with someone else, moving furniture in the bedroom. Heat blasts through him while he tells himself it shouldn't matter what she does. What is she to him? She is nothing, white trash, the baby is white trash, best forgotten. Bonaparte climbs back into his cage and spins on his wheel. Its whirring does not obliterate the noise from upstairs. Reese tries on his Happy Feet and turns on the television. Boys with guns argued on a bus and started shooting at each other. The boys weren't hurt, only innocent bystanders. A man is dead and a girl blinded in one eye due to a bullet grazing her face. An ex-husband bit off the nose of his ex-wife whom he was sexually assaulting. He claimed it was an accident, that the nose fell into his mouth so he spat it out. *What if Katrina is being sexually assaulted?*

His knocking receives no response. He begins to pound on the door while calling her name. Finally, like Serge Hollyduke before him, he uses his head as a battering ram.

A large-gutted man in bikini briefs swings open the door. "What the fuck do you think you're doing?"

It takes Reese a moment to recognize the bouncer from the topless bar who suggested he stick to the Keg. "Is Katrina there?"

"She doesn't want to talk to you. She thinks you're a fucking nutbar."

"That's because she's not used to people being nice to her," Reese says loudly, hoping to be overheard. "She doesn't think she deserves to be treated decently."

"Does this mean you don't want her to suck you off?" the bouncer inquires. "I'll give her the message." He starts to close the door but Reese pushes against it.

"Katrina!" he shouts. "Don't do this!"

"You keep at it," the bouncer warns, "I call the cops."

"I waited for you at Edwina's!" Reese shouts. "We learned the foxtrot!"

The bouncer shoves his weight into the door, nearly crushing Reese's fingers. Hearing the deadbolt lock behind him, Reese slides down the door and sits on the floor. In his head Fred sings, "Must you dance every dance with him, won't you change partners and dance with me." Oh, to be one of the protesters living in a tree in a futile attempt to stop the destruction of forty-seven thousand trees to make room for a freeway. Reese could piss off the edge, believe that he is making a difference, taking a stand. But the thumping overhead grinds the delusions out of him. The freeway will be built. Katrina will kill the baby. Climate change–induced disasters will become commonplace, respiratory illnesses and cancers will escalate. Munitions makers will continue to profit. Money will be made by those who need it least, who will never, ever have enough.

He begins to howl.

"You get a better lumbar response in the pocket coil," the saleswoman advises. "Less movement, better contouring. Plus, if you have a sleeping partner you don't feel them as much."

Looking up, Reese notes that she has several chins. "What kind of bed do you sleep on?"

"Oh, I bought a Bedford. It was an end of the line. It's too firm, I want to sell it to my uncle." Her name tag reads Muriel Seranno. She's friendlier than Mary Jane Lovering, who is glowering at Reese from the bedskirt display. Muriel is very round and therefore difficult to imagine on a firm bed.

"Does your uncle want to buy your bed?"

"I've only slept on it a year. It's a quality mattress, it just doesn't have a pillow top so you really feel the pressure points. The Sensation series, plush or firm, doesn't come with a pillow top."

"I'm not sure I like the pillow top."

"It provides contouring."

"Do you know anything about green mattresses?"

Muriel holds her index finger against one of her chins. "You mean the natural fibre ones? We've got the Four Seasons Collection." She leads him to more beds, which resemble all the other beds. "They've got breathable, cleaner, non-irritating and non-toxic materials *plus* a hundred percent cotton cover."

He lies on one, clings to it, hoping to fall in love with a natural-fibre bed. It feels like all the other beds.

"That's the Azalea, then there's the Iris and the Orchid. Try them, make yourself comfortable." Muriel Seranno doesn't seem enthusiastic about the Four Seasons series. "There's silk and wool in them."

"Would you buy one of these?" Reese asks.

"To be honest, there's no bacterial resistance in them so I'd worry about mildew. And fireproofing. You wouldn't want to drop a match on one of them. Personally, I think all that green stuff is a bunch of bunk."

"I have a mildew problem. I live in a basement."

"Oh," she says, understanding for the first time just how low on the social scale he is. "What are you sleeping on?"

"A futon."

Although she maintains an air of professional courtesy, he senses that Muriel will soon join Mary Jane in her appraisal of him. "I'll let you browse," she says.

Avril told him that the people of the First Nations say that we must consider the welfare of our descendents for seven generations, if we are to be wise stewards of the Earth. Reese hasn't shown the revised script to Sterling. He is planning to road-test it with Avril, hoping that her numbers will be so impressive that Sterling will have no cause for complaint. It has become apparent, however, that the general perception in the office is that Reese and Avril are getting it on. As they sat in the boardroom, reviewing the script, several people poked their heads in and immediately said, "Oohh excuse me" in hushed tones. Serge, pacing outside, contained his anger. He and Avril greeted each other civilly, although he didn't respond to Reese's "Good morning."

A gaunt man who looks as though he hasn't slept for several weeks flops down on the Orchid beside Reese. "Have you tried a Dax?" he asks with some urgency.

"A what?"

"They don't sell them here. D'you ever go to Buffalo?"

"No."

"They're a shitload cheaper in Buffalo. They scalp you here."

"I thought you said they didn't sell them here."

"Not here. At the Ultimate."

"The what?"

"The Ultimate Sleep Shoppe." The man begins scratching first his head then behind his ears. "It's *the* place for discerning sleepers." He rolls onto his side and beckons Reese closer. Over the gaunt man's shoulder Reese sees Mary Jane Lovering and Muriel Seranno watching them with loathing. "Those mooers don't know squat about natural latex and calibration," the man whispers.

"Do *you* have a Dax?" Reese asks.

"Are you kiddin'? They're made in *Sweden!*"

"Have you tried the Tempur-Pedic system?" Reese asks. "They're also made in Sweden."

"They smell."

"Really? I hadn't noticed that."

Mary Jane Lovering is fast approaching. "How may I help you gentlemen?"

Melody Lesko, the bookkeeper, bites into a submarine sandwich while Wayson begins disassembling her keyboard.

"My throat was so sore," she says, "I figured I had throat cancer because they're saying saliva mixed with nicotine is deadly. I started bawling and my numb-nuts brother thought it was because I was moved. The whole time I was thinking, 'There's him marrying some bimbo half his age and I'm dying of throat cancer.' I don't care what anybody says, men and women are not equal."

"Does he love her?" Reese asks.

"Does he what?" Melody Lesko, without a cigarette for the last twenty minutes, is becoming edgy.

"If he's marrying her, he must think he loves her."

Melody squints at him. "How old are you?"

He phoned Betsy to make certain that Gateway had delivered the groceries and to tell her he'd bought some Happy Feet. He tried not to think about what colour her hair might be. She told him she wanted to paint the bathroom in the condo sienna and gold.

"People do marry for love," he says.

"You're a romantic." Melody twitches for nicotine. "How quaint."

Reese rolls his neck. "There are lepers in Iran who love each other. It was in the paper."

"Don't believe everything you read."

"Crumb," Wayson announces. "You put crumb in keyboard." Wayson regularly chastises staff for eating around the computers. Sterling, back from reading the *Sun* in the john, grabs Reese's elbow. "A word, boyo."

Nick Dizon is already in the office sitting in Reese's chair beside the drawer containing the plastic shoes. "Nice socks," he comments. Before him are papers which Reese suspects to be the Voice of First Nations script.

"What's this about not answering your e-mail?" Sterling demands.

"Who said I wasn't answering my e-mail?" Reese responds.

"Dirwin Roach. He's not too happy about it."

"I'm sorry."

"He seems to think you don't take Plasmacluster Ion Technology seriously."

"Really?"

"Whatever the client's shtick is," Sterling says, "we show respect. We never and I mean *never* ..."

"Tell them the truth," Reese interjects.

"Not if it interferes with their shtick."

"The client is king," Nick Dizon intones.

"And what the fuck," Sterling adds, with growing intensity, "does Iraq and Afghanistan have to do with Indians?"

"Exploitation."

"Nobody wants to know about burnt babies, alright? They want to hear success stories, they want to hear that Joey Smallfoot has his own barbershop thanks to them. They want to know that Susie Wildflower is off the streets and studying social work, you get my drift? Positive, think *positive*."

"What exactly," Nick Dizon says, "is your relationship with Avril Leblanc?"

"We're friends."

Nick and Sterling exchange dubious looks.

"You don't need me to tell you," Sterling says, "we don't mix business with pleasure."

"No," Reese responds.

"No what?"

"I don't need you to tell me."

"And what's with the bakery kid? I told you to fire him." Sterling rubs his gut and Reese hopes that the clip left behind from his gallbladder surgery has become infected again. He waits for Sterling to buckle with pain. "Did I not tell you to fire him?"

"Holden?" Reese can smell the plastic shoes.

"Don't act dumb with me," Sterling says. "Why haven't you fired him?"

"His numbers are improving."

"Get rid of him and the girl."

Nick Dizon leans back in Reese's chair and rests his feet on the desk. He's wearing stylish, obviously leather, loafers. Before Muriel Seranno noticed Reese's plastic sandals and learned that Reese slept on a futon in the basement, she advised him that he must flip his mattress monthly and therefore would be wise to buy a Simmons Fantasia with a pillow top on both top and bottom which, for two days only, was being offered with a bonus sheet set, bed frame, headboard, or pillow. The fanged salesman at the pillow store had cautioned Reese that he must put his pillows in the dryer monthly to rid them of dust mites. Suddenly, all this required maintenance is too much. "Life's a ball of plaster dust," Reese mutters.

"Did you hear what I said?" Sterling demands, still rubbing his gut but showing no signs of collapse. "I want them both gone by morning."

The Daxes are non-flip. Swedes don't have time to waste heaving mattresses. "They go, I go," Reese says.

"Suit yourself," Sterling responds.

Reese realizes too late that without employment there is no hope of getting his children back. He legs lose power while Nick Dizon doodles diamonds on the Voice of First Nations script. He draws squares around the diamonds then adds more diamonds and draws squares around them. "Our feeling is, Reeso," he says, "you haven't been happy here. You've got to believe in your causes and we respect that. You've got integrity and that's admirable."

Sterling pulls out his comb and arranges his hair. "The truth is, boyo, you belong on a boat in the North Sea getting radioactive waste dumped on you."

"Where would we be without activists," Nick sighs, drawing squares around more diamonds. With no power in his legs Reese is forced to lean on the desk, a desk which he hates but has come to accept as crucial for survival, like the Robert Bateman reproductions and the fake leather chairs. He has adapted to this life of corruption, greed, and wilful ignorance. Like Tony of the Firestone franchise, he has eaten shite to preserve his car and his house. He has eaten shite and now has nothing. He begins to shove the desk into Nick Dizon.

"Take it easy, boyo."

"You're killing us," Reese says in a voice hoarse with self-loathing.

"Hands off the desk," Sterling commands but Reese continues to shove it into Nick Dizon, who has a look of terror about him. Never before has Reese been able to terrorize Nick Dizon. "You leave your car running," he sneers, "your lights on, dump your garbage, batteries, wash your fucking car, hose your fucking interlocking bricks, pour poison down your toilet, your drains …" Nick Dizon manages to slide off the chair before the desk hits the wall, causing Sterling's sailboat pictures to crash to the floor. Sterling gasps and looks at Reese with fear, *fear*! "You've ploughed up prairies," Reese continues, spitting out the "p"s in *ploughed* and *prairies*. "You've razed forests, drained aquifers, *spewed* nuclear waste …" Both the pods stand with their arms held out at their sides as though unsure where to run. *No more* will Reese have to listen to their lies. *No more* will he have live with the boat pictures. *No more* will he have to face the crucifix Sterling hangs above his desk before meetings with the Family Values people. *No more* will he have to hear about testosterone gel. A song of freedom reverberates through him. "Where do you think it's going to go, *boyos*?" he demands, his arms sawing the air again. "Each year an area of rainforest *the size of Poland* disappears!" The pods, slack-jawed, back up against the wall, giving him room to flail.

Oh yes, he has dreamed of this day, his *last* day when he could shout in their faces. "By 2025, boyos, 5.8 million acres of ocean shoreline in *America alone* will be destroyed to make room for human sprawl!" Statistics flood his mind. "Yo' Norte Americanos consume twenty-five percent of the global energy used each year despite being only *five percent* of the population!" He feels power returning to his legs and begins to bounce on the balls of his feet. Consonants torpedo from his lips. "You've caused mass extinctions and now the looming spectre of climate change is *in your face!* Who's next, boyos?!" He'll deliver a knockout punch, he will! "In twenty years breathing's going to require *gasping!* Who do you think's going to save us? Jesus Christ? Is He gonna rise up and carry you to heaven?!"

They suddenly grab him, one on each side.

"Choose *life*, boyos!!!" Reese bellows as they begin to force him out of the room he hates but can't live without. He digs his heels into the puke-coloured broadloom. "Hold on, wait a minute, wait! Wait!" He braces his feet against the door. "What ... what about my severance package?!"

"Don't scavenge," a woman in short shorts shouts at her dog. The dog continues to ogle Reese's Jamaican patty. The woman's thighs jiggle as she strides towards it. "Naughty boy." She hooks her leash to its collar.

"He's welcome to it," Reese says. He offers the patty to the dog, but the woman jerks the leash as the dog is squatting to relieve himself. "Wonderful," she tells it, "don't let me hurry you, Walter, take your time." She leans over the dog. "Would you like a magazine?"

Reese left his plastic shoes in the desk. He can't go back for them. As he was leaving, staff kept making demands, not under-standing that he was no longer in charge. Marge wanted to know if Huntington's disease affected the bowel. Holden chased him with photos from the party and held up a shot of Reese biting into a steamy. "You got pink eyes," Holden said. "It's that alien probe." Reese turned on him and Marge, who'd inadvertently bumped him with her walker. "Do I look like a fucking people person to you?" Reese said. He takes another bite of the patty, hoping for food poisoning. Derek, before he began taking blue pills, believed that all food not prepared by his mother was poisoned. He'd make Roberta bite the prepared food before he would chance it. That he was willing to have his mother poisoned always puzzled Reese. "Why doesn't he ask me?" he asked Roberta.

"He doesn't trust you."

So we poison the ones we love. And trust.

The song of freedom has left him. He is just another fuck-up on a bench. Teenaged girls wearing revealing clothes slouch by in flip-flops. "Tara's had it done to her belly button," one of them says. "Every day she wears, like, a totally different thing in it." A grey-haired man on the bench opposite watches the teenaged girls when he should be watching his four-year-old who is wandering below the monkey bars where a swinging foot could easily knock her unconscious. The grey-haired man, wearing sunglasses even though it's overcast, resumes studying a printout. The four-year-old skips towards Reese. "I know how to spell my name," she tells him. "L-u-c-y." At the Patti Hut the radio blared about another car bombing. Forty-seven people dead. One hundred and thirty-six injured, some are blinded, some will lose limbs. Does it matter when over the next year the population of the planet will grow by 72 million?

"Where're your children?" Lucy asks.

"I don't know."

"You're not allowed in the park without children."

"I got fired."

"What's that mean?"

"I don't have a job anymore."

"Oh." Lucy runs to the slide. Bigger boys monopolize the play structure. Lucy watches in fear and awe as they stand on the swings and the teeter-totter. They ignore her as they challenge each other to swing higher. Will they grow into politicians or corporate execs who bloviate while the biggest mass extinction since the dinosaurs takes place? Does it matter?

Bernie was not happy to see him. He wanted to watch *Action Star*, a reality television show in which young men and women compete to perform suicidal feats. Bernie is determined to drive the car again. He has failed the driving test five times but wants to try again. That he backed into a school bus does not deter him. He feels maimed without his vehicle.

Somewhere in this world, Clara believes that her father didn't want to take her swimming. Somewhere in this world Katrina is with, or without, the baby.

The challenging boys scoop up gravel and approach the street. As the light changes, they hurl the stones at cars then run in all directions. Tires screech and drivers step out of cars to yell at the scattering boys.

The only way to hurt them is through their cars.

An old woman eating a Mars bar sits on the bench beside Reese. Coughing, she rummages in a dollar store bag and pulls out a small plastic lantern. "What d'you think?" she asks. "All you do is put a battery in. They make nice gifts. I keep buying them and giving them away. Today, I decided to get one for myself." Enslaved children in battery-recycling factories squat in Reese's mind, pulling apart the poison with bare hands. Does it matter?

"I told my daughter they'd work nice on the balcony," she says, "you know, tied to the railing. She don't use the balcony in the daytime because of the kids but at night it would be nice, don't you think?"

Mrs. Ranty yanks his ears. "Hel-*lo!* Forty-two million kiddies enslaved worldwide!!"

"Mosstly girlss," Scout Leader Igor clarifies, "*domessteec zslavess,* zseeex-year-oldss getting fucked in every orifice!"

"It's a dis*grace!*" Mrs. Stinkman shrieks.

The old woman waves the lantern in front of his face. "A little sparkle on the balcony would be nice, don't you think?" Reese thinks he nods. Why do the aged confide in him? Do they see in him themselves — still moving despite considerable resistance? Does he appear secure, a post to which they can tether their increasingly unruly minds? What can it be like to have lived through wars; to remember a time before television and plastic and unaccountable multinationals, when bread and milk were delivered by horse-drawn carts? What can it be like to watch peers succumb to death while you continue to eat Mars bars and buy dollar store lanterns?

"And look at this," the old lady says, pulling a small child's umbrella from the bag. "Isn't it the cutest? Made in China. How in the world do they make that for a buck?"

Does a self-righteousness evolve because you have survived? How do you not go insane? How do you endure this private war between what's real and what isn't? Maybe he should audition for *Canadian Idol*. Distraction *must* be possible. Smile, though your heart is breaking.

eese has never been to a peace vigil before. Gusting winds repeatedly blow over the "War is Not the Answer" sign. He only came because Avril, clutching his plastic shoes, was waiting for him outside the basement apartment, and because he felt so despised by the world, his family, Gwyneth Proudley. Holden was with Avril. They looked apprehensive as Reese approached, as though afraid he might yell at them. "You weren't yourself on leaving base camp," Holden said. "Marge was a bit startled. She thought you *were* a people person."

"He *is* a people person," Avril said, "under normal circumstances."

Reese offered them what was available — tap water or Swiss Miss. Avril accepted neither. She was disappointed that the Voice of First Nations client owned casinos. "Why didn't you tell me?" she asked. Reese slumped on one of the eighties' chairs and listened for movement upstairs, even though he'd told himself that he'd accepted that the baby was dead.

"He made a pass at her," Holden said, "when she told him her granddaddy was a shaman."

"I don't think he's a good representative for First Nation Peoples," Avril said.

"He's got the cash," Holden pointed out. They sat in silence. Bonaparte spun on his wheel. "Everybody knows the chiefs keep all the cash anyway," Holden added. "They use government handouts to fix up their houses."

"What do you mean 'everybody knows'?" Avril demanded. "*I* don't know that. Do *you* know that?" She looked at Reese, who tried to appear absorbed in offering Bonaparte sunflower seeds. Holden turned on the TV, which showed bleeding red cowboys throwing ropes around the necks and legs of bleeding red horses, the narrator explaining that wild horses are still being rounded up, but not for riding, for pet food products. "How could anybody do that?" Avril gasped. The horses, lathering sweat from the struggle and rendered graceless, collapsed in the dust. "That is so like man," Avril said. "Kill, kill, kill." A car polish commercial came on. "No buffing," the male voice announced, "just wipe on. Still beads after fifty-two washes." A car was shown being washed presumably for the fifty-second time. A man's hand holding a cloth darted into frame to wipe the car's hood. "Still has that showroom shine," the voice-over said.

Reese is having difficulty understanding the purpose of transients holding a peace vigil outside a closed city hall. The world is not at peace, therefore there is no peace to be vigilant about. Avril advised him that he could offer a prayer if the mood struck him. "People just pray when they feel like it," she said. So far no one has prayed and they're being harassed by a drunk in a sombrero. "Fucking pinkos!" he shouts at them. "Fucking Arab lovers!" The peace vigil transients tighten their circle and hold hands. Some of them close their eyes and begin to hum. Soon they're all humming. The drunk kicks over the peace sign. "Fucking cowards, if you had your way we'd all be speaking fucking German!" The grey-haired black man beside Reese is wearing a T-shirt that reads, "Do Not Disturb, I'm Disturbed Enough Already." His grip tightens as his baritone humming increases. To Reese's left is a slight woman who introduced herself as Heidi. Her high-pitched hums resonate through his hand, up his arm and into his head. His only defence is to hum himself. He hums until his lips tingle. Heidi has told Reese that she worked in a bookstore and that the most depressing period in her life was when Bill Clinton's book came out. She sold fifty-two copies in one day. She also asked him

if he knew about America outsourcing torture, jetting detainees
to Syria to get their testicles electrocuted and their limbs boiled.
Heidi reminds Reese of his sister and he wonders if she had a
brother who made jails out of chairs and blankets and forced her
to be a prisoner. While he tries to think peaceful thoughts,
Katrina's dead baby keeps surfacing, bloodied and shrivelled.
Why, when he tells himself repeatedly not to think about something because there is *nothing* he can do about it, does he continue to think about it? Why is he continually treading water around
Gwyneth Proudley when there's nothing he can do until he meets
the woman? Why is he reconstructing the meeting with Sterling
and Nick Dizon, flagellating himself for not having held his
ground? He had to beg for a pink slip. He *grovelled* in front of
Nick Dizon. He does not want to revisit this moment of humilia-
tion, but of course his mind drags him there repeatedly. Along
with Katrina in the bath with blood congealing around her.

Tears dribble on the cheeks of some of the hummers.
Suddenly he feels a communion with them. They care enough to
join hands in a hostile city to further the idea of peace. His ears
begin to tingle. He squeezes Heidi and the black man's hands in
the same manner he would squeeze his children's hands to assure
them that he was there and that he loved them. Without opening
their eyes, Heidi and the black man squeeze back.

Betsy's hands and forearms are stained brown. The grout in the
tiles is now rust coloured. Her favourite house frock looks as
though it's been smeared with chocolate milk. "Why didn't you
change into something you didn't care about?" Reese asks, staring at the remnants of the Natural Light Golden Brown with
built-in highlights in the sink.

"Too much trouble." Brown and orange-haired she broods in
her armchair, once again sidelined by life's disappointments. He
offers to play rummy, turn on the TV, mix a drink. She uses a
toothpick to dig at the dye under her fingernails.

"Dad's coming home."

"I don't want him seeing me like this."

"You look fine." Bernie doesn't want to come home. He'd rather stay with his Funny Valentine. He has a new neighbour who also watches sports. They get lively over men smashing into each other, throwing and hitting balls.

"Maddy's cleaning lady broke her hip," Betsy says. "They put her in the hospital and she didn't want to eat anything so they opened her up. She was a mess inside so they sewed her up again and left her on life support till her kids said they could pull the plug." She starts to unwrap a Crispy Crunch. "She never talked about stomach trouble. How could she be a mess inside when she never talked about stomach trouble?"

"Maybe she was trying to hide it."

"What for?"

"So she wouldn't have to go to the hospital and be opened up and sewn up again."

Betsy bites the chocolate bar. "Sounds fishy to me. I don't see how you can have your gut twisted up and not know about it."

"Do you want to go out for something to eat?"

"I can't go out looking like this."

"You look fine."

"He can come home if he wants," Betsy says, "but *I'm* not looking after him."

"Well, I wanted to talk about that. I've asked a nice Filipina lady to help you. She even cooks."

"I'm not having strangers in the house."

"He's going to be in rough shape, Mum. He may soil himself, that sort of thing."

"Why doesn't he just *die?*" She has never before stated her preference so vehemently. Her ruthlessness reminds him of when she transformed him into a latchkey kid. Without warning his mother wasn't home after school and he had no choice but to look after snotty Chelsea. Within days he lost the key that Betsy had tied around his neck. She put a spare under a flowerpot. He lost that one too. She put a key on a chain around his neck so that he would feel its weight and therefore notice were it to slip off. Nothing would prevent her from working for

Dr. Brewer with the harelip and the small dogs. As a child this seemed to Reese like betrayal. He had no understanding of his parents' precarious finances.

"I don't think he wants to die," Reese says.

"Why not? What's to do here? Gripe and moan."

"Maybe you guys could start playing bridge again, have some people over, and Menmen could prepare sandwiches."

"Who's Menmen?"

"The Filipina. She says she'll cook whatever you want. She can even make brownies, she said, chocolate, butterscotch, or even peanut butter."

The word *brownie* catches his mother's attention. She chews vigorously while bunching the Crispy Crunch wrapper. "When's he coming?"

A shapeless, balding man on the other side of Linden orders another rum and coke. He's reading *Men Are From Mars, Women Are From Venus*.

"So this Nova Scotian," Bob says, "is nuts about dogs and hates humans. But he doesn't hate humans in Nova Scotia so he gets in his car with a shotgun, a nine-millimetre semi-automatic, a machete, a throwing knife, and six thousand rounds of ammunition. Guess where he goes?"

Linden doesn't guess so Reese says, "Hollywood?"

"Shit no, he comes here, everybody hates Toronto. So he goes down to the beach with all his gear preparing to ambush and guess what happens?"

"He blows up?" Reese asks.

"He meets a dog. He starts talking to the dog and I guess the dog talks back because the guy turned himself in. What's that about?"

"Alienation," Linden says.

"Here's the best part. He used to work as a prison guard. He wanted to commit a crime so he could get into jail. He said the guys've got it made in prison: room and board, medical, dental. Is that not gorgeous?"

What can be said of a world in which a free man yearns for prison?

"Guess what book he had in his car? Come on, guess?"

Linden doesn't guess so Reese says, "*My Life* by Bill Clinton?"

"*How to Win Friends and Influence People*. Is that not gorgeous?"

"Have you fired *your* gun yet, Robert?"

Bob makes a frantic "be quiet" gesture before asking some tightly necktied men if they want another. While opening beers he glances at the TV where zebra are being stalked by female lions on the Serengeti. "I *love* this channel," Bob says. "You really learn stuff." The large male lion doesn't want to share the zebra carcass. Not having stalked and killed the zebra he has no right, other than being king of the pride, to make off with the carcass. During the night, when an adventurous cub tries to get a bite of the carcass, the big male lion kills it. In the morning, its mother tries to lick the cub back to life while its siblings hop around it. The king, unmoved, continues to gorge on the zebra. A day later the mother begins to eat the dead cub. Soon its siblings are chewing at it and dragging its head around. "So much for the noblest of beasts," Bob says.

"No different from humans," Linden points out. "Killing whoever threatens."

"In defence of territory and resources," Reese adds.

"Programmed to kill," Linden says.

"We're running out of territory and resources," Reese says.

"Then what happens?" Bob asks.

"Dog eat dog," Linden says.

One of the tightly necktied men loosens his belt. "They freeze you but you've still got this thing down your throat," he says. "The whole time I was gagging. Meanwhile the doctor's doing a play-by-play for his students and they're all taking turns looking down my throat and talking about how some cancer's tripled in the last decade and I'm thinking, 'Christ, I've got some-thing!' Next they're talking biopsies and taking chunks out of me and getting real excited about it. For a week there I was shitting bricks. Dr. Champion was his name, he was a champ alright."

"There's a shift coming up," Bob tells Reese, "if your girlfriend wants it."

"She's not my girlfriend."

"Kyla's sister's getting surgery and she needs Kyla to look after the kids."

"When do you want her to start?"

"Does she have a name?" Linden asks.

"Who?"

"Your girlfriend," Bob says.

"She's not my girlfriend. Katrina, her name's Katrina." He realizes he doesn't know her last name.

"Tell her to give me a call, we'll set something up for the weekend."

"Thanks, Bob."

"I'm not making any promises. We'll try her out, see how it goes."

"Robert," Linden says, "have you ordered your glideshoe safety system yet?"

"My what?"

"In case of terrorist attacks we can buy glideshoe kits that will enable us to glide down steel rails outside our high-rises. Unless of course we prefer to jump."

"Is that a joke?"

"No joke."

"That's if we leave our panic rooms," Reese says.

Gwyneth Proudley has left a message informing him that she can see him in two days but that he must call to confirm. He replays her message several times to decode its hidden meaning. If she has suffered a family tragedy, she is hiding it well. The imminence of this meeting causes a buzzing in Reese's body. He shakes out his arms and legs before trying a variety of positions on the futon. The sounds of bombing, aircraft, and machine gun fire coming from Katrina's TV limit his ability to release muscle tension. Despite his tiredness, his eyelids remain open. Derek, before the blue pills, used to complain that his eyelids felt heavy, that he could barely keep them open. Roberta took him to their G.P. who checked him out and said, "He'll live another day." Derek assumed this meant he only had one more day to live and refused go to sleep for fear of waking up dead. Reese read *The Lord of the Rings* to him for over an hour until finally Derek lost consciousness. Reese sat in the dark for another hour in case the boy woke up. He planned to stroke his forehead if he woke up. Who is stroking his forehead now?

Katrina doesn't answer but the door is unlocked. He approaches with caution, fearing the worst as he avoids stumbling over the exercise equipment. He finds her unconscious on the orange couch and immediately feels for a pulse, remembering the lack of pulse in the swollen-footed man in the bed beside Bernie's. After a few seconds he feels her heart's steady rhythm. Asleep, her child face dominates and he tries to imagine the child dreams she once had. Did she always want to be a Broadway star? Did she belt out "Tomorrow! Tomorrow!" in her backyard? On TV, men are falling from the sky in flames, spewing blood from severed arteries, Tommy-gunning enemy prisoners to death. Reese finds the remote and presses the power button.

"Why'd you turn it off?" she asks.

"I thought you were sleeping."

"It helps me sleep."

"It's a war movie."

"It's about D-Day. It has a happy ending."

"Are you alright?"

"Why wouldn't I be alright?"

"For obvious reasons."

She tightens the belt on her bathrobe. "What I do with my private life is no concern of yours."

"You asked me to go to the clinic."

"I haven't gone to the clinic, alright. Just buzz off."

He feels a general lightening, as though he might levitate. She stares at the blank TV screen. "Who was that girl who was hanging around?"

"What girl?"

"She had your shoes."

"Oh, that's Avril."

"Who's she?"

"Someone I work with."

"What is she, like, a size zero?"

"Actually, I don't work with her anymore. I got fired today."

"Get out."

"I'm serious."

She looks at him. "Didn't they like your shoes?"

"That may be part of it."

"What was the girl doing here?"

"She brought my shoes. She was also fired. And the guy who was with her."

"So are you, like, forming a union?"

"We went to a peace vigil."

"Get out." She turns the TV back on and more men fall from the sky. "This is way better than Vietnam movies. One of our bouncers was a Vietnam vet. He used to sit on a chopper and shoot people. He said ever since, no matter what he's doing, every ten minutes he sees shit in his head like a sampan he gunned down and a woman and her babies falling out of it and kicking around while he was shooting them." The light from the war movie bounces off her face.

"I think I'll go back downstairs," Reese says.

"I'll turn it off if you want."

"Please."

She turns it off. The parents of the garbage-producing hockey players are shouting at each other again.

"There's too much violence in the world," Reese says.

"You just noticed that?"

He sinks into the orange armchair. "Why?"

"Duh, humans are at the top of the food chain. Who's going to kill us if we don't kill each other?"

"A friend of mine owns a bar and needs a waitress. I told him about you and he said you should call him."

"Excuse me?"

"I just thought you might like a different job. It's a nice bar."

"There is no such thing as a nice bar."

"I mean, some nice men go there. *I* go there. Anyway, here's his card."

"You think men won't look at my tits if I have a shirt on?"

He remembers his preoccupation with Kyla's breasts. "I just thought you might be more comfortable."

"*You'd* be more comfortable. I'd make no money."

"I think Kyla does alright. She supports her kid on it."

"She probably lives in a dive."

"No, I've been to her place. It's quite nice, I mean, it's small. She has a lot of bead curtains."

"What were you doing at her place?"

"Just visiting."

"Isn't that special. My rent's a thousand here."

All he knows about Venus is that it is surrounded by poisonous gas.

"You're picturing me working in this 'nice' bar," she says, "supporting my kid."

"I wasn't picturing anything."

"There is no kid. There will be no kid."

"I know that."

"It's tomorrow at 12:15."

He crashes to earth. "Guess they don't stop for lunch."

"Is that supposed to be funny?"

To avoid reflection or speculation, he checked the Net this morning for information about Dax mattresses. In the photograph a Swedish-looking woman in a white negligee with spaghetti straps lay on her side with one arm draped over her pillow. In another shot she lay on her stomach with her hands folded under her cheek. In another she lay beside a man in a white T-shirt and pyjama bottoms who was reading a book.

"I'll understand if you don't want to come," Katrina says.

"I'll come." The Ultimate Sleep Shoppe's web site claimed they had styles of the highest quality brands to fit every budget, and fast delivery — with a great selection to choose from, satisfaction guaranteed. The ad featured a shot of a bare-chested man on a bed with a woman beside him in a spaghetti-strap negligee. She gazed at him while he seemed only partly engaged with her.

Katrina closes her eyes again. He watches her while listening to the yelling parents next door. He thinks of the cells inside her busily multiplying, unaware of tomorrow's lunch date. At six weeks isn't there a heartbeat? A soul? He feels a howl pending, forcing its way up his intestines, stalling in his throat. He knows he must not reveal his distress to Katrina. He must be — like the men on the Ultimate Sleep Shoppe and Dax ads — there, but not fully committed. Absolute commitment is perceived as weakness. He rolls his neck. "Do you think we could watch a Fred and Ginger movie?"

He leaves early, taking care not to wake her. He slept on her bed because she remained unconscious on the orange couch. He found her mattress reasonably comfortable and searched for the label, which was somewhat faded — "Springwell." He feels strongly that today he *must* make a decision about a bed. It is his destiny. Bicycling to the Ultimate Sleep Shoppe, he is nearly killed by a roofing truck pulling a fast right, and by a cab door opening. It cheers him that he's avoided these hazards, that his life continues to be worth preserving. Inhaling polycyclic aromatic hydrocarbons at a light, he remembers again that he must inform Roberta of his job loss. He will, he decides, after his meeting with Gwyneth Proudley. His life will begin or end after the meeting with Gwyneth Proudley.

He left a note for Katrina saying that he'd pick her up at eleven. He couldn't spend the morning with her, was afraid of what he might say or do while awaiting the execution. Does it matter when breathing will require gasping and dogs will be eating dogs? In his head Fred sings about life being short, you're getting older, you don't want to be an also-ran.

The salesman has a trim moustache and receding blond hair. His name is Chad, which doesn't sound Swedish. The sound system is playing Bryan Adams, who doesn't sound Swedish. "Why don't you tell me your needs?" Chad inquires.

"Comfort, really. I've tried a lot of mattresses and haven't fallen in love with any."

"Plush or firm?"

"Both."

Chad smoothes his moustache, looking concerned. "What are your feelings regarding independent versus integrated coils?"

"To be honest, I can't really tell the difference."

"Have you tried the Wellness Series? The Lumbar Response or the Chiropractic Pillow Top?"

"I don't think I like pillow tops."

"May I ask why?"

"I like to feel stable on a bed. I don't like to wobble."

This new information gives Chad pause.

"Have you heard of Springwell?" Reese asks.

"Springwall."

"Yes. I slept on one last night and found it reasonably comfortable." The baby's heartbeat won't leave him.

"You hadn't slept on it before?"

"No." Heartbeats on sonogram monitors look like bright, pulsing stars.

"Was it a new bed?"

"No. It belongs to a friend."

Chad narrows his eyes slightly. "We don't carry Springwall."

"Oh really? Don't you like them?"

Apparently considering Springwall unworthy of comment, Chad peruses the sea of mattresses. "Have you tried the Silverwing Perfect Sleeper?"

"I don't think so."

Chad leads him past and around many beds then gestures for him to try the Silverwing Perfect Sleeper. It feels like all the other beds. Reese senses that Chad is anticipating a positive response and Reese hates to disappoint him. He tries several positions on the Silverwing until finally he blurts, "I was thinking I might try a Dax."

"A Dax?" Chad murmurs after a quick intake of breath.

"I've heard they're really good."

Chad glances down at Reese's plastic sandals. "If you don't

mind my asking," he says, "I wonder if you might give me a ball-park figure of what you're intending to spend on a bed?"

"I'm not so concerned about the cost as the comfort."

"I see." Chad smoothes his moustache again. "Dax," he begins carefully, "provides scientifically engineered mattresses designed to transform your life. But I must warn you, there is a price tag."

"I understand."

Chad leads him to a curtained area behind which there are only Daxes. "The system involves a myriad of coils that allow the bed to shape itself gently to your body, reducing pressure points and therefore the number of times you shift or move about to get comfortable during the night." He gestures towards a bed. Reese doesn't so much lie down as climb into the Dax, reminding him of settling into a well-calibrated water bed.

"Never underestimate the importance of the height of a bed," Chad cautions. "Dax offers metallic legs that can elevate the bed. Or you can choose mahogany for a more traditional height. Some customers prefer to leave the bed low to the floor for that sleek European look." What chance would the baby have in the wars over territory and resources? "The company," Chad murmurs as though in church, "promises a variety of health benefits, some postural but, most importantly, increased deep sleep." Floating on the Dax Reese tries to imagine himself sleeping deeply. He can't remember the last time he went to bed and didn't wake until morning. He is beginning to feel alarmingly relaxed, as though his body is dissolving. "It all has to do with natural latex," Chad whispers. "I'll leave you alone for a few minutes."

There is bird shit on his hand. He continues walking, unsure of how to dispose of it. He can't wipe it on his clothes and he has no Kleenex. He holds his hand palm upwards so as not to drip. People think he's gesturing to them and look at him strangely.

"Sir? Wake up, sir. We don't allow people to sleep here." It is Chad, leaning over him.

"Was I asleep?"

"I think you may have found your mattress."

"What time is it?"

"Eleven-fifteen."

"What?"

He rides faster than he has ever ridden, takes chances he has never taken. Drivers honk, pedestrians scowl but death, he knows, will not strike. He is destined for more suffering than this.

Katrina sits without moving on a steel and vinyl chair. She doesn't look up when he enters. He grabs her hand as he sits beside her. "I'm so sorry," he says.

"Don't sweat it."

"I fell asleep. On a mattress. I've never fallen asleep on a mattress in a store before."

"You were *shopping?*"

"I need a bed." Other patients watch them: a young girl in a private school uniform and what must be her mother because they both have squints and slits for mouths. And a dull-eyed black girl with cornrows and fuchsia fingernails. Beside her a white man, wearing a ponytail and camouflaged combat pants, fidgets while glowering at anyone who glances in his direction.

Katrina's hand feels lifeless. Reese puts it back in her lap. In a corner, a girl with smeared makeup and tangled hair sobs. The receptionist, behind glass, does not look up. It hasn't changed much. Barren walls and people. A place where life stops.

"Can I get you a glass of water or anything?" he asks.

Katrina shakes her head. Reese looks at his watch. "I guess they're not on schedule."

"I guess not."

As he was leaving, Chad advised him that they offered free delivery, set-up, and removal of the old mattress. Reese's first thought was how wonderful to be free of the rock-hard futon. But then he thought of Clara, Clara on it with him, saying, "Where's that paw" and gripping his hand in hers.

"I barfed this morning," Katrina says. "I don't know if it's nerves or what. One big barf-a-thon."

"Are you nervous?"

She looks at him with loathing. "What do you think? It's a cinch, right? I go in there and they just kind of slip it out like it's a tampon." She looks away again. "I don't even want you here. You should go."

"I'd prefer to stay."

"Why?"

"I'm not sure."

"Suit yourself."

The man wearing a ponytail and camouflaged combat pants taps his foot incessantly. His girlfriend in cornrows picks at her nail polish. Reese doesn't know what he's doing here, what he's hoping to achieve. Roberta often asked him what he hoped to achieve and he always lacked a response. Although, in the midst of the action, achievement didn't seem to matter. The doing mattered, the getting through the day without major mishap. Getting through the day without causing harm to himself or others. If the world were filled with underachievers concerned with getting through the day without causing harm to themselves or others there would be no massacring of children.

"I fucking hate this," Katrina says.

Why must the competitive spirit be rewarded? Why must we win at all costs, without looking at the bodies underfoot?

"They must, like, totally overbook."

As Katrina predicted there was a man out front in plaid wielding a "Please don't kill me, Mummy" sign. There was a whiff of the unwashed about him. "Did the man with the sign bother you?" Reese asks.

"I told him to go jack off someplace else."

A woman in a lab coat calls a name but no one says "Here." She speaks quietly to the sobbing girl with tangled hair. She calls another name and the girl with cornrows stands up as does the fidgety camouflaged man.

"Excuse me," the mother with a squint and a slit of a mouth says, "we were here first."

"Like hell you were," the camouflaged man says.

"I don't care, Mother," the squinting girl in the private

school uniform interjects. "I don't *care*." One of her legs, crossed over the other, swings at high speed.

Unfazed, the woman in the lab coat checks her notes. "You are ...?"

"Christine, my daughter's Christine Granger."

"She was taking a piss, alright?" the camouflaged man says to the squinting mother. "She was in the fucking can when you came in, alright?"

"Watch your language," the mother says.

He points to his camouflaged crotch. "Watch this."

"Sir," the woman in the lab coat says. "You'd better wait outside."

"Nobody," the camouflaged man says, "tells me to wait outside, alright, *nobody*."

The woman in the lab coat sighs. "Well, then, we'll just have to phone the police, won't we?"

War, even in here. Reese wants to take Katrina away from all this, wrap his arms around her big bones and fly away somewhere. But then she's standing, nose to nose with the camouflaged man. "Why don't you fuckin' chill," she says, "and do us all a favour, keep your cock to yourself." She turns to the girl with the corn-rows. "Go with the nice lady, honey. Dreamboy'll still be here when you get back." She flops back into her chair and closes her eyes leaving the camouflaged man with no one to fight. He feels in his shirt for cigarettes while muttering "f" and "c" words. Reese points to the no-smoking sign.

"I fuckin' know that, alright?" the man says, leaving, slamming the door. How many more babies will he spawn, Reese wonders, how many more lessons will he not learn?

"You okay?" he asks.

"Peachy," Katrina says.

"My daughter's next," the squinting woman says.

"We *know* that," Katrina says. "Don't worry your pretty little head about it." Only the buzz of the phone interferes with the steady hum of the fluorescent lighting. Even the sobbing girl has quietened. She sits hunched, pulling on strands of her hair. In

Reese's head the Bee Gees are singing about too much heaven. They were singing in the Ultimate Sleep Shoppe. Aren't they all dead now? Or, like Englebert, will they croon on forever in mattress stores? While dogs are eating dogs will the Bee Gees, and Englebert, continue to chant about loving you, babe, in suits made by cowboy tailors? Is there a point at which the plastic surgeon throws up his hands? Does it matter?

He feels a weight on his shoulder — Katrina's head. This must be why he's here. This must be what he was hoping to achieve. Very gently, he rests his cheek against the warmth of her hair.

"Are you okay?"

"Stop asking me that." She looks no less tense, no less tortured. She crosses streets, heedless of lights.

"What do you want to do?" Reese asks.

"I don't know."

"Do you want to go home?"

"No."

"We could go down to the water and stare at the lake," Reese suggests. "I always enjoy doing that."

"It's too far."

"We'll take a cab."

The Rasta driver tells them Toronto used to be a great city but now it's like Detroit.

"Why do you think that is?" Reese asks.

"Nobody give two cents about anybody else."

"Yes, but is this a new development?"

"Toronto used be good, no garbage, that kind of t'ing."

"What changed?"

"Greed, mon."

Reese doesn't touch her as they walk, doesn't put a comforting arm around her. He doesn't know what's expected of him, if anything. He is awed by her bravery. The lake is a mix of blues, lighter by the shore, darkening towards the horizon.

"It's shimmering," she says, which surprises him because he hadn't thought she'd notice the beauty of it, the expanse.

"Every time I see it," he says, "it's different."

"Silvery."

"Do you want to sit?" Dog people walk by, courting couples and mothers with strollers.

"I want to go out on the pier," she says. "I want to be in the middle of it."

With Nikes in hand she marches ahead and sits on the end of the pier with her tattooed legs dangling over the water. He starts to follow, pebbles pinching his feet and sticking between his toes. Maybe she wants to be alone. Should he leave her alone? He pretends to be looking for stones. He and Clara used to look for what she called "sea glass": glass that had been part of a bottle or jar but had been shattered and worn smooth by time, surf, and sand. He spots a blue piece of sea glass, a rarity, and slips it in his shirt pocket to give to her when he sees her but then remembers that he might not see her, and this causes a sudden weakening which forces him to sit. Pebbles pinch his butt and his ribcage shrinks, bones press against his heart.

Towards the end that he did not see coming, just before the mouth guard and the Portuguese water dog, Roberta was reading a book about the Bodymind. Everything came down to molecules, she told him. Emotions cause physical reactions that can weaken or strengthen the immune system. Words said thoughtlessly can induce a chain reaction of physical responses. Reese's words, in particular, instigated rashes and elevated heart rates. "Look what's happening to me," Roberta would say, pointing to reddening skin on her neck or legs. "You have no idea of the effect you have on people." He has no idea of the effect he is having on Katrina. He's assuming he is having no effect, that he is just the turfed divorcé howling in the basement. But then why did she save the baby? Why did she say, "I can't do this," and walk out, shouting, "You win, dickbrain!" at the man in plaid? Did Reese affect any of this? And if so, is he partly responsible? He would like more than anything to be partly responsible, to hold the baby while it drools on his shoulder, to walk it back and forth in the dead of night. To be one of the first faces it comes to know and love. To trust. He would like this more than anything. Except getting his children back. He notices that some of the plastic is beginning to tear away from the nylon of his sandals. This undoubtedly causes molecular changes in him that are not good for his immune system. A tanned man of solid muscle sprints by then stands on his hands for an impossible length of time. Reese waits for his legs to tip, for some sign of mortality but the man remains inverted. What can this be doing to his molecules? The man's grim expression offers no hint as to the altered state induced by the prolonged handstand. Abruptly the knees bend and the man resumes his sprint only to stop at the monkey bars where, among the children, he hangs upside down. Reese put his feet through rings once, to impress Roberta with his athleticism. He couldn't get his feet out of the rings but hung there, trapped until she shouldered his bulk while he pulled off his shoes and slid his feet from the rings. She was laughing, he was laughing. They did laugh sometimes.

He glances back at the pier and sees that Katrina is gone. He looks around for her. How could this happen? How could he *let* this happen? He stumbles in pebbled sand to the pier then scrapes his feet on concrete as he runs its length. At the end he looks down. No bubbles are visible, no trace. He begins to call for her as he called for Clara that day she vanished on the departure level. The dog people, the courting couples, and the mothers with strollers stare at him. "Katrina!" On the boardwalk he puts the sandals back on and begins walking one way and then the other. What about the coast guard, isn't there a coast guard? Able-bodied men braced to rescue? A dog woman wearing a visor grabs his arm. "Is she a border collie?" she asks. "There's a border collie without a leash back there."

"She's a human," he says. The strap on one of his plastic sandals snaps as he struggles through sand to the lifeguard station. Tanned and disinterested youths with "STAFF" printed on their T-shirts look at him. "My friend ..." Reese begins "... she ... I think she may have fallen in the lake."

"Did you see her?" a gum-chewer asks.

"No. She was there one minute and gone the next."

"What makes you think she fell in then?"

"Well, she's … she's pregnant."

The gum-chewer looks at a doughy girl who also has STAFF printed on her shirt.

"Where'd this happen?" the doughy girl asks.

"I don't know if it did happen. But if it did, it happened off the pier a few minutes ago." He points to the pier.

"We'll take a look," the gum-chewer says, moving at sloth speed.

"Thank you. As soon as possible would be appreciated."

"We'll get right on it," the doughy girl says without moving.

"Thank you. I'm really quite worried."

"No problem." They still don't move. Are they waiting for him to leave? He trudges through pebbles and sand until he reaches the boardwalk and sits on its edge, waiting for action. On an episode of *Baywatch* there was a lot of running to the rescue in bikinis. The youths with "STAFF" printed on their shirts do not run and Reese wants to surrender to it all: lethargy, corruption, brutality, the cheapness of the human spirit.

"Where've you been?" she asks, suddenly behind him. "I've been looking all over for you."

"*I* was looking for *you*."

"Isn't that special."

"I was worried."

"You worry too much. I needed to take a leak."

He sees the STAFF stepping like eighty-year-olds into a boat. "They're rescuing you," he says.

"Get out."

"I thought you might have jumped."

"It's polluted."

"Does that matter?"

"No way I'm going down swallowing that cocktail."

The STAFF begin to paddle towards the pier.

"I should probably tell them you're not drowning."

"Don't bother," she says. "It gives them something to do."

A Great Dane slowly lowers its haunches as it prepares to defecate. Its owner, a middle-aged woman dressed like a teenager, stands at the ready with a plastic bag. "Come on, Silas," she tells the dog, who is clearly aging and without mobile joints or bowels. "Hurry up," she urges. Why the hurry? Reese wants to know. Why *always* the hurry?

"If you thought I was drowning," Katrina says, "why didn't *you* try to rescue me?"

"I wasn't sure you were drowning."

The STAFF, close to the pier now, look over the edges of the boat.

"Your sandal's busted."

"Yes."

"Lance left a pair behind that've got little plastic nubby things on them that are supposed to massage your feet."

"They'll be too big."

"They're adjustable, they've got Velcro. He said they drove him nuts because he could feel them all the time so he couldn't forget about his feet. But you probably wouldn't mind thinking about your feet. I get the feeling you think too much about your feet."

The Great Dane shudders as it tries to meet its owner's timetable. A small dry turd appears, which the middle-aged teenager immediately snatches. "Good boy, Silas." The tanned solid-muscle man begins to do one-armed push-ups.

"I would like to help you look after it," Reese says. "If you'd let me. I'd really like that."

"Talk is cheap."

"Seriously, I mean, I love babies, children ..."

"It's adults you have a problem with."

"Yes."

"You may not know this, but children turn into adults."

He stares at a windsurfer struggling to keep his sail upright.

"You figure yours'll be different, right?" Katrina asks.

"Probably not."

"So what's the point?"

"I have to believe it's possible." The tanned solid-muscle man switches arms.

Katrina pushes her feet into the sand. "I don't know what I'm supposed to do with this baby."

"Love it."

"I've never loved anybody. Like, not even my parents." The windsurfer falls into the water and clings to his board.

"I killed somebody," Reese says.

"I know."

"How do you know?"

"Duh, like, it was on TV."

"I didn't mean to kill him."

"He was a pig, right?"

"Possibly."

"So, one less pig isn't something to sweat about."

"He had a wife and children."

"Maybe you did her a favour."

Katrina's willingness to be on his side, to give him the benefit of the doubt, is completely unfamiliar to Reese. He is accustomed to explaining himself to no avail, to being judged and condemned. "I don't think any child can be happier without a father," he says.

"You'd be surprised."

"No man has the right to kill another man," he says, quoting Avril Leblanc.

"Is this, like, some kind of hair shirt?" she asks. "Are you, like, lost without having all this stuff scratching at you? Because it seems to me you must get off on it, otherwise why would you cart it around."

"I can't forget it."

"Nobody's telling you to forget it. Just live with it. It's done, it's over. Same with your wife."

He realizes that she's suggesting he *be* with his remorse and sorrow. That it just live there, quietly, beside him. "Why are you having the baby?" he asks.

Her toes emerge from the sand. "Because it's over, all that." He doesn't know if she's referring to her Broadway career or furniture-moving with the likes of Lance and the bouncer. "And who knows?" she says. "It might be my last chance." He thinks he knows what she means, the awareness that the curtain is coming down, that the show will not go on. The sun moves out from behind a cloud and Reese feels at one with the sky, the water, the earth, Katrina. They are all damaged. Like the sea glass they were once part of a whole, which has been shattered. Like the sea glass they will go on, tossing and turning.

And the heartbeat will only grow stronger.

26

"So this guy," Bob Vinkle says, "inherits all this cash after he puts his mother in a home. Guess what he does with it?"

Linden doesn't guess and Reese is thinking about his feet in Lance's sandals. The plastic nubby things do, in fact, massage his feet. This does nothing to alter the tension contorting the rest of Reese's body, tension that has increased due to the purchase of a five-thousand-dollar bed and the impending meeting with Gwyneth Proudley.

"He's one of those types," Bob continues, "who's got to spend to feel alive so he gets this idea he's going to buy a house in Italy since him and the wife go there every year to taste wine or whatever and she takes Italian classes. So they get on a plane and find a villa for a million and a half bucks with a pool and five bathrooms and olive trees and plum trees and I think even a lemon tree or something. And he can't stop talking about it. He comes into the bar and jabbers about Italy, how he's going to get Silvio the gardener to press his olives for him and squeeze his plums. Then he starts in on what they're going to do to the villa, the pool, the bathrooms, the walls, the kitchen. And all I'm thinking is, *Italian tradesmen*. I mean, who in their right mind wants to do business with Italian tradesmen? Anyway, I don't say anything. He tells me I got to go visit, which I'd never do because his wife thinks he's a drunk and I'm responsible. So they go over there and guess what happens?"

"They write a bestseller about renovating an Italian villa," Linden says.

"There's *wasps*," Bob says. "Like, not normal wasps, *big* wasps, red, the size of your little finger. And they're buzzing and buzzing, driving the wife nuts. So they ask Silvio the gardener if he can do anything and guess what he does? Come on, guess."

"Sprays them with weed killer," Linden says.

Bob shakes his head. "He pours diesel fuel down the chimneys."

Reese left Katrina sleeping on the orange couch. They'd been watching Fred and Ginger dancing on roller skates. He'd so badly wanted to talk about the life growing inside her, about how she is going to find out what love is.

"Meanwhile," Bob says, "they've got guests and *everybody's* freaking about the wasps. So they call in the wasp police, eight Italians who show up in the evening when the wasps are sleeping. They climb around on the roof and say they don't see any wasps. Next day the buzzing's worse, the wasps are getting pissed what with the diesel fuel and the Italians poking around at them. The husband and the guests leave, which means the wife is alone with the wasps and guess what kind of animal?"

"Rats," Linden says.

"Worse."

Intensified anxiety has caused a slight tremor in Reese's hands. He grips his beer to immobilize his fingers.

"Wild boars," Bob says. "The guy told me wild boars there are like coons over here. They're nocturnal and charging at the garbage and the beemers. So the wife is getting more and more worked up about the buzzing and the boars, and pissed off that the Italians don't speak English. So the gardener gets the eight guys back and they spray some chemical around but still say they can't see any wasps. By this time the wasps are getting mighty pissed and the wife is so freaked she leaves her million-and-a-half-dollar house to stay in a hotel until she can get an exterminator. Silvio the gardener tells her the exterminator's going to cost her but at this point money's no object. So the exterminator shows up six days after he said he would and sprays some chemical around and tells her to set fires in the chimneys. Guess what happens?"

"She has an affair with Silvio," Linden says.

Bob shakes his head. "Next morning there's dead wasps all over the joint. But, there's also *live* ones, and the exterminator tells Silvio there's probably eggs in between the bricks. So the wife hops the next plane out of there. The husband says he doesn't want to go back but they have to oversee the doors getting put in. I said, 'Can't Silvio watch them put in the doors?' He says they're custom-built, you don't just hang them and go. It just goes to show."

"What, Robert?" Linden asks.

"Never dream of an Italian villa."

"Never dream," Linden says. His wife is no longer in the padded room. He doesn't know where she is.

"More money than brains," Bob says.

"What made them needful of five bathrooms?" Linden inquires.

"Guests. They can't stand each other so they have to have knobs around to tell them how fabulous their house is." Bob had a date with a single nature lover. They met at Vinkle's because Bob is still under house arrest. She told him that the only TV show she watches is *Survivor* because she dreams of being stranded on a tropical island and having to forage. "You would not want to see this woman in a bikini," Bob told them.

"But was she a soulmate?" Linden asked.

Bob pours Reese another draft. "Your girlfriend came by."

"She's not my girlfriend," Reese says.

"I liked her. We're going to try her out."

Katrina told Reese none of this. "When did she come by?"

"Yesterday. Or maybe the day before. She didn't look too pregnant."

"They don't look pregnant right away, Robert," Linden says.

Katrina went with Reese to the Ultimate Sleep Shoppe. Chad greeted them enthusiastically and suggested that Reese and Katrina lie on the Dax together. "We're not together," Reese explained. "I think I'll just order it. I mean, I can return it, right?"

"Within thirty days. We guarantee next-day delivery."

"You mean tomorrow?"

"Is that inconvenient?"

"No, it's just I have an appointment."

"Morning or afternoon?"

"Afternoon."

"Fine. I'll make a note. Will this be on your credit card?"

"Yes." He handed over his card, fearing that his tremor was visible.

"A queen, I presume," Chad said.

"A what?"

"Queen-size."

"You don't need a *queen-size*," Katrina said. "It'll take up your whole apartment."

"She's right. A double will be fine."

"What did you decide about the legs?" Chad asked.

"Oh, I think the adjustable would be best. It has to be off the floor. I'm in a basement."

Chad twitched slightly at the thought of a Dax in a basement. John Lennon's "Imagine" was on the sound system and Reese tried to imagine a world with nothing to live or die for but then remembered that he was acquiring a very large possession from Sweden.

"It's going to be weird having you all the way down there," Katrina said. "You'll still come up and visit, right?"

"Right." Although he wasn't sure. Once he has his Dax he may never surface.

Bernie phoned and was very upset because a doctor had recruited his Funny Valentine to help with a research project, leaving Bernie surrounded by "Blacks and Indians." Betsy phoned to discuss the wallpaper she wanted for the condo, "A mulberry pattern would be nice." Reese drains his beer glass. "I spent five thousand dollars on a bed today."

"Shite," Bob says.

"I've never had my own bed," Reese explains. "A *quality* bed."

Bob and Linden look at each other then away. On TV, a big-eared reporter looks directly at Reese. "To preserve the family honour," he tells him, "fundamentalist Muslims, gaining power in this fractured country, are murdering their raped wives, sisters, and daughters." Women in burkas are shown scurrying with bowed heads through the bombed out streets of Baghdad. One of the reporter's ears looks slightly lower than the other. Reese has one ear slightly lower than the other. He feels a connection with the big-eared reporter who must have been called Dumbo as Katrina was before her plastic surgery. "Women," Dumbo says, "who expose their hair or try to get jobs to support their starving children are also murdered by their husbands, brothers, and fathers." Reese looks around to see if anyone else is hearing what Dumbo is saying. If they are, it doesn't seem to bother them. He plugs his ears with his fingers and stares at water rings on the bar. "One woman," Dumbo continues, only slightly muted, "was killed for getting a job as a hairdresser. Due to the resurgence of fundamentalism in post-invasion Iraq, men are not sentenced to death for honour killings. They live in crowded cells with their honour."

"I shot my gun," Bob says. "All these years I've been sticking it in my mouth and the frickin' thing's busted."

"Was the gun in your mouth when you discovered this?" Linden asks.

"I figured a bullet in his windshield wouldn't hurt."

"Oh, Robert."

"Every fall that bitch's been after me to go up in one of those hot air balloons. She'd go on about the fall colours and how amazing they'd look from a hot air balloon. Six hundred bucks for two hours in one of those things over the Hockley Valley. So guess what?" Nobody guesses. "She went up with that assistant of hers."

"It's not fall," Linden points out.

"She's getting sixty percent of my pay so she can go up in a balloon with that jerk-off." On TV, thirsty Iraqi children scramble over bodies to gulp sewer water. Reese scrawls his finger through the water rings on the bar. Tightly necktied men order more beer while complaining about shrinking budgets and growing costs and the price of gas.

"Up at my cabin there's beavers," Bob says. "They mate for life, right, or anyway until one of them dies, then they mate for life with some other beaver. The point is, they've got this mutual goal, right? Fix the dam, get the food in for winter, keep the babies safe from predators."

"Aren't those *our* goals?" Reese asks.

"Whose?"

"Human beings."

"Humans want a little more than just plain survival," Bob says.

Reese, unharnessed by his fourth beer, feels as though one of his arms or legs might jut out unexpectedly. "Why?"

"What d'you mean 'why'?" Bob asks. "You want to go back to pounding spearheads?"

"I don't see what's wrong with just plain survival," Reese says. "Living *with* nature. Why do we have to destroy every-thing? Why can't we just fix the dam and look after our babies?" He looks at the tightly necktied men who are staring longingly at an ad for a metallic-hued car. "Awesome," they say.

Mrs. Ranty grabs Reese's nose. "Thirty to forty thousand people die of starvation *every single day!*"

"Every five sseconndss," Igor adds, "a child diess of hunger."

One of the tightly necktied men stares at Reese. "Did you say something?"

"They're only poor brown people," he blurts. "Thirty to forty thousand poor brown people dying of starvation daily is no big deal. It's not like it's *news.*"

"It's a dis*grace!*" Mrs. Stinkman shrieks.

Reese, standing now, feels his arms beginning to flail. "How many photos of skeletal children with bloated stomachs do we have to see?" he demands. "How many rotting corpses? Whatever we do to the planet we do to *ourselves!*" Nobody clutching bev-erages appears to make the connection. Their mouths gape, their pasty skin sags, their waistlines bulge. "What about *your* chil-dren?" Reese persists. "Don't you care about *your* children?"

"Easy, bro," Bob says, coming out from behind the bar and putting his arm around Reese's shoulders.

"Don't you see?" Reese pleads. "We're making human existence *unsustainable!*"

"There's not a whole lot the little guy can do about it, brother," Bob says. "It's got to come from the higher-ups."

"We *elect* the higher-ups!! *We* buy cars, *we* buy plastic and chemicals ..."

"And mattresses," Linden adds.

Reese falls to his knees, humbled by guilt and too weary to stand. "My life may be over tomorrow," he wails. "They might take my babies away from me tomorrow."

Bob signals to Kyla. "Get him a coffee."

"All I want is to fix the dam," Reese whimpers. "Why won't she let me fix the dam?"

He places one foot in front of the other in Lance's sandals with the plastic nubby things. He marvels that his heel strikes the pavement, admires how the load is shifted to the arch then the ball of the foot before being pushed off the toes. He can trust his feet. Trust. Where did that go? As children betrayed his children, forced them to tell lies, give answers, relinquish snacks, he tried to explain about trust, that only very few could be trusted. "Why?" Clara wanted to know.

"Some people might want to hurt you."

"Why?"

"If you know more than they do, they might not like that."

"Why?"

"Because you might make them feel stupid."

"Not on purpose." So much of it, the mistakes, not on purpose. It distressed Clara that she couldn't trust anyone. You give them your trust, you give them your heart to chew on. He never said this, only cautioned her not to lie as Sidona had instructed her to when they dawdled in the washroom instead of returning immediately to class. "If the teacher asks us why we're late," Sidona told her, "tell her my tooth was bleeding."

Lies.

Tomorrow he will tell the truth. Gwyneth Proudley will be trawling for lies. If he hesitates, if he stammers, looks away, all may be lost. Not on purpose.

The light is on in the bedroom that was once his. Is Roberta sleepless? Suffering doubts, regrets, fears despite her pharmaceuticals? Is she considering calling the whole thing off? In his head Fred and Ginger sing "Let's Call the Whole Thing Off." In his head is the beginning, all that potential, and confidence that there were years ahead. Arm in arm shopping for a stroller, testing them, rolling them around the store, imagining "the baby" sleeping soundly in them. He carried the chosen one in the box to the car. Humid spring air kissed him. There were years ahead.

He must make room for the Dax. He hadn't noticed how crowded the basement had become with newspapers, hamster supplies, and Sterling's discarded chairs. He borrows a dustpan and broom from Katrina, who is still sleeping. Focusing on the task at hand reduces his tremors. He discovers ants on some spilled Swiss Miss. He busies his mind devising a plan to get rid of them without using toxic chemicals or brute force. Roberta systematically killed centipedes and beetles on their honeymoon. She mashed them with a flip-flop then slid them onto hotel stationery and deposited them in a glass. Reese, uneasy on the bed, tried to look engrossed in a brochure describing man's destruction of coral reefs. When the glass was full, Roberta took it to reception and demanded to be moved to a higher floor. They were upgraded to a penthouse suite containing a king-size bed. It required great effort to reach Roberta across it.

He knows she is not the villain. She is his son's first and only love, who rescued the fallen baby robin, grabbed the extension ladder while Derek hopped fretfully around her. "Can't we feed it?" he asked.

"It would die, sweetie, it needs its mummy to feed it."

"I don't want it to die. Don't let it *die!*"

She searched for an hour among the trees and eavestroughs until she found a robin's nest. Reese, depleted from trying to calm the hysterical boy, handed the weakening chick up to her. Later, on her quality bed, Roberta muttered, "It'll probably die anyway. The mother won't want to touch it with the smell of human all over it." Reese took her hand then and kissed it.

Katrina's screams cause him to take the stairs two at a time. She's on the toilet. "Don't come in," she shouts, kicking the bathroom door shut with her foot.

"What's wrong?"

"Blood."

"How much?" She doesn't answer and he fears that she has been muzzled by grief. "It doesn't necessarily mean anything," he says to the door. "Lots of women spot blood when they're pregnant." He presses his ear against the door but can hear nothing. "Please come out." When she doesn't, he slides to the floor and tells himself that the embryo must have been flawed, that nature knows best. "Please let me help," he pleads, knowing that she won't and that he can't. He hears cars passing. There will always be cars passing, long after there are no people there will be cars, piled up, deserted, eroded, leaking chemicals. There is no room in this world for another child. What was he thinking?

Kicking against the door wakes him. "Move it," she says. He stands as quickly as his cramped body will allow. "Sorry," he says. Skilled at masking her sorrow, she pushes past him to the orange couch. He follows at a safe distance.

"Sometimes it's like you're my dog," she says.

"Sorry."

"You should go downstairs."

"Okay."

Never dream, Linden said.

He lets Bonaparte out of his cage, watches as he dives into the garbage can. He turns on the TV. Tom Cruise and a blonde are disrobing, swallowing each other's tongues, bleeding red. He turns it off.

27

The bed is massive, preposterous, obscene. The deliverymen push and pull it through doors, sweating and swearing in Albanian. The mattress jams in the stairwell. "Maybe you should take it back," Reese says. Anxiety caused by the impending Gwyneth Proudley meeting has him peeing frequently.

"You chose a good bed," the larger Albanian says. "*I* sleep on dis bed and I'm a pretty big guy. Dis is a quality bed."

The smaller Albanian nods agreement.

"Best bed I ever slept on," the larger one adds, shoving it further down the stairs. "And I've slept on all kinds. Most of dem wear out. Not dis bed." He uses his foot as well as his hands to manoeuvre the bed. "My moder sleeps on dis bed. So does my sister. And my moder's sister." Why not his father? Or his brother, or his father's brother? Do only women and very large men sleep well on this bed? The Albanians speak to each other in Albanian while they yank and squeeze the Dax. Reese hopes that the noise will alert Katrina, that she will smile down on him, saddened but reconciled. How much blood is involved in a miscarriage anyway? Did it pour from her? Was she crying, whimpering in pain? How long was he asleep? How *could* he sleep?

"What are you doing sleeping in da basement?" the larger Albanian asks.

"Oh, well, I just rent."

"You shouldn't be putting a bed like dis in da basement."

"Well, I don't really have a choice. I'm divorced."

"Oh," the larger Albanian responds before saying something in Albanian to the smaller one. They both look at Reese differently with this new understanding.

"I guess you've got big plans for dis bed," the larger one says, winking at Reese as he rams his shoulder into the Dax. The smaller Albanian begins to giggle. To Reese's horror the song "You Picked a Fine Time to Leave me Lucille" is going through his head. He hasn't heard this song for years and didn't enjoy it when it was popular. While the Albanians abuse his bed, he is hearing about five hungry children and no crops in the field.

"Don't worry," the larger one says. "We'll get it in dere." He twists the Dax as he forces it around a corner. Reese returns to the bathroom to pee and cut himself shaving again. He must remember to remove the bits of Kleenex before his meeting with Gwyneth Proudley. A news announcer blares that a famous boxer has been found guilty of raping his eleven- and nine-year-old daughters repeatedly. The older one has written a book about the abuse, and is not able to forgive herself for failing to protect her younger sister. The boxer forced his penis into their mouths before he progressed to sexual intercourse. He's been sentenced to seven years in prison. How is it possible that such a man should ever be allowed to walk freely again? He's refusing psychological treatment and continues to protest his innocence. "He's starting to believe his own lies," the older daughter says. Reese hopes that Gwyneth Proudley isn't watching the news. He hears knocking on the door. "You coming out?" the larger Albanian asks. "I need you to sign dis."

Reese opens the bathroom door. "You're leaving it then?"

"What?"

"The bed?"

The larger Albanian looks at the smaller one then back at Reese.

"Sorry," Reese says, "of course. That's fine." He signs the paper without reading it. How many times has he signed documents without reading them?

"You'll sleep like a baby," the larger Albanian assures him, but Reese isn't sure he wants to sleep like a baby. His babies woke frequently and wailed into the night.

"Do you want us to take dis?" the larger Albanian asks, pointing to the futon.

"No," Reese responds, urgently.

"Enjoy," the larger Albanian says, looking mildly concerned. "You're bleeding, by da way."

"Oh, really? Thanks, I'll …"

"No problem."

The smaller Albanian, still nodding, follows the larger one out.

Then there is only Reese and the Dax. He attempts to stare it down, to dominate it. It floods the apartment, forcing Sterling's chairs against the wall. Reese misses Bonaparte, his nocturnal ally, who is in a rodent REM state. He returns to the bathroom to perform first aid on his face. He suspects that his light-headedness is due to the smell coming from the mattress, probably from the off-gassing fire-retardant chemicals that are currently being found not only in humans but in the livers of polar bears. He opens his window that faces the underside of the deck but it sticks, allowing a meagre six inches of airflow. He should leave and allow the bed to air out. He can't stay here with the bed. He leaves the door ajar, hoping to create a breeze.

He looks at his watch again. Beside him at the Burger Palace sits a well-fed man who points out that Reese has bits of Kleenex on his face. The man introduces himself as Dermot Horgan and presents Reese with his card, seeming not to notice Reese's tremor. Dermot Horgan is a developer and miffed about the grief the city has given him about cutting down trees to build condos. "These weren't *historic* trees," he says. "We're not talking hundred-year-old oaks here." Dermot Horgan talks at length about the condos, describes the granite tiles, the slate and hardwood floors, the eight-foot-high doors, the ten-foot-high windows. "Now that's rare," Dermot Horgan says. "How often do you see an eight-foot-high door?" Reese feels no urge to rant about the tree-killing and the energy inefficiency of eight-foot-high doors and ten-foot-high windows. He has been muted by the Dax and a feeling of impending doom. The newspaper he's staring at to avoid Dermot Horgan announces that male bass are producing eggs because of the human hormones in processed sewage dumped into rivers. Reese looks at his watch again. Two hours and twenty-four minutes before his life begins or ends.

The identical twin Zellers clerks avoid him. Directionless and with mounting panic, Reese searches aisles for a sign that reads "Bed Linens." Future landfill surrounds him: plastic, melamine, fibreboard, chrome, aluminum. Every breath of toxic air weakens him. He leans against boxes of U-assemble wardrobes.

In the distance, like a mirage, appears a sign that reads "Bed Fashions." He must get there, will get there, focusing on the floor tiles, taking it one tile at a time. Around him immigrant shoppers from the Third World cram the products of Third World labour into carts. With diminished lung capacity, Reese stumbles into "Bed Fashions," propping himself against stacks of packages labelled "bed-in-a-bag," which include not only sheets and pillow cases but a comforter as well. "All made een Bangladesh," Scout Leader Igor informs him.

On closer examination Reese learns that the Wabasso Prestige bed-in-a-bags are 70 percent polyester and 30 percent cotton. He wants pure cotton. "Hel-*lo!*" Mrs. Ranty taunts. "What about those little brown cotton pickers?"

"Zsome are born deeformed," Scout Leader Igor reminds him. "It's a dis*grace!*" Mrs. Stinkman shrieks.

An aisle over, Reese gropes packages of sheets labelled "Prima Cotton Rich," which are 60 percent cotton. What about thread counts? The more expensive sets have higher thread counts. A heavily made-up woman pushing a stroller stops near him and also stares at the Prima Cotton Rich sheets. Her tight clothing makes bending over to study sheet labels awkward. The baby in the stroller sucks wearily on a pacifier. Reese tries to smile at the infant but she only stares back with eyes that could belong to a woman who has lived through wars.

"Do you understand what the thread count means?" he asks her mother. "I mean, obviously it means more thread, but does that make the price difference worth it?"

"I want burgundy," she says. "D'you see any burgundy?"

"No, they're mostly floral."

"It's not my fucking funeral," she says, grabbing the stroller, jolting the old soul within, and stomping to another aisle. Reese tries not to fear for the child's future with an embittered mother. His body temperature rises as he realizes that he may have to spend close to a hundred dollars on quality sheets for his quality bed and that they will be funereal and only 60 percent cotton. Miraculously, the word *flannelette* catches his eye. One hundred percent cotton flannelette sheets decorated with purple sheep, hearts, and Eiffel towers are only $29.97 for a double. Clara would *love* these sheets. She has always loved purple and she has always loved sheep. He pictures her in her purple pyjamas decorated with clouds jumping into the sheep, hearts, and Eiffel towers, pulling them up to her chin. He buys them for her because he has to believe she will see them. He has to believe that. Hugging the sheets to his chest, tile by tile, he wends his way to the exit.

He arrives early. The waiting room is small with no chairs, only foam cubes upholstered in primary colours. Parents watch warily as their son jumps into, onto, and over the cubes while emitting primal noises. Reese, attempting to breathe normally, settles on a cube and looks at his watch again. Around him are toys, many of them broken, and parenting magazines. He picks one up and reads about the emotional roller coaster ride of the working mother. Is Gwyneth Proudley a working mother? Does she leave her disturbed children to diagnose disturbed children?

"When is your appointment?" he asks the father of the frenzied boy.

"Twelve-forty-five."

First impressions are important. He doesn't want Gwyneth Proudley's first sighting of him to be trembling on a cube. There's a corridor outside leading to the offices of other professionals.

Reese paces it and, in an effort to subdue his tremors, practises his foxtrot. Lance's sandals with the plastic nubby things make squishy sounds on the linoleum. He repeatedly checks to see if the parents and the boy have been admitted into the inner office. The boy has begun to swear at his parents who speak to him in hushed tones with growing intensity. Reese breathes deeply as he foxtrots in an effort to *be* with what is, to free himself of his hair shirt. Katrina said he'd be lost without it. What is a hair shirt exactly? A feeling of obligation? A moral compass? A conscience? How can we be free of what we've done? The world is full of people who are free of what they've done, who have put the past behind them. Politicians, for example, or the boxer who raped his daughters. No, Reese thinks, the world needs more hair shirts.

The door to Gwyneth Proudley's office swings open as he is attempting a sashay. The short and wide person is neither the parents nor the boy. "Excuse me," she says, passing him with purpose. He notes grey hairs as she exits to the ladies' room. He fears, of course, that she is Gwyneth Proudley, that she has caught him ballroom dancing. Disgraced, he walks back into the waiting room where a woman wearing a cast on her foot is putting on a raincoat. "Whoops," she says, as he squeezes past her. "Make sure I don't step on you." She points to Lance's sandals. "Do those work?"

"In what way?" he asks.

"Do they feel good?"

"Certainly. But you're aware of them."

She's tying on a rain bonnet. Why, when it's not raining? "Aware of who?" she asks.

"Your feet. You think about them more."

The door swings open again and the short, wide, and greying woman nods at the woman in the rain bonnet. "*You* take care," she tells her. Gwyneth Proudley strides into her office where the parents of the frenzied boy are visibly waiting.

You take care. Like Bambi Ootes she will speak of taking care in a world where little care is taken, where care is taken not to care — to be free of hair shirts. Already Reese feels his chances diminishing. Not only has she seen him sashay, she is prone to false sincerity. He picks up the parenting magazine and reads about "quick meal fixes," the difficulties of raising a mixed race child, and three-hundred-dollar "butt-lifting" jeans. He studies exercises to firm up his buttocks and thighs and learns that he should have started Botox injections in his thirties to delay the signs of aging in his forties. He hears little from the inner office, only the occasional primal noise from the boy. What are *his* children doing? Hunching over desks, rubbing out mistakes with erasers? Rubbing out mistakes. Sometimes he'd shout at Derek, to make himself heard, understood. How could he shout at him? The boy's shoulders would tense, his jaw would tighten. Reese would apologize, put his arms around him but it was too late. Always too late.

He looks at an ad for Disneyland, "The Happiest Place on Earth." Visit the Animal Kingdom, it tells him, and see Lucky the dinosaur, who is the first ever free-roaming audio-animatronics figure. Reese puts down the magazine.

She reminds him of the smart girls in high school who played ball hockey. There was a small band of them who seemed not to see him. They would stand at their lockers talking through him. They won prizes for hockey and academic excellence. He visualizes Gwyneth Proudley in the bright yellow shorts of the ball hockey uniform. He sees her chasing a ball and thwacking it.

"Do you enjoy dancing?" she asks.

"Actually, I just started taking classes. I didn't want to but a friend made a deal with me regarding composting. She would compost if I went to dance class with her." He senses that Gwyneth Proudley will let him talk at length, hang himself with verbosity while she observes his every nervous twitch and stammer. "I guess," he says, "you're wondering why I'm here."

"Why are you here?"

"Well, I …" He searches in vain for the notes he has made in his mind, notes that he has edited, rewritten, and underlined. She watches without facial expression. "I wanted to give you all the facts," he blurts. "So you wouldn't have a one-sided view."

"What are the facts?"

Reese clasps his hands in an effort to subdue the tremor. "Just that I'm a normal, concerned father. I love my children and I want what's best for them."

"Good." She doesn't move but remains on her cube with her hands folded in her lap.

"I just thought," he continues, "that it might be helpful to contribute some background information about my daughter and my relationship with her." When Gwyneth Proudley doesn't respond or even nod understanding, he continues, "And, of course, I should probably give you my perspective on my relationship with my spouse." His hands escape him and begin flapping around. "Please understand that I'm supportive of your meeting with my daughter and I want to do whatever is in her best interests." This sounds too rehearsed, he knows.

"Good."

Her stare is unwavering and he fears that in his desperation he will blunder and antagonize her, put her on the defensive, or, worse still, close her mind to him. "Did Roberta mention the futon?"

Gwyneth Proudley shakes her head, still staring.

"Well," he says, trying to maintain the eye contact so as not to appear shifty, "there was this futon in the basement for guests and ... and after we ... after Roberta decided that we shouldn't sleep together, I slept on it. Which was fine by me, the thing was, when Clara couldn't sleep, she'd come down to the basement and sleep with me. You see, normally she wouldn't be allowed to sleep with us because Roberta thinks children shouldn't sleep with their parents. But since it was just me ... I mean, it was fine by me if she wanted to sleep with me. I had no problem with that." He is losing proprioception of his hands but can't look to locate them because this would mean looking away from Gwyneth Proudley. His hands orbit just outside his sightlines. "Anyway," he adds, "I think this irritated Roberta. In fact, I know it did because she told Clara that big girls don't sleep with their fathers."

"What did Clara do then?"

"She kept coming downstairs. I mean, she has nightmares sometimes, you know, of monsters with green hair and stuff, and she wakes up scared. I couldn't tell her she had to go back to her room. She just needed to be held." A general constricting of his throat and chest warn him that sobs are pending and he knows this would be disastrous, the abusive father seeking pity. He can no longer meet Gwyneth Proudley's glass eyes and instead looks at the sandbox, toys, and two large dollhouses. How does it work? Pretend this is Mummy's house and this is Daddy's basement apartment. Which house would you rather live in?

"I wanted to explain my feelings to you," he persists, "to let you see me."

"What are your feelings?"

No one has asked about his feelings and suddenly he can't feel any. "A lot of things, you know, betrayal obviously, and confusion, misunderstanding."

"Those aren't feelings."

"No, well I ..." Perhaps he should have allowed himself to cry to demonstrate that he *has* feelings but now the impulse has left him. He is cold and dry on his cube, hating this woman who can end his life. Like the Dax she is immoveable, a blight. He wants to kick the cube out from under her.

"You see," he says, "I still think Roberta and I can work this out."

"Have you tried counselling?"

"No."

"Usually when people hope for improvement in a relationship they seek help."

He can't admit that he has never met a therapist who didn't display behavioural problems. "It's all happened so fast. I mean, it feels fast to me."

"You feel stressed."

"Yes."

"Stress," Gwyneth Proudley says, "is sometimes a smoke-screen for a deeper hurt."

"There's no question there's a deeper hurt."

"You feel a lack of control, you want insight into experiences that have confused or troubled you. You've been experiencing anxiety, depression, grief."

"All those things."

She still hasn't moved her hands from her lap. "Therapy is a journey. Not always a comfortable one."

"I'm sure." Is she offering him a deal? If he agrees to see a therapist, she'll let him see his daughter? Is that what this is about? He feels indignation brewing. His toes clench against the plastic nubby things.

"A therapist can help you identify your unproductive patterns," she says, "the triggers that upset you, the underlying issues. This is particularly important when you are facing a life-change."

He looks back into her eyes, which have no depth, only reflection. He sees himself, fumbling, trembling, wretched, full of bile. "Personal growth costs money," he says, "which I'm spreading a little thin these days." She continues to stare at him and he senses that she is unconvinced, that she has heard fathers protest their poverty before. Even though the earth is cracking beneath him, he must continue to go through the motions of civility. "I love my daughter," he blurts, more loudly than he'd intended. "I would do anything for her, I would *die* for her. I would never hurt her. I would *kill* anybody who hurt her." Gwyneth Proudley still doesn't move and he wants to grab her by the throat and throw her in the sandbox. He wants her to experience pain, *his* pain.

"Let me explain what I intend to do," she says. She points to the two dollhouses. "I will use a form of 'play interview' to avoid the stress that direct questioning would place on your daughter. I will have her arrange the toy furniture to recreate two homes, one Daddy's and one Mummy's. Clara will play out the activity in each home and I will observe her activities to find out how she views the home and the people in them. I will give her two anatomically correct dolls to play with to determine if any indication of abnormal behaviour or sexual abuse exists."

"I live in a basement apartment. It's not a house."

"Has Clara been there?"

"Not since Roberta made these accusations."

"She hasn't made accusations. She has expressed concern."

"Whatever," Reese says. "I'm not allowed to see Clara until this is settled."

"But your daughter has spent time there before?"

"Yes, although I didn't have any furniture then. Just the futon. And a tent. I have four chairs now, and a bed. And sheets."

"Good."

"But she hasn't seen them," Reese emphasizes.

"But she has played with you in your apartment?"

"Yes."

"Good."

He has never heard anyone say "good" so frequently. Never before has he considered what a useless word *good* is. I guess you're feeling pretty *good*, he wants to shout, sitting on your cube, playing God! It must feel pretty *good* to be a *good* person with *good* patterns and *good* relationships and no unproductive patterns or underlying issues!!

She stands, indicating that the meeting for which she will undoubtedly charge him is over. "My recommendations will be based on my observations, nothing more."

"Of course."

"I suggest you consider counselling. My sense is that you need acknowledgement of your pain."

"Possibly."

"We are all fellow travellers." As she opens the door for him she says, "*You* take care."

There continues to be no report of a mouse infestation in the franchise across the street. Bob is considering acquiring rats.

"What about wild boars?" Linden suggests.

Reese's forehead is on the bar. He can't lift his head.

"Your girlfriend was in earlier to do the lunch shift," Bob says. "She needs a little work on serving lady customers. I told her, 'You can't just slap food in front of them and go, you got to ask if everything's alright, can I get you anything else, that kind of thing.'"

"Why only the ladies?" Linden asks. "Don't the gents like to be asked if everything's alright and if they would like anything else?"

"They're happy looking at her tits, brother."

Bob shakes Reese's shoulder. "What's up? You about to puke or something? Not on my carpet, laddie."

Reese, still unable to lift his head, pushes himself away from the bar. Like a glacier, Gwyneth Proudley is expanding inside his skull, weighing him down, forcing him to his knees. He slams his head into the wall.

"What the fuck?" Bob asks.

The pain brings distraction. It is real. He can control it. He slams his head again. Somebody tries to grab him but he stumbles onwards, banging into obstructions, people, tables, doors. People shout at him. He can't lift his head. She's still in there, staring, swelling on her cube, cramming his skull. He could walk into a car. Where are the cars? He stands in the street, looking for a car. He lies down. The asphalt feels warm beneath him. A car will come. There is no sound in his head, just the squelching of her flesh against his skull. A tire will crush her. He will wait.

A bulbous-nosed streetcar driver leans over him. "Are you alright? What happened?" People crowd around, sniffing for blood. Reese is surrounded by feet in dirty shoes. A dog licks his face. Strange hands prod him. He scrambles to his knees and clutches the arm of the streetcar driver. "Can I get on your car?" he asks.

He sits at the back, far from the driver who wants him to go to the hospital. People, wasted from worry and woe, get on and off the car. Reese looks at no one and nowhere. He keeps his mind on the wheels in the tracks beneath him. The seat beside him fills and vacates. People cough and blow their noses. He sways with the predictable movement of the car, keeping his mind on the wheels in the tracks beneath him. Until metal collides with metal and the car stops. The coughers and nose-blowers crowd to the front of the car. Men's shouts are heard. "You didn't fucking signal, asshole!"

"I did so fuckin' signal! You ran a fuckin' red!"

The streetcar *must* keep moving. Reese exits through the side door. The men *must* stop arguing. One is tall, black, and hooded with cargo pants falling off his ass. The other, squat, white, and hairy-legged in running shorts, repeatedly jabs his finger into the chest of the hooded man. "Don't touch me, man," the hooded man warns.

"You didn't *fucking signal*," the hairy-legged man repeats. "I got witnesses." He looks around for witnesses, sees Reese lurching towards him.

"The streetcar *must* keep moving," Reese says.

"Who the fuck are you?" the hairy-legged man demands. "Did you see this nigger signal? No way did you signal, asshole."

"What'd you call me?"

"Asshole, asshole. Where'd you learn to drive, the jungle?"

The blow impacts Reese's head where the wall had offered comfort. Searing pain obliterates the woman on the cube. He wants more of it. Hits that will pummel her flesh, crush her bones, mash her eyeballs. He pushes himself into the cyclone of their fury.

Serge Hollyduke is pacing outside the basement apartment in the rain. "What happened to your face?"

"What are you doing here?"

Serge holds out an envelope. "I signed for this, figured it was important, barristers and solicitors and all that. Have you seen Avril?"

Reese fumbles the envelope, drops it in a puddle.

"Because I've been calling her old number," Serge says, "and some dyke says she doesn't live there anymore and she won't give me her new number. I said, 'Don't lie to me!' I told her I've been getting counselling and I'm, like, totally changed."

Reese picks up the envelope. Already the print is smearing. He should leave it here, to be washed away.

"I still love her," Serge says. "I know I have issues and I'm facing them, totally. Could you tell her? I'm just asking for another chance."

The envelope tears easily. The letter opens. He scans it under the porch light. The word *divorce* zaps him, cuts him off at the knees.

"It's not like I did anything on purpose," Serge says. "I get a little emotional sometimes, that's all. She'll listen to you, *please*, could you talk to her?"

"We all want another chance, Serge!" Reese yells into the drowning man's face. "It doesn't happen. Forget it, *it's not going to happen!* Get the fuck off my yard!"

While laying the flannelette sheets, on which his daughter will never lie, Reese loses complete control of his body. He collapses on the Dax, convulsing with grief, trying to remember the feel of her, the smell of her, the sound of her. He *can't* remember. No sooner has he expelled one sob but another heave begins. It's as though he has swallowed poison, he can do nothing but retch. The purple sheep, hearts, and Eiffel towers are soaked from his sweat and tears, making it difficult to breathe. He presses his face deeply into them, hoping for asphyxiation. Gwyneth Proudley's treacherous stare reappears to him and he pounds his swollen head into the Dax. The bed springs back, unperturbed.

When his body, racked by lack of sleep, can no longer produce the muscle contractions necessary to express concussive despair, he lies motionless. *Five hungry children and no crops in the field.* He pushes himself onto his back and sinks into the Dax. Without the familiar futon pressures against his shoulders and hips, he feels cut adrift. The bed seems transmissive of vibrations caused by movement. If he moves, the bed moves. A twitching foot causes spasms in his neck. He tries not to twitch but suddenly his legs feel bound in Saran Wrap and he must shake them. The bed quakes, shouting at him through the echoing of integrated coils, scolding him for dreaming of another chance. He tries to silence the bed by spreading his arms and legs across it. Momentarily he masters it but then his breathing reverberates through the mattress. He tries to stop breathing. *Why* won't the bed leave him alone? He tries to jump off but has no strength. He slumps to the floor and listens for noises upstairs. Katrina will tell him the truth about the bed. He crawls up the stairs.

"What?" she demands in her fuzzy bathrobe. "What're you doing on the floor?"

"My legs aren't working properly, too tired or something."

She sighs massively and leans against the doorframe. "What happened to your face?"

"I tripped."

"Who'd want to beat you up?"

"I've got my new bed," Reese says, "and I ... I'm finding it difficult to relax on. And I wondered if it was just me, you know, because I'm not used to it."

"This is retarded." She trudges downstairs, over to the bed, and flops down on it. He waits. She rolls onto one side and then the other. She lies on her stomach and then on her back. How can someone who has lost a baby continue on? Serve women lunches while men look at her tits? "It's too soft," she declares.

"Really?"

"And too springy. Why'd you buy it?"

"I fell asleep on it in the store."

"You fell asleep because you're fucking wasted. You look like one of those hostages. They're going to cut some woman's head off, some woman who *helped* people, like, not some jerk who's stealing their oil or something." Katrina stuffs his five-dollar pillow behind her head and stares at the ceiling. "Some fucking world."

Reese crawls towards the futon.

"I saw this guy on the street," Katrina says, "really screwed up with CP or something, like he could barely walk and his arms were flopping around. Anyway, I tried not to stare but all of a sudden the guy is, like, limping towards me and I look around and there's this old lady who's tripped behind me. The gimp is helping her up. Briefcases walk by but the gimp helps the old lady."

Reese hauls himself onto the futon and also stares up at the ceiling.

"I felt good for about an hour after that," Katrina says. "It was, like ... so human."

Should he mention the miscarriage? Offer condolences? He's afraid to comment because he doesn't realize the effect he has on people. He has too many underlying issues, too many unproductive patterns. Bonaparte begins to spin on his wheel.

"How was your meeting with the shrink?" Katrina asks.

"She thinks I should be in therapy."

"Get out."

"She thinks I need someone to acknowledge my pain."

"What a wank."

Neither of them move, staring skyward.

"Are you crying or something?" Katrina asks.

"My wife is divorcing me."

"Is this a surprise?"

Why does everyone think his marriage is over? Why does *everyone* but him think his marriage is over?!

The noose tightens around his neck. "Clara … she had this umbrella. With Daffy Ducks on it. She was crazy about it, carried it everywhere. I told her not to use it as a walking stick but she … she wouldn't listen. The handle broke off and she was crying and I told her to *stop crying*." His convulsions begin again, sobs swallowing words. "I was shouting at her," he chokes, "telling her I'd warned her not to use it as a walking stick. How could I shout at her?"

"It's the principle of the thing."

"Why is it always a negotiation?"

"Beats me. We should be more like the gimp."

He presses his palms into the futon. He knows there are stars out there and that in the end nothing remains but the cosmos. Yet the fact that his life has ended and here he is still carting his body around, the fact that tomorrow will be more of the same, childless, struggling to put one therapeutic sandal in front of the other with no destination in sight, causes a numbing of his person. Like the frostbitten, if he doesn't move he will lose function.

Chad doesn't want the bed back. "Our policy is that you keep the bed for at least a week before returning it."

"Why?" Reese demands. The phone is becoming sweaty in his grip.

"Sometimes it takes a little while to adjust to a new sleeping system."

"I can't even lie on this bed. It's alive."

"It's the exact same model you fell asleep on in the store."

"I was exhausted." His tremor has developed into a spasm. He sits on his hand on the Dax.

"Maybe last night you weren't tired," Chad says. "We all have sleepless nights, particularly when we're on a strange mattress."

"I *was* tired. I'm *tired* of this bed. I want it out." Reese hears a clicking sound, maybe Chad's tongue.

"Let me get my supervisor. He's been selling these beds for twenty years. He knows everything about them." Chad puts him on hold and Reese is forced to listen to propaganda about the excellent quality and guaranteed customer satisfaction at the Ultimate Sleep Shoppe. At least he was able to walk this morning, steadying himself against the walls.

"Ivar Olstrum," a voice that does sound Swedish. "Please, how may I help yew?"

"I don't want this bed. I want to return it."

"Yes? Yew say it is too springy? What kind of floor is it on?"

"Linoleum."

"That would be yewr problem. Yew need a carpet under the bed. A carpet will dampen the springs."

"I don't have a carpet."

"In that case, I recommend yew buy four felt-and-rubber furniture coasters."

Reese can't believe that Ivar Olstrum is suggesting he buy four felt-and-rubber furniture coasters after he's just spent five thousand dollars on a bed. "I don't want coasters. I want the bed gone. Chad said I could return it within thirty days." Panting with fury, Reese holds the receiver further from his mouth so as not to alert Ivar to his growing hysteria.

"Yew say it is too bouncy?" Ivar inquires.

"Yes. And wobbly. It reverberates. My friend got on it and she agreed with me."

"Were yew both trying to sleep on the bed?"

"Not at the same time. She was testing it for me." Reese's heart is where his brain should be, slamming into his skull.

"There are many springs in the bed," Ivar says. "That is how it works. All the springs work together. There is going to be some movement. Perhaps yew need yewr own sleeping area. Perhaps yew need a queen."

"I don't need a queen! This bed is wrong! I feel it, *all the time!* I feel too much on the bed!!"

"It is a quality bed. I am sure if yew keep it yew will get used to it."

"I don't want to get used to it! Do you have any idea how much *poison* is in this bed? People probably get poisoned *making* this bed. Do they wear masks, protective clothing? I bet the materials aren't made in Sweden, I bet little brown and yellow people produce the materials for a dollar a month. I bet children go *blind* integrating your coils. I bet women give birth to *fish* thanks to your mattresses. And are they *recyclable?* How long do you think you can keep stuffing the planet with your mattresses and your toxic waste? How many more trees are you going to kill? How much more energy are you going to burn? You're *killing* the planet!!" Sweat drips from Reese's temples and armpits. His right foot is in spasm. Ivar puts him on hold. *You picked a fine time to leave me, Lucille.* The bed has turned to quick sand, sucking him into oblivion. He tumbles to the floor while listening to the supreme sleep options available at the Ultimate Sleep Shoppe.

"Are you still there, Mr. Larkin?" Chad asks.

"Yes."

"We'll send someone for the bed. It may take a couple of days."

"I know what you're doing. You're hoping I'll get used to it."

"Is morning or afternoon pickup better for you?"

"Anytime."

"Fine. I'll make a note."

"I want it gone by the weekend!"

"We'll see what we can do. In the meantime you might want to try the coasters."

Reese slams the phone down. He has been swindled. Fooled. Destroyed. He crawls to the futon like the gimp whose every movement meets resistance, like the pleading, people-helping hostage whose head was severed hours ago. Clara is asking him to tie her shoe. As he bends down, she throws her arms around him and presses her face into his neck. Her skin warms him and he can feel her breath on his neck. Then she's gone. *Gone!* He gasps, sucking in the bed's toxic air. There is only poisoned air in here with the bed. He must get air. He pulls himself up on one of Sterling's chairs, leaning on it. He can't go outside, can't face the tightly necktied men in awesome cars. *Can't* go out there. He hobbles to the window and presses his nose against the sooty screen. He begins to howl.

Her grip hurts his elbow. Street noise and exhaust engulf him. He can only take small steps, staring at his sandals, far away, all the way to the ground.

"Stop," Katrina says, "it's a red light."

He can't remain upright and falls into her. He feels her catching him but his weight drags her down. He will drag her down.

"Let's sit for a second," she says.

The bus shelter smells of urine. The bench is metal, hostile.

"You've got to get a grip," he hears her say.

Why? There *is* no why. Fragments of memories gash him. With every movement they pierce and gouge.

She pulls him into the pharmacy, hurting him, why is she hurting him? Fluorescent lights blind. He could die here, let him die here.

She waves at the pharmacist. "Hi, my friend's in trouble. I mean, I think he's having an anxiety attack or something and I wondered if you could give him something. I mean, we don't have a prescription, but I just wondered if there was anything …"

"See your family doctor." He has the eyes of a Syrian interrogator.

"He doesn't have one," Katrina says. "I mean, he has one but he doesn't want to see her because she's friends with his wife and his wife's divorcing him."

The pharmacist looks back at his monitor. "Go to a walk-in clinic."

"So what you're saying is, there's, like, nothing over the counter for nerves?"

"See a doctor."

"Fuck you," Katrina says. She pushes Reese into the blood pressure chair. "Wait here."

An old woman wearing a neck brace and rubber gloves and a hat with earflaps stares at him. A man with a bandaged eye prods him. "You using that thing?" His hands clench the chair arm, shaking it. "What the fuck you sittin' there for if you're not checking your pressure?"

It's safer on the floor. He stares at a bloodied Band-Aid. And a *lucky penny!* He grabs it to give Clara, reaches for her hand, where's her hand?

"Get off the floor, Reese."

She drags him into the food court, hurting him again. Blasts of Mick Jagger, grease, and neon. *Can't get no satisfaction ...* Too many people chewing and touching him. He could die here, let him die here.

She pops open a can of Sprite, holds a pill in front of his face. "Swallow."

"What is it?"

"Tylenol with codeine. Take six and you'll get stoned."

Why not all of them? He grabs the bottle, slips on a French fry, goes down, head smacking into tiles.

28

"If the truth be told," Dr. Fitch with the receding gums tells him, "you're experiencing a reactive depression." How long has it been? Days? Weeks since she's been prefacing statements with "If the truth be told"? Does this mean she's lying the rest of the time? Weeks of *lies?* He hates her clothes, all those little pockets with zippers. "What I'm saying to you, Reese, is that it's going to take more time."

"What is?"

"Your recovery."

Recovery? Impossible. Whatever he's done, whatever's been done to him, will live forever in his flesh no matter how many times he re-covers.

The ping-pong balls keep clacking. In his head. He tries playing, can't keep the ball on the table — it whizzes past him — which stops the clacking but annoys the shuffling man in oversized shoes, who tells him, "You're a shit-arsed player. I'm not playing with no shit-arse."

The staff don't want Reese here. Take your meds and go home. There is no home.

He loiters in the lounge, stares through the wire mesh into trees at squirrels keeping busy, always busy. Back in the Chekhov play. *We must work, Uncle.*

At what? He can hardly move, spends all day working up the speed to take a shower. What if there is no soap? What if there *is* soap but just a slippery remnant that will slide out of his grasp and clog the drain? He'll have to dig for it, bend down, banging his head against the illegal shower stall while being subjected to the previous tenant's pubic hairs caught in the grill. Then his mother will call to complain about the Filipina. "She can't even fry a decent pork chop."

Betsy can't reach him in the lounge. In his chair. It used to belong to a man who spoke at length about the mind-control methods of Martians. Now it's Reese's chair. Nobody bothers him, not even the violent ones hauled off to "emergency services" and thrown into body nets. The others bang things, fart shamelessly, scream, pat his neck as though he were a dog, urinate in the wrong places, but they don't scare him. Not like the shopaholics, the car-idlers, the water-wasters, the tree-killers, the garbage-heavers.

He sits between the anorexics in "group." Both girls are hooked up to IVs that feed them the nutrients they refuse to take by mouth. The more skeletal has almost no covering flesh. The other says that she wishes she looked like the emaciated one. "I'm jealous of her bod. She's flat, I'm *totally* bloated." She pinches her abdomen to display an eighth of an inch roll of flesh between her thumb and forefinger.

Dr. Fitch unzips one of her pockets and digs around for a throat lozenge. Her laryngitis hasn't stopped her yakking. "My goal," she says, "is to assist the group in helping you to learn more about your relationships with others." Behind her sit three fresh-ly scrubbed psychiatry residents who nod whenever she speaks. "Look around the room," Dr. Fitch says, sucking on her lozenge, "and try to describe how the other members of the group are important to you."

Reese looks at the man with a severe muscle-wasting disease, belted to his wheelchair, a sheet loosely covering the twigs of his legs; at the seventy-year-old obese woman inexplicably paralyzed from the waist down, who claws at "insects" on her arms; at Marjorie who has been a paraplegic for a year since jumping out a third-storey window.

Fitch perseveres. "Is there anything you would like to change about yourselves?"

"Not me," the skeletal anorexic says. "*I* don't have any problems."

"Me neither," the bloated one agrees.

"I'd prefer less contact with people," the skeletal one admits. "I don't trust anybody, they're constantly trying to force me to eat."

"Yeah," the bloated one agrees. "People are always misunderstanding me and trying to change me."

"Would it be helpful," Fitch inquires, "for you to be understood in *this* group *today?*"

Marjorie has spittle dripping from her mouth.

"Nothing good's ever going to happen to me ever again," the severely wasted man moans.

"I'll be happy to listen," the obese insect-clawing woman says. "My mamma always told me I was a good listener."

"Reese," Fitch asks, "how are *you* feeling about what's happening in the group?"

"Is something happening?"

"Do you feel misunderstood?"

"Constantly."

"Right on," the bloated anorexic says, handing her Diet Coke to the skeletal one.

There is a dull silence while the doctor looks meaningfully at the patients, who avoid eye contact.

"I killed a pigeon once," Reese offers, "bashed its head with a rock, swung it around until it was still. I hated doing it. I wanted my mother."

Dr. Fitch leans forward to examine him more closely. "Why do you think you killed the pigeon?"

"To impress Dudley Dancey."

"Who was?"

"We were in Scouts together."

"Is that something you'd like to change about yourself, would you prefer that you'd never killed the pigeon?"

"Ditto most of my life."

Fitch nods thoughtfully as do the psychiatry residents

behind her. "My sense is," she says, "that you all have a lot of pain inside, and that if you learn to deal with it directly, you won't have to express it in indirect ways."

The patients appear preoccupied with personal maintenance.

"Is it time for puddin'?" the severely wasted man asks.

Reese doesn't want to get in the truck. It's too early. Why are they putting him in the truck? Katrina shoves him from behind.

"Where are we going?" he asks.

"Somewhere nice. Have you got your drugs?"

"Yes." He always has his drugs. All he has is drugs.

She pushes him in the back seat. "Buckle up."

"Where are we going?"

Bob Vinkle is behind the wheel. "It's a surprise, brother,"

"You're not supposed to drive," Reese says.

"Who says?"

"Your doctor. He said he'll have to cut off your legs if you drive."

"What's *he* know?"

Katrina climbs into the front seat and stares at him in that anxious way she always does now. "How are you feeling?"

"Alright," Reese says. Mostly he doesn't feel. If he starts to feel he takes more drugs. He no longer hears voices. Bob's truck seems too high, too wide. It could run over people, children. Don't think of children. He doesn't want to be going who knows where with these people. "You never leave the bar," he protests.

"Never say never, pal," Bob says.

"But what about house arrest?"

"What about it?"

"You could get into serious trouble."

"Trouble's my middle name, brother."

They drive past malls, parking lots, car dealerships, fast food franchises, industrial parks, housing developments. No trees. It doesn't matter.

They're "rustling up some grub" in Bob's cabin. Reese can hear them laughing. Ha ha ha. He has never heard Katrina laugh before. He stares at the pond, swatting at bugs. Where are the beavers? A blue heron swoops down, gangly-legged, slowly flapping. With its spear beak it jabs a frog buried in mud coming up for air.

There is always drowning.

They're packing up, shoving things into the truck. Bob caught a fish he wants to show off at the bar.

"Can I stay here?" Reese asks.

"What? Now?"

"I don't want to go back."

"You have to go back."

"Why?"

"You have to fight this thing."

"I can't fight it." He feels nauseated all the time, his head is too heavy, he wants to lie down.

"What kind of attitude is that, brother? You have to fight her."

"I can't." He leans his forehead against a tree. The bark feels rough, real.

"You can't stay here without a car," Bob says.

"I don't need a car."

"How are you going to get supplies?"

"I'll walk."

"It's six miles to the store."

"I'll walk."

"This is retarded," Katrina says. She and Bob exchange anxious looks.

"I don't want you going psycho here," Bob says.

"I won't go psycho," Reese says.

"Have you got any money?"

Reese feels in his pocket, pulls out five dollars and change.

"Here," Bob says, handing him bills. "I'll check up on you in a week. There's canned food in the cupboard, beans and shit. Make sure you eat."

"Have you got enough drugs?" Katrina asks.

He has drugs. All he has is drugs. Please go, why won't they *go*?

Then they're gone, monster tires grinding the dirt road. Katrina looks out the rear window and waves.

All night he hears noises; buzzing, hooting, chirping, pond frogs — life throbbing all around him. He hates it. He sleeps during the day, wakens, remembers, goes back to sleep. His mouth tastes of rot. He wades into the murky pond. Bugs fly into his eyes. All those movies in which they walk, unflinching, until the water is over their heads. He stands chest deep, his feet sinking in muck. What's in this water anyway? Leeches? Are they already clinging to his legs, sucking the blood out of him? He squelches deeper, gulping pond scum. He sputters and flails. Pond slime plugs his nose, his mouth, his ears. He turns back, struggling in mud, swatting at bugs.

He lies down again.

He can't find the can opener, only an axe. He hacks at the can. Pork'n beans splat over the grass. He sits inside the screen door and waits for the bears. A woodpecker keeps rat-tat-tatting. Bugs buzz against the screen. He waits. The bears don't come. His teeth feel fuzzy. He finds a toothbrush, catches sight of himself in the medicine cabinet. He hasn't shaved, looks like a criminal, a child molester. He lies down again.

The screen door screeches then slams shut. Is it a bear? Finally? "Cottager Mauled by Bears." Roberta will find out eventually, suffer remorse. Maybe.

"This isn't helping anybody," she says, switching on the overhead. He squints as she strides around in her wraparound skirt, flashing thigh, revealing the familiar veins. Her face looks different, though, she's cut her hair, looks like a flapper. Who's she kicking up her heels for now?

"What are you trying to prove here?" she demands. She looks younger with the hair gone. "You look awful, and you smell. Have a shower, please, and then we'll talk. Is there food here? Tea or anything?"

He doesn't answer, listens while she rummages around the kitchen. He could escape out the window. She'd go looking for him, maybe get lost in the woods, mauled by bears. He would grieve. Maybe.

"Do you want some tea?" she calls out. "Does anybody ever *wash* these cups? How can you drink out of these?"

What's she want? It's a long a drive. She must have a mission. Is she planning an overnighter? Maybe he should shower, wash off the pork'n beans. He doesn't want to sleep with her, though, doesn't want her here. Bob is *his* friend, how does she know about Bob's cabin? Did Bob betray him? Is that what brothers are for? He grabs a mildewy towel and creeps to the bathroom. He doesn't want her to see him. Behind the door he asks, "Is there anybody with you?"

"Who would be with me? The children are with my mother."

That curling-frenzied sow. What is she saying to them? "Your daddy's gone AWOL."

She washes dishes while he's in the shower causing fluctuations in water supply. He is alternately scalded and frozen.

Already the place looks better, he has to admit. She's yanked open the blinds and windows. The sun is slinking behind the trees across the pond. Soon the beavers will resume fixing the dam.

"Sit," she says and hands him tea in a cup that no longer has brown rings inside it. "You can't run and hide from me," she says. "That doesn't help anybody."

Who says he's running and hiding? Has he said *anything* since she got here? Does he *need* to say anything? He crosses one leg over the other to appear casual, a man of leisure in the woods in one of Bob's plaid shirts.

She puts her cup down. "Gwyneth reported that Clara hasn't been molested. She says she's evidencing separation stress. Apparently it results from frequent transfers between the parents. Parents are reluctant to part with the child and are stressed out about it. The child picks up on it and acts out."

He could have told her that.

"Anyway," she says, "she's recommended that Clara's stress be minimized. She's proposing a schedule that would reduce the number of transfers by increasing the length of each visit."

Is this real? Can this be *real?* He feels his face, his bristles feel real.

"I know it's been strange," she says.

He grips the piece of blue sea glass and the lucky penny. He's been saving them for Clara.

"I've told my lawyer," she says, "to incorporate Gwyneth's recommendations in the settlement. But I want you to act normal, Reese, I want you to get a grip. The kids can't see you like this."

"Why?" he asks.

"Because you look like an insane person."

"No," he says. "*Why?* How could you think I could do that?"

The sun has been swallowed, the stars are breaking out. Her face is in darkness. The forest noises begin, the pond frogs start their racket. For a long time he waits.

"It happened to me," she says, more quietly then she has ever spoken. "It happens all the time. Nobody knows about it. We tell ourselves it didn't happen. Then our babies turn into little girls and we get ... we get really scared."

He can't see her, wants to see her but is afraid to turn on the light, to frighten her.

"My father would come and kiss me goodnight," she says, "and it progressed from there."

All of his pain, *all of his pain* cannot compare to this.

"Gwyneth says I should have told you long ago."

She never mentions her father. Her father died of a heart attack. He took Reese curling once. Reese kept slipping on the ice. Her father had liver spots and hairy hands. He ran for public office.

"I really can't talk about it," she says.

"That's okay." He listens for some sound from her, some movement.

"I'm so sorry," she says.

He knows she is silently aching, far removed from him.

"It's okay," he says.

The winter has been hard, the pioneer life. Waking up in cold and darkness. Muscles he'd forgotten he had have resurfaced due to the endless gathering and chopping of firewood. Reading the *Little House on the Prairie* books to his children has provided relief. His hardships can't compare to Pa getting buried alive in a sudden snowstorm, or the ice freezing over the cows, or starvation, scarlet fever, Indians with skunk pelts hanging over their groins.

Bernie's Ford Escort, on loan, resents country roads. Twice it has skidded into snowbanks, causing Reese to pine for Pa's horse and sleigh, with the fur and the hot stone for his feet. Having no phone has its advantages. Betsy can't call. Although Reese always visits before he picks up the children, pulls banana skins out of the toilet and listens to his parents' complaints. Bernie and Betsy stand united in their disapproval of Menmen, the ultra-tolerant Filipina who keeps the house spotless and the cupboards stocked with Crispy Crunches and Campbell's soup. Finding fault with Menmen has revitalized Bernie and Betsy's relationship. They even, occasionally, share a television while conspiring behind her back.

Another upside of cabin confinement has been living rent-free with nobody to torment Reese but himself. Clara calls him Rip Van Winkle and braids his beard. He puts on a show for the children, tobogganing, snowshoeing, roasting marshmallows. He doesn't want them to see the black holes inside him. Derek builds endless forts with snow and broken branches. He stays out for hours. Reese takes him Thermoses of hot chocolate, checking for signs of frostbite, and lingers, hoping for signs of communication. Derek says "thank you" and waits for his father to leave.

When Reese returns the children to Roberta and is alone, huddled by the woodstove, he is aware that the drive is gone, whatever drove him. The need to save the world. Why bother? Once humans have destroyed themselves it will only take one hundred thousand years for Earth to heal. A drop in the bucket of time. Nature is already running rampant around the ruins of Chernobyl, wild boars charging about despite traces of radioactivity. So it will be with planet Earth when mankind ceases to exist. Remnants of concrete and steel will be visible but the plants and animals will once again rule.

How could he live with her for twelve years and not know that she had been sexually abused by her father? How could he not sense it? How could she not tell him? Is it possible to really *know* anybody?

He had a snowball fight with Derek and the boy hit him in the face, said sorry but clearly was not. Will Reese ever know *him*?

Clara he knows. Maybe.

But all that effort to live worthwhile lives, pursuing careers so that they could buy a house and go to movies and buy clothes and go on holidays. What was that about?

The drive is gone.

When his mind tires of tormenting him, when exhaustion due to the pioneer life renders him inert, he succumbs to the snowbound quiet. Isn't this what he wanted? Isolation? A panic room?

Slowly, by tiny increments, he is developing a confidence in his solitude, an appreciation of the value of unstructured time. He even has brief moments of feeling linked to the whole matrix, despite knowing that there are far too many people for nature to digest, that we are all going down together, that as the planet sickens, so shall we. He has begun to suspect that he is privileged to be able to contemplate his life before it is over, to function without mediation, to be apparently going nowhere.

30

The ducks trail him in the canoe. He tosses them breadcrumbs, hears the *ka-whop* of a beaver tail warning other beavers of his presence. Since the spring he has been hoping to see a beaver. He allows the canoe to drift. A frog hops, a water snake slithers, a snapping turtle glides below the surface. No beavers. Next to humans, isn't the beaver the most proficient of North American inhabitants at manipulating the environment for its own benefit? For thousands of years humans have been able to harness fire and manufacture tools to assist them in modifying their surroundings. Beavers manipulate their environment using only instinct, paws, and teeth. And they do it without destroying each other, or other species.

The canoe snags in a drift of yellow water lilies. Reese puts down his paddle and lies flat, staring up at parading clouds. His children are coming today for three consecutive weeks. He has cleaned and cooked and fussed, even shaved his beard. The prospect of sharing unstructured time with them while apparently going nowhere for *three whole weeks* makes him both giddy and joyous. To his amazement, Derek didn't protest when the plans were made. Probably because the boy has developed a fascination with the stream that nurtures the pond. Shoeless, he splashes about as it bounces downhill in a rocky bed, mirroring a spectrum of colours. He searches for tadpoles, fish, frogs, water spiders, and what he calls fool's gold — rocks that glitter under the sparkling currents. Derek has, Reese believes, discovered the womb of the world.

They still rarely speak and have not, as Reese dreamed, bonded over the canoe.

The true miracle is that the boy likes the baby. He carries him around and shows him bugs and caterpillars. With the baby, Derek has been seen to smile. Reese is careful not to comment on this relationship. Katrina sees nothing abnormal about it, nothing abnormal about Derek. He's just a kid, she says, and so he is with her. They play cards and are both sore losers. Reese makes popcorn to reduce the tensions while Clara paints. He has been buying larger and larger paper as her visions expand. Roberta calls her work abstract impressionism but to Reese they reveal Clara's emotional centre. Depending on the day, the presence or absence of sunlight, the effusiveness or sobriety of the trees, the shapes of the clouds, streaming or muscular. Whether it's a sickle moon, a half moon, a full moon, all of these factors affect Clara's paintings. He has pinned them to the walls of the cabin. Soon there will be no dark wood visible, only Clara's soul.

There is cause for anxiety, of course, EI running out, genocide, famine, pestilence, a blackening planet, nuclear holocaust. Moments of panic still seize him when he looks at the vast uncertainty ahead. But this is what he has now, this time alone and with his children. Even though he realizes that this kind of focused intensity on his own small world is bad for planet Earth, it is what enables him to put one foot in front of the other. When he ponders his life, the losses and gains, he accepts that it is *his* life, and that it will always be filled with losses and gains that rarely balance.

When the baby cries and Katrina, seeking refuge from her week at Vinkle's, can no longer cope, Reese carries him out into the night and within seconds Emerson quietens as he listens intently to the forest sounds. They walk under the cosmos, fearless of bears, and Reese feels so incredibly lucky.

Katrina continues to rail against life's injustices and Kyla's sister, the budget daycare provider who leaves Emerson to cry himself to sleep at nap time. Reese has offered to care for the baby, let him roll around in the grass and pick berries. But Katrina remains suspicious of the hermit life. She doesn't want Emerson growing up "some kind of freaked-out wild boy." She and Bob are dating, which could prove fatal. Bob says she's got more balls than any man he's ever met. He drives her and the baby to the cabin after closing on Fridays. With his children asleep beside him, Reese can hear Bob and Katrina giggling and moving furniture.

There is a fallen tree beside the pond, hidden by shrubs, where Reese sits to watch and listen. Sometimes Clara sits with him and says, "Where's that paw?" They hold hands and silently point out creatures to each other: the heron, misguided seagulls, butterflies, barking geese, a woodchuck straddled on a leaning bough of aspen. Sometimes they sit in the rain and watch droplets form circles on the pond. Sometimes they hear the loon. One day, they will see a beaver.

Peter Bregg/Hello!

About the Author

Cordelia Strube is an accomplished playwright and the author of six critically acclaimed novels. Her first novel, *Alex and Zee*, was shortlisted for the W.H. Smith / Books in Canada First Novel Award, and her third novel, *Teaching Pigs to Sing*, was nominated for the Governor General's Award. Her play *Mortal* won the CBC Literary Competition and was nominated for the Prix Italia. She lives with her family in Toronto where she teaches at Ryerson University. Her most recent novel is *Blind Night*.